Allison M. Dickson

The Last Supper

ALLISON M.
DICKSON

THE LAST
SUPPER

The Last Supper
by Allison M. Dickson
Published by Hobbes End Publishing, LLC, a division of Hobbes End Entertainment, LLC

1st Printing
Hobbes End Publishing: trade paperback, August 2014
Printed in the United States of America

The Last Supper
All rights reserved.
Copyright 2014, Allison M. Dickson

ISBN: 978-0-9859110-5-8
Library of Congress Control Number: 2014931951

Produced by Vincent Hobbes
Cover and internal design: Jordan Benoit
Internal illustrations: (CC) spektrgraphix.com

For information, contact:
Hobbes End Entertainment, LLC
PO Box 193
Aubrey, TX 76227
www.hobbesendpublishing.com

For Dad. I'd travel all the scary roads with you.

Acknowledgments

This book has been one the longest labors of love I've ever endured, from its genesis way back in 2009, to its final release. But I don't think I would have been nearly as happy with it if it hadn't gone through the tender loving care of all the great folks at Hobbes End. Jairus Reddy, Vincent Hobbes, Jordan Benoit, and Abby Miller, and everyone else who saw the potential of this wet behind the ears girl from the very beginning, and edited and polished her first novel to a high shine.

I am also incredibly thankful to my dear friend, author Ian Thomas Healy, who on the morning I told him about the strangest dream I'd just had about a man sitting down to eat a poisoned feast, said I needed to write it down immediately. And so I did. The Last Supper started life as a fifteen thousand word novella I wrote in a frenzied two days, and it eventually grew into the more epic and fantastical piece you're holding right now. If not for that dream, and more importantly if not for that encouragement to write down that dream, it would have faded back into the ether from whence it came.

A huge thanks also goes out to all the beta readers who had their eyes on this book, among them Craig Wessel and others who found holes for me to plug and other ways to expand this world. My undying gratitude goes to my husband Ken, who read this book once it was finally finished and proclaimed it worthy, and who will always be there to soothe my overly self-critical doubts when they pop up like those dreaded serpent weeds. I would like to thank my beautiful children, Natalie and Elias, both of them rebels in their own way, who give me hope for a better future. Thanks to Ray Nicholson for his honest reviews, which are always helpful and appreciated whether he likes the piece in question or not.

My final shout-outs have to go my closest confidants of the craft, my girls Jaime Hobbes, Jennifer Greene, Kate Jenkins, and Kirstin Jewell, who read things when they're at their ugliest, ask all the right questions, provide plenty of laughs, and keep me sane in this increasingly insane and competitive business. We gather regularly around our invisible water cooler, only I like to imagine that it's filled with margaritas. Perhaps some day that will be a reality.

Allison M. Dickson

Introduction

I came across Allison M. Dickson's fantastical mind a few years ago. Although seemingly by chance, I prefer to believe it was fate.

I was a latecomer in the world of eBooks but, once I purchased my first Kindle, I was immediately pulled in. I couldn't download enough books.

I found myself downloading a host of short stories. I believe the truest artwork of a writer is a solid short and, whether accident or fate, I came across a little gem titled *Dust*.

I was hooked. The plot, the characters, the prose—*Dust* became an addiction. When I finished, I read it again. And again. There was something different about this indie author. Something special. Dickson's writing touched me in a way only the highest caliber writers do. I kept going back to the beginning, believing I had accidently downloaded a work by Stephen King. But I hadn't, and quickly realized I'd just discovered a new talent—a raw talent—who was just beginning to make waves in the indie world of books. *Dust* triggered an emotional response so powerful I immediately sought out more of Dickson's work. Before long, I had read all of her titles, and knew it was time to contact her. Because of this simple short story history was created, and *The Last Supper* was to be released.

A friendship emerged that I hope to keep forever.

A bit more about *Dust* before I move on. Quite simply, it's the story of a man who has taken refuge in a post-apocalyptic world. The recently destroyed world offers him no comfort as he comes face to face with his own tragedy, his own madness, his own demise.

> *"For now, I'm holding tight. In a prison camp, you learn to get comfortable with dread the same way you get comfortable finding bugs in your food and sleeping in your own piss. Still, this is better than Hanoi at least. I got clean air, plenty of food and water, stacks of crosswords and Louis L'Amour, and all the Johnny Walker I can stomach. Now it's just a matter of seeing how long my mind can hold out."*

In this small excerpt, you can feel the man's resentment. Resentment for having survived. Dickson's awareness of human nature creates a believable character, one whom I truly feel saddened for. I root for his survival and, if it so comforts him, his death. In this short passage, Dickson gives the reader hope that maybe he will endure. Maybe he will come out of his hidden shelter and reemerge from the ashes a better man, in a better world.

We are given a moment of hope.

Although *Dust* takes place in a world of gray, a million colors exist in Allison Dickson's tale, her characters, her prose. She takes the reader through an emotional journey, where in one instant she creates hope, and in the next despair.

"... Instead of a sun-drenched welcome back into the world, I see a lawless, gray-drenched landscape filled with cannibals and savages fighting over the few remaining scraps of sustenance on our now alien planet. On those days, I polish the stock on my Winchester and summon the gumption to live out another day. I read another book, play another song, or just sleep and dream of all the ghosts whose words, faces, and songs fill my mind. And when the voices get too loud, I have a few nips of Johnny Walker and it suddenly feels all right to join the conversation."

These small examples are but a speck of moon dust of her overall talent with words. More interesting is her ability to capture what a real writer should—human nature. Dickson is a keen observer, a watchful eye who understands just how humans truly operate. What makes them tick, what makes them react to horrible circumstances. She captures this human nature in its truest form, then grants it back in glorious fashion.

Dickson accomplished something with me that few writers ever do.

She made me believe!

Dickson is a masterful storyteller, and crosses many genres without worry. I believe, however, that dystopian fiction is her best. First, she doesn't ignore the elements dystopian fiction must contain. Neither is she ignorant of them. She is well aware of what makes dystopian literature great, and uses these elements to her advantage.

There must be an authority, a figure or entity or government that controls all. Perhaps it's even alien, or maybe a tyrannical leader, but it must be something beyond our control, beyond our will to alter. Something unstoppable. Something all-powerful.

Second, there is dread. Gloom. Darkness and despair. A good dystopian tale must be a nightmare, a place from the underworld where we never want to venture. A sense of darkness must take hold for dystopian literature to work, a sense of hopelessness, an unwinnable battle.

Next, there must be conflict. This conflict cannot be trite, though it can be common, even generalized, of human behavior. This conflict must be reasonable, and it must pull us in with vice grips.

Lastly, there must be tragedy, and there must be hope. These two elements work together. They are the yin and yang of dystopia, and without them, the reader will not care.

Sure, there are other elements of dystopia, but these basic few are a good start. And a dystopian writer must have a good understanding of these elements, and their importance, before he or she attempts to write a story in this genre that once was.

In the previous excerpts from *Dust*, Allison Dickson captures the essence of a dystopian tale. She fills the curious reader's mind with an uncomfortable sensation of the unknown, and allows him or her to believe that maybe, just maybe, this character will find refuge from the darkness. Isolated and alone, Dickson creates an ominous feeling where you are smack dab in the middle of the plight, and there's no going back. She creates hope, no matter how small; it's enough to urge us forward, to keep turning the pages. And then, just as Dickson allows us to hold on to this hope, she dashes it away with the not so subtle reminder that, above all else, dystopian fiction is a tragedy.

At the time of reading *Dust*, I was seeking out the next best author. Someone suitable for an up and coming small press to sign. I was looking for a new talent, someone who didn't follow the rules, and whose writing inspired me. My job was talent seeking, something I feel I've always had an eye for.

After *Dust*, and after reading the rest of her work, I began to pursue Allison Dickson like a stalker. I couldn't help myself. I had to know more about her, about what made her tick. And more importantly, I had to see if she was willing to submit a story. Anything would do, for all her work was amazing in my eyes. And as luck would have it—or fate— she was open to the idea, and the rest became history.

First, she was published in the second volume of *The Endlands*, a short story anthology. And though this was satisfying, it wasn't enough. I needed more, and soon after, she finished and eventually submitted two novels.

First, was her debut novel, *Strings*. It's a horror tale like no other. It's been well received, and has set the stage for her future as a writer. It set her up in fine fashion to take on the horror world by storm, and it's still going strong.

That being said, this book, this carefully crafted tale called *The Last Supper*, was originally meant to be her first. *Strings* was to follow. I fought this until I won the battle, for I felt *The Last Supper* was something that needed time. The readers, her fans, needed a prelude, an opening band, before the big show. Not that *Strings* is any less of a novel, it's just different. And though I'll always hold horror close to my heart, dystopian literature is dearer to me, as is *The Last Supper*.

Dystopia will always be my one true love.

I often call dystopian fiction the lost genre. There is an intricate nature of this genre, delicate in that it often balances between horror and science fiction. At some point, the genre was lost. At best, it became a sub-genre, despite the decades of dystopian greats. I never understood that.

Now, can *The Last Supper* be classified as dystopian? Often times, its own creator labels it sci-fi. In a way, this is true. There even exist a few splashes of contemporary fiction within its pages.

My answer is yes, *The Last Supper* is most definitely within the realm of dystopian fiction. I'd further that the book maintains the groundwork of being able to compete with the best in this genre—that her writing can compete with Bradbury, or Wells, or Orwell. And though dystopian seems to be removed from most lists of genre, it is still alive and well inside the pages of *The Last Supper*.

Now that we've defined this, the next question is, why do we care? The answer to this is simple at first. Dystopian fiction has impacted modern literature more so than any other genre. The greats, the dystopian writers made mandatory in high school English class, have stood the test of time. They've earned their place, and are worthy of being discussed.

We covet Huxley, Wells. We still discuss Orwell, Bradbury.

But why is dystopia so appealing? What is the allure to stories where there cannot possibly be a happy ending?

Isn't life tragic enough? We live in a chaotic world. You see it every time you turn on the news. It's filled with sadness, mostly. This sadness seems to outweigh the good things. Tragedy defeats triumph.

We can blame the media. We can blame culture. Blame whatever you want, it seems as if the world has gone to hell, and there's no escaping it.

Yet strangely, we're attracted to this misery. We can't take our eyes off it. Whether it's a sickness, or simply fear, the way of the world horrifies most of us, and yet we watch it pass by, longing to see what happens next.

Much like I wonder what events unfolded after Montag's grand escape, I'm curious what events will unfold in our own future.

And this is the same curiosity that makes dystopian literature such an interesting genre of fiction. Dystopian fiction causes us to ask questions about our own future.

How far will humanity decline?

Can we achieve a utopian dream?

Or is our civilization doomed from the start?

Now we can ponder the ways of the world, but that's not the task. The question is: why do we love dystopian fiction?

Books like *1984, Fahrenheit 451, Brave New World, The Time Machine*—these stories have all traveled down the deep rabbit hole, searching for the same answers we ask ourselves. Questions about our future, questions about our past.

How did we get here, and why? And more importantly, is it stoppable? Can we alter our destiny, can we create a utopia, or is that but a dream?

With the recent success of *The Hunger Games, The Road*, and others, this genre has seen a reemergence, both in literature and film. Also, a newer, younger generation is now exposed due to this success, opening the doors to the genre that once was, and perhaps shall be again.

You see, there is something about a dystopian story that touches our innermost psyche. Our deepest fears. On the surface, the plot may even be fantastical, but the elements within the genre are what matter.

The successful zombie series, *The Walking Dead*, captures this momentum. And though zombies aren't the most real of fears, and though the show dances in the horror genre, I'd make the claim that it's more of a dystopian television show than horror. Even though the subject matter seems trivial on the surface, *The Walking Dead* touches our hearts as we journey with the cast into impossible circumstances.

Dystopia is scorched earth. Dystopia is a dismal future. Yet we read or watch in awe, wondering what will happen next. Dystopian writers play with our fears, specializing in a chaotic world where anything is possible. Wars and rumors of wars, famines and disease—dystopian writers have long since written on these subjects, which have eventually come to fruition. They question what the world will one day become. They question if our future is survivable, and explore the human element of our distress.

If you think about it, our future isn't far off from fiction. The great dystopian writers were on par with their future, our present, and predicted modern events and technology as if they were prophets.

Cell phones.

Drones flying overhead.

Artificial intelligence.

Satellites and robot technology.

These subjects perhaps were created by sci-fi writers, but dystopian writers exploited them.

What separates dystopian fiction from sci-fi? Not much, actually. The two genres cross blend, and do it well. However, science fiction explores the future, and often is bright, hopeful. Dystopian writers explore the same future, usually realists, and often conclude a bleak outcome. Whereas sci-fi sparks our imagination, giving us hope of a better future, dystopian fiction does the opposite. It causes us worry, that our future will continue spiraling downward, and that the life we have today, despite our advances and technologies, will not save us from our ultimate fate.

War and tyranny.

Death and destruction.

Depression and despair.

Oppression and transhumanism.

In Dickson's own words, she describes a dystopian world in Dust, perhaps without actually knowing she is defining the genre as well:

> "The world had gone to seed. There were wars, political scandals, busted economies, and freak viruses competing with an even bigger plague of human stupidity."

Dystopian fiction is exactly this. So why should it appeal to us? How could it appeal to sensible, intelligent readers? Why do we eagerly flip to the next page of *Brave New World*, knowing deep down that the ending will be as dreary as the world created within its pages?

Why do we read *1984* when we know the fate of Winston can't be good? Are we naïve enough to believe he will survive the oppressive society he's trapped within?

Do we really think Montag can remedy the trouble he's found because of a simple curiosity about a book and a young, outspoken girl?

The answer is no, the readers of dystopian fiction are not naïve. We do not hold such illusions, for the world around us is headed for disaster. And we read it because we opt to forget our present by reading about the future. Because at least the future isn't now, and we don't yet have to face it. This is a defense mechanism of sorts, and it works well to entertain us, and protect us at the same time.

We love the lost genre of dystopia because of fear. That's right, fear. Much like we watch horror movies, curled up eating popcorn, and wondering why the woman ran up the stairs instead of out the door, and wonder what we would do in her place. We do the same with dystopian fiction. We watch with a sick fascination as the world destroys itself, and wonder what we would do.

Fear is the driving factor in how we view our own society. For example, we fear death. So what do we do? We choose to ignore death. We do so by entertaining ourselves, by buying things that make us temporarily happy. While ancient civilizations revolved life around death, we opt to forget about it. We fill this void with things, then buy more things when those things fail to complete us. Happiness is never achieved, and when death comes, it comes at a great surprise. We force our own view of immortality to deal with it, and when our time comes, we deny death, and wish to overcome it.

This is but one fear, and dystopian fiction uses this fear to motivate us. It binds us to characters, to the conflict within the pages. It allows us a choice—it makes us take sides. And most importantly, it makes us acknowledge our own duress of the world around us, confirming we are on the right side.

The sad fact is, our world is filled with death and mayhem, and there is no escape from it. Dystopian books allow us to shed some light on what's wrong with our own society, and not necessarily fix it, but at least comprehend it.

Whether coming to terms with the massive social engineering feat of social media, and that it is destroying human relationships, to accepting the fact that technology will one day outsource humans, dystopian writers allow us to peer inside ourselves. They allow us to acknowledge our fate, even if we don't want to. And though fear drives us, for it's filled with tragic conflict in this genre, it also allows us to choose sides. This reaffirms our belief that our fears are indeed right, and that we're not alone in them. That someone else, even if a fictional character, shares the same woes as we do. This shared fear is what makes our own fears bearable. It keeps us moving forward.

I'll end with this: *The Last Supper* is one of the best books I've ever read. I say that objectively; this book touches my soul. I care for Dickson's character John, as I do for Winston and Montag.

I wonder if our world will see a Justification.

Will I see a Last Supper?

I will remember the following words to my grave, the opening lines of one of my favorite books of all time.

"My last supper has a salad. I've always hated salad."

The Last Supper has all the proper elements of a great dystopian novel. It stands out from the others, settled in a small group of books such as *1984*, *Fahrenheit 451*, *Animal Farm*, *The Time Machine*, and *The Road*. I tend to believe—because belief is what fiction is all about—that one day in the future, *The Last Supper* will be a classic.

That is, if we make it that far.

In closing, this novel has it all: fear, the all-powerful control of the Justification, crop blights and serpent seeds, all mixed with a pleasant undertone of religion. The story takes place in a fantastical world, overgrown and overwhelming, containing equal parts tragedy and hope, and will surely touch your soul. With Allison M. Dickson's voice, her raw talent and crafty prose, I hope you embark on a journey as I did, and never forget *The Last Supper*.

Vincent Hobbes

THE LAST
SUPPER

Chapter 1

My Last Supper has a salad. I've always hated salad. It isn't that I don't appreciate a good vegetable now and then, but I can't think of anything I'd less like to eat in my final moments than a bowl of limp lettuce leaves with a few pale shreds of carrot mixed in. You can ask any condemned man what he'd like his last meal to be, and if he says salad, there probably was something wrong with him to begin with. But maybe, it's what I deserve.

I learned early in life to avoid most of the food that came out of the ground, unless it was from a Divine Rite Farm, one of only a handful of areas left not affected by the weeds. You can take your chances on what grows outside those areas, but you would probably live to regret it. Even so, not even the "safe" food is safe. Cancer's the biggie—that's what took my wife—but birth defects were common not so long ago and most folks only needed to have a few kids born looking like a Cyclops before they realized maybe there was something to all those crop warnings.

But the Last Supper is a whole other breed of food. Like any other standard-issue death kit, it's *supposed* to kill you.

Like the McDonald's signs of old used to say, billions have been served. I earned my meal ticket, though, and I'd be lying if I said part of me didn't want it. I didn't know a whole lot about this world before leaving the homestead, where everything was green and safe and nobody knew any different, but I've seen enough things now to realize how very doomed we are. People haven't lived anywhere in a long time; they've merely survived. Yeah, I'd say we screwed it up big time.

—

The box my Last Supper came in even has a facsimile of Da Vinci's painting on the front. The irony is enough to kill me all on its own. *Take of my body and eat; take of my blood and drink*, it says in flowing script. I never did enjoy that particular sacrament, my knowledge of it only sufficient enough to pass the yearly Justification exam.

Oh yeah, that reminds me. Justification. I suppose that's the reason I'm here in the first place, and why millions have been before me. It's a simple enough test for those who don't know better, impossible for those who do. Then there are those, like my devout and now deceased wife, who fall through the cracks. All you have to do is prove your worth to this crippled but highly regimented society, and you can continue breathing. Fail, and your final gift is a poisoned repast. More irony for you, I suppose. Poisoned repasts have been a specialty of the human race for some time, long before the weeds came and destroyed everything. The weeds were ours too, by the way, but I'll get to those. I recall John 3:16. *"For God so loved the world He gave His only begotten son, that whoever believes in Him shall have everlasting life."* I guess God decided we weren't much worth saving this time.

He probably gave up on His creation the way you give up a piece of burnt toast when you can't scrape off enough of the black stuff.

I just discovered a packet of oil and vinegar in the bottom of the box. It pads the blow of the salad, but only a little. At least there's dessert: a big, thick wedge of chocolate cake. I can't even remember the last time I saw chocolate. Had to be when I was barely big enough to see over the table. The God-fearing pricks would probably say they prayed extra hard to make the cocoa beans grow, but I think most of the good stuff, like chocolate and sugar and all the things we used to think of as "sinful," comes from the Divine Rite labs nowadays. It's much easier to control it for the masses that way. There may be a lone plant or two in the tropics still doing nature's work, but I wouldn't know. I can only hope with the naivety of a child still wishing for the existence of the tooth fairy that the Blight didn't destroy everything. It's a big planet after all, and even after everything that's happened, I can't quite become a full-blown cynic.

I believe I will start my meal with the cake. If there was ever a time to buck tradition and have dessert first, it's now.

The other parts of the Supper include a hunk of charred meat (species indeterminate), and a small loaf of bread that feels like it's at least a few days old. There's also a small bottle of the fermented grape juice the Rite calls red wine, enough for a single glass. That's plenty for me, since I'd like to be able to write everything I have to say with a clear head.

It might not sound like much, but all this food would be a marvel for most. Meat is a luxury because livestock requires grass and grain to feed, and what little is left has to go to feed the humans. The ones that roam the wild and eat what grows out there . . . well, I'll get to some of them in a bit. Wouldn't want to spoil my appetite.

I just took my first bite of the cake. It's greasy and thick and it coats my tongue against another flavor that reminds me of gasoline. That's probably the poison. Suddenly, the generous slice doesn't seem like such a gift. The salad is the only thing that might taste even remotely clean in all this, so maybe I should be a little thankful it's here.

I just read the short letter accompanying the meal, the standard message, I think. My wife received its twin with her own Supper:

To ensure a painless and dignified passing, we present you with a meal handcrafted by our expert chefs to your exact tastes as specified on your Justification Exam.

Except maybe the salad.

The Divine Rite will place your earthly remains in a planter with a beautiful tree to be placed in one of our scenic Memorial Gardens designed with the comfort of your eternal rest in mind. The Holy Uniter would like to thank you for your service to our nation and to the world.

You may be wondering why they use us for tree fertilizer, but that's not too weird when you think about it. The disposal of bodies posed a challenge in the beginning. Burial wasn't just inefficient with the number of dead involved. The roots of the serpent weeds make digging next to impossible. It's a network stretching far beneath the ground, so thick and hard it takes enormous earth movers to break through them. And if you do, well, they start growing back before you get more than a few loads of dirt out. It's almost like they're intelligent.

Let me rephrase that. They *are* intelligent.

But crematoriums were a poor solution to the problem. The skies were black with the smoke. Even worse, the weeds seemed to thrive off the acidic rain the emissions produced, so the Rite came up with a real bright idea. They used a caustic powder to dissolve the bodies instead. It didn't work on the weeds, but that was a good question if you were already thinking it. It worked like gangbusters on human flesh and bone, though, and there was just enough residue left to make fertilizer for a potted plant (Divine Rite Certified, of course), which the departed's family could then plant in a Memorial Forest, one of those hallowed patches of ground the weeds hadn't taken over for some reason. The Rite would say it was God's providence, but it was just a simple game of evolutionary luck in our favor.

I think I've rambled on long enough, though. There is a much longer tale beyond all this, and I have only a little while to tell it if the Supper works the way I think it does. Things happen too fast to allow for even the smallest amounts of self-indulgence or cathartic blathering. Nonetheless, it's a tale that needs telling, even if no one else ever reads it, because maybe if I know it and hear it deep down in my heart, I'll be able to move on to the doing that needs done, even if it hurts my heart more than words could ever say. Even if it will never bring back the ones I've lost.

At any rate, I'd better continue before my steak gets cold.

Chapter 2

It wasn't like the world didn't see it coming. The devil was in the pollen, and it took decades for people to start connecting the dots. Reports of increased asthma, skin diseases, cancer, and anaphylactic shock made a little murmur in the news-wires from time to time, but it was when the birth defects started popping up in clusters too big to ignore that folks started to panic. And the Blight, of course. Can't forget those. There was a whole host of new "super weeds" out there, and industry people couldn't just cover up the tidal wave of pic-tures and videos and anecdotes normal folks were passing among themselves, even if the media was largely ignoring it. In the old world, where people were accustomed to sharing everything from what they ate for breakfast to the last time they had sex, it was natural that word about our agriculture problems would spread like the weeds themselves. And be just as hard to lie about.

The companies involved weren't complacent. They ex-punged data, silenced whistleblowers, and spun lies into gold. Denial and ignorance reigned among groups who dis-agreed on who had spliced what gene into what that caused the Blight, or whose Super Weed Killer eventually gave way to the species that we came to call Serpent Weeds. There were big suits out there still insisting on the safety of genetic modification in light of the atrocities, their lies becoming so robust and defiant they even attempted to make the weeds sound like a good thing. Not long ago, I even found old literature advertising a big annual festival called Salad Days, where supporters of these big agro companies would gather and "Eat the Future!" as they called it. That not only included the contaminated plant life, but the animals that fed upon it.

Naturally enough, many of those participants were the first to go, and when the founder of the Salad Days events died of a particularly aggressive form of flesh-eating cancer, the festivals stopped altogether and the chorus of dread became a lot more monotone.

In a last fit of desperation, the government ordered planes to drop loads of specially developed herbicide from the skies to kill the invaders. It poisoned what good crops remained and contaminated the groundwater, but the weeds grew bigger and hardier. Fire was another option, but that beast was difficult to control. It wiped out as many homes and towns as it did people, and new weeds sprouted up right through the ash. Freezing with liquid nitrogen seemed to hold them at bay for awhile, but there weren't enough resources to keep it going, and as soon as the weeds thawed, they bounced back twice as hard.

As for the few crazies who survived that initial glut of Salad Days stupidity, well, a lot of them gave rise to what we know as Divine Rite today. It takes crazy to make crazy, after all, and you have to be a particular brand of lunatic to come up with ideas like Justification and The Last Supper.

But I don't really need to go into the rest, do I? There isn't enough time, for one thing. More importantly, the "how" of it doesn't really matter anymore. That's because after things really turned south, we can only guess what happened. Histories of the rise of the Divine Rite were wiped clean of all their warts, and the truth only lives on in those brave enough to share it. I received the barest glimpse of it before I arrived where I am now, and I can tell you there is a whole hell of a lot more involved here than a simple gene splice gone wrong. It was a cataclysm far beyond Biblical, and I'm not sure anyone will ever really know the facts, or if the facts at this point would even make a difference. They couldn't undo what's been done.

It might surprise some people to know there were still thriving and established communities in this country, even at the height of the Blight. They were small and heavily quarantined, of course. The Rite designed these electrified domed nets to hang over the residential areas and farms that trapped most of the serpent weed pollen and allowed for a sustainable amount of subsistence farming.

Most of the people who lived under those nets were asleep. I know, because I was one of them. Our news was every bit as filtered as the air, and we were blissfully ignorant, "doing God's Work" and passing Justification accordingly. Well, most of us were, anyway. There were a few who knew it was all an illusion, that the Rite was just another group of tyrants from a long line of them stretching back to the time of Jesus himself. I got to know some of those good people very well, and so will you.

Under the net, most people had to follow some basic rules. Stay free of drugs and alcohol, make your productivity quotas (that's hold a job, in plain speak), procreate according to the mandate of the local Divine Rite poobah and, of course, go to church three days a week.

Our little patch of fertile land was called God's Hope. Not too imaginative, but creativity is rarely a valued commodity among the pious. If you ever needed an example of how well Justification worked, you could look to my hometown. The grass grew green and tender, the people were smiling and content, and there was always enough food to keep their bellies full as long as nobody bred out of turn.

I lived in God's Hope until I lost my wife. After that, I just sort of floated along like a dead leaf on a stagnant pond.

Tumors invaded Linny's pancreas, and two years later, she died. But it wasn't from the cancer. When it was her yearly trip to the Exam center in the center of town, she drew the short straw. Months of illness had made her too weak to attend church. She also lacked the strength to care for the home or perform any of her required civic duties. In the cold, impartial eyes of the Divine Rite, her continued existence was no longer Justified.

They took no appeals. There wasn't even a department for such a thing. Linny had violated the algorithm, and if they made an exception for her, they would risk a possible revolt. Later that evening, there was a knock on our door and sitting there on the welcome mat Linny had stitched herself with the ladies from the Fellowship was a box bearing the same Da Vinci painting I'm looking at right now. We sent our twin daughters, Beth and Kaya, to spend the night at friends' houses, and once they were gone I yelled and screamed. I begged her to throw the goddamn thing away, not caring who was in earshot of that particular forbidden blasphemy. But it didn't matter. She started to eat, even as I gathered our meager possessions and shoved them into bags. Escape was my first resort, giving up was hers. I still want to hate her for that, but what's the point? She was dying anyway.

Her dessert had been lemon pudding, and she started with that, just as I did with my chocolate cake.

"We all have to go at some point, John," she'd said between small spoonfuls of the yellow stuff that looked a bit like something you'd squeeze out of a nasty pimple. Apart from her red-rimmed eyes, her face was a sheet of white. "We'd be just as dead when they caught us, and I don't have the strength to run anyway. We both knew when the cancer came this might happen." Her face brightened for a second. "Perhaps they're doing me a mercy! That must be it, after all of my devotions and tithes. You can't be mad at them, dear. This is better than the cancer."

I clenched my fists. To hell with that, I wanted to say, but she wasn't listening anymore. The food was already doing its job.

She gazed at the steaming, deadly entrees before her. It had come out of the box hot, as if someone had baked it right on our front porch. That was the creepiest part. "Have you ever seen anything like this? I haven't seen such food since I was a little girl."

It was so unnatural looking, so . . . manufactured. I wondered where it came from.

She held out her hand to me as I plopped down across from her in resignation. I watched her eat the plain omelet and the flat biscuit that accompanied it and I dug furrows into my leg with my other hand to keep from slapping the fork away.

We started talking about the girls and how we thought they would turn out. They had both been coming up on their fifteenth birthdays and their first Justification exams. We agreed that Beth was a cinch, but Kaya, a natural rebel forever with a question in her mouth, would bear watching. Tears and the Lord's Prayer accompanied Linny's last bite, and I carried her unconscious body to bed, where her shallow breaths slowed and eventually stopped. I wrapped her body in a sheet and left her there. Then I walked out back, where I fell asleep on our picnic table under the cold and uncaring stars.

When I awoke at the chilly crack of dawn, she was gone, along with all her possessions and the remnants of her Supper. Not even a picture of her remained. It was as if my wife of twenty years had never existed. This was all standard Divine Rite custom. They sent their goons out like thieves in the night to collect their victims. I never even heard them come. The Rite claims they do this "for the expediency of the grieving process." In other words, out of sight, out of mind. Eventually, with no personal effects to remind you of the one you lost, you start to question whether he or she was in your life to begin with, and you forget. Or at least, that's what they hope, and for a few days I lived in that foggy space between memory and reality. Then I received a second delivery: a little fir sapling in a crude clay planter, with a neatly printed note attached. Every word of it has since been branded into my head.

On behalf of the Divine Rite, and by extension Holy Uniter,

Urban IV, we present to you this remembrance gift. You are free to plant it in your nearest designated Memorial Forest, or if space and local ordinance permits, allow it to grace your own yard, where it will eventually provide you shade as well as comfort. Please note the pot is designed to be planted with the tree, as it serves as a source of additional fertilizer for the growing specimen.

In Grace,

Clarence Wolf

Senior Spokesperson, Divine Rite, Kansas Parish

And there it was. The tree. The "specimen." They took Linny and everything that was hers and then they brought her back. I suppose if they hadn't, I would have continued my quiet, unquestioning life in God's Hope, eventually forgetting I even had a wife. I wondered why the Rite would do this, why they would prod someone's grief this way, but I eventually figured out it was like everything else they do. It was a test. If I could endure this cruelty, I could endure anything they threw at me. But I failed that test. Seeing my wife reduced to nothing more than white specks in dirt, plant food in a world consumed by rogue plants, ignited a white-hot rage that's driven me ever since.

That evening, the girls and I planted their mother in our backyard, pot and all as instructed. I think it was the last thing I ever did by Divine Rite code. Beth wept openly, but Kaya was uncharacteristically silent, stonily looking off to the horizon as I dug the small hole and placed the fir and its pot inside. Beth helped push in the dirt and kissed its branches. One of the tree's sharp needles poked her in the lip and that only made her cry harder. Kaya refused to touch the tree. After I filled the hole, she said, "So I guess we're done then," and strode off toward the open prairies where she spent most of her time those days.

Beth curled up next to the tree and held one of its delicate boughs as if it was her mother's hand. She was fifteen years old, but at that moment she was five all over again with golden pigtails, ready to poke her thumb back in her mouth. Lost in my own grief and anger, I had no idea how to comfort her, so I didn't, and every horrible thing that happened afterward was made worse by that inaction. If I had held her close and shared my grief with hers, maybe . . .

But what's the point of maybes?

A couple hours later, after Beth had fallen asleep next to the tree, Kaya's angry footsteps thudded on the porch. I was sitting in the small, newly emptied parlor, gazing at the spot where Linny's rocker and needlepoint supplies once sat. Kaya's slender figure darkened the doorway. With her short haircut and big blue eyes reddened from crying, she looked like an angry pixie.

"There was nothing you could do, was there?" she asked, her voice trembling like a dam fit to burst.

I shook my head, feeling weak and without the answer she so clearly wanted. "I suppose not."

"She was going to die anyway, you know. From the cancer." Her voice cracked on the last word, but she remained dry-eyed. She had more courage and strength than anyone I'd ever known, and I saw a lot more of it in the events that soon unfolded, but right then I was struck by how different she was from everybody in God's Hope, and it wasn't just the boyish haircut that made the long-haired ladies in town turn their heads. There was a fire in her, a vitality that reminded me of my mother, or what little I could remember of her.

I wanted to open my arms to Kaya, but that wasn't how she operated. She had to be the one to break down first. One wrong move and she could clam up for good, or make me lose my hand in one of the many booby traps that guarded her heart.

"Yes, the cancer would have gotten her eventually. Probably by Christmas," I said. "She'd been getting weaker every day. This was what your mother wanted."

"But why did *they* take her?" she screamed in the darkening room. "She was almost dead anyway and they took her from us! They had no right! They had no fucking *right*!" She burst into great, heaving sobs, and that was my cue. I went to her and let her melt into my chest, but as I stroked her head and held her close, my arms felt numb.

Chapter 3

Grief is a cruel captor, and you never know what kind of warden you'll have until you're locked inside its prison. I waited in my cell for the ultimate catharsis, something that would come crashing through the bars and carry me away like a flash flood sweeping away debris from a forgotten riverbed in the wilderness. I waited for salvation, or the "Voice of God" that so many desperate souls insist visits them in their greatest time of need to deliver them from the darkness. But there was no cleansing deluge, and I grew more and more certain there was no God. Not the God I'd grown up envisioning, anyway.

In the weeks following Linny's death, I started going into work less, and eventually stopped going in at all. That alone was grounds for Justification failure, but the linchpin was when I stopped attending church. Without Linny, I felt like I'd been cast out from the herd. The eyes of people I once considered friends regarded me as if I were a strange bird carrying a contagious disease. It wasn't that I stopped believing in a higher power altogether. After everything I've seen, I like to think I have somewhere greater to go when I die. But I couldn't do my sort of believing next to people who were beholden to the Rite's idea of righteousness.

Kaya and Beth drifted further away as well. They both passed their first Justification exams, but my relief was bittersweet at what was only to be a year-long reprieve from the inevitable. Eventually, one of us would fail. The deck was stacked.

The only thing that did come to rescue me from that prison of grief was my rage. Its waters were dirty and cold, but they motivated me. I eventually came to see the Divine Rite's true nature: cold-blooded murderers disguised in holy-rolling benevolence. The fires of hatred burning in me by that point could only be quenched by acts of subversion.

Writing seemed a natural place to begin. I purchased a red leather-bound journal, a luxurious item in such lean times (I can't say now what became of it), and I began a journey of self-expression forty years in the making. It was slow going at first. I felt like a kid tempting rebellion by sneaking out of the house only to stop at the end of the driveway. One night, I took my chair out back and opened my journal next to Linny's tree. With her by my side, the anti-establishment floodgates opened and out spilled a river of hate near impossible to dam back up again. I was trembling by the time I finished, and a little sick to my stomach. My thoughts were no longer in my head. They were physically "out there" now. I could have burned the pages, sure, but I could no more do that than deface my own child.

After that, it became ritual.

I focused my writing mostly on immoral acts because they provided immediate payoffs. I detailed a fantasy in which I drowned Stanley Robbins, the supervisor on my line at the textile mill who docked an hour of pay for even one minute of tardiness, regardless of the excuse. But it wasn't just the pay that took a bite out of your ass. It was the points that would be deducted at Justification. Not a lot for one instance, but a chronic problem of showing up late could prove lethal.

In the story, I held his fat, screaming head in a steaming vat of indigo dye until it was puffy and black. Petty and juvenile maybe, but then again, I'd never had much of a childhood.

The rebellion also had a considerable effect on my libido. I won't lie and say I didn't feel guilty about it. I did. But I think my urges were more about "going against the grain," and less about "cheating on Linny." In the confines of our small garage, where I kept our bikes and a work bench for unfinished projects, (and well out of sight of Linny's tree) I wrote about the younger redhead with the shapely hips and tilted green eyes who ran the general store with her father Harry. Genevieve. She and Harry came to God's Hope not long after I proposed to Linny. I remember her being small for her age, and frail, but she eventually blossomed into something almost unnaturally beautiful, and was the only other woman in all of God's Hope who occasionally made my thoughts stray to forbidden places. And I was sure I wasn't the only husband in town who felt that way, given the number of sharp glances I saw from their wives at the Fellowship if their eyes lingered a bit too long as she passed by. Linny was a little less disapproving that way, and was probably more gracious to the girl than most of the other women had been.

In more recent weeks, however, my thoughts about Genevieve became a little less occasional and a little more regular. The material I wrote about her was pretty light, and honestly too ridiculous to share here. But after those particular writing sessions, I found the only source of relief was to masturbate, which of course was very frowned upon by Divine Rite, and something I hadn't even dared try until then. I soon found it contributed more to my awakening as a hot-blooded rebel than anything else, and I learned that the release of one's libido after decades of keeping it tightly regulated can be a bit hazardous, with excessive preoccupation leading to carelessness, as I soon learned.

My acts of sedition might have begun with pen and paper, but they definitely didn't end there. I grew restless with the pages after awhile. I wanted to move beyond the security of my home and my trusty journal and start seeing if I could spread my little disease of awareness to a few other members of the town.

I began by taking late night strolls and ripping down Divine Rite propaganda posters from the trees and bulletin boards, but eventually I decided it was best to leave them up, after performing a little "corrective artwork." One night, I decided the Holy Uniter would look better wearing a crown of dicks, and I hastily made the alteration with a red paint pen while looking over my shoulder every millisecond or so. After finishing the masterpiece, I scrawled "Crowned Dick of the Divine Rite" across the top and crept home, shaking with manic giggles I later screamed into a pillow with my bedroom door shut behind me.

The next morning, after hours of tossing and turning, certain the Hand of God, the Rite's most elite police force, was going to pound down my door any minute, I swung my legs out of bed at first light and dressed. When I arrived at the Pavilion, a small crowd had already assembled around the bulletin board. A few (mostly kids) smiled and laughed openly, but most appeared somber and afraid.

A young man in official patrol robes walked up to the board and ripped the poster down without ceremony. "Everybody move along here, before I decide to start asking questions," he shouted at the already dispersing crowd. I lingered for a moment, though. The officer, who didn't appear much older than my teenage girls, locked eyes with me. I suddenly felt naked, as if he knew I was the perpetrator, as if there was a gob of betraying red paint on my face that told the whole story. I turned on my heels and walked away, breaking into a full run the closer I got to the house.

When I walked in, the girls were just sitting down to breakfast. Both looked startled by my sweaty face and sloppy clothes, but Beth's expression was particularly suspicious. She raised her eyebrow in an expression that looked so much like her mother that it hurt my heart. "What are you doing leaving the house looking like that, Daddy?"

My mind fumbled for a few seconds. Why the hell would I leave the house so early in the morning, anyway? "Just . . . felt like a little jog, I guess," I said. She didn't seem convinced.

"I was hoping to hear you'd visited the Fellowship. Reverend Blackwell has been asking after you."

"Screw Reverend Blackwell," Kaya muttered. She was stirring a bowl of porridge without much interest. "He's probably grubbing after more money, anyway."

Beth gaped at her sister and crossed herself. "Where did you even hear that language?"

"There are other books than the Bible, you know. And stop talking to me like I'm your kid. Seriously, you're worse than mom."

"That's enough from both of you," I said, taking a seat at the table. It was the first time in awhile we'd all sat together, but I might as well have been sitting on the moon for how distant I felt from them.

"I plan to pray for you, Daddy," Beth murmured. "For you both."

"Thank you, sweetheart," I said. My heart wasn't in it, but if it pacified her suspicion even a little, I was all for it.

Kaya snorted. "Sure, Beth. Pray your face off. While you're at it, maybe you can ask the Big Man Upstairs to put some extra dessert in Daddy's Supper, since he has one coming any day now."

Beth stood up fast and glared at us both. "It's like both of you are trying to fail Justification now. Mom didn't have a choice, but you do. You're both being so selfish. She would be ashamed if she could see you right now." She stormed out of the house, leaving Kaya and I to endure the pregnant silence Beth left in her wake.

Finally, my other daughter sighed and stood up. "She was right about that, Dad. About Justification. I probably won't pass my next one at the rate I'm going, and I'm pretty sure you won't, either. This family is fucked." She walked off in the direction of her room, and I didn't bother to call her on the obscenities. What right did I have after all of mine? Besides, she was right. I pulled her porridge to me and ate a few bites before putting my head down on the table.

If I'd known that would be the last time the three of us would ever sit in the same room together, I might have tried harder, but hindsight is a cruel mistress and she spins one hell of an illusion out of our regrets.

—

Of course, no good rebellion against the establishment is complete without the consumption of illicit substances, and with the way things had deteriorated at home I needed the kind of escape that could only be had in a bottle. Drinking and drugs, of course, were not part of the regimen of anyone who planned on passing Justification, and it was difficult to get any in large quantities outside a Sin Bin, facilities where people surrendered their last year of life so they could live in complete debauchery. But liquor was easier to get than one might think. Like most "forbidden" things in God's Hope, it wasn't exactly illegal. It was just another tempting piece of fruit the Rite liked to have lying around for the weak of will, and the price for succumbing to such things was deadly.

The lack of large agriculture wasn't much of a hindrance for the making of potables either. Nearly any grain is distillable, any fruit or starchy vegetable fermentable. You could lay hands on some liquid lightning for a small price and little effort, and you barely had to leave your own backyard if you knew a few techniques, or the right person. For me, that person was James L. Turpin.

Turpin had been in God's Hope for as long as I could remember, though for most of my life people simply referred to him as "the old fella." He escaped Justification by being just over fifty when it became law, which made him part of a very rare Exempt Class. It should also be noted that the average minimum age of the high ranking Divine Rite officials at the time coincided with the age of exemption. No man should be hoisted by his own petard, after all. Turpin lived the sort of life that incited fear and loathing in most people, but envy in a select few who were courageous enough to admit it. I was the former for many years, but now I was one of the latter.

His place was a massive stretch of land the locals referred to as "The Bunker," one of many military posts left behind after the Blight, where a combination of disease, weeds, and ensuing civil skirmishes decimated too many people to fill a proper army. The Rite reclaimed some of these sites to build Cradles, which were outposts where they trained and housed the Hand of God agents, but most were left to the weeds or the simple reclamation of time and the elements. Turpin apparently had some ancestral claim to the land, though most of those details were a little murky in an age where most pre-Blight deeds and records were destroyed. He was allowed to keep it so long as he agreed to remain on it and stay away from the regular townsfolk. As I later found out, that's exactly how Turpin preferred things anyway.

I gazed at the rusted remains of an M1 tank with a bird's nest tucked inside the gun turret on my way up the long driveway. Signs posted around the perimeter of the property warned of the presence of mines, and this probably kept most intruders away, but the legend of Turpin frightened more people than the possibility of obliteration by landmine. You didn't associate with him unless you were determined to flunk Justification. It was as simple as that.

Though older than dirt, he was hale enough to subsist off his land with little help, and he made most of his money through the sale of his homegrown ethanol fuel to neighborhood farms and businesses. Depending on who you were speaking to, Turpin was an "evil atheist" who performed abortions and put hexes on local missionaries. Others claimed he shot intruders with devilish pre-Blight weaponry hidden in an underground cache somewhere on his property. But the most popular anecdote, and the one that was actually true, was that he ran a "poison factory." That was God's Hope lingo for booze.

He might have been the town's answer to the urbane wizard with the taboo apothecary, but Turpin's medicine came from copper kettles and unmarked mason jars rather than bubbling cauldrons. I'd never before taken a drink of any alcohol apart from the thimble of sour grape juice at Sunday Mass, and I had no idea what intoxication actually felt like, but now something within me craved a glut of Turpin's poison. I guess it was just a part of the natural progression of things that led to me sitting here now.

I followed a sturdy wood fence, which crested a few feet over my head, until I reached a gate into which security cameras and an ancient intercom had been set. I let out a few breaths to ready myself and pressed the call button, not even sure if it would work. A buzzer sounded at the main residence behind the fence. A couple seconds later, a soft and quavering voice sounded from the speaker.

"Yes?"

I should have expected something like this, given the guarded set-up of the place, but I stammered out whatever came to mind first.

"Hello, uh, Mr. Turpin. My name is John, uh, Welland. We've never met, but I had, ah, hoped—"

"Ah yes, Welland. The one whose wife just got the Supper." Though the audio was tinny and laced with static, I could detect notes of sympathy along with a touch of accent that was downright exotic in this part of the country.

"Yes, uh, that's right, Mr. Turpin." Although I had written about it plenty, speaking aloud with others about my dead wife was still unfamiliar to me, and I fought the lump that rose in my throat at the mention of her name. There was another buzz and a locking mechanism in the fence clicked. The imposing doors swung open, officially welcoming me into a new era of my life.

Turpin stood just on the other side with a little rectangular clicker in one hand and a cane in the other. For a man considered old by any period's standards, he stood tall, as if the years had only spared a glance at him before moving on. His frame was thin, but he had a small paunch of a belly, and a weather-beaten face covered in a straggly silver beard. Beyond Turpin, I saw a well-manicured yard filled with cushioned wicker furniture and antique propane heaters, which he must have worked like hell to bring back into operation and polish to a high shine. Brightly colored paper lanterns decorated the fence and added a sense of whimsy to the place. A lush garden stretched away from the side of the house. I could make out carrots, lettuces, beet tops, and a hearty crop of Lazarus, a bland hybridized grain the Rite developed after the Blight that was good for making rough bread and porridge and not much else. In the middle of it all, a modest log cabin sprouted rambling additions to either side making the structure resemble a bird carved by a novice whittler.

I stepped forward and stretched out my hand. "Thank you for seeing me, Mr. Turpin."

The old man's grip was firm, but his smile was soft. "I figured we'd meet at some point after I heard the news 'bout your wife, boyo. Goddamn shame what happened. I ain't seen that sort of travesty 'round here in many a year. By the way, most of the friendlier persuasion just call me Turpin."

"Turpin it is," I said.

He regarded me for a moment, like someone trying to measure me for a task. "Ya do know that just by bein' here, yer sacrificin' any standin' ya might have with the Rite. Not too late to turn back, boyo."

I tried on a smile that felt a little forced given how anxious I felt. "I walked all the way up here. The least I could do is have a drink."

"Understood. Well, we can't let any more time waste away, then." He led me toward the porch, where two cozy rocking chairs sat. "I have to say, it's good to see a new face in the place. What sorta tonic tickles yer fancy today?"

"Um. I'm not really sure what I'm looking for." I felt a little embarrassed to say so, as if I should have had a list of items prepared before I even came up here.

"So, a tastin' it be. Follow me. We'll line up some glasses and figure out what kinda man ya are." He walked with a spry gait up the creaky porch stairs and into the house. I followed, my nervousness slowly melting into amusement. In a few minutes, I'd be passing the ultimate point of no return, worse than writing some cuss words in a book, defacing a poster, or even masturbating. I was going to violate an explicitly written Divine Rite covenant; I was going to Spoil God's Temple.

The amount of stuff inside Turpin's place was almost overwhelming. Books lined every wall of the living room, from floor to ceiling, and heaped every other flat surface. I saw both foreign and forbidden tomes—Dostoyevsky, Nietzsche, Salinger, Rushdie, The Kama Sutra—mixed among even more contraband: colorful comic books featuring costumed heroes of old, and glossy pornography magazines featuring swells of bare breasts and acres of skin.

A battered copy of a book called *The Population Bomb* by Paul R. Ehrlich rested on the arm of one of the room's two well-worn wing chairs with a stub of pencil and a pair of old spectacles on top. Over the fireplace hung an ancient American flag I had only previously seen in history books. Fifty stars on a dark blue field, red and white stripes; a relic of a dead era if there ever was one.

Hundreds of black and white photographs and newspaper cutouts adorned tables, desks, and available wall space. A few of the grainy pictures featured an impossibly young Turpin in a military uniform.

The room smelled of paper, warm spices, and a distinct sourness I later came to associate with the making and drinking of booze. It was comforting rather than offensive. I could have spent years in this house soaking up the smells and every scrap of culture and knowledge it offered.

Turpin rummaged in his kitchen cupboards, and set down bottles and jugs of various sizes and colors on the rough-hewn but well-oiled countertop. From a shelf above his sink, he took down a few tiny glasses of the sort I'd only seen at Communion.

"I got fake bourbon whisky, malt whisky, and gin. It's fake bourbon, because the real stuff is made with corn, and as we all know, that particular grain went to the devil long ago. I make do with a mix of Lazarus, malt, and rye. Malt and rye are dear, but luckily I can make a lot of liquor with what little I can get. There's vodka from Lazarus or potatoes—I prefer the potato stuff, personally. I got some moonshine that I make from plums that grow here on the property. Good for cleanin' engines, and it'd melt the good looks right off yer face, but some folks like it. I wouldn't recommend it for anyone who doesn't have a death wish or a titanium liver, though. Rum's the only thing I don't got. Sugarcane's even more dear than the grain. It's only for fuel. And of course I got a few experimental ales." He hoisted a clear jug of pink-ish-gold foamy liquid. "This here's my latest. I call it Turpin's Strawberry Piss. Tastes better'n it sounds." He let out a wheezy cackle that endeared him to me a little more, and I loosened up the rest of the way.

I stared in fascination at the menagerie of bottles, reveling in a language that might as well have been foreign for all it meant to me at the time. "Uh, you pick," I told him. Turpin gazed at me for a moment and poured me a shot of clear liquid that smelled like pine. Or cleaning solvent. I took a cautious sip before knocking it back. It seared my stomach, and I gagged.

I was not a gin man.

Then I tried a few more things. It turned out I was a bourbon man. Turpin approved.

Chapter 4

The old man opined a lot in his slurred and shaky speech as he rolled cigarettes from homegrown leaf. We discussed the mundane—kids, crops, small town gossip—but after we emptied a few glasses, our discussion turned to the Divine Rite. After all, why would anyone else darken this man's doorstep, if not to rebel against the powers that be?

"They got ya kids by the scruffs of yer balls and most of ya don't even know it. Or worse, don't even *care*. Oh, ya used to care, all right. Why, in the beginning of this Justification business, there was a nasty little revolt, ya see. The streets ran red with the blood of those who tried to stand against it. Of course, they wiped out damn near a generation of people in the process. Rounded 'em up and beheaded 'em, or stuck 'em in those ghastly Cradles for experiments."

There were several Cradles throughout the country. The nearest one was a few hundred miles away. Talk of experiments were only rumors, but most thought of them as schools where ordained folks left God's Hope every year to study or join the Hand of God. "My daughter Beth had talked about going away to the Cradle from time to time. Linny and I used to think that might be best. But now . . . Now I'd rather set myself on fire than see her work for these people."

Turpin nodded and took a drag off his smoke. "Yep. Most folks think they're doin' right by their kiddies raisin' 'em by the Divine Rite code, but it's mostly because they're afraid." He looked at me shrewdly for a moment and then asked a question I hadn't expected. "What became of *your* parents, boyo?"

Ordinarily I would have diverted the topic. My parents were a sore subject not even Linny would bring up but once in a great while, usually when she was mad at me for something, but the alcohol had opened me up some.

"They fought against the Rite. I don't remember much of it, though. We moved around a lot. It was a small-time group mostly made up of troublemakers. More of a nuisance than a real threat."

"Aye. But sometimes a bunch of little acts put together make for a lot of change."

That much was true. They'd vandalized a few Exam centers and committed a little bit of tech warfare. While most computer technology was done away with in this part of the world, the Rite still used terminals for the Justification process, and pretty fancy ones at that. Skin tests to tell if you were lying, machines that analyzed your voice patterns, stuff like that. One time, a nasty virus infiltrated their testing software and shut the whole system down. My folks' little organization took credit for it, and I remember the celebration they threw for it too, but the victory was short-lived. Justification was back online after a week and more robust than ever.

After awhile, the Rite offered amnesty to those who turned themselves in and agreed to stop their acts of rebellion. It was one thing to be a principled fugitive from imminent death, but another to receive a second chance at legitimacy. My parents had been among those lucky few they granted clemency, mostly because Mom had become pregnant again and didn't want us kids dying in a gutter or a Cradle.

I have one vague memory of Mom holding her barely pregnant belly and stroking my head as she cried. I was too young to understand it then, but life on the run was wearing on her. It wasn't long afterward the Rite issued us fresh papers and a new start in God's Hope. I was in school again. One of their schools, sure, but I was around other kids and living out in the open. That's also where I met Linny. Our families bonded almost immediately, and it wasn't until she died that I spent a single day without the person who eventually became my wife.

One day, not long before my mother was due to deliver the baby, a rebel group bombed a Divine Rite parish office. Dozens of clerics and other high ranking officials were killed. Linny's family greeted me at home after school, but my parents were gone. My mom had left me a note scratched on a scrap of paper, which only said she loved me. I never heard from either of them again. As for what happened to my unborn brother—at least she believed she was having a boy, though there was no way of knowing for sure—I dared not to think.

I washed away the bad memories with whisky and winced at the fire that trailed down my throat. "I sometimes think they're still out there breaking laws, making things harder on the bastards. Just a dream, I suppose."

"It's a good dream, boyo. It's a better life than tryin' to live by the Holy Algorithm."

"The Holy Algorithm," I spat sarcastically. "Sanctimonious fucks."

Turpin laughed. "Ya got that right. They have a pretty detailed formula for figurin' out who passes and fails those tests, but it all comes down to the same answer. Ya can stray outside the line once or twice over the year and not get yer Meals on Wheels of Death. But if ya make it a lifestyle, they got no use for ya. *Humanity's* got no use for ya, according to The Holy Algorithm, and they're damn sure gonna tempt ya until ya slip up. The Rite *wants* more people to slip up so they can do away with 'em, or put 'em in Sin Bins where they can turn a profit on the drugs they supply 'em with. What's left are only the most perfect ones. Or so they think."

"It's sick," I said.

"Sure it is. It ain't gonna work though, for the same reason most religions don't work. Believe it or not, most folks are wise to the system. They fall in line not because they think it's the right thing to do. They're just afraid of the consequences. But most of the people in this town aren't much different from you and me. It's why I got such a thrivin' trade." He puffed the last of his cigarette and put it out on one well-worn boot heel. "But eventually, somethin's gonna give. The Rite will reach a point where they'll have to deal with the folks like you, the ones who played the game and lost anyway. Those twisted bastards can make millions of people disappear, but they can't make people's grief go away. Anger is grief's best friend, and with anger comes revenge. Ya probably know all about that."

I glared into my mostly empty glass, knuckles white against the molded mason jar logo, and thought about how it would feel to wrap my fingers around the throat of the face-less official who'd decided my wife was no longer Justified.

"You bet I do."

Turpin swatted at a fly circling his wizened head. "They got hooked on the power Justification gave them. The ability to decide whether people live or die with such precision is something not even God has perfected yet. They aren't only *playing* God, boyo."

"They think they're better," I said.

"Right ya are. After other countries started following our lead, we got ourselves a New World Order practically over-night. But they're ignoring the big elephant in the room. And that's folks like us. Folks like you." Then he leaned in, his old, watery eyes agleam and said, "Ya know what elephants do when they get treated badly enough, don't ya?"

I laughed. "They trample the whole goddamn circus." The language of blasphemy felt as natural in my mouth as my own tongue.

Turpin didn't smile, but his rheumy eyes twinkled. "Yer goddamn right they do."

Chapter 5

The summer whittled away as I spent more and more time at the Turpin stead. I received a letter from Stanley Robinson at the textile plant giving me one last chance to keep my job before he sent in his final report to the Justification office, but I ignored it. There are only so many woven shirts an enlightened man can dye, so many days of indigo-stained hands, before the repetition becomes so maddening that you either quit or start making good on the murderous fantasies written in a certain red journal.

I decided I would talk to Harry down at the general store to see if he had a need for someone to make deliveries or stock shelves, but even the excitement from possibly working alongside Genevieve faded from my mind as I awoke and set off for another day at the Bunker. Helping the old man with his chores and reading through his extensive book collection didn't count as a job by Divine Rite standards, but I felt busier and more fulfilled than I had in years and I was content to live off the dwindling remainder of my nest egg until it was gone.

I'd also taken up a new form of defiance, my most daring one yet. I wrote Haiku-style poetry on little slips of paper and left them lying around in various public places: park benches, grocery baskets, store shelves. One of my last trips into the Divine Rite Fellowship was to leave a slip of paper in one of the Bibles.

Divine Rite is Wrong
Peddles death, yet we don't act
Where is your outrage?

I realize I'm no poet, but it no less felt cathartic to envision my words spreading around like viruses, in the form of hushed dinner conversations or murmurs at church social events. A waiter on the nightshift at the Daily Bread Café may have swept one up into his dustpan and become curious enough to read it. Would those seventeen syllables awaken a longing spirit in him and spur him into action? Would he then write a poem of his own or just pass mine along? Even if only five more people read it and spread it on to another five, I'd consider that an accomplishment. The population of God's Hope wasn't very big, a couple thousand at most, but even if a tenth of them became intrigued enough to write something, it could change the whole chemistry of the place.

Looking back, I suppose my hopes were a little high, but we sure changed things all right. Many paid the price for heeding those little whispers on paper, and are still paying it. It's one reason I'm sitting here right now, choking down this damn chocolate cake. And salad.

A week after I quit my job, I received a letter from Reverend Blackwell asking after my lack of attendance at Mass, and of course my lack of tithe contributions. Divine Rite considers it theft from the church if you give them less than 40% of your income. The price for living in a heaven-bound society, I suppose. Penalties are stiff for lack of payment. Excommunication is the standard, and it makes receiving a Supper all but inevitable.

It was time to make a decision. My actions over the last half year probably already spelled certain death, and this would be the thing that clenched it for sure, but the consequences of failing Justification seemed muffled somehow. Like seeing the fin of an approaching shark from the safety of the beach, I knew it was there, but I arrogantly assumed it would never actually reach me. Maybe my name and number would just fall through the cracks. I was just one man. The Divine Rite couldn't actually account for every living soul inside its net, could it?

Like I said, it was arrogant. Naïve, even. But I was having too much fun feeling alive. The poetry, the blasphemy, the taste of Turpin's aged bourbon, it had fundamentally changed me. You might be wondering what sort of father that makes me, that I should have been thinking of my girls during all this, but when you're only living in the present, you don't really think that way. As it was, we hardly spoke. That last breakfast we had, the morning I ran home from the town square, set the stage for many days where we hardly saw each other at all. Beth buried herself deeper in her religious studies, and Kaya volunteered at a local preschool. I spent those days either at Turpin's, or sleeping off a drunk from the night before.

I should have tried harder. I know that now. They were my kids, and it was my job to open the dialogue, but I think after a certain point, when I knew I was lost for good, I reasoned my absence from their lives was a way of protecting them. What they didn't know couldn't kill them.

Beth never asked where I spent most of my time, but she didn't have to. I knew rumors were circulating about how much time I was spending with Turpin, and the conclusions were easy enough for an infant to draw. But Kaya made a comment when she brought in the clean laundry on one rare afternoon we were sharing the house together.

"Your clothes smell of whatever it is you've been drinking."

I had nothing to say to that.

The morning of the day when everything changed, I received an envelope in the mail reminding me of my overdue tithes. I put in my final contribution to the Fellowship: a single dollar bill with *Thou Hast Forsaken Me* scrawled on it in black ink. I suppose if I had left out the blasphemy and just sent the dollar, the course of my life might have been different, but that's the whole point, isn't it? I didn't want things to be the same anymore. My home was broken. My life was shattered. This was the moment that would prove whether I was ready to live by the words rather than just think them. I suppose I was ready, because when I put the envelope into the Fellowship drop box, my heart didn't so much as skip a beat. I was in this thing for real now.

In that, I felt a large measure of freedom. I'd struck up a new path, and although I knew my own death was on the horizon, the world seemed a little brighter right then.

I decided to swing by the market to pick up something special for dinner. It was time for our broken little family to huddle together again as a single unit so I could finally explain all this to them and let them know I wouldn't be passing Justification when the time came in a few months. Beth would never understand, and I couldn't blame her. After all, hadn't her mother and I helped instill some of that piety in her just by raising her here, and exposing her to a life of Divine Rite indoctrination? I thought maybe Kaya would be on my side, though. She had somehow escaped the propaganda with her rebel's heart intact.

I was just heading into the store when a voice made familiar after hundreds of sermons, prayers, and benedictions called out from behind me.

"Brother Welland, is that you?"

I turned and saw a man draped in black robes with red piping and the insignia of a serpent wrapped around a crucifix, the official Divine Rite pastoral garb. He was in his late sixties, but there wasn't a single gray hair anywhere in the thick head of black. His blue eyes were like two Alaskan lakes, and the smile on his face only seemed to go about a millimeter deep.

"Good afternoon, Reverend." I choked out the words, convinced my heart would leap out of my throat after them. I thought I could stand by my convictions, but this was too soon. By his cool expression, I knew my antics were finished. He would soon take me by the arm and escort me directly to the Justification center. There would not even be time to say goodbye to my girls. I had a wild thought that maybe there wouldn't even be a Justification exam, that he would call on the Hand of God, and off to the Cradle I would go.

"I was beginning to wonder if something had happened

to you, John. If not for the regular attendance of your daughters, I might have been even more certain about that. Did you receive my letter?"

The tithes. Maybe he hadn't received them yet. My heart slowed, but only a little. "Yes, I've, ah, been keeping my own spiritual counsel lately. I sent my tithes this morning." I was sure I looked as guilty as Cain after the murder of Abel, and felt disgusted with myself for my reflexive need to kowtow to this bastard.

The Reverend's face remained ever glacial. "Money alone does not guarantee salvation, John, neither with the Lord nor with . . . anyone else."

The hidden threat behind those words had a way of steeling me up a bit. "My wife gave a hell of a lot more than money, Reverend, and it didn't exactly guarantee her salvation either." My voice got a little raw toward the end, but I held it together. Barely.

Blackwell cleared his throat and his eyes softened a little at the mention of Linny. "Perhaps not here on earth, but salvation is awarded in heaven, as I'm sure dear Linda would agree from on high."

"I find little comfort in that," I muttered and stepped past him.

"The church is your source of comfort, not your enemy, John," he called after me. "Do not stray from the flock when you need it most. It may not be too late for you to redeem yourself!"

He'd soon be changing his mind about that.

Inside Camden's Goods, I stocked up on basic essentials, adding a trio of pheasants, some red lentils, a sack of wild rice, a basket of peaches, and a jar of raw fireweed honey to my usual order. Genevieve seemed surprised by the change as she rang things up. "Wow, Mr. Welland, what's the occasion?"

"Nothing much. Just thought I'd fancy things up a little."

"I'd say. I hope I'm not being forward at all, but . . . You look well. I know people are talking, but I don't listen."

Talking. I had a good idea what they were talking about. "Is the gossip about my friendship with a certain old man on the outskirts of town?"

She didn't drop her eyes. The green irises seemed to be giving off their own internal light, and I was transfixed. "That's right. But Mr. Turpin is a good man and a friend. You won't get any trouble from my father and me."

I grinned. "Thank you for saying so. Seems my alliances are dwindling around here."

"You never can tell. Most folks around here, they're just afraid." She wrapped the pheasants and put them into a cloth sack with the other items. "I hope you know how to prepare these. They're delicate little birds. Wouldn't want your good money to go to waste."

"I'm not much of a cook. I'm afraid all I ever picked up from Linny was how to make a sandwich and boil some mush for breakfast. I don't know what I'm going to do when the girls finally pack off."

She handed me the bag. "If you're interested, I could show you a few things. I like cooking."

At that point, her cheeks were the same color red as the journal in which I'd written about her.

"I might have to take you up on that." I handed her a small

stack of bills and watched her count them out and make change with her roughened yet graceful hands. A guilty voice tried to worm its way up from my subconscious to remind me I was a married man, but I tamped them down. Linny was gone, and nothing would bring her back. I had to get used to that fact.

"Here's your change, Mr. Welland. Would you like Ernie to deliver these to your house for you?"

I shook my head as I put the change back into my wallet. "I think I got—"

The words lodged in the back of my throat like a large piece of ice cube. For a moment, I didn't breathe at all. Something had changed on my God's Hope citizen card. The "J" hologram in the bottom right-hand corner was now red. Three months early. Someone raised an alarm, and I was pretty sure I knew who. My mouth went dry and I could feel my eyeballs bulging in their sockets.

Genevieve's smile faltered. "Are you okay?"

I stuffed the money back into my wallet, folded it closed, and managed a weak smile. "Oh, it's nothing. I just noticed it's almost time for my next J.E."

A shadow passed over her expression for a second. "Oh my. That's never great news," she said. "Are you worried a little? Especially after . . ." She trailed off, but she didn't have to complete the sentence. Everyone in town knew this was coming.

I shrugged, trying to play it casual. No need to drag her into my troubles. "To tell you the truth, I hadn't thought about the test a whole lot until just now. I've had my mind on other things, I guess."

"Are you going to take it now?"

"Nah. I figure I'll try to enjoy my night." To be honest, I wasn't sure I would have much of a choice in the matter. They were probably waiting for me at the house. Maybe even outside this very store.

Her eyes remained watchful. "I'll be wishing the best for you. If you need anything at all, you come find me."

I nodded, though I wasn't sure what a young grocer could do to get me out of this jam. "I'll do that. And call me John, okay?"

"You got it, John."

Once outside, I darted straight home, my mind awhirl with the certainty I was running straight into a trap. By the time I arrived on the porch, I was staggering and so out of breath, I could barely register my relief at seeing no Divine Rite people in the vicinity.

The door to the house flew open and Kaya popped out.

"Did you run all the way here? You're sweating buckets, Dad." She scooped up the grocery bag and carried it into the house.

"I guess it's a little hot out," I said and closed the door tight behind me. I pulled the curtains shut and slumped down in the living room chair.

"Well, Beth is having dinner with the Shaffers tonight so—HOLY COW!" she shouted.

I shot up to my feet. "What? What is it?"

"These birds! They're gorgeous! What's the occasion?"

"Oh."

In my current frenzy, I'd forgot all about them. "I wanted to make something special for you two. We haven't spent much time together lately, and . . ." I trailed off, realizing how very little time we actually had. Hours, not days.

Kaya frowned. "Dad, what's going on? You've quit your job and have been spending all your time up at that Turpin place. Everyone knows your number is up, and your own kids can't even get through to you. Now you're acting like someone's coming to bust down our front door."

Here it was. The talk we'd desperately needed to have for so many weeks, but everything would have to be condensed. "Yes, I know."

"I should go and get Beth. She needs to be here for this."

"Later," I said.

That turned out to be my greatest regret, but at the time, I also knew I wouldn't have been able to broach this conversation so easily if Beth were there. I needed to get Kaya on my side first, and then maybe we could tell Beth together and hopefully bring her around as well. Although the girls were twins, Kaya differed from her sister in nearly every way. Where Beth was all sunshine and gentleness, Kaya's personality was grim and introspective. While Beth carefully chose every word and thought, Kaya never minced words in the best of times, and often found herself in hot water with authority figures. I was afraid her tendency to avoid conformity would make her a prime target for the Divine Rite. She had the sort of personality those people just loved to break and mold in their favor, or just strike from the equation altogether. Now I intended to put those attributes to good use. Maybe she would help me out of this jam. It might sound odd for a forty-something man to put the hope for his future into the hands of a sixteen-year-old girl, but her quick-thinking resourcefulness was exactly what I needed.

"We need to talk first. Just you and I. Beth wouldn't understand this the same way you might, and I need you to hear me out."

Taking a seat, she seemed to lose a little bit of her harsh posture. It was probably the desperation painted all over my face that did it. I no longer felt like the adult in the room.

"Okay, Dad. Tell me."

"Kiddo, I'm in trouble, and it's all my fault." I began telling her about some of the things I'd been doing since her mother died. The journaling and poetry, the defacing of the Divine Rite posters in the center of town. When I told her about Reverend Blackwell and what I did with my tithes, her eyes grew as wide as tea saucers.

"Oh my God, Dad! You're nuts!"

"Yeah, well, I guess now's the time I actually have to answer for all that. My Exam is due, three months ahead of schedule. And I think we both know what the end result will be."

She glared at me. "Wait, you're not actually going to take the test are you? They killed Mom for missing four days of church. You might as well open your wrists right here and have done with it."

"Calm down. I never said I was actually going to take the damn thing."

She sat back, looking relieved. "Well that's good at least. What do you plan to do?"

"To tell you the truth, I was hoping you had a suggestion. What would you do if you were me?"

Her eyes locked onto mine, slate blue on slate blue. It was

the one physical feature of mine she shared. "If I were you, I'd make like the wind and blow out of here. See how far I'd get. You never know. You might make it. I'm sure you're not the first. Lots of people around here have disappeared over the years."

She was right. There was always a family or two a year who was there one day and gone the next, though there was no telling whether they got Suppers eventually, or something worse once they ventured outside the boundary of the net and into the mutated wilderness that lay beyond it.

"I'll have to talk to Turpin. He's a pretty worldly guy. He might have some ideas."

Kaya folded her arms. "Well, you won't be doing that alone. I'm coming with you."

Chapter 6

I balked and protested, like any other father would when his kid starts speaking madness. "Do you really think I would let you do that?" I asked. "I've already lost your mother to this. I would kill myself if the same happened to you, or worse. I got myself into this."

"That's nice of you to say, but it's a little late to talk about risks, don't you think? You think I didn't see this coming? I've been waiting for this conversation for months, having it over and over in my head. Especially this part. There is no way in hell you're leaving me here with these people. I'm no more one of them than you are." The stubborn jut of her jaw nailed it home. She'd gotten that from her mother.

She left me speechless, and under her gaze I found I could do little more than stare at my lap.

"I have something to show you," she said. "Stay here." She got up and ran to her bedroom and returned with a hand-bound scrapbook in her hands.

I easily recognized the book, and the cover's glued-on posies that Linny had pressed flat in our large family Bible ages ago. Kaya had been keeping things in it since she was about eight. Her first communion, a golden lock of hair from her first haircut, pictures she'd drawn of the family when she was little that looked more like a clan of smiling scarecrows than people. "I've been finding scraps of paper all around town with words written on them," Kaya said as she flipped through the pages. "Ordinarily, I wouldn't pick up pieces of litter, but I found the first while I was sitting on a bench in the town common. It blew up to my leg and stuck on my pants, like it wanted to be found."

My heart started pounding, but I didn't say anything. Not yet, anyway.

"I felt like someone out there was talking directly to me when I read those words," she said. "I carried that piece of paper with me everywhere. It was soothing. It made me feel like I was a part of something bigger, that I wasn't the only one in God's Hope who hated the Divine Rite. After that, I picked up almost every piece of white scrap paper I found, hoping for another poem. It became a fun little game, I guess." She landed on the last two pages of the book, and my heart, which had already accelerated to a galloping pace as she spoke, stopped cold in my chest. I gazed down at about a dozen of the little Haikus I'd surreptitiously written and left about town. My little "viruses."

She carefully separated one from the page and looked at it. "A few minutes ago when you said you had written poetry, my mind didn't make the connection. I honestly didn't think you were capable of something like this. But this one: 'Your tyranny kills, Murder in the name of God, My soul died with her.'" Tears sprang to her eyes. "You wrote these, didn't you? I mean, I always wondered, but I still couldn't quite bring myself to ask."

My throat clicked as I swallowed the hard lump that

formed there. "Yes. I wrote them."

"Then how could you expect me to not feel the same as you? To not *do* the same? She was my mother," she yelled, thrusting the book at me. "You do these things, and yet I'm supposed to just be some ignorant do-gooder, like Beth?"

"Beth is not ignorant," I said. There wasn't much conviction in it, and I felt terrible about that, because what did it mean other than I had already given up on her seeing the truth?

"Sure, Dad. Whatever you say. You can't just brush me off because I'm your kid. I'm in this too, whether you like it or not."

"What do you want me to say, Kaya? My first instinct is to protect you, not to send you into the mouth of the beast with me. If the tables were turned, you would think the same."

"I doubt that. I wouldn't ignore my kids when I needed them most either."

We sat quietly for a minute, the tension in the air not quite broken. There was nothing I could say that would have convinced her differently. And why would I try? She was right. Finally, she sighed and pulled another one of the slips of paper from the book in front of her and read the words written upon it: "I do not fear death. I will not sit complacent. I am not your slave."

I put my face in my hands and choked back a sob. Up until that moment, I had never been so frightened and confused in my life. Was I actually considering making my daughter a fugitive with me? And what about Beth? Would she come willingly, even if I begged her? The dark part of my heart thought she would not only refuse to come, but she would turn us both in for our own good. I hated myself for those thoughts then, and I hate myself even more for them to this day.

Kaya placed her cool hand on the back of my neck, bringing me back to the moment at hand. "Dad, don't do this. You didn't do anything wrong. Well, not everything."

I laughed. "That's good to know."

A knock on the door made us both jump, and I flew to my feet as if something hot had poked me.

"Sit down," Kaya said. "I'll get it. Your face is a mess." She wiped her own eyes and smoothed out of the front of her skirt. "Besides, it's too early to be *them*." I never knew such a small word could feel so ominous. She went to the door, but I followed her so I could see who it was.

Kaya looked through the peephole and turned to me. "It's the lady from the market. Why would she be here?"

I thought of the pheasants and the offer of cooking lessons. It couldn't have been a worse time, but she'd come all the way out to the house. Good manners prevailed.

"Go ahead and let her in."

Standing on the porch, Genevieve Camden's perky, all-smiles demeanor from earlier was gone. Her eyes were now hard, green flints and she wore a cloak over her head with a leather satchel slung over her shoulder. "Hello, John. We have some business to discuss."

"Cooking lessons?" I asked, and immediately felt stupid. What is it about a sense of humor that likes to rear its head at the worst of times?

"Saving your life," she said. "Can I come in?"

Kaya and I stepped aside and gestured Genevieve into the

house. I offered her a chair, but she insisted on standing. "I'm sorry to barge in, John, but we have to move fast. You're in trouble."

"What do you mean?" My stomach did another flip-flop.

"We've been watching you for a while, my people and I. Me and my people. We just learned that the Hand of God is en route here to scoop you up."

When I had earlier considered the possibility of the Hand of God coming to get me, it was in jest. The group was like a mythical force children usually spoke of in order to scare other children. No one had ever seen them here. They usually roamed the countryside for strays and non-believers. And now, they were coming for me. But why? Then I thought of my last conversation with Reverend Blackwell. And my tithes. Stupid question.

"You've been watching me?" I asked.

She reached into the leather satchel, pulled out a large folded sheet of paper, and handed it to me. I opened it, and for the fifth or sixth time that day, I felt like I was having a heart attack. The crudely defaced visage of the Holy Uniter smiled up at me from beneath his red crown of dicks.

"An officer ripped this down," I said. "I saw him."

"That's Andrew. He's one of ours." She looked around the room. "Get yourself a bag. Pack only what you need. We're getting you out of here."

"Are you a rebel group or something?" Kaya asked. I could hear little seedlings of excitement in her voice and I knew she was beyond my reach now.

Genevieve's smile was tight. "Something like that. I'm your conductor on the Absolution Railroad."

"What do you mean railroad?" asked Kaya dubiously. "There aren't any active train tracks around for five hundred miles or more."

"It's not a literal railroad. It's a network of safe passages and hideouts eventually leading to the coast."

"And then to where?" I asked.

"Look, they could be within a mile of here. I don't intend to be around when they arrive, and you'd better not be either. Get packing." She turned to Kaya. "You too, kiddo."

"Where are we going now?" I asked.

"Our first safe house not far from here. Tomorrow, I'll take you to the next place along the line. But we'll worry about that later." She stepped to the window and looked up and down the lane before turning back to us. "John, you can either take five minutes and pack a bag or ask me even more questions and leave with the clothes on your back. Your choice."

I started for my bedroom then stopped. "What about Beth?"

Genevieve drummed her fingers on her folded arms. "John, the less anyone knows about the railroad, the better. Beth is safe right now, assuming she's ignorant about what's been happening with you lately."

"Trust me, she doesn't know anything," said Kaya.

"Hey, wait a minute! I'm not going to leave my daughter to face those goons!"

Genevieve's face remained impassive like granite. "Andrew will watch over her. If he sees she's in danger, we'll bring her in, but right now the less she knows, the safer she is. Now hurry and pack. And bring any weapons if you have them. You have four minutes."

As we retreated to our rooms, I thought of the last night I saw my mother and father. What would Beth's memory of me be? I couldn't get past the feeling that her heart would be broken beyond repair.

After a moment of rummaging, I stuffed three shirts, two pairs of pants, a wad of socks and underwear, and a bar of soap into a knapsack. I grabbed the crude bedroll I kept on my closet shelf for the occasional camping trip and lashed it all together with some twine before hoisting it on my back. Next, I grabbed my shotgun from beneath my bed. The old Winchester pump-action was considered an antique over thirty years ago when my father gave it to me, but I'd always taken good care of it. Its .410 gauge shells were useless for anything beyond shooting the occasional bird or squirrel, which made the weapon allowable under Divine Rite guidelines, but it was better than nothing. I loaded it with five shells and pocketed the remaining eight I had left in the box and slung it over my shoulder.

I emerged into the living room moments after Kaya, who wore her backpack and the hunting knife I gave her last Christmas tucked into her belt. Genevieve had turned off the lights and was keeping watch from the house's front windows. Her face was a pale oval in the darkness. "We need to run hell bent for leather. I can't stress enough that you do *whatever* it takes to avoid capture. Kill them if you can."

I nodded, though I didn't think I'd be able to do that. We followed the red-headed woman as she broke into a trot across the yard and into the field toward the tangle of woods beyond. Our journey on the Absolution Railroad had begun.

Chapter 7

Once we reached the cover of the woods, we slowed our pace a bit to catch our breaths. My lungs felt like they'd been doused in oil and set on fire.

"I don't understand. Why are they coming after me?" I asked.

Genevieve grunted. "Reverend Blackwell raised the signal that you were a Nil."

My blood turned cold. Nil. A bureaucratic term for atheists, pagans, or other types of non-believers. You could murder a child and be punished less severely than you would if you were a Nil. It was a bad place to be.

"So I guess that means I don't get a Supper if they catch me," I said.

"They would much rather try to reprogram you or use you as a guinea pig. You're now a valuable asset to the Divine Rite, John. Congratulations."

"Lovely," Kaya muttered from beside me.

"Try not to worry. Everything will be okay if we do this right," Genevieve said. The darkness made her face one great shadow, save for the whites of her eyes, which were glassy with fear. We started walking again while she talked.

"There are a few things you need to know about these

people. Although they're sadistic ghouls, the Hand of God is very superstitious. That's their weakness. Every force travels with a Sentinel, who is a person they consider a direct messenger to God, guiding them. They will not act without this lifeline. Take him, and they'll retreat."

"That's it? That's all it takes?" I asked, incredulous. I'd never heard about these Sentinels before, but then again, I didn't know much at all about the Hand of God. It was their mystery that made them so formidable. But taking out one of them in order to drive them all away seemed too easy.

Her voice took on a dry tone, as if she'd been expecting my reaction. "Sure, all you have to do is fight through a phalanx of agents who are armed with Staves and electric sticks to get to him. Should be a piece of cake."

"So what you're saying is it's impossible," Kaya said, her teenage ears well tuned to the language of sarcasm.

"It is," Genevieve admitted. "Unless we get away."

"Have you ever faced them before?" Kaya asked.

Genevieve was silent for a moment. "Sort of," she muttered, but didn't elaborate. Instead, she turned and ran deeper into the woods. Kaya and I looked at each other, shrugged, and followed her.

Five minutes later, a high-pitched siren warbled into the sky, shredding the night's silence. It was in the direction of the house, which was about two miles to our backs.

"Shit! They've discovered you fled. We need to move faster." She broke into full run. Our shoes crunched on dead foliage as branches slapped and scratched our faces. It was then that I realized we were in one of the Memorial Forests that dotted the God's Hope landscape. A living graveyard. I kept my eyes trained on Genevieve's bobbing flashlight and hoped I wouldn't entangle a foot in the thick undergrowth.

"How much farther?" I barked, gasping and trying as hard as I could to ignore the stitch forming in my side.

"A good piece yet. Watch out for the Staves. If we see them, they're very close."

I had barely enough time to wonder what she meant by "Staves" when a glowing white stick whizzed through the air and impaled itself into the ground less than a foot in front of me. It gave off a pure, bluish-white glow. I recoiled and tripped over my own feet avoiding it. Genevieve slapped a hand over Kaya's mouth to hold in her scream. Another Stave slammed into the tree beside me, just above my head. It quivered and made a faint ringing sound with the impact. I reached up to pull it out.

"Don't touch it!" Genevieve whispered. "They're trying to form a perimeter around us. If you touch one of those, they will know exactly where we are and home right in on us. Keep moving."

We charged through the woods with Genevieve in the lead, Kaya in the middle, and me bringing up the rear. I flinched as I heard more of the Staves slamming home behind us; each of them gave off a different harmonic tone, and I thought suddenly of old church hymns.

I pushed myself harder, sure at any moment one of these Staves would impale me or Kaya through the head. One came so close I felt the wind of it against my cheek. I dodged as a couple more struck the path before me. The toe of my boot caught in a thick nest of roots, and I fell into a prickly juniper bush.

Kaya stopped and looked back.

I gestured for her to keep going. "I'm fine! Just keep—"

A streak of white light moving so fast it looked like a falling meteor impaled Kaya's backpack and pinned her hard against a tall fir. She shrieked. "Daddy! It's got me!"

"Kaya!" I yelled and rushed to her. Genevieve arrived at the same moment and pushed me out of the way just in time to avoid another of the deadly glowing Staves.

"Did it touch you?" Genevieve asked.

Kaya, who quivered like a girl in the midst of a high fever, shook her head and wept silently.

"We're going to slip you out of your pack then," Genevieve said. "Just be very careful not to touch—" Another Stave implanted itself in the tree, this time mere inches away from Kaya's belly. Two impossible shots, perhaps guided by their Sentinel. The three of us screamed in unison.

"They have a read on us, John."

As if her voice cued it, the Staves in the tree began to glow a sinister red.

Genevieve yanked out one of them with some effort and handed it to Kaya, who took it with trembling hands. She then opened her leather satchel and removed a pistol that looked about as old as my shotgun, which I pulled from my shoulder and clumsily aimed.

I didn't bother to tell her I couldn't even raise a hand in anger, let alone shoot someone. I'd thought about it in recent months, but that's not the same as doing. Kaya looked steady enough as she stood grasping the Stave, but her breath shook and her face was bathed in light the color of blood.

"Where are they?" I asked

"Up ahead." Genevieve pointed with her weak light. "About fifty yards."

"What do you mean? It's too dark to see."

"They *are* the darkness," she murmured, sounding close to tears herself.

A voice issued from that black void. "John Solomon Welland, make no further attempt to escape us. We have no wish to kill you."

My insides turned to cold jelly. Not because of the command, but because there was nothing human about those voices. I thought of bees or grasshoppers.

"What are they?" I asked in a shaky whisper.

Genevieve motioned around her face. "They wear masks."

"There is no shame in being a Nil," the voice continued. "God has a plan for us all. Yours is to be cared for and returned to the light."

"Oh shove it," I replied, my mouth suddenly on autopilot. "You can't hide under the cover of darkness and talk to me about the light. You're hypocrites and murderers."

The adrenaline pumping through my veins, my indignation at being hunted like a dog, made me defiant, and my face grew hot with anger.

"Come now, John. Do you think God doesn't see the hypocrisy of pointing a gun while accusing others of murder?"

This voice was closer. Close enough that its buzz caused the hairs on the back of my neck to stir

"We don't have the same God! You're a perversion!"

I steadied the .410's barrel in the direction of that voice. If I waited any longer, the agent would be on me.

"I guess this is it," I whispered to the two women beside

me and squeezed the trigger.

The report was deafening as the shotgun kicked back in my arms like a startled animal. A shrill electronic scream erupted into the night, and I saw motion in what I thought was a solid black void as the HOG agents scattered.

The .410's range was weak and at this distance, the shot pattern had plenty of time to dissipate into a harmless spray of grit, but they were definitely startled. If we could scatter them enough to get to the Sentinel, it wouldn't matter if we were outnumbered.

I pumped and fired another blast as we advanced on the mob. We were close enough that I could see beams of white light shooting out from between columns of black. The Sentinel, I assumed. Genevieve blasted two rapid shots from her giant pistol, which was far louder than my shotgun.

As we drew closer, I could see the HOG force more clearly, illuminated by that ethereal light behind them. I frantically counted a dozen. They wore hooded black robes, their faces draped in shadow, but I saw each one had a white glove on his left hand, and in the other they held long sticks tipped with blue arcing electricity.

Genevieve screamed a hoarse battle cry and charged toward the mob, firing her pistol, her braids flying behind like streamers. Kaya followed her lead and impaled one of them through the stomach with the staff Genevieve had handed her. I gaped at my daughter, who displayed a savagery I had never seen before.

Three of the shadowy figures advanced on me, and I turned and filled the world with more gunfire. The shot was far more effective in close range, and I dropped two of them.

I dodged the other one in enough time to avoid the shock of his weapon and butted him in the side of the head with the gun stock. He dropped like a bag of sand. I had enough time to see Genevieve blow away another pair of HOG agents before I shot one point-blank in the chest. The hood on his robe fell back and I caught a glimpse of something that looked like a gas mask. I picked off a couple more of the charging zealots as my mind fought to keep a count of my precious eight shells of ammo, but honestly I couldn't remember how many shots I'd fired. Before too long, I would hear a dry click. I just hoped it wouldn't be until after I killed the Sentinel.

A burning, tingling wave erupted in the center of my body, and I fell to the ground convulsing. I bit my tongue hard enough to bring tears to my eyes, and the coppery tinge of blood filled my mouth.

"On your knees, Nil," the HOG agent hissed just before a spear of red light erupted from his midsection. He fell and Kaya stood above me, her face splattered with blood that looked like war paint. Her eyes were feral from the kill, and I was thankful we were on the same side.

"Are you all right?" she gasped as she yanked her spear from her victim's still-quivering body. The electric stick had temporarily paralyzed me, but I was getting enough sensation back to nod my head.

"Yes. Go."

She ran back into the fray.

I gazed around at the ensuing battle. Genevieve and Kaya were standing back to back fighting off another pair of agents with the red Staves. The Hand of God seemed to have lost track of me as I lay among the fallen, and I gazed at the source of the light coming from the center of their now decimated phalanx.

Although my legs tingled with pins and needles, I began to crawl toward that pulsing beam, hoping the darkness and the chaos would shield me long enough to have a clear shot at what was in the center of it all.

The three HOG agents still guarding their guide shifted again, and I finally saw the supposed direct lifeline to God. My breath stopped cold in my chest.

The Sentinel was just a boy.

I lowered my gun as Genevieve cried out from behind me, "Shoot him, John! We can't hold out much longer!"

The boy was on his knees in a praying stance, his shaven head bent in stern consternation. He seemed completely unaware that he was exposed, or of the fight surging around him. White robes draped a body too emaciated for walking, and the white light gave his skin a near transparent pallor.

"Goddamn it, John! Kill it! Kill the Sentinel!" Genevieve screamed. This time she sounded closer, but struggling. I looked back over my shoulder and saw the side of her face bleeding freely.

"He's just a little boy," I said. "I can't do it."

"DADDY!" Kaya's screams dissolved into shaky gibberish as an agent took her down with his electric stick. She lay on her stomach, immobilized as one towering brute held her down beneath his foot. I screamed to the sky and shot at them, but one missed, and I knew in my heart that I only had one shot left. In that moment, there was no other choice. It was either kill the kid or save Kaya. I then realized that killing him would accomplish just that. I leveled the shotgun at the praying little boy, and prepared to squeeze the trigger, hoping like hell the ancient gun wouldn't pick that moment to seize up or misfire.

"Please forgive me," I whispered and closed my eyes so I wouldn't have to see him die.

Suddenly the world filled with more light and the roar of a large engine. A series of gunshots rang out from behind me, and the remaining HOG agents dropped dead.

"Christoph, go after any stragglers! Don't shoot the boy, though. We'll need him."

The voice was as familiar as my bedroom slippers, only I'd been more accustomed to hearing it over glasses of bourbon. I tried to get up, but the world was losing coherence. Halos of yellowish white light surrounded the cars, the people, and the trees as if the dawn had come early. My limbs felt weighted with lead. I saw Kaya and Genevieve receiving rescue, and I called out to them from my place amid the dead, unsure if they heard me. A singing chorus filled my head, and I thought maybe I was dying after all.

Chapter 8

The white light dissolved into a starry night sky, and I soared like a crane over acres and acres of a crop I had only ever seen in books. The mature corn was illuminated by an impossibly bright gibbous moon, breathtaking and haunting. I wondered if I was dreaming of a past I'd never before experienced. In my lifetime, most of the vast stretches of American land, once fertile for farming, had been consumed by the serpent weeds, or the destructive forces people had used to fight them.

After a closer look, I could see a narrow road cutting through the ocean of stalks, and a vehicle of some sort zooming along it. I was too high up to make out any other details than the two beams from the headlights cutting into the dark ahead. When I tried to move closer, I hit an invisible barrier that stretched like elastic and then pushed me back.

What I saw next filled me with black horror. A hungry wall of millions (perhaps billions) of swarming things was consuming the fields, the world, and it was rapidly catching up to the fleeing vehicle. I thought of the great locust plagues described in Revelations.

Soon, the swarm would engulf it. Those people didn't stand a chance. I tried calling out to them, but my voice felt muffled, like I was screaming from the inside of a glass jar.

The halos and the white light reappeared in my vision, just as they had after the battle with the Hand of God, only the deafening drone of the locusts accompanied it. My eyes burned and watered, the sound threatening to liquefy my brains. I put my hands to my ears only to realize the sound was coming from inside my head. I screamed my voice bloody as the inevitability I feared unfolded. The truck, and everything visible in the world below me, disappeared in a tsunami of swarming black.

The noise cut off as abruptly as it began and the darkness became light. I no longer flew among the stars. Instead, I sat in serene mid-morning sunlight, cross-legged beneath a flowering plum tree. Pinkish-white petals fluttered down around me like sweetly fragrant snow. I knew this tree. Turpin had pointed it out to me on one of my many visits. He told me he planted it on a hill to the northeast of his house to ward off evil. "Silly Japanese superstition," the man had said. "But there ain't nothin' wrong with playin' a few safe cards, 'specially if they're so damn pretty."

I looked to the southwest, and saw the corrugated aluminum roof of Turpin's house peeking out from a canopy of trees.

I was at the Bunker, but I was not yet awake. This suspicion was confirmed when I turned back to face a young bald boy kneeling before me. The Sentinel. A deep bluish-white aura surrounded him, making his pallid complexion look almost transparent. I could see the web of red capillaries, a network of purplish veins beneath his skin. The plum blossoms that landed on his smooth head slid off onto his lap and piled onto his loosely clasped hands. The hands of a child.

I felt more exalted by the small figure than afraid, but words still evaded my lips.

"I am Ezekiel. We don't have long," he said. His voice was so small, so childlike, but I got the sense he was much older. Something about his spirit, I guess. Also, there was something strange about the presence of him. He was flickering in and out, like he was made more of light than of substance. I resisted the urge to reach out and touch him, just to see if my hand would go right through.

"Are you . . . okay?" I asked.

"I have been in the *Élan Vital* much longer than is recommended, and my body is exhausted."

"What's that?" I asked, deciding to avoid pronouncing the exotic phrase.

"It is the essential life force. It allows me to see that which most do not."

"It allows you to speak with God?"

The boy shook his head. "That is what the Hand of God believes, but I do not speak directly with any omniscient entity, for there are none."

I was more confused. "If you don't believe in God, then how is it they allow you to live?"

The boy managed a weak smile. "I never said I didn't *believe* in God. I said there *wasn't* one. One requires an act of faith. The other is a matter of fact. Of course, neither the Hand of God nor the Divine Rite care what I believe or know about their superstitions. They use me, and others like me, for our gifts. I'm not much different from you. I'm just another tool."

"What exactly are your gifts?"

"I seek out the life forces I am ordered to seek, and I enhance the perceptions of the agents so they can better see and stalk their... prey. You can think of me as something like a power booster. But none of that has anything to do with my true power. I am nothing more than a placebo for them, really. If someone told them a rock could speak with God and guide them on their journeys, they would carry a rock instead."

"So this..." I gestured to the dreamlike surroundings. "They don't know about any of this?"

"Not as much as they think. My work with the *Élan Vital* is more related to what the Buddhists call Nirvana, only in a more sustainable and tangible form. I can use it to manipulate objects. I sometimes have the ability of prophecy. Often, I just retreat here to escape the darkness in the world."

I couldn't blame him. I did much the same thing after my eyes were opened to the truth of the Rite. "Are there more like you?"

"People like us have been around since time's beginning, though in far smaller numbers in proportion to the world's population. After the Blight, the Divine Rite scooped us up and experimented on us to see what our abilities could do for them. My powers are limited to a small range, and they lose potency the longer I am here. Of course, if they simply used human instinct and deductive reasoning, they would be able to find you and other Nils without my help, but they forgot how to rely on themselves, and so without us they lack the resolve to do what they do. That's their one weak spot."

"What exactly happened back in the woods? I... I almost killed you."

The boy cracked a sunny, innocent smile, which almost made me love him a little in spite of his creepy white-eyed stare. "You wouldn't have killed me, John. No one has ever faced down a Hand of God army and successfully killed a Sentinel. Your mission was successful because I allowed it to be."

"You sabotaged them?"

"When I sensed you, I received a powerful vision. That is my strongest gift, actually. I see the future, or at least a likely version of it. Few like to entertain such a talent, least of all the Divine Rite. They don't want to chance learning of a future in which they are not in absolute power. Nonetheless, the vision I had of you was so strong I felt obligated to save you. I placed them in a state of induced confusion from the moment you fired your weapon."

The inside of my mouth felt lined with sandpaper, and I wasn't sure I could speak, but I had to ask him the obvious question. "What was your vision of me?"

The boy's smile widened. The sound of buzzing locusts was coming back along with the light, but Ezekiel's voice trailed out like the last vestiges of smoke from a freshly extinguished candle.

"You will see soon enough."

—

I awoke in Turpin's living room feeling stiff and out of sorts in the early morning light. The place still felt asleep, but I recognized Harry Camden, Genevieve's father, hauling up a crate of something that looked like potatoes from the cellar.

I sat up, wincing at the aches in my joints. It was the most concrete sign that I was no longer dreaming. And then a gut-wrenching little reality set in. Beth wasn't with us, and I was a fugitive. Everything about my life had been turned upside down.

"Kaya?"

"She's sleepin' in the other room," Turpin said from behind me. I turned and saw him standing with a couple of steaming mugs in his hands. "Come on in the kitchen and have some coffee, boyo. We'll catch up on things."

I stood and my knees and spine crackled. "How long was I out?"

"Oh, a good while," he answered. "The little fella's still out cold and it's been about six hours since we dragged you all in here."

I accepted the mug and took a gulp of the hot liquid inside. Turpin's version of coffee was strong, black, and contained copious amounts of whisky.

In case you're wondering, it wasn't really coffee. Arabica plants were among the first to go extinct in the Blight, even before the corn. The substitute was a combination of fermented herbs and roots that was more like a strong black tea, and it's what I'd always thought of as coffee. Turpin waxed poetic about real coffee beans early on in our friendship, calling them true nuggets of God's grace, their demise proof of how far we'd fallen as a species. He said there were still places in the world that had small stocks of the stuff, but it would cost a fortune to get them.

"Are the girls okay? Kaya went down. I remember that. And Beth . . ." I trailed off. It wasn't necessary to say more, given the knowing nod of Turpin's head.

"Nothin' but a few cuts and scrapes, mostly. Andrew's lookin' out for yer Beth, and we haven't heard anything. Be easy. They're the lucky ones. It was you and the boy that scared us, at least until Genevieve said you two were communicating in yer minds, and that we should leave ya alone. She seemed to know a bit about it." He was quiet for a minute as we sipped our drinks, but I knew what the next question was going to be.

"What'd you two talk about?"

"So, this is the safe house, then?" I asked, deciding to avoid his question for a moment.

Turpin nodded. "I suppose ya wonder why I didn't mention it to ya sooner, given all our talks about the Divine Rite and such."

"The thought did cross my mind."

"Little movements like ours have tiny shots at greatness. We ain't the first to do what we're doin', and we probably won't be the last, but I like to think we have more chance than most who have tried to buck the status quo. We have a good network of folks that're inside and outside the Rite."

"I imagine it would be hard to do without people on the inside."

He shrugged. "And it's not as uncommon as you might think, either. At the end of the day, they're still politicians just out to make a deal."

I felt a little bile rise up into my throat. "Too bad I couldn't have made a deal for Linny."

"I know, boyo. She was gone before we even got word she was on the choppin' block. We can't help everyone that needs it, much as we'd like to. Every little thing we do has got to be timed and carried out just so, or we're all dead. We couldn't save yer Linny, but we're damn sure gonna make sure you and yours are kept out of harm's way."

"Well, I thank you for it, Turpin. As does Kaya, I'm sure."

The old man looked humbly at his feet. "I only wish we coulda done more for yer other one. We'll do our best to watch over her, though. I can promise ya that."

I stared into my mug for a few minutes, hoping my frustration would subside. Watching over Beth was supposed to be my job, but the futility of my anger only seemed to make it worse. We couldn't change the course of things now. It had all happened too quickly. Backtracking on a rescue mission would endanger everyone here, and I didn't have to confirm with Turpin to know that was true. I also realized right then if I had sent Kaya to fetch her sister last night, I might be separated from both of them now.

"What can you tell me about the boy?" Turpin asked.

"He's some sort of prophet, I think. He said we escaped the HOG because he made it possible."

Turpin nodded. "I'd believe it. We never would have made it to where ya were if it hadn't been for him."

"How so?"

"I was sittin' on the porch with Christoph—you'll meet him later—when I saw that boy come right through the fence. And by *through*, I mean like Jacob Marley walkin' through Ebenezer Scrooge's bedroom door, and just about as frightenin' too. I was a few sheets to the wind on some of this new grain alcohol I been testin' out for the motor scooters, so I wouldn't have believed my own eyes if Christoph hadn't shot up from his chair and cocked his rifle at him. The boy didn't even notice, and even I coulda told Christoph that ya can't shoot ghosts anyway. He told us the Hand of God had ya surrounded in the woods about a mile out and that we had to help you. I didn't hesitate. Don't know why, since I hesitate any time someone orders me around, but that boy had some power of persuasion I couldn't shake. In fact, I don't think I coulda stopped myself from doin' what he said, even if he was leadin' me right off the side of a bridge. I grabbed Christoph and Harry, and we piled into Christoph's truck and followed the boy right out there, like he was a rabbit on a fence at a dog track."

He snorted laughter and reached into his shirt pocket for his tobacco pouch. "I've seen a lot of strange things in my day, boyo, but divine apparitions is a first."

I shook my head. "I wouldn't call it divine, exactly. He said there was no God. He called it some kind of life force. Some foreign word I can't remember. Evan vial. Something."

"*Élan Vital*," Turpin corrected me, the term rolling easily off his tongue.

"That's it. You know it?"

He casually flicked a hand. "Came across the term once or twice in my readin'."

"I never heard of it," I said.

"The Divine Rite schools don't teach much philosophy outside what you'd find in the King James Bible."

"He also said he could see the future. It was—"

Turpin sat forward sharply and cut me off with a raised, gnarled hand. "Don't tell me any of it," he said fiercely. "And don't tell anyone else either. Whatever that boy told ya stays between the two of ya, and it's best ya try and forget about it yerself."

I frowned at him. "What I was going to say is that he didn't tell me much of anything. But why are you so worried about it?"

"There's prophecy, boyo, and there's *self-fulfilling* prophecy. One is usually bullshit and innuendo, and the other is even worse. We don't wanna get caught up in that. Whatever happens, happens because we make it happen, and we'll just leave it at that." He sat back in his chair and took another sip of his coffee. I noticed a faint tremor in his hand, which was something new.

Turpin knew more than he was telling me, but this was no time to push the man. Instead, I asked him what was next.

"The Bunker's been compromised. Divine Rite listed you and the women as fugitives last night, and they'll be bangin' down our door soon. Our folks on the inside have been trying to throw off our scent, but it won't work forever. If you'd been a typical case, things would've been a little easier. When someone just misses an Exam, it takes a little bit of time to cut through the red tape and find out why. Sometimes people just forget. It happens. By the time they know somethin's up, the runaway is usually halfway to the coast before they send out the dogs. But they're a lot more aggressive with Nils. They don't like 'em out roamin' the countryside. They think Atheism is some kind of catchin' disease, and they ain't gentle with the infected."

"I noticed." The memory of the jolt from the electric stick was still fresh, and I was sure that was like a flutter of an eyelash in comparison to what happened in a Cradle.

"We're gonna clear outta here and move to the next stop

on the railroad and hope like hell it hasn't been sniffed out by the time we get there."

Then something occurred to me. God's Hope didn't have any open borders. The only way in and out of the net that I knew of was through a main checkpoint, after presenting the proper papers that showed permission to leave. It was an elaborately designed passage meant to keep the air from out there, and any rogue bits of pollen floating in it, from getting into God's Hope. That wasn't going to work this time.

"How are we going to get through the net without going through the checkpoint?"

Turpin was quiet for a moment. "None of these decisions are easy, boyo. Usually, when Genevieve took folks out of town, it was through an underground passage here on the Bunker property. But now there's too many of us, not to mention our vehicles. The only way out of the net this time is to go through it."

"But the weeds . . ." I stopped right there. I knew the stakes were going to be high, and I should've anticipated this. Our escape was going to kill the town. Maybe not right away. It would take some time for the pollen to germinate, but God's Hope would be consumed sooner or later.

And then what of Beth? "We can't let my other daughter stay here, Turpin. This place is going to hell fast."

"Soon as we get to our next stop, we'll have Andrew bring her in," he said. "We're sorry events happened the way they did, but we can only move forward, boyo."

I clenched my jaw. He was right, but I didn't have to like it. "Where is the next stop?"

He tipped his mug at me and drained the last of his coffee. "There's another safe house about thirty miles northwest of here, a town called Old Babylon. The weeds took the outer part of it about twenty years ago, but the inner part's under a net and still doin' pretty well. We have a friend there who's on our side. He'll get us passage on a river boat to the next part of the journey."

I thought of what the landscape might look like outside God's Hope and shuddered. "How bad is it out there?"

The old man leaned back in his chair, clasping his cane between his legs. "The landscape's rough passage for vehicles, and we could draw the attention of some things out there that are . . . nasty. But it's been done before."

"What sort of things are out there?"

The old man waved his hand. "Best we don't think about it now. It'll only mess with our nerve." He didn't seem to realize his vague statement had already done just that. I hadn't been on the outside since I was a boy, and the memories of those days, before God's Hope, were foggy.

"Turpin, I'm sorry I brought all this on you. Really, I am."

The old man cackled. "If ya learn one thing about bein' a rebel, boyo, it's that ya get used to movin' around a lot. I'm sure yer folks understood it. I been here longer than I ever been anywhere, but that was just luck and half-dumb anyway. Truth be told, I like it here and if ya couldn't tell, I'm gettin' on in years a little, so I was slowin' down a bit. But whether ya came or not, it was time to move on down the line. I'm just glad yer along for the ride."

I was glad to be along too, but there was a shadow on my heart. Not only for Beth. My mind turned back to the locust swarm I saw in that strange dream, and how no matter how fast that car tried to outrun it, there was no hope of escape.

Chapter 9

We spent the duration of the afternoon stowing most of Turpin's valuables in one of the Bunker's many underground military caches. The rumors about that had been true after all. While I was down there, I traded in my sorry .410 for something with a little more bite: a lighter and more compact M4 carbine that Christoph disassembled, cleaned and oiled, reassembled, loaded, and handed back to me in working order.

The German giant, who was the group's closest thing to an artillery expert, also handed me an armful of hand grenades to stow in my pack, though he expressed doubt as to whether they would work.

"They are older than Turpin's grandmutter, but we'll try our luck," he declared in his thick, guttural accent. I wondered how he ended up in a place like God's Hope given the Divine Rite's strict policy against foreigners, and I asked Turpin about it later.

"Christoph's mom, dad, and sisters snuck out of Germany when their own version of the Rite started clampin' down about thirty years ago. They had money, apparently, and it bought 'em a ticket over here. I guess whatever system we have here is a petting zoo compared to the German solution.

Not much of a surprise, really. Over here, the Rite hired 'em on as entertainers at a Sin Bin, if you could believe it."

I shivered at the thought. Sin Bins were basically like roach traps, from what I'd heard. One could get in easily enough, but getting out was impossible. It never occurred to me to travel to such a place, even in the depths of my own despair over losing Linny. A year went by so quickly, as I'm sure most of the lost souls in those places learned when they were presented with their own steaming plates of death and no way out.

"When their meal ticket arrived, they attempted an escape. Christoph is the only one who made it. Far as I know, he's the only one to ever escape from a Sin Bin alive. I met him in the place I lived before I came to God's Hope, and he's been here ever since, helping folks get to safety. Lives under a number of assumed identities that a couple of our folks inside the Rite helped him cook up. But I think they gave up on finding him long ago."

Back out front, I found Harry fueling up four green motor bikes, one of which had a sidecar hitched to it that would carry Turpin. Like most motorized vehicles in the world, they were pre-Blight salvage jobs. Harry had retrofitted these with engines that could run on Turpin's homemade ethanol. They also sported fat, heavy-treaded tires, and springs capable of handling the countryside's rough terrain. Homemade leather saddlebags hung from their flanks and they would carry most of our lighter goods. The other vehicle, Christoph's black custom-made hulk of a pickup truck, would carry himself and the boy, extra fuel, food, and of course plenty of weapons and ammunition.

When I first greeted Harry, he shook my hand so hard in his calloused, meaty fist that my shoulder popped a little. He too was a big man, but I liked the unconsciously graceful way he carried himself. Though he looked as if he would be clumsy and unrefined, he was as dexterous at chopping carrots for a stew as he was at dismantling engines. He kept his shaggy mop of red hair, which was the same shade as his daughter's but heavier on the gray, tied back with a hank of rawhide, and he never deviated from his standard outfit of clean t-shirts and rough leather vests. His weather-beaten face was a complex map of deep lines and genuine good nature. I had always liked the man, but never got to know him before now.

I learned through Turpin that Harry used the town's general store as a front through which he showed several of God's Hope's doomed residents to the Absolution Railroad. That had all changed after last night, and he would be joining us on the run. I'd assumed this upset to his life would have angered him, but he was enthusiastic about the change. "I was starting to go a little stir crazy anyway, to tell you the truth. My produce guy is taking over the store. He's got a boy about Genny's age, and they'll both do a fine job. It's great to have you with the group, John. When Linny died, I wondered if maybe you'd come our way."

"I never would have dreamed it would come to this," I said. "I only hope I don't get you all killed."

Harry's smile revealed a yellowed set of handmade dentures. "No regrets, brother. I couldn't deny anyone a chance to stick it to these assholes. Especially after what happened to your wife. You got balls, I'll tell you that. That poetry you wrote was top-notch stuff." I thanked him and wondered what he would think of me if he knew what I'd once written in my journal about his daughter.

About two hours later, the seven of us convened in Turpin's sun-dappled dooryard: Harry, Genevieve, Christoph, Turpin, Ezekiel, Kaya, and me. The Sentinel remained in his coma-like state and Christoph held the wrapped-up boy in his arms as easily as he might hold a bundle of blankets. Kaya sported a small bandage on her forehead and some scratches on her arms and cheeks that were yellow with iodine. She seemed less feisty than usual, but otherwise no worse for wear. The feral zeal that had been in her eyes as she speared HOG agents the night before was gone, at least for now, and I breathed a sigh of relief. Genevieve avoided eye contact with me, as if she knew I had a laundry list of questions she didn't want to answer.

Turpin gathered us around in a semi-circle. "Christoph knows this countryside damn near better than anyone here. He's gonna take us way off the beaten path and break us through the net. There may be an alarm, but there are stretches where the detectors have gone bad over the years, so we could get lucky. The ride'll be long and bumpy, especially if yer on one of these," he said, tapping one of the scooters with his cane. "We'll look for signs of any other fugitive distress along the way. There are always some out there. They'll have left a signal if they had a chance. Keep your weapons at the ready."

We mounted our bikes, Kaya and I a little unsteady on ours because our riding experience had been limited to the brief training lesson Harry gave us an hour previous. Turpin slipped into the sidecar of Harry's slightly more sophisticated ride outfitted with a radio that would allow him to communicate with Christoph's truck.

"Are we really doing this, Dad?" Kaya asked. "We're going . . . out there?"

Worry was painted all over her face, but did I detect a spark of anticipation in her eyes? Yeah, I think I did. "We are indeed going out there, sweetheart. Don't be afraid."

"I'm not. At least not much. But Beth . . ."

"I know," I said.

"They won't hurt her. I'm sure of it."

I looked back at her. "What makes you say that?"

"Because she's like them. If anything, they'll turn her against us. Probably use her as bait."

I felt a stone drop in my gut. Never in my life did I wish more for someone to be wrong. But a whisper of agreement danced around in my head, nonetheless, and I focused forward, saying nothing.

With Christoph in the lead, we left the Bunker for the last time. Once we'd pulled onto the dirt road, Turpin closed the big gate with his remote, and pulled another small clicker out of his tweed jacket's breast pocket.

"What's that?" I asked, pointing to the device.

"Christoph armed the house with a remote incendiary device," Harry explained. "Once we're out, the Bunker will be no more."

We set off along a path that cut through a field at the heart of the Bunker, a place that was probably once used for soldier training exercises but had since been left to the whims of nature. The sun threw a grid-shaped shadow from the net high above. The pattern was one of those things I was so used to seeing that I never really saw it anymore, but I noticed it today. Probably because we were about to leave the net behind. In many ways, it was a bit like feeling naked.

The path went on for a mile or so and let out on an access road running around the perimeter of God's Hope. It was mainly used for maintenance of the net, according to Turpin.

Kaya was soon steady enough on her bike and pulled ahead of me to ride alongside Genevieve. A few minutes later, Kaya was throwing her head back laughing at something the other woman had said. The two appeared to get along well, which was nice to see. Kaya never had much in common with any of the prominent women in her life. Through the years, it had been Beth and Linny with the stronger bond, but it seemed like Kaya had finally found a kindred spirit in the older girl, and that made me happy, despite the worry that all of it could go wrong at any moment.

Harry signaled a stop when we made it to the part of the net Christoph intended to break through. The German giant hurried out of the truck with a tool kit and a large pair of cutters usually reserved for pruning bushes, and set about his hasty surgery on the thin network of wire protecting God's Hope from the deadly pollen of the world beyond. After he worked a few minutes on the junction box that electrified this zone of the net, he started cutting. I braced for the piercing bray of an alarm, but we were only greeted by silence. After he cut a hole wide enough to fit the truck, he got back in and drove through, with Harry and Turpin following close behind. Genevieve went next and Kaya and I looked at each other. Although I couldn't actually see any pollen flecks, I knew the damage had been done.

"You ready for this, kiddo? Point of no return."

She grinned. "I think we passed that awhile ago. Gotta keep going or else." With that, she powered her scooter through the hole in the net and into the alien landscape on the other side. Already I could see the knotted twists of the serpent weeds twining up the trees that lay beyond. I took a deep breath and followed her out.

Turpin held up the clicker and pressed the button. A second later, I heard a distant "FOOM."

"Guess it worked," Kaya said.

Turpin nodded. "I'd say yer right, little lady. Let's go while the gettin' is good."

Everyone's motors fired up and we were off in a single file line along the first of many broken roads in the world outside the net.

In a gesture that reminded me of Lot's wife turning back to get one last glimpse at the flaming Sodom, I looked and saw a column of black smoke climbing high over the trees of the Memorial Forest. Somewhere back there, a flowering Japanese plum stood guard against evil, and I hoped it would survive the fire. Turpin's home, which was also home to all those who sought refuge from the brutality of the Divine Rite, would be reduced to a pile of ash and rubble by the time anyone arrived to investigate. A new phase of the rebellion had begun. We were committed now.

Grimly, I turned back to the road to catch up with the rest of the group.

Interlude

I had to put the cake aside. It was too much. After the third or so bite, I felt like I was eating mud. Or maybe shit. I guess that's a more accurate description of what it is anyway, but that doesn't seem to sway most folks. Linny had gone to hers so willingly, but here I am, resisting inevitability until the very end. It's in my blood, I suppose.

The salad wasn't much better. The lettuce was like bits of peeled skin dipped in grease. This wasn't the first time I've seen vegetation with a fleshy feel to it, but I'm getting way ahead of myself. There are so many dreadful things between that and the time we left God's Hope and entered God's Worst Nightmare that I wonder if I'm going to have the strength to tell it all.

Maybe the wine will help. It couldn't taste worse than the cake. It's like every Communion I ever took in a single glass. How bad could that be?

Chapter 10

It was rough going at first. The road was little more than two deep wheel ruts with tufts of serpent weeds growing between them. It was also littered with rocks, sticks, potholes, and ancient human detritus that threatened to throw us from our seats every fifty yards of so if we weren't careful. The German's truck was ahead of us by about a mile to scout for any Divine Rite stooges or other obstacles blocking our way. Twice he had to radio back to Harry that a newly fallen tree or an impassable thicket of weeds was blocking the roadway and we had to wait while he cleared it. Of course, cutting the weeds was futile for the long term, but it was enough for us to make passage.

We finally exited the woods about an hour later to see the decimated world sprawled before us like an alien tapestry. The serpent weeds twisted and coiled around each other like their reptile namesakes, crawling up any vertical surface. A towering structure in the distance that might once have been a grain elevator was covered in the vines, their strange orange flowers looking like flames in the late morning sun. Solitary trees stretched to the sky like prisoners begging God for clemency as the pervasive weeds dug into their trunks and limbs, sucking them dry.

The few buildings we saw looked like random humps in the weed-covered landscape as the plants had eventually grown to consume them in full. In the distance, some herd animals, perhaps cattle or bison, roamed around in the poisoned pasture. I thought it was a trick of the eye, but it looked distinctly like a few of them had more than one head. Mutants. Sadly not uncommon, even in God's Hope on the limited amount of livestock people raised on the Lazarus grain, but these were worse. Even the birds looked strange, almost like reptiles, with leathery wings and bald, scaly heads. A few of them circled overhead, probably waiting for a fresh carcass to skin. Maybe they were checking us out. Even the sky they flew in looked funny. I hadn't realized until then that the net over the town provided an illusion of normalcy. Out here, the horizon, tinted by the unchecked pollination of the serpent weeds, was the color of infected piss.

Kaya, who had been largely silent since we drove through the net, stopped her bike and gazed at the world around her in dawning horror. Then she screamed and started batting at her head.

I jumped off my bike and ran over to her. "What is it? What?"

"Something bit me! Get it off me, Daddy! Get it off!"

Frantically, I moved to the other side of her, where I saw an enormous fly trying to light on her neck. But no ... it couldn't be that. My mind fought the idea. No fly could possibly be so big. I could see its eyes, green clusters on either side of its head. Its buzz wavered from a bass to a baritone as it moved to avoid Kaya's swatting hand, intent on getting another taste of her.

Already, a red welt was forming where it had bit her the first time, and I became infuriated. I flung both arms at it. "Get off her! Go away! Shoo, goddamn it!"

Finally, it seemed to lose interest and flew off, just as Harry and Genevieve arrived where we were. "What's going on?" Genevieve asked with a frown of worry. "Kaya? Are you hurt?"

"A f-fly bit me . . . this thing. This gross thing . . ." She started crying and I took her in my arms like I had so many times when she was a little girl, whether it was a skinned knee or hurt feelings. Those days weren't all that long ago, and I guess as her father it would never be long enough. She shouldn't have been out there with me, but it was too late to take it all back.

Harry inspected the bite and put a little bit of salve on it from a kit he kept in his bag. "Those flies are more a nuisance than danger. You'll be all right, kiddo." He patted her shoulder.

"What *is* this place?" she cried. "I knew it would be bad, but I never thought it would be this bad."

I knew what she meant. I hadn't been outside God's Hope in thirty years, when the weeds were only just getting started, but they were far worse now than anything I remembered from those days. At least I had some idea of what to expect, though. Kaya was completely new to this side of the net. She may have heard rumors from some of the kids she hung around with about what lay outside, but nothing could have prepared her for this. It was like we'd stepped onto some hostile jungle planet.

"It breaks my heart too, kiddo," Turpin said from his seat

in the sidecar. "I remember what the world was like before the Blight and the weeds and the Rite. It weren't perfect by a long shot, but I'd take it in a heartbeat over this abomination. Seein' the world like this, it never gets easy. Ya just learn to soldier through it, I guess."

No one argued with him. After a minute, and a few sips of water, we kept moving.

An hour later, we entered more woods, only it was a little generous to call them that. During the height of the Blight, the government had leveled or burned the areas most impacted by the serpent weeds. Fire, followed by a heaping dose of toxic herbicide, was the only thing that worked to stop the growth for a time—at least until the weeds adapted, and they always did—but it made entire regions uninhabitable.

Word had it some places didn't suffer from weed infestation at all, that for whatever reason, conditions for growth weren't ideal. Of course, deserts were as arid and devoid of vegetation as ever, but places in high altitudes in the west, as well as some of the coastal areas, also seemed to have avoided the worst of it. Naturally, those were also the places most heavily populated by the Rite, with their citadels, Sin Bins, and of course Donum Dei itself, the epicenter of the Divine Rite, where the Holy Uniter and his special cabinet of God's army held sway.

I later learned that serpent weeds were the least of the west's problems, but we'll get to that horror soon enough.

What remained of this forest were tangles of dried out weeds and vines clinging to jagged white tree trunks petrified from decades of exposure to the elements. There was a stunted canopy of sorts from the few trees that had defied the odds, but they were twisted and bent, like poorly smithed metal heated and stretched and then cooled too soon. Their leaves lacked any sort of color or symmetry, looking like scraps of tissue paper glued to the branches. It was odd to attach an emotion like suffering to a tree, but it was the best description I could think of. The patch was eerily silent too. No birdsong, no insect calls, no rustle of scavengers in the undergrowth. It was completely barren.

Christoph called back to say there was another trunk to clear from the road, so we all ate some dried fruit and drank more water while we waited. "I call this place the Weeping Woods," said Genevieve. "The trees almost look like they're crying, don't they?"

It was like she'd plucked the thought right out of my head. "Yes."

"The fire wasn't the worst part. Life comes from fire. It was the herbicide they used. It bleached the ground. Scorched it for good. Nothing will ever grow here now."

"Are there a lot of places like this out there?" Kaya asked.

Harry removed a bag of pheasant jerky and passed it around. "Even one is too many," he said. "They scorched thousands upon thousands of square miles before they realized the cost of killing the weeds would make things even worse. Then I guess they figured it was better to have some semblance of life, even if it choked out the human race, than this. The segregation of the population and putting settlements under the nets came not long after."

Christoph called in with the all clear, and we got back onto our rides. An hour later, Turpin raised his cane as a signal for us to stop again.

"We're about out of these woods and ten miles from our next stop. Start keepin' yer eyes peeled for any signs. Harry, Genny, ya know what to look for. Christoph has a good jump on us and has been lookin' already, but ya can never be too careful. A lot of 'em are hard to see."

He turned to Kaya and me. "Fugitives from the Rite have a particular code they use to talk to each other. They're symbols usually written with coal or chalk that don't look like much to ordinary folks, but that's the point. Hobos back in the pre-Blight days and long before used a similar code to alert their brethren to danger or places with food or supplies. There's too many of 'em to teach ya at once, but if ya see any mark on boulders, trees, or on the ground that look man-made, give a holler."

"We should try to wake up the Sentinel," I suggested. "He may be able to see if the Rite is up ahead."

"We'll be lucky if he ever wakes up at all after what he was put through," Genevieve said softly.

"What do you mean?" I asked. "Is it a permanent coma?"

"Something like that, yes." Her voice took on a harsh edge that made me step back a little. "Sentinels have a pretty limited shelf life as it is. The Hand of God pushed this one to the breaking point, and he'll probably be of little use to us. Your little conversation with him probably finished him."

There it was. Since we'd left Turpin's house, she'd been distant with me. Even a trifle cold. And now I think I got it. She thought I'd hurt this kid somehow, when not even two days ago she was screaming for me to shoot him.

"Wait a minute. He brought *me* in, first of all. Second, do you think this is *my* fault? Maybe you should have given me a little warning, before we went on that little suicide mission against the Hand of God, that I'd have to shoot a little boy."

Her cheeks flushed red, but she didn't drop my gaze. "If I'd told you, you never would have considered it."

"How many Sentinels have you seen, anyway? Ezekiel told me no one has ever successfully faced one down before."

"Both of you need to shut your traps," Harry interjected. "We don't need to be having this conversation right now."

Genevieve raised her hand. "I have this, Dad."

Reluctantly, the big man stood down and folded his slab-like arms across his chest. Kaya watched us all wide-eyed, as if we were participating in a game of badminton with a live hand grenade.

Genevieve dry scrubbed her face, steeling herself. "I was raised in a Cradle. The reason I was so sick as a child when we came to God's Hope is because I was part of the same program as that kid up there."

Kaya gasped, and I'm sure if there had been any flying insects, I would have sucked a few into my mouth as well. "How did you get out?" she asked.

"I was born on the inside." Her eyes moved to her father and softened a bit. "My parents worked for the Rite."

"Genny," Harry cut in again.

She placed her hand on Harry's shoulder. "Don't worry, Dad. If they're going to be part of this group, they should know the truth like everyone else."

He nodded, though it looked like it pained him to do so. I sympathized with his need to protect his daughter, but I was too curious to let her stop.

"Tell me everything," I said. "It's okay."

"I don't really remember my mom. She was a Proselytist, which is basically a recruiter of sorts. I don't even really remember my time as a Sentinel. It's all really foggy." Her eyes shifted. It was too quick for most people to catch, but as the father of two teenage girls, I had a bit more practice at that sort of thing. She was lying, at least about that part, but I saw little sense in calling her on it. If she remembered how bad it was and wanted to forget, that was fine by me. "Anyway, I guess my mom had become involved with some of the resistance groups that were floating around at the time. Eventually, she told Dad, and he joined too. You and I have that in common, John. Rebel parents."

"Yeah, I guess so."

"She was set up, though. Someone ended up getting caught, and they slipped her name as a bargaining chip, or maybe under torture. There was no saving her. Actually, we probably would have all been killed if Daddy hadn't made a deal. He was a well-respected Samaritan at the time, and he had some pull."

I wasn't surprised to hear that Harry was a Samaritan, a kind of healer not unlike the doctors of old. He was gentle but dexterous, and seemed to have a way with making salves, judging by how quickly the redness faded from Kaya's fly bite.

"That wasn't it," Harry said. "Esther and I had made a pact long before, when we decided to turn to the good side, that the first one of us caught would take the fall and assume all blame. That way at least one of us could be spared to raise Genny." He sniffed back tears. "She beat me to it."

"How old were you when you became a Sentinel?" Kaya asked.

"They're tested for their abilities at about a year old," Harry said. "Genny's were showing long before that, though. The first sign was she never cried. Not because she *couldn't*. Oh, she'd howl like the best of them if she hurt herself, but she never cried because she needed anything. She could tell us exactly what she wanted, just by putting a picture in our minds. Soon enough, though, she was talking. At three months. Early even for a Sentinel."

"Wow," I said.

"They agreed to spare Genny and me, provided we cut all our ties with them," Harry went on. "We had to agree to subject ourselves to Justification every year, just like any ordinary citizen, and we'd get no special treatment because of our background. They ordered us to God's Hope with enough money to settle down. We played it straight for a while, but it didn't hold. I never got over what happened to Esther, and the guilt ate me up inside. I eventually met Turpin, likely under the same circumstances as you. A grieving man looking for a little medicine. The rest is more or less history. He gave me direction, and I took it."

"If you don't mind my asking, what became of your wife?" I asked.

Harry looked at his shoes. "She was shipped off somewhere in the mountains. One of their prisons or death camps," he muttered thickly, and the real source of his pain was exposed. The thought of his wife suffering so that he and their daughter could live probably ate at him like acid every day. That he managed to stay so open and friendly was a miracle.

"That was also part of the deal," Genevieve said. "The price for clemency with these people is never cheap. We don't know how or when she died, but it's never painless or quick in one of those places."

"Do you still have any of your abilities?" Kaya asked.

Genevieve shook her head. "Not really, no. Like I said, Sentinels have a limited shelf life. Maybe five years. Eight is the oldest I've ever heard, and you only really ever see that in girls or twins. Around the start of puberty, the path to the *Élan Vital* becomes blocked. No one knows why. I might have some lingering psychic intuition. It's helped me stay safe as a conductor on the Railroad, or at least I like to think it has. But I can't do anything like Ezekiel. Actually, I don't think any Sentinel can do what he can. Sabotaging a whole army of HOG agents and then pulling you into the ether like that. I can't imagine the mental strength that had to take. It would have killed me."

"I think you're selling yourself way too short there, darlin'," Harry said. Genevieve shrugged, but said nothing.

We sat in silence for the next few minutes, and I let all the new information wash over me. A beep issued from the radio mounted on Harry's bike. He picked it up and pressed the Talk button.

"Monticello here. Go ahead," he said.

"*Red Baron here. I cleared the road. But the boy woke up.*"

We all gazed at each other. Awake? So much for that coma, I thought.

"Has he said anything?" Harry asked.

"*He only said one thing and then passed out again.*"

"What was it?"

"He said Babylon is burning."

Chapter 11

We raced for the rally point Harry arranged with Christoph over the radio. Kaya and I lagged behind due to our inexperience on the bikes, but we managed to avoid wrecking at the breakneck pace we were keeping. Soon we emerged from the Weeping Woods and entered a town that could only have been abandoned, judging by the number of forlorn buildings crumbling under a carpet of weeds. We followed Harry through a narrow alleyway, dodging trash and other debris, and came to a stop in a lot behind a large corrugated metal building where we were to wait for Christoph.

I finally had a chance to take in the horror of the town, one of several we would see on our journey that had been left to the whims of the devilish landscape. This place was among the worst hit I'd seen. Cars with weeds spilling from their windows sat on rotting tires. One of them looked curiously bent in the middle, as if the vines had hugged it to death.

Tangles of vines were spread across the lot like a green rug amid chunks of concrete and blacktop, where it seemed they had burst right through from below in their quest to consume everything. Had people here seen that, or were they long gone by then? I certainly hoped it was the latter. I tried to imagine what it must have been like and shuddered. No signs of human life remained, apart from their faded business signs. I could see the sun-faded hamburger of an old fast food restaurant lying in the street before its defunct building. Fast food . . . it was almost as mythical as corn these days. I could still make out old graffiti painted on the crumbling brick façade: *DON'T FEED THE WEED!*

Turpin told me many stories of the riots from the early days of the Blight, back before most folks wanted to admit there was a Blight, back before the Salad Days insanity, back before the serpent weeds were considered anything more than a nuisance, like dandelions. There were activist groups, who were closer to the truth than most wanted to believe or admit, who accused the big food companies of putting the mutant weeds into the food in order to stay in business when the corn and wheat crops began to go. They saw the writing on the wall. And in this case, it seemed, they'd written the writing on the wall.

Harry helped Turpin out of the sidecar so the old man could stretch a little, and I gladly stepped off my bike for a spell—the seat was making my ass numb—but I didn't want to remain in this haunted place for long. The weeds seemed almost vital here, like they could wrap around us like snakes and crush us to death.

"Where are we?" Kaya asked.

"Morning Sun," I said. When they all looked at me like I'd gone crazy, I pointed to a faded sign above the doors of the metal building. *Wear Parts and Equipment,* and below that: *Morning Sun's Foremost Heavy Equipment Outfitter!*

"Ah, yep. Morning Sun," Turpin said. "Just another abandoned burg along our road."

"I don't like it," Kaya said. "It feels haunted."

Harry nodded. "That's what the Divine Rite thinks too. A remnant of the old days. One of the first towns to go down from the weeds before Justification ever got a foothold. You'll rarely see agents here, which is why it's one of the resting points on the Railroad. Of course, that doesn't mean they won't send someone in if they have good reason to, but it's safe enough. A little spooky, but otherwise harmless."

The roar of an engine cut through the dead silence, echoing off the building fronts. Kaya and I, already strung tighter than piano strings, went for our weapons. "It's okay," Genevieve said. "It's just Christoph."

The black truck roared into the warehouse lot, kicking up clouds of dirt in its wake, and ground to a halt. The driver unfurled his impossibly large body from the cab and hurried over.

"Is the boy still out?" Turpin asked.

The German nodded. "I drove a little farther west to Shepherd's Bluff before turning back. You can see the Hymn River Valley stretching on to Old Babylon from there. I saw no signs of fire."

"Are you sure that's what he said? Babylon is burning?" Genevieve asked.

"Yes, I'm sure."

"Well that doesn't make any sense," Kaya said.

"It does if he's speaking prophecy," I said. "He said his main gift was seeing the future."

"Forget about it," Turpin said, visibly irritated. "If the city ain't burnin', it ain't burnin'. If it's prophecy, then we aren't gonna waste our time on it."

"So we just keep going?" I asked.

"That's right, boyo," Turpin said. "We're gonna ride to Old Babylon, but we'll be high on our guard. If we smell a fire before we get there, we'll figure somethin' out, but we really ought to make that stop if we can. That's where we catch a boat to carry us down the Hymn, where it joins the Colorado River near a town called Eudora. From there, we'll be able to get horses to take us along the Colorado and through canyon country, and on to the coast. We've got a small window to catch the boat, and we want to catch it. Riding to Eudora on back road terrain will be nigh on impossible, and we'll likely hit a lot of Divine Rite presence. On a trade boat, we'll move faster and have a better chance of passin' without notice, especially at night."

"How long until the next boat from the coast?" I asked

Turpin shrugged. "It's a dangerous voyage. They only chance it a few times a year. This boat is the second one to go out and probably the last one before the winter, if I remember correct. If we miss it . . ." He trailed off, but he'd said all he needed to say. If we missed the boat, we'd be stranded and likely caught by the Rite.

We decided to have a meal before carrying on with the rest of the journey. Christoph and Harry removed a small cook stove from the back of the truck, and they heated up some bean soup into which Harry sliced some of his home-made venison sausage. After the meal, I walked over to the passenger side of the truck cab and peeked in.

Ezekiel lay on his side across the bench seat, wrapped in a blue and white quilt, his sleeping head propped on a pillow. One of his hands curled into a fist under the shelf of his jaw and the other lay on the blanket like a deflated jellyfish. Dark circles of exhaustion and malnourishment ringed his eyes, and his small lips were a purplish hue as if he had been eating handfuls of blackberries. If it hadn't been for the faint flutter of the blanket over his chest, I might have believed he was a corpse. For reasons I can't quite explain, other than I guess I felt compelled to do so, I opened the door, leaned into the cab, and clasped his hand.

A barrage of images flooded my mind and I jerked back, rapping my head on the truck's door jamb hard enough to raise a painful knot later.

I was back in a familiar landscape. Dead, bleached tree trunks, twisted weeds, garbage, wheel ruts. Hallmarks of the Weeping Woods. It felt like I was looking through someone else's eyes, and the side-to-side list as he or she walked along was a little nauseating. Suddenly the person stopped and knelt down, and I saw large feet clad in scuffed black boots. A gloved hand, also black, reached out to clear away dead brush, revealing a fresh tire track. Everything inside me went cold.

My link with the boy was suddenly severed, and the images blinked out like birthday candles on a puff of breath. I realized, at least on some semi-conscious level, that Harry was yanking me out of the truck. I opened my mouth to speak, but my tongue lay there like a dead slug. It was only after the large man slapped my face that the world came back into focus. The first sensation I noticed, other than the hot stinging of my cheek, was the smell of urine and a wet spot on my jeans. In my trance, I'd pissed myself.

"John! Are you okay? Talk to me, son," Harry yelled into

my face.

I looked up at him and said the only thing that needed saying. "I think we're being followed."

Chapter 12

I first changed my clothes and had a few sips of Turpin's bourbon before I told the group what happened. Harry looked particularly troubled.

"Ya got any inklin' who it could be?" Turpin asked him.

He shook his head, but the frown on his face said he might have thought otherwise. "I need some time to think about it," he muttered.

I asked Turpin who he thought it was.

"Can't say for sure, boyo, and I don't got enough info to venture a guess, but I will say it's odd for Divine Rite folk to travel alone, 'specially through haunted lands like the Weepin' Woods. If ya saw what ya saw, then I'll just say we're ahead of him by a good bit, and if he's on foot he won't have much hope of catchin' up. If we go now, we'll make the safe house before anybody can catch up to us."

We decided that was the safest bet, and after packing back up, we hustled out of Morning Sun through the town's wide main boulevard, where there was more room to skirt around cars and busted blacktop. In the sky, late afternoon golds and blues began yielding to early evening's oranges and pinks. I lagged behind, still a little unsteady from my encounter with the boy. Genevieve circled her bike around so we could ride side by side.

"How are you holding up?" she asked

"I'm hanging in," I said, feeling a little cautious with her. I used to think she liked me, but now after all this business with the Sentinel, I wasn't sure.

"You shouldn't have touched him like that, John. What were you thinking?" She didn't say it in a scolding way, but she was grave.

"I wasn't thinking. I was just going on instinct, I guess."

"He has some sort of a psychic connection with you. I can't deny that. But his mind is very delicate right now, and whatever it is with you . . . you haven't been fully tested. We could have lost both of you back there."

"What do you mean by fully tested?"

"The Hand of God always feared us. They keep the Sentinels weak and underfed on purpose. They've studied us for years to see how they can better use us, not only to guide them on their missions, but to shape the minds of those who resist the Rite. The Sentinels didn't do so well, but the subjects they linked with were even worse off."

"How so?"

"Ezekiel could have killed you if he wanted to. He could have ruptured an artery in your brain or turned you into a vegetable. If he was at his full strength, he could have even bent you completely to his will to do God knows what. Of course, I've never seen Sentinels do it out of hand. Normally they have to be directed to do so, and only under duress. It's . . . morally counter-intuitive."

"Like murder?" I asked.

"Something like that."

I remembered the brief few seconds after Harry and Christoph pulled me back from the boy, when I could neither move nor speak. If I'd stayed with him much longer . . . I shuddered. "I guess I'm just lucky, then."

She glanced at me. "I don't know if lucky is the right word. Those guinea pigs back at the Cradle, they died. All of them, according to my father. He doesn't know of a single person who has survived a direct link with a Sentinel like you've done twice now. And yet, here you are, pretty much the same as you were, save for a little piss in your pants. Yeah. I'd say that's definitely more than just luck."

There was that note of accusation in her voice again. I ground my bike to a halt in the middle of the street. Suddenly it seemed too hard to drive and think at the same time. The others, who were ahead by a bit, eventually stopped too and looked back. Genevieve signaled for them to wait a minute. "What are you trying to say? Three days ago, I had no idea what a Sentinel even was. Maybe you could tell me what all this means instead of acting like I should have some clue."

She glared at me for a moment, but then her features gradually softened and she looked away. "I'm sorry, John. I don't mean to sound angry with you. Or like I think you're hiding something. It's just that I didn't expect any of this. It reminds me of difficult times. I wish I had more answers, but I don't."

I touched her arm. "It's okay. I know what that's like. My childhood wasn't very good, either."

She looked back up at me, her green eyes alight with hope. "John, maybe that's it! Maybe you were a Sentinel yourself as a child."

Her idea hit me like a brick. "Impossible," I said. I'd never been within five hundred miles of a Cradle at any point in my life that I could recall.

"Are you sure? My memories are foggy too. I only remember as much as I do because of my father."

I entertained the idea for a minute, only because she looked so desperate for answers, but it didn't fit. Certainly, there were fuzzy patches in my memory. I guess I'd blocked out the worst things, especially from the days before God's Hope, but my parents were fugitives from the law. They weren't in a Cradle. Maybe Genevieve was dancing close to the truth, but she wasn't quite there yet.

"Maybe we're close to the right idea, but we just need to think on it a little longer," I said, not wanting to trample all over her hopes.

"Yes, perhaps. Whatever the answer, you are definitely special, John Welland. And you need to be much more careful."

She revved the little engine of her scooter and set off to catch up with the others. I sat looking after her for a minute before I continued along in quiet meditation. Eventually, I found myself immersed in old memories, trying to recall any instance in my life where I exhibited some sort of extrasensory perception, or any time when I could pluck thoughts out of someone's head or put something into theirs, the way Harry had described Genevieve's abilities as an infant.

I thought of the two times I'd forgotten my and Linny's wedding anniversary. That wasn't particularly psychic. Or the one time I'd decided to surprise her by buying her a dress that ended up being two sizes too large. I thought of our first official "date." I'd taken her to a place that served fish, even though she'd always hated the stuff. I had known her for years by then, had grown up with her in fact, but I completely failed to remember that little detail. Being her quietly thoughtful self, however, Linny didn't admit my goof to me for years.

I laughed a little. Intuition was definitely not my strong point. Of course, if I'd once had the abilities of a Sentinel, I would have been very young. Genevieve had said they were all done in before age eight, and usually by age five. Most people in general can't remember much before age four, and I could recall very little about my life before moving to God's Hope at ten. Any memories I did have felt like they belonged to someone else.

There were no Christmases, no birthday parties, no school lessons, no bullies, no friends. I remembered my mother singing me to sleep, and my father teaching me how to tie my shoes, but their faces were like unformed clay in my mind now, decades after their sudden departure. I guess it's easier to forget with age, or without any older family to help dredge things up. I didn't have so much as a single picture of them, and I would probably pass my own mother on the street without recognizing her.

I was in the midst of that profoundly disappointing thought when I heard Kaya cry out up ahead. "*Hey*! It's one of those sign thingies, I think!"

She hopped off her scooter, one tan and sleeveless arm pointing to a rusted stop sign in the intersection. Someone had drawn a simple diamond shape with a tiny cross in the middle of the red octagon using a piece of coal pencil.

"Dear God," Harry said and pulled his shotgun from the

holster in his saddlebag. I followed his lead, pulled my M4 to me, and a few seconds later remembered to flick off the safety switch.

"What is it?" I asked, blood pounding in my ears. I didn't like the idea of another fight, but at least I had a better gun this time.

"It means 'be ready to defend yerself,'" Turpin said, and pulled out an antique revolver that looked more like a blunderbuss. Genevieve removed her trusty pistol from her leather satchel. Kaya, who didn't care much for firearms, pulled out a weapon with which she'd always had a passing familiarity growing up in the country: a slingshot. Only this one was no child's toy. It had a pistol grip, an arm support for stability, thick tubular thrust bands, and even an adjustable sight. Christoph had fashioned it out of a dismantled handgun and some other spare parts, and gave it to her along with a heavy bag of metal ball bearings that could kill a man as easily as a bullet. I saw her make some practice shots with it earlier that morning and she was deadly with the thing.

"Who could it be? Hand of God?" My voice trembled and my gut clenched like a fist. I wasn't sure I would ever be able to go into battle without my bowels turning to water.

Harry shook his head. "Maybe, but I doubt it. I don't think any of them would want to camp out in a place like this."

"What about the guy Daddy saw following us?" Kaya asked as she dropped a ball bearing into the slingshot's cup.

"Doubtful," Harry said. "We haven't had any rain lately. That mark could be weeks old. Just the same . . ." He grabbed for the radio, nearly dropped it, and called for Christoph. A flying insect that looked like an overgrown grasshopper lighted on his shoulder and he flicked it off impatiently.

"*Red Baron. Go ahead,*" called the German from up ahead.

"I don't suppose you saw a warning symbol on a stop sign on your way through here?" asked Harry.

"*Nein. I saw stop signs, but no symbols on them.*"

"Shit!" Harry hissed. "I need you to halt and make your way back here. We may need—" Harry stopped talking, but his mouth hung open as his face went white.

A familiar buzzing sound, one I remembered distinctly from a recent memory but couldn't quite place at that moment, rose from behind us. I looked and saw a black cloud of locusts rise up between a former hardware store and a shack of a building that the dirty red and blue striped pole lying in pieces before it denoted as a barbershop. Their droning chorus filled the world and set my teeth on edge. The sound felt like it could chew a canal through to the center of my brain, plant its barbed roots into the soft tissue, and kill everything around it.

"Let's go!" Kaya shouted over the infernal murmur of the advancing swarm. Harry's big hand fastened over her wrist.

"It's too late," he said.

"What the hell is it, Harry? What are we supposed to do?" I demanded. He said nothing. Meanwhile, Turpin sat with his head bowed, as if in meditation. He was no help.

Genevieve looked fearful, but also a touch accusatory. She scowled at her father, spots of scarlet high on her cheeks. "Daddy, what do you know?"

"I just need you to trust me, Genny. Can you do that?"

She didn't reply, but raised her gun to the advancing cloud, lips drawn tight.

"Hold up your weapons, but don't fire," Harry said. "If it's what I think it is, we're gonna have a hell of a bigger mess on our hands if we shoot at it."

The swarm stopped about ten feet away and compacted into a very familiar shape: four limbs, a stout trunk, shoulders, and a head. The drone took on a higher pitch as the swarm solidified from the ground up. I recognized the boots from the vision I had inside Ezekiel's head.

Harry crossed himself. "A Heretic. Dear Lord, I didn't want to believe it, but it's true."

"A *what*?" Kaya asked.

The man-thing's features began to distinguish themselves, and the buzzing dissolved into the encroaching evening like the whistle of a teakettle removed from the heat. Before us stood a thick and sturdy man-shape, about my height, with dark skin that seemed to quiver. I made a revolting realization that it wasn't actual skin, but a mass of tightly compacted exoskeletons. He didn't wear clothes, exactly, but his body was shaped more with the suggestion of pants and shirt, as if they'd been molded to his body. His hair was a cap of curls I soon figured to be tightly compacted antennae. Even more inhuman were his eyes, which had very little white. His gigantic irises were grass green and flecked with glints of glowing orange. His pupils were like tiny dots of ink.

No one on our side seemed inclined to speak the first word. We just stared, as if uttering words would undo everything we'd just seen. The being stepped a little closer and smiled. His teeth were as glossy and black as the rest of him.

"I believe the ginger-headed gentleman called me a Heretic," the man said. His voice was reedy and vibrated slightly.

Locusts appeared to be flying in and out of his mouth as he spoke. "I don't like that word so much, for I do have a maker. But you can use skin-walker, metamorph, mimic, or even freak and weirdo. Or you can just call me by my given name, Anansi." He bowed with a flourish, his curls gleaming in the late afternoon sun.

"Anansi," Turpin muttered. "Interesting name, though I recall from my folklore that he was a spider and not a locust."

"Ah, well what's in a name anyway?" Anansi grinned. The orange in his eyes flared like freshly stoked embers.

"Did you make that there?" Kaya asked, gesturing to the mark on the stop sign.

"Guilty as charged, my lady," the mimic said. "Before I introduce myself, I like to let people know to expect something. On the few occasions I've popped up without any sort of warning, the poor people have either fainted or died from fear. Dead people don't make for good bounties."

"So that's what you want, Heretic?" grumbled Harry. "A bounty?" I observed he hadn't yet lowered his weapon. I kept mine at the ready, and so did the others. Anansi didn't seem too bothered one way or another.

"Tut tut, Harry. I don't think you're in a place to be forgetting your manners. Nonetheless, let us not waste our time on trivialities."

"Who's the bounty on?" Turpin asked.

"Well, all of *you*, of course. However, the Hand of God was most interested in recovering the Sentinel and this gentleman and his daughter." He gestured to Kaya and me, and my stomach clenched again. "But if I bring all of you, well, that would buy me far more favor. I'd never have to work again, I suspect, though I probably would if asked. I do so love my job."

"Good luck trying to get us all," Kaya said. "Maybe you didn't notice, but we outnumber you."

Anansi threw back his head and laughed. Its timbre was high and rich, and it reverberated off the nearby buildings and cars. "Outnumbered. You really are quite adorable, young woman. Far feistier than your sister, I'll grant you that."

I snapped at the mention of Beth, and I advanced on him, leveling my gun at the locust man's strange face. His smile only grew bigger, though. Anansi wasn't afraid of being shot, and probably welcomed the challenge.

"Where is my daughter, you freak? What did you do to her?"

"Don't worry, Mr. Welland. She is currently in a safe location. And she is completely unharmed. I always deliver my cargo safely. You may even get to see her when we get to Donum Dei."

I shuddered. Donum Dei. If Beth was there, it meant we had the attention of much bigger fish than the local or even regional magistrates. We had gone Big Time.

"What are we worth to ya, out of curiosity?" Turpin asked, as if he were dickering over a piece of furniture and not our lives.

"More than you could pay me, old man."

Turpin nodded, as if he'd expected Anansi to say just that. "We're a little lean on money, that's true, but what else? It ain't just the cash yer after. Not much use for cash in this day and age except to bond a man to his word."

"He doesn't work for money. Heretics earn points that go toward their freedom from working for the Hand of God," Harry said. "He's a prisoner in a Cradle, probably caught swarming over the border from Africa where his kind come from, but he gets work release privileges."

Anansi bowed his head. "Correct you are. And I should say that this final payload will release me from my bond quite handily."

"So you get to go back to Africa?" Kaya asked.

"They'll release him to a Heretic colony, but not before they make sure he's unable to disperse into his little locust cloud again."

Anansi revealed more of his abundant teeth in a shark-like smile that made me cringe. "Impressive, Harry! You haven't forgotten much from your own stooging days have you? But yes, I'm afraid the gentleman is correct. I don shackles of my own, you see." The "skin" around his wrist shifted, revealing a band of red and green lights twinkling around it.

"Why don't you just stay in bug form and fly away forever?" Kaya asked.

Anansi's face grew serious. "It really wouldn't be much fun for me, or anyone else for that matter. The longer I'm in swarm, the more separated I become from my mind, and the more havoc I tend to wreak. Have you ever seen a true locust plague anywhere outside the Bible, dear girl?" Kaya shook her head. "Well, ask the old man about it sometime. I'm sure he could fill you in on the devastation it can cause. Either way, I prefer being human. I feel a little less . . . spread out." He uttered a giggle that sounded about a half-step down from mania.

"So your idea of freedom is to move from one prison to another?" Genevieve asked.

His gravity returned, only this time it bordered more on anger. The rapid shift in his moods was terrifying, and I worried he would suddenly drop the pretense of discussion and scoop us all up.

"Living among my own people is no prison, my dear. It is my dream."

"Oh, I'm sorry, it's a 'designated colony,' where you can't even be your true self," she said. "A prison with walls and a prison without walls is still your choice. That isn't real freedom. You would be no better off than we were in God's Hope. It too was a prison in disguise, only none of us had your remarkable ability. No wonder the Rite wouldn't allow you to wander freely."

"And what would your suggestion be, if I may ask?"

"In exchange for letting us go, we would set you free from the Rite," Genevieve said.

For the first time since setting down, Anansi's confidence faltered. Shoulders slumped, eyes down, he said, "You drive a hard bargain, and you seem quite charming, but you ask me to risk too much. Even a prison without walls is a fine reward if it gets me out of that wretched Cradle. And this bracelet I wear is part of me. All of me. You could not remove it without risking my life. And if I do not bring you in soon, or if they discover I've tampered with the bond, they will track me down and kill me off piece by piece."

Turpin looked at him. "Let's just say we could remove the bracelet without anyone bein' the wiser. Make it so it never even existed. Would ya reconsider?"

I looked at him wide-eyed. What in the world was the old man thinking? He was bluffing, of course, but he was also playing with fire.

Anansi laughed again, only this time it was more somber. "It's a useless question, but sure, if you could remove the bracelet, I could make an exception. While you're at it, why not make the weeds disappear and the Hand of God into a flock of geese?"

"Believe me, boyo, if we could do that, we woulda done it by now."

"But you think you can give me your freedom."

"That's right," the old man said. "No prisons, with or without walls, without the shadow of the Rite hangin' over ya. With all yer abilities intact. Same thing all of us are searchin' for, really."

"I imagine it every waking moment, old man, but I have no guarantee you're any closer to it than I am. You're on the run. That's a far shot from being free."

Turpin nodded. "Yer dead right, boyo. Our journey's only begun and the odds are stacked against us, but I'm offerin' ya a real adventure and a chance to earn yer freedom the honest way, with honest folk who wouldn't dare exploit yer abilities, and who would fight by yer side every step of the way. And ya would have a chance to walk or fly with yer own people in Africa again. Maybe even liberate the colonies too."

Anansi gazed at the ground as Turpin spoke, his dark face shrouded in deep contemplation. He looked up at the mention of his homeland, his strange eyes shining with cautious hope. "All this, provided you can get this bracelet off," he said, now sounding like he believed. Turpin had that effect on people, but damn if I knew how the old man was going to come through.

The answering roar of Christoph's truck startled the shapeshifter, but Turpin stayed him down with a steady hand. "Don't worry about that. Our special tool just arrived.

Glancing at me, the old man said, "I think this'll all work out just fine."

Chapter 13

Harry and Turpin hailed the approaching truck and headed toward it. The two of them walked with their heads nearly touching, speaking in harsh but hushed tones as if engaged in an argument. I couldn't hear it, but I was pretty sure it had to do with Turpin's harebrained plan and Harry's clear disapproval. Genevieve headed off to join them while Kaya stayed with me, looking warily at our new guest. Anansi, meanwhile, rested on his hunkers with his strange eyes turned up to the sky. I took a few steps closer and squatted down next to him.

"I want to know how my daughter ended up all the way in Donum Dei, and why."

Anansi sighed, but he didn't look at me. "I don't have much to tell. The Hand of God gives me orders, and I carry them out. No additional information is necessary. The first order of business today was to bring in your girl and then track you down. I always do as I'm told. Until now."

Despair filled me. "That's it? Is there nothing else you can tell me?"

The man was silent for a few minutes, a polar opposite of the flamboyant spectacle he was in his introduction. I think the prospect of freedom was sobering to him. "It was an unusual job, I will say. I'd never had to deliver anyone directly to Donum Dei before. I usually take them back to the Cradle. Your daughter was quite a valuable commodity, but I do not know why."

The only thing I could think was that they wanted to use her as leverage to get at the rest of us. Beth wasn't a player in this game, and I could see no other reason for her involvement.

"You swear to me she's unhurt, because if she isn't—"

"I'm nearly positive she is well."

"How can you be so sure?"

Anansi finally locked his eyes on mine, and I mustered all of my courage to hold his electric gaze. "Because of all the people I've had to bring in for the Divine Rite, she is the only one who didn't put up a fight or show fear. She stepped out of your house and simply stood there on the porch. I told her who I was and where I'd been ordered to take her, and she nodded as if she'd been expecting me. So I gathered her up and away we went."

"What do you mean you 'gathered her up?'" I asked.

He laughed quietly. "You'd have to see it to believe it, my man. Maybe one day, I'll show you. Just for fun-like."

Before I could question him further, Harry trotted over, his expression as stony and cold as a rock face. "On your feet, Heretic. Provided you have no tricks up your sleeve, we're going to try and free you from your bonds."

I jumped to my feet first. "They have Beth at Donum Dei," I said to Harry.

He nodded slightly. "I understand, John. But that doesn't change our current direction."

I couldn't believe what I'd just heard. "What do you mean

it doesn't change our direction?" I shouted. "If my daughter has been kidnapped by these scumbags, I can't leave the country! We never should have left her. She should have been here with us the whole time."

Harry placed his big hands on my shoulders. "Listen to me, my friend. I said *current* direction. Our final destination has changed. We would never let the Divine Rite have one of our own for free. However, we have neither the provisions nor enough information to just go blazing all the way up there without a plan. We'll end up getting ourselves captured or killed and that won't help anybody. If the Heretic is correct, she's not in any immediate danger. She's an important piece of leverage to them. We're going to meet our man in Old Babylon, formulate a plan, and do it right. Okay?"

I wanted to say more, but the man was right. It could have been worse. They could have decided my troubles were my own and abandoned Kaya and I to this rescue mission alone. Harry gave me a companionable clap on the shoulder and turned his attention back to Anansi. "You ready to be freed, bondsman? Or do you have any funny business to get out of the way first?"

The Heretic grinned. "Not me, my man. If you can get this bracelet off without alerting the HOG, I'd be so thankful that I'd stick with you for the pure entertainment value."

Harry looked at me. "We're going to need you too, I think."

I frowned. "What for?"

"You'll see," he said. "Come on."

We followed him over to the truck where Christoph towered over Turpin in a parody of physical opposites. The passenger side of the truck stood open, and Ezekiel had been propped up in the seat, the blanket draped over his bony knees like that of a terminal patient. His closed eyes were sunken deep into their sockets. I looked over at Genevieve. Her face was pinched with worry.

"If anyone here could remove Anansi's wristband, it's Ezekiel," she said. "The question is how to do it without killing Anansi."

The shapeshifter got a look inside the truck. His eyes flared and his dark, quivering features went still with shock bordering on reverence. "Moon and stars above. It's really him," he whispered.

Genevieve frowned. "What do you mean? He's just a Sentinel. You've undoubtedly seen them before."

"Yes, but . . . he's different."

"How do you mean?" she asked.

"This one is almost like a God himself. Some think he's the Messiah, though they'd never say it out loud. But they sure are angry that he's missing."

Genevieve sniffed with disdain. "God, huh? He's a kid who's spent most of his life suspended in a half-trance. Why would anyone think that?"

Anansi frowned at her. "Kid? This is no kid. He's legendary." He regarded Genevieve closely for a moment. "You're telling me *you've* never heard of him? You were one of them. I can see the shadow of it on you."

She gaped. "How would I—"

"Never mind that for now," Harry said, almost as if he didn't want her to finish the thought, and that made me curious. But it was the wrong time to dig deeper.

"John, Genny says you seem to have a special link with the

boy. I think you'd be able to act as a sort of shunt between him and Anansi to help channel his power in such a way that it doesn't kill the Heret—bounty hunter."

I was dumbfounded. "Uh . . . do you think that will work?"

He shrugged. "I don't have the first idea what'll work here. We're all in this guessing game together. But I think it's as good an idea as any."

"Well why doesn't Genevieve do it?" I asked. "She used to be one of them."

"I already tried," she said. "I grabbed his hand, but I got nothing at all. He seems to only work for you, John."

"But I have no idea what I'm supposed to do."

"I understand," she said. "I'll do my best to try and guide you through it." She switched places with me so I stood right between Ezekiel and Anansi, who was still too exalted to remove his eyes from the sleeping Sentinel. "I want you to take Anansi's hand, the one that has the bracelet on it. Study it for a minute. Then I want you to conjure an image of it in your mind. Take your time. I want it to be crystal clear. When you're sure you have it, I'll give you Ezekiel's hand. Imagine the white energy that flows from him into you is moving through that arm, down through your belly, and out your other arm in a thin stream toward the band of lights. Does that make sense?"

I uttered a shaky laugh. "As much as something like this can make sense, I guess."

Genevieve put her hand on the back of my neck. It was warm, and I felt instantly soothed by her touch. "I have no doubt in you, John. I never have. We'll be here to catch you when it's done."

"Damn right we will," Harry said. "Now let's get to it. We're losing daylight fast, and I'd like to be to our next stop before dusk."

I began the process of clearing my mind. Inhaling and exhaling, I imagined all my worries were boxes in the middle of a white room that I could push to the side. It was a little exercise I first learned from Linny in the aftermath of my parents leaving, when I'd lie awake at night crying, wondering why they'd abandoned me, and where they'd gone. I'd later boxed up my worries when she got sick and I fretted about work, money, and how we'd make it through. I did it after she died, though less successfully. And now, her voice was in my mind, guiding me again.

Pack up all the bad things that will fit and push them to the side of the room. Good. Now focus on what's left in the middle. It should be just you, John.

Except, it was never just me left over. It was also her. She *was* the middle. As I stood bookended by two examples of nature's newfound madness—a psychic little person who could apparently bend minds, and a bounty hunter that possessed the ability to transform into a swarm of locusts—I realized how much I missed her, and how much I'd give to be together in that little white room again. It had always been an illusion, sure, but it was a comforting one.

I packed up my worries about Beth and what was happening to her in Donum Dei. I packed up my guilt over the pain and fear Kaya had experienced since leaving God's Hope. I packed up my terror that we wouldn't live to see the next day, let alone the distant dream of whatever our final destination was. Soon, I started seeing floor space. With the "boxes" out of the way, I held out my right hand to Anansi, who grasped it tightly, and I did my best to ignore the odd rigidity of his skin. I studied the band around his wrist for a moment and closed my eyes.

"Best of luck, my man. I have faith in you," he whispered.

"Don't speak. I barely have any faith in myself," I said and focused all of my energy on remembering his bracelet. It was seamlessly integrated into his flesh. Just blinking red and green lights with a strange insignia twisting through them that looked almost engraved. That must have been what made it work, but that also made it the weak point. And I knew if I didn't do this right, it would also be what would alarm the Hand of God that something wasn't quite right with their Heretic.

I envisioned the energy bypassing this somehow, allowing the lights to still work, even when the functional part of the bracelet was removed. That way, nothing would change on whatever device the Hand of God was using to track him.

I thought of a toddler performing delicate surgery with a battleaxe and felt inept compared even to that. What was I doing here?

But there was Linny in my head again, reminding me I forgot to put another worry into a box. That there wasn't room for that here. Not now. *Do this for our daughters*, she said, and that was enough.

Holding this image firmly in my mind, I held out my other hand for Ezekiel the way a surgeon holds his hand out for an instrument, and braced myself.

The boy's cool, small hand settled into the palm of mine and I clasped it tightly. At first, nothing happened. I was sure it was going to fail. The image of the broken bracelet, with that important delicate insignia, began to flicker and degrade like a dream upon waking. "Ezekiel," I whispered. "Help me."

Suddenly a flash, like the sun heliographing off a giant, shiny mirror, filled me with a physical force that threatened to turn my brain into a pile of steaming jelly. I struggled to control it, but I faltered and it nearly overtook me. I wanted to drop the boy's hand, but we were bound in our bodies and minds by the energy.

The *Élan Vital*.

I believe I screamed, but I could hear none of it. The light ate up all my other senses. I became one with it and, in essence, I realized I could manipulate it, squeeze it like ethereal clay in imaginary hands.

I forced that light into a tiny point and pushed it down through me like a piece of food down my esophagus, into my belly. Its density was enormous, like a million nuclear furnaces squashed to the size of a child's marble. I could only hold it a moment or it would break free and incinerate me, and everyone in the world.

I hurled that tiny ball up and out toward Anansi's bond. It left a tracer of illumination behind it like a comet's tail as it sailed toward the insignia. The force of the collision was unexpected. It was a supernova. It not only broke the bracelet; it obliterated the thing to a time before such things ever existed. As far as the Hand of God was concerned, Anansi never existed. The bracelet was nothing more than the tiniest quark floating on an invisible cosmic wind, where it would become part of another star in another galaxy in another universe.

I couldn't verify this, but I just knew. The way I knew that right then all my traveling companions were looking at me like I was some wondrous new species of animal. The way I knew they were now a little afraid of me. The way I knew I had also wet my pants again.

From that nebula of light and certainty came an image that shattered whatever control I had over the infinite forces flowing through me, and with a *POP*, it winked out of existence. I floated in a void of comforting blackness, yet the picture remained. One that would haunt my dreams until now, and one that will likely haunt me in death.

I stood on a high peak with the world a desolate panorama. My hair had gone white. Men and women, including those from the Divine Rite in their torn and tattered robes, bowed fearfully at my feet—starved, frail, terrified. A cracked and barren earth screamed for sustenance beneath a blackened, forbidding sky. In the distance, a city's forgotten skyline pitched and yawed like a crone's rotting teeth. Carrion birds circled above us, diving down to feast upon the abundant remains of the wasted and defeated bodies that died in supplication. Amid all this horror, my face terrorized me most. It was the wild-eyed rictus of a madman.

—

I awoke on a hard metal bed that squeaked and jounced back and forth at the behest of a noisy, laboring motor, and I realized I was in the enclosed back of Christoph's truck. The boxes of our provisions jangled and jittered on either side of me, and I noticed with some relief they'd been secured with lengths of twine. My throbbing head, blood-encrusted upper lip, and the salty tang of my own urine spoiled any relief at being alive. I grimaced and moaned in discomfort.

"John? Are you awake?"

Genevieve.

She jumped to my side from where she must have been sitting against the truck's tailgate and hovered over me like a fire-haired apparition, her concerned eyes reddened and puffy, as if she'd been crying. She sighed and laid her head against my chest. I remained in stunned shock for a moment before I reached up to stroke her sweet-smelling hair. My arms felt like they'd been weighted with lead, but the sensation of holding her was too good to let go.

"I was so worried we were going to lose you," she said. The thickness in her voice and her irregular sniffles told me she was weeping again.

"Be careful," I warned. "I'm a mess. I think I'm going to have to pick up some diapers if I'm going to make a regular habit of communicating with Ezekiel."

She sat up and wiped her streaming eyes. "I don't care how dirty you get, so long as you don't scare us like that again. Kaya nearly had to be sedated, but she's fine now."

Lovely, I thought. More trauma for my traumatized kid. I was doing swimmingly at this whole single parenting thing. Linny would have been so proud.

"What happened?" I asked. I tried sitting up, but it was too soon. The world started spinning as soon as I made it up to my elbows. I collapsed back to the truck bed and tried to hold back the urge to vomit. There looked to be a bucket sitting nearby holding my previous failures.

"Anansi's bracelet shattered almost immediately after you were all linked together. It was amazing, John. I had expected it would take a moment for you to get going, but it was as if you knew exactly what you were doing."

"Interesting," I said. It didn't seem all that immediate to me.

"Yeah. Anansi jumped up and started whooping and hollering, thrilled that it worked. I thought it would end right there, but it didn't. You just held on to the boy and he held on to you. We tried to separate the two of you, but you wouldn't come apart. It was like we'd glued your hands together. Then you opened your eyes and mouth, and this bright white light spilled out of you. You screamed so loud. Kaya just about fainted dead away, but Anansi caught her. Daddy and Turpin . . . I never saw either of them look scared a day in my life, but both of them looked too weak to stand. Christoph held them up by their arms and just stood there watching it all with his eyes squinted."

"And what were you doing?" I asked.

She bowed her head. "I was still trying to pull you apart."

"And? What happened to you?" I forced myself upright and fought through the ensuing vertigo.

"I think we shared something. Some sort of, I dunno, vision. You were standing on a mountain, and all of these people were gathered there before you."

I closed my eyes. "Yes, I also remember that. I barely recognized myself. My hair was completely gray."

"Yes, you looked quite different. I barely recognized myself, either."

I started and knocked my aching head on the back of the

truck's cab. "What? You were there?"

"Oh believe me, I was standing right next to you. And about nine months pregnant, I would guess by the swell of my belly."

"*WHAT*?"

"I know. And look." She reached for her satchel, and un-buckled the clasps. She removed a folded silver object with her name engraved on it and handed it to me. "It's a mirror. Open it."

I found the catch and opened the clamshell case. My weary, bloodshot eyes, my bloody nose, and my pasty complexion first greeted me, but it only took a second to register the biggest shock: the thick swatches of pure white hair running through the formerly solid dark brown.

"I don't understand any of this," I murmured and handed her back the mirror. "I didn't see you with me in that vision. I'm sure of it. People were dying, and the earth was in ruins. And I'd gone completely mad."

Genevieve's brow furrowed as if I actually had gone mad right then. "You weren't crazy. You were happy. And the world wasn't in ruins. It's already in ruins. But in my vision, it was green and thriving. People were happy. They were cheering for you."

I covered my face. "This doesn't make any sense. Why would we see two completely different things?"

"Probably because either of our visions is possible," she said.

Chapter 14

We rode the rest of the way in thoughtful silence, and when the truck came to a halt and the engine shut off, I bounded out the back despite the lingering dizziness. I came around Christoph's side of the truck, where he was just hanging up the radio. "The others will arrive shortly," he said and stepped out.

I looked in the cab and saw Ezekiel stretched out across the seat again, eyes closed. I shouldn't have felt disappointed, but I did. "I was hoping he'd be awake."

"He was," Christoph said. "He fell asleep a few minutes after we got back on the road. You can try waking him."

I shuddered at the thought of touching the boy again so soon. "I think I'll wait."

I gazed around, but saw only the shadowy hulks of buildings silhouetted against the moon-bright sky. We stood in front of a ramshackle church with boarded up windows and a broken steeple. Weeds spilled out from behind the boards and out of the top of the roof like funny hair. Divine Rite Fellowships were ornate, imposing edifices that usually sat in the geographic center of the town like castles. This was a building from a lost age.

"This is Old Babylon?" I asked with little enthusiasm. I'd

expected something different from God's Hope, but not a place that had more in common with Morning Sun.

"This is the outer rim," Christoph said. "No one lives out here. It was lost before they could get their net up We will finish the rest of the trip on foot and come back later for the supplies."

"What did we bring all that stuff for, anyway?"

"Payment for our passage. Excuse me for a moment," he said and walked off to a distant patch of weeds to urinate.

"Are you feeling better?" Genevieve asked from beside me. I jerked a little at the sound of her voice, not expecting her to be there. My mind kept going back to her vision of me and comparing it with my own. She said she was pregnant. Was it my baby? What did that mean for us? I wasn't sure how to even discuss that issue with her, and she didn't seem like she was in much of a hurry to do it, so I let it lie for now, recalling Turpin's previous words on the danger of prophecy.

"A little, yes."

She gestured for me to follow her to the back of the truck where she started gathering our things and supplementing our packs with extra food and water from the supply boxes. She opened a bag of black walnuts, helped herself to a few, and handed the bag to me. I took a few tentative bites, but before long I'd eaten most of them and had also torn into more of the pheasant jerky from earlier. I was hungrier than I thought.

"We're going to see a man named Akiva Paine. He's another purveyor of goods, similar to my dad's shop, only he tends to deal more in, well, novelty items."

"What sort of novelty?" I asked.

"Cannabis, special mushrooms, and opium-based drugs mostly. Liquor too, like Turpin, although not as good if you ask me."

"Wow, so the town is full of a bunch of stumbling drug addicts, eh?" I asked, mostly joking.

Genevieve shook her head. "Not that I'm aware of. The people seem normal enough, at least for rustic folk. They could have tapped into the hydro plant downriver, the same one that powers God's Hope, but this lot shuns such things. Most of them still buy into the whole 'modern technology is evil' gambit."

"I take it you don't? Wouldn't you say all we're dealing with now is the result of someone misusing technology?"

"After some of the crazy stuff I've witnessed, I think there is far more to fear than simple human invention. The Sentinels and Anansi, for instance. Some say it was the result of exposure to the weeds, which, yes, are man-made. But I think there's more to it than that."

"Like what?" I asked.

"Back before the Blight, advanced technology provided us everything we needed. People billed the supernatural as unexplained, but mostly fake. No one believed in magic. When that world went away, this was all people had left to turn to. Their gods, demons, and everything in between. The Divine Rite in particular saw its use and exploited it."

"That still doesn't answer why I never saw it in God's Hope," I said.

"God's Hope was nothing more than a bubble. An experiment. Wouldn't you agree?"

I nodded. "I guess so."

"That's not an accident. The Rite loves social experiments. Justification is their crowning achievement, but they have many more subtle ones than that. I've seen a lot of this countryside, and I can tell you that no two places under their control are alike. Different customs, different technologies, different goods to import and export. The only thing they have in common is Justification. God's Hope was an 'All Things in Moderation' experiment. We had some electricity, indoor plumbing, and access to certain grains, vegetables, fruits, some medicines, and very limited livestock. There were no heavy gas-powered machines, but we could have scooters, and of course there was no presence of supernatural abilities. It's the closest approximation of what the world was like about a century before the Blight."

I nodded. "Seems about right. So you're saying there are places that are the exact opposite?"

"Well, the Sin Bins for one thing. But there are still actual cities out there, from what I hear. Ones that are like the pre-Blight era that the Rite rebuilt, at least to some extent. They have lots of cars and electricity and other technological wonders, but they're also filthy and full of vagrants. The Divine Rite has fenced them in like animals, only the people there are so blind with their own greed and sloth they don't even realize they're prisoners. I'd no sooner live in one of those places than I would in a Cradle."

"Sounds like a Sin Bin, but without all the fun."

She grinned. "That's a good way to put it. Old Babylon is even further behind than God's Hope was. It has no electricity, and their people shit in outhouses. Their land wasn't hit quite as hard by the weeds, even before the net went up, so they can grow more grain and herd more livestock. And they boast that they haven't lost a single person to Justification since their founding. I don't know if that's true, but I wouldn't doubt it given how simply they live."

"So why does Paine deal drugs?"

"As far as I know, none of the citizens partake, and he wouldn't sell to them even if they came asking. He ships the goods off down the river to the Sin Bins."

"Sounds like a hell of a deal. And you trust this guy? Seems like someone who deals so closely with the Rite is likely to swing wherever the wind blows. Turpin never had that problem."

Genevieve's eyes sparkled in the moonlight. "I wouldn't go so far as to say he's like a father to me. He's a strange old goat, and he isn't easy to warm up to, but Paine has been with us for a very long time, and he believes in the cause and has no true loyalty to the Rite. He's the only real bet we have in these parts. Without him, the Railroad would fail, but there's never anything wrong with watching your back in these times."

"Ezekiel said Babylon was burning. Maybe it was metaphorical. Maybe he meant we were going to get burned here." And oh how right I turned out to be.

She shrugged. "I guess we'll see. We're kind of in a bind either way."

"Whatever it means, I don't have a good feeling about this place."

She studied my face for a moment. "Is that just intuition talking, John?"

I shrugged. "I don't know whose thoughts are whose right

now." Since the latest encounter with Ezekiel, my feelings and perceptions felt sharper. For instance, I knew right then that Genevieve's heart was pounding inside her chest, but not because she was afraid. She was excited, maybe even a little aroused. Some wild part of me wanted to reach out for her right then, but the buzz of approaching motorbikes put a stop to that.

Genevieve handed me my pack and we stepped away from the truck. Christoph sat in the cabin with his head bent studiously over something. Though the dome lights were on, I could only make out a mass of fabric and straps.

Turpin, Harry, and Kaya arrived a few moments later. "Just in time too," Harry muttered. "I have to piss like the dickens." He hopped off his bike and raced toward the same stand of bushes Christoph had used earlier.

Kaya was off her bike before she got it stopped all the way, and when she flew into my arms, I nearly fell backward from the force.

"You scared me so much, Daddy." I took a moment to reflect on how much she'd called me Daddy since we left God's Hope. That phrase had previously been abandoned around the same time as the stuffed animals and baby dolls. I didn't mind. After the last year of us barely speaking a word to one another, I needed to hear it as much as she needed to say it. When she pulled away, her eyes went right to my newly whitened hair. She grinned a little, but there was concern in her eyes. "I guess that will take some getting used to."

I ran my hands through it, noting its new coarseness. "I hear skunk stripes are the latest fashion."

"What did you see when you were doing that? When you

and Ezekiel were . . . stuck together?" she asked.

My eyes flitted for a moment over to Turpin who stood regarding us thoughtfully with his rheumy eyes, and I didn't think this was the best time to start talking prophecy again. "I don't really remember much. It was pretty intense." I lied. She didn't look very convinced by the lie either, but she didn't press it. We'd both seen enough for one day.

I looked around and noticed we were missing someone. "Where's Anansi?" I asked.

As if to answer my question, the din of the locust swarm approached from the east, backlit by the silvery moonlight.

"His preferred method of travel," Harry said, coming back from the bushes. He didn't sound particularly thrilled.

I repressed a shiver as the beat of a million wings coalescing into a single entity blew back the hair from my brow. When the shapeshifter stood before me in human form again, every bit as odd looking as before, I had no more than a second to regard him before he grabbed me into an enormous bear hug and spun me around as if I were nothing more than a child's doll. I tried to ignore the tough and brittle feel of his skin, and the way it seemed to thrum beneath my hands with the life of a million separate beings. He set me back down on my feet, eyes flaring with orange and green phosphorescence.

"You're amazing, my Lord! Simply amazing!" Anansi cried. "I owe you more than you know, John Welland. I owe you my life. *All* of my lives." He quickly dropped to one knee, his arms spread wide, and bowed in a deep expression of fealty.

"On your feet, Anansi," I said, feeling more ridiculous than I ever had in my life. "You owe me nothing. I didn't even know what I was doing."

"As you wish," he said and stood up. "I suppose I forgot myself for a moment. I am always a little eccentric after a flight, my Lord."

"Let's stick with 'my man,'" I said.

"Indeed, indeed, my man."

"We'll camp for the night and go into town tomorrow," the old man said. "No sense in gettin' the man outta bed, given the change in plans."

"Akiva Paine?" I asked.

"Yep. I assume the young woman got ya up to speed on things." He rummaged in his bag and pulled out a flashlight. "I'm beat. Christoph, ya know where to hide yer vehicle."

I looked at Harry. "We're going to sleep in there?"

He nodded. "Sure, why not? It's a roof over our heads, and we've stayed here before. There's a parish house out back too. It's not in the best of shape. You can hear rats in the walls and the weeds are pulling it down, but it's still sturdy enough."

"Is Turpin okay?" Kaya asked. "He doesn't seem himself."

Harry shrugged. "He's been quiet, but it's been a long day, what with the Heretic and all."

"Dad, you can stop calling him that," Genevieve said.

"Force of habit, sugar."

Christoph moved the truck into a camouflaging grove of dead firs and covered it with some nearby clumps of weeds. At least the things were good for something. He came back with the sleeping Ezekiel bundled up in his arms. "I will sleep with him in the parish house," he said. Harry gave his approval and the rest of us moved into the church.

The inside was a ruin.

People had desecrated the place with graffiti and brute force over the years. Rotting fabric from the altar lay in tatters amid pools of water from the leaky roof. The splintered remains from what must have once been a mighty crucifix littered the floor, and Harry started picking through it for kindling. The few intact pews lined the walls, which cleared a space in the middle of the floor for four shabby cots placed before an enormous fireplace. Turpin was already sitting on one of the beds while Harry started arranging the wood pieces to build a fire. I went over to help him.

A thin layer of dust covered everything. Kaya kicked up a gray cloud of it when she dropped her bags on the floor and stifled a couple of sneezes.

"It's been a little while since we've had to stop here," Harry said.

"Well I'm glad you all found suitable shelter," Anansi said from the doorway. "I'll be sleeping outside. I've never been much a fan of closed-in spaces, as you can imagine. Besides, I am excellent at standing guard. Nothing like a few hundred thousand pairs of extra eyes to watch out for the Divine Rite, eh?"

"That sounds just fine. Thank you, Anansi," I said.

"I'll go out back and join Christoph and the boy in a little while," Turpin said. "But I figured I'd offer you all a nightcap before turnin' in." He held up a dark brown bottle filled nearly to the top.

None of us refused.

The adults sat before the fire, passing the bottle between us. Kaya asked if she could have a sip, and I allowed it. We weren't part of normal culture anymore, and the kid had seen more in the last two days than most adults did in a lifetime. I figured she earned a swig of fire water. The first one sent her into a fit of coughs, and Turpin clapped her on the shoulder. "Welcome to the Liquid Bravery Brigade, little girl." We all laughed, but she refused the bottle after that, and that was just fine with me.

Anansi, who initially claimed alcohol had no noticeable effect on him, was soon slurring his words and told the room he was getting drunk because he was going outside. That broke us up even more and in the laughter, the stress of the day slowly began to melt away. Only the hot rock of worry in my gut over Beth remained, but I felt I could at least cope with it for the time being. One step at a time, I kept reminding myself.

Before the Heretic headed outside, he pulled me away from the circle.

"What is it?" I asked.

"I, uh, don't know the best way to tell you this, but I didn't want to tell the others because I don't trust them yet. Especially the big red man," he said, referring to Harry. He looked at the floor and shuffled from one foot to the other like a child about to be doled a stiff punishment for breaking a vase.

"Don't worry yourself, Anansi. Spill."

"I've been to Old Babylon before. It's a strange little place. Always has been. Most folks are very suspicious of outsiders. Folks like me in particular, as you can imagine."

"I understand."

"So glad that you do, my man, but listen. I've passed through there as I said. Not in my human form, mind you. The Divine Rite values my ability, but they probably wouldn't bat an eyelash if anyone there wanted to cut my tenure short with the right kind of pesticide. I'm not the only one who can do what I do, even if I do consider myself one of the best."

I tried to imagine what a full clan of people like Anansi must be capable of and stifled a shiver.

"Usually, I just swarm around the place. Sometimes to take a nibble of the greenery. I have to be careful what I eat around Old Babylon, though, because there is a lot of wacky weed, if you catch my drift. And poppies. That stuff and me do not play well together, my man."

I was getting a little impatient. He spoke a mile a minute and flitted around the point like a hummingbird around a honeysuckle patch. "Anansi, where are you headed with this?"

"So as I was saying, the place is surrounded by farmland. Most of it barley, oats, potatoes, cukes, beans. Lazarus grain for their livestock. But the last time I was there ... I saw corn."

My eyes grew wide. "Corn? You're sure?"

"Indeed, my man. Acres and acres of it rolling off into the distance to the northeast of town."

My mind briefly drifted to that dream I had of the fields of ears, the fleeing truck, and the locusts. All those locusts. "People haven't been able to spawn an edible corn crop since the Blight, and it's forbidden by the Rite to even try. How is this even possible?" My questions felt hollow on my lips. I wasn't doubting Anansi's story, but I was concerned about the sudden reality of my vision.

"I don't know, my man. That's why I'm telling you something isn't right in that town. I vote we bypass it."

I glanced back at the circle of people sitting around the

weak illumination of the heater. Turpin, Harry, Genevieve, and Kaya. The girls were both laughing at something Turpin was saying while Harry looked on with an amused grin. "I'm not sure I'll have much luck persuading them," I said. "Turpin and Harry especially know more about this whole thing than I do. They're kind of the ones in charge here."

Anansi nodded. "I know all about chain of command, my man. Just tell them about what I saw. They'll listen to you. Especially now. You're special."

"I'll do my best," I said, though I didn't feel very hopeful. My newly discovered abilities weren't necessarily going to make me leader material.

He stretched, his jaws cracking open in a massive yawn that exposed more of his crowded black teeth. I noticed there were several rows of them and took a moment to be thankful I was on the right side of that mouth.

"It'll be great sleeping as a free man," he said. "I only wish the same for my people back in the Cradles and the colonies. Maybe one day they will feel it too. Maybe you are the Messiah, my man."

I shook my head. "I'm a little uncomfortable with that title, Anansi. Maybe you better not use it so much."

"Soon, I will not be the only one using it. I saw you in that white dream from earlier, my man. They all loved you, but I think you fear yourself. I think you're confused about all these new things and not sure where all of it will carry you. But I saw great things. Beautiful things." He turned and strode off into the night, kicking a tin can out of his way as he did and whistling an unfamiliar tune. He looked as carefree as a child frolicking in a meadow. After a minute, I went back inside.

"What did he have to say?" Harry asked after I settled back down into the circle. The liquor and laughs seemed to have lessened his animosity toward the shapeshifter a bit.

"I have a question for you all first," I said. "About how many passengers do you ferry through Old Babylon on a regular basis?"

Harry was the first to speak. "Not too many. Three or four times a year, I'd say."

"Except this year," Genevieve said. "This is our first trip since January. It's been a slow year."

Turpin spoke next. "Almost every year the Railroad sees fewer passengers than the one before it, I'm sad to say. I dunno if it's because people are becomin' better at gamin' the system or because they're just too beat down to fight any-more. I think it's the latter. Justification's doing its job keepin' folks in check."

"So it's been about eight months since you've been to Old Babylon?" I asked.

"Yes, that's right," said Genevieve. "But if you're worried about it still being a viable refuge, we usually keep our ear low to the ground to make sure the pipeline is still open. We get semi-regular correspondence from Akiva Paine by radio, and as of a couple months ago, nothing seemed off."

"Have you seen much of the town or the surrounding ar-eas other than Paine's place?" I asked.

Genevieve nodded. "I stop in the town and visit with a few of the shopkeepers when there's time. It's a quaint little place. Orderly. Usually, I guide the passenger in, make the drop, and head back. I couldn't afford to be away for too long. People would notice. Paine probably won't be too happy to see so many of us. He usually doesn't like handling more than two visitors at a time. It's why we brought so much stuff to trade. We hope he'll relent if we tempt him with enough goodies."

"I see," I said and drifted into deep thought again. I began to feel the underpinnings of dread worm its way through my gut.

"Dad, what is it? What did Anansi say?" Kaya's open and concerned expression is what got me. I had to make sure this place was going to be safe for her.

"Corn. There's corn in Old Babylon, and apparently lots of it."

"Impossible," Turpin grunted. "He's puttin' creepy crawlies in yer brain, boyo."

"No, he isn't," I replied, putting a bit too much force into my voice than I'd intended. "He would have no reason to lie about something like this, and I would be able to tell if he was."

Turpin peered at me, white bushy eyebrows raised. "How would ya know that?"

"Because he looked terrified," I said. "He saw it with his own eyes. And he was just recently through here, so he has a more up to date picture of what's happening." I thought to bring up the vision I saw with Ezekiel about the cornfields and the locusts, but I decided to leave that out. If I ventured beyond simple intuition, I'd lose the old man's confidence for good.

"Well, we still have to go in," Harry said. "Akiva Paine is the only ally we have in these parts, and we need the provisions before heading north to Donum Dei. Paine would be able to give us more guidance on how to get there than anybody."

I nodded. "I get that. I know we have little choice, but I'm saying we should keep our eyes peeled. Anansi said something wasn't right about the place, and I see no reason to disbelieve him."

"Yet," Harry muttered.

I rounded on him, the last of my patience draining away. "What's your story with him, Harry? If you know something about Anansi the rest of us should know, spill it."

The big man scowled at me for a minute, and then sighed in resignation. "It's not him exactly, but then I wouldn't know for sure. I saw his kind pretty regularly way back when during my days at the Cradle, usually bringing people in and never bringing them back out again. A Heretic carried away Genevieve's ma when the Divine Rite pegged her. I saw it happen. I'll never forget the way all those screaming bugs crawled in and out of her before they carried her off. If you'd seen it happen to your Beth, I'm not sure you'd be as willing to warm up to the guy."

I opened my mouth to press Harry further, but Kaya cleared her throat and shook her head subtly as if to say, "Bad idea, Dad." She was right. I'd heard enough to understand, and no amount of pressure from me was going to make Harry's mind open up. And I didn't think I could blame the man after what he told me.

Turpin stood up slowly in a series of cracks and pops. The level of liquid in the brown bottle had dropped considerably. "Get some sleep, comrades. We'll head in early tomorrow." He cocked his gaze at me. "And we'll have a pair of eyes on each side of our heads, just in case what Anansi says is true."

We slept the best we could, which wasn't very well at all.

Chapter 15

Christoph roused us about two hours before dawn as the faintest hints of daylight tickled away the stars. I felt rested enough despite my worries and the certainty I'd be plagued with nightmares about Beth being overtaken by a billion swarming locusts and carried off to Donum Dei. We convened around the church steps and noshed a quick breakfast of the pasty, tasteless gruel Harry heated up on the cook stove. The thing with the fabric and straps Christoph had been working with in the truck last night turned out to be a sling, which he'd fashioned crosswise in front of him to carry Ezekiel. He looked like the world's biggest parent with the world's biggest baby. With the high-powered rifle slung across his other shoulder, the look went from comical to absurd. Anansi pulled me to the side again before we set off.

"I won't be going into Old Babylon with you, my man."

"Where will you be?"

"I'll be . . . near. And I'll come at the first sign you need aid."

"Anansi, do you think we'll need that? Aid, I mean?"

He took my hand and placed an object into it. It was a thin, hollow tube of wood with a tiny notch carved out of it. "Take this," he said.

"What is it?"

"That, my man, is an object of special importance. When you blow it, it won't make a sound. I will hear it, though. Even from a few miles away. And when I do, I'll come. It will also work on others of my kind. The Divine Rite uses similar ones made of silver. I made this one myself, after the ways of my kind. When you show it to any of them, my people will become your people, John Welland."

"John, let's head out!" Harry called from where he stood with the others by the road.

"Stay safe," I said to the shapeshifter and headed off.

Genevieve led us briefly south until we came to the outer boundary of the town's dome net, which like the one at God's Hope, kept the land free of serpent weed pollen. This time, however, we didn't want to disable it and leave the town vulnerable. But the main obstacle would be getting in through the checkpoint, where Divine Rite guards, or maybe even Hand of God, would be on duty.

On the way, we discussed our strategy. Christoph, being the most capable of the group in a combat situation, would be the one to approach any personnel and disable them. Normally, there weren't more than two, so it would be an easy enough job for the giant, and by the casual way he talked, it sounded like he'd done something similar to this before. We found a small grove of deformed trees to wait under while Christoph crossed the next half-mile or so to the gate. Harry took Ezekiel and sat with the boy in his lap while the rest of us stood around with our arms folded.

"It could all end right here, you know," Kaya said. "If he can't take them down before someone sounds the alarm."

She had dark circles under her eyes, and her normally spunky hair lay flat against her head like a golden swim cap. The stress was visibly weighing on her now, and I felt another pang of guilt.

Genevieve, seeming to sense this, placed a gentle hand on Kaya's shoulder. "Best we try to think positive about these things. Christoph is a very capable man. This isn't the first time he's taken out some stooges."

"Thanks, Gen. I'll try." Kaya looked at her with an almost fawning expression of gratitude, and I was a little jealous. My daughter and I were close, but she always approached me and any of my advice with a measure of skepticism. In contrast, she almost seemed to worship Genevieve. I should have been relieved at the bond between the two of them—Kaya did need someone else she could count on, she needed a friend—but I guess I was just a little tired too.

After about fifteen minutes of waiting in awkward and un-easy silence, Christoph radioed to Harry.

"Red Baron here. All clear."

Harry fumbled for his walkie-talkie, nearly dropping it on Ezekiel's head. "Excellent! How many were there? Over."

A brief pause and then, *"There were none. The checkpoint was empty."*

We all looked at each other. An abandoned net was not a good sign. Not at all. "What should we do?" I asked.

Turpin shrugged. "We stay the path, boyo. Don't see as we got much choice at this point."

I blinked. "But if the checkpoint's been abandoned, it could mean the town—"

"It ain't the town we're here for," Turpin said. "It's Akiva

Paine. And I'll bet ya my last dollar he'll be carryin' on with his business regardless of what's happenin' in Old Babylon proper."

No one else seemed interested in joining the discussion, so I dropped it, but not easily. The place could be burned down

Babylon is burning.

or ravaged by some sort of unholy weed-mutated beast, maybe even decimated by an unknown virus, but Turpin was right. We didn't have much choice. Bypassing this place without a plan would mean certain death, and not only that, we were curious. We had to know what had happened, or was happening, in there.

We reached the checkpoint about twenty minutes later. Christoph stood outside the gate that led into the "decon" chamber where people coming and going would be doused with gases containing various herbicides. Of course, it wasn't known whether these gases were lethal to humans or if they did in fact stop the spread of serpent weed pollen, but it and the nets were the only available defense we had. That the outside of these gates were more often than not coated with a fine sprinkling of the yellow grains, particularly in the springtime months, was proof that more of it was being kept out than in.

The German had been right. No one was here. He looked a little disappointed by this, like he'd hoped to follow up his hasty breakfast with a fight.

"Where do you suppose they went?" Harry asked him.

Christoph shook his head. "Wherever they went, they didn't go easy. Look here."

He pointed to cracks in the glass booth, where the guards usually sat when on duty. A hole had been busted clear through the door before it was ripped partly off its hinges. Dark drips on the dry packed dirt were likely blood. I could even see channels in the dirt that looked like someone's heels being dragged.

"Insurrection," I murmured.

Turpin cackled. "Perhaps so. We can only hope. See, boyo? It could be a good thing."

For some reason, I didn't feel comforted by this. If the people of Old Babylon had risen against their Divine Rite leaders, who's to say they would be kind to any outsiders? They could be a bunch of ruthless savages by now.

Nevertheless, we all stepped into the plexiglass chamber and waited for Christoph to pull the gate shut. A light on the lock turned red and the solar-powered machinery began to hum. Soon a white colored gas filtered down from above, and I thought morbidly of things I'd once learned in school about gas chambers and hoped like hell this thing hadn't been rigged to kill anyone coming in. The vapor smelled oddly floral, and it made the inside of my nose itch, but I wasn't experiencing any other symptoms. Kaya took my hand and squeezed it, and for that I was grateful.

A few minutes later, the light on the door opening into Old Babylon turned green, and Christoph swung it open. As we filed out, Kaya looked at me and said, "My first time through one of these things. It wasn't so bad." I gave her a reassuring grin, tamping down any thoughts about cancer or lingering after-effects on our lungs or kidneys that might kill us in our sleep later.

We followed the Hymn River, taking a wide, determined course around the Old Babylon town proper. From there, we turned west, making sure to stay off any main roads. "It's not far," Genevieve said when Kaya asked her when they would arrive. "You'll know it when you see a fence and a change in the greenery."

After about an hour, the sky had brightened to a pale violet, and swaths of pink streaked across the eastern horizon. Our pants were wet with the dew that had collected on the long grasses overnight. It was nice seeing pristine land again. We passed houses still sleeping away the morning. A few birds greeted the coming dawn with some light music.

As Genevieve promised, we ended up at a sturdy metal fence about six feet high. When I made to grasp the top so I could swing over it, Harry grabbed hold of me and yanked me back. He pointed a little ways down the fence to a contraption with shiny black solar panels attached to it and a sign with lightning bolts. The fence was electrified. I guess not being attached to the power plant didn't exactly preclude such things as electric fences in Old Babylon, but Akiva Paine had a valuable crop to protect. On the other side, about an acre of tall, dark green plants with feathery leaves grew in long, lush rows. I learned about the look of this plant not long after I met Turpin, though I sometimes heard people in God's Hope speak about it in hushed, fearful tones. We'd reached the cannabis field.

Beyond that, the land dropped off into a little valley, and I could just see the top stories of Akiva Paine's massive estate. The architecture was nearly ancient even before the Blight. I would guess it was over two centuries old, based on the tiled roof and the stately white pillars that towered along the front of the place. Lush vines of purple flowers cascaded over window boxes and wrought iron railings, reminding me a little bit of serpent weeds.

"It's bougainvillea," Genevieve said from next to me. She must have seen me noticing. "Beautiful, isn't it?"

"Yes, but a little disturbing too."

"It is. A lot of these vine-like plants are scary in the age of plants run amok. That stuff can take over entire buildings if you're not careful, but Akiva Paine likes to live dangerously, I guess."

I didn't need to see the bougainvillea to know that.

Genevieve turned to address the group. "Be careful you don't step on any of these plants when we go in. Paine is apt to be a curmudgeon when he sees all of us here. It'll be worse if he sees his money trampled underfoot."

"How do we get in?" Kaya asked.

Genevieve led us over to a grassy patch and set her things down. "We wait. Paine will be out soon." Kaya and I sat with her while the other men stood watch. I asked Genevieve what her thoughts were on our chances of making it to Donum Dei. She shook her head.

"I don't have the foggiest idea about that place other than what the Rite tells us in its propaganda. I don't even think Daddy has been there, but you're welcome to ask him about it. I know that we alone are not going to be enough to get up there, overpower Urban and his people, and get Beth out."

I agreed, but I also knew something she didn't know. "I've come to think this isn't a rescue mission. I think they're expecting us, and I think Beth is up there of her own accord."

Kaya swung her head around. "What do you mean her own accord?"

I told her about Anansi's account of Beth not resisting his arrival, how she went willingly and appeared to be in no danger when he left her.

"Assuming he's even telling the truth, that doesn't prove what you're saying," Genevieve said.

"I agree, Dad," Kaya said. "Beth might be on the holy roller side, but she's no stooge."

"I didn't say she was a stooge, hon. I think it's possible she's there under the belief that she's helping us. Either way, it doesn't matter why she's up there. We're going to get her out."

Genevieve nodded. "We're with you all the way, John." She looked at me plainly, her green eyes gleaming in the morning light, not with lust but with a mix of pride and compassion that made me fall for her a little more. At some point, I'd have to deal with those feelings and the near crippling guilt they caused, but for the moment I just let myself enjoy it.

As if sensing these things, Kaya cleared her throat, and I dropped the other woman's gaze. I glanced over at my daughter, who grinned and rolled her eyes in a "You're too much, Dad" expression she saved for the times I embarrassed her. She seemed okay with the possibility of me moving on from Linny, but I wondered what she would have thought if I'd told her I could barely remember what her mother looked like anymore.

I tried in that moment to call up Linny's face in my mind and only got a collage of broken features. Her long, slender nose, her straight blonde hair usually pulled back with one of the turquoise and silver hairclips her mother gave her on our wedding day, the tiny mole on her left temple, the expressive crook of her left eyebrow when one of us—usually me—was being unreasonable. I couldn't form all those things I loved so much into a single picture. Our daughters were the closest composites.

Kaya looked back at Genevieve. "So do you really think this Paine guy is going to help us or what?"

Genevieve answered with a bit of hesitation. "I won't lie. He may take some convincing at first, but he'll come through. I don't expect he will provide us with detailed maps of the country between here and Donum Dei. As far as I know, no such maps exist. But I think his dealings with the Rite will give us more information than we have now."

"Are you going to ask him about the corn?" I asked.

Genevieve rolled her eyes. "You mean provided there actually *is* any corn? You know how ridiculous that sounds, don't you?"

"Still doesn't mean we shouldn't check it out," Kaya said.

"Let's get settled in first. We'll have enough on our plate just bargaining with Paine. My first goal is to convince him to even let us stay with him."

I nodded. "Fair enough."

Kaya raised a pointing hand. "Looks like our wait is over. Is that him?"

We all stood up to get a better look. A stooped figure in gray trousers and a wooly cardigan hobbled along one of the cannabis rows with a long walking stick in one hand and the long barrel of a shotgun slung over his shoulder. A straw cap with a flat brim was perched askew on his head. As he drew closer to the fence, I saw he wore gold-rimmed spectacles not unlike Turpin's. We held back as Genevieve approached the fence.

"Good morning, Mr. Paine," she said, confident as ever. When the other man spoke, it was clear he was either slurring drunk or missing a number of his teeth.

"What the christing morning glory're you thinking bringing all these people here, Ginger? Our arrangement's always been no more than two folk at a time." He held up two gnarled fingers and showed her both sides of them for emphasis. "Two! And you go on and bring the whole christing lot of God's-Bloody-Hope with ya. This'd better be good, girlie." His rheumy eyes wandered to Kaya, and he regarded her (and her body) in such an open and evaluating way I disliked him immediately.

Genevieve cleared her throat. "I apologize for deviating from protocol, Mr. Paine, but matters were complicated by the Hand of God. They intercepted John, Kaya, and I as we were heading for Turpin's safe house. Our covers have been blown."

"And you think that's my problem?" Paine shouted through his mushy mouth from which little flecks of spittle flew like heavy snowflakes. "I got enough on my plate with the up and comin' harvest. This ain't no time to be hidin' a buncha fugitives." He pronounced the last word like *fooshatives*.

"We came with our own provisions, as well as a wide selection of items just for you, Mr. Paine," Harry said. "Mr. Turpin has a selection of fine grains, tobacco, medical supplies, and ethanol just on the outskirts of town in a safe location."

Turpin reached into his shirt pocket, pulled out a leather pouch of his homegrown weed, and handed it to the man. Paine took it while eyeing the old man with a trace of contempt. "Turpin's leaf is good, but not as good as he thinks, if you ask me." He sniffed at the pouch with caution, and his face softened a little. "This ain't too bad, though. You got more of this, you say?"

"There's several ounces back in Christoph's truck," Turpin said. "Once ya take us in, we'll send him and Harry back with one of yer hands to fetch the rest." He didn't seem ruffled at all by Paine's demeanor, which probably meant this was how the man always was.

Paine fetched a deep sigh and peered at us for a moment from beneath the brim of his hat. His eyes lingered a bit on Kaya again, but she stood her ground. I looked a little closer at the old man and saw a cluster of small red sores in the corner of his mouth. Combined with the liver spots and pallid skin, he didn't look very healthy. I had no idea until later how unhealthy he truly was, but my intuition, which was stronger than ever, told me to sleep with both eyes open.

"You got two days," he said. "After that, you're not my problem."

Chapter 16

The inside of Paine's house was no less miraculous than the outside. The front door opened onto a grand foyer with seemingly acres of parquet flooring that shimmered almost preternaturally from decades of lacquering and heavy polishing. Thick dark wood moldings with meticulous bead and scrollwork spanned through the other rooms in an endless parade of luxuriant excess. The walls boasted a wide array of complementary colors—bold salmons, plums, and dark greens—and a staggering amount of hanging artwork. A spiral staircase wound lazily up to the second and third stories.

There was a spicy, earthy aroma I had difficulty recognizing. When I asked about it, Paine said, "That's mutton vindaloo. Or my version of it, anyway. I got someone who brings me some unusual spices from time to time. This stuff'll melt your bloody face off. Maybe you'll see come dinner."

I wasn't sure whether to be excited or afraid.

"I only got two rooms to spare at the moment. Took on extra hands for the harvest. If you'd been here two days earlier, you would've had your pick. I wish I had a better place for the big fellow, but I got but naught unless he wants to sleep in the stables."

"I'll sleep on the floor," Christoph said.

Paine warily eyed the sleeping bundle hanging from the German's shoulders. "Am I gonna have a problem with what you got there? I don't want no more trouble than I got already."

Christoph shook his head. "He always sleeps."

"Good. Make sure he stays like that and you'll be right fine by me."

A man emerged from the kitchen. He was sallow-skinned with greasy hair and a dusty jacket with scuffs at the shoulders. Red sores also blossomed on his face, in both corners of his mouth and in the creases of his nose. One was weeping a clear fluid. He removed a dirty handkerchief from his breast pocket and dabbed at it. His eyes concerned me most. They were flat and dead, like marbles left and forgotten beneath a child's bed. I would have thought him a walking corpse if he hadn't spoken.

"Should I show them to their rooms, Mr. Paine?"

"That'd be fine, Antony. Once you're squared away up there, come on down to the kitchen and we'll have us a little chat. There's food, too."

We followed the insipid butler up the staircase to the third floor. By the time we made it, we were all huffing a little, except Antony, who seemed to slither more than actually walk. "Each of the rooms has two bunk beds, which should suit for all but the big gentleman. We have extra sleeping pads, blankets, and pillows for you, sir."

"That's fine," Christoph said. He seemed to have little interest in the butler. His eyes instead crawled around the place, perhaps looking for trap doors, security, emergency exits, or people to shoot.

Antony stopped between two open doors in a hallway lit with flickering gaslights. "You will find oil lanterns just inside each door. Also, if you need to use the restroom, this house is equipped with an elaborate privy system. I will show you how to operate it momentarily."

"Privy? You mean like an outhouse?" Kaya asked.

Antony grinned and revealed several empty sockets where teeth might once have been. The rest were going black with decay. I felt my stomach turn a little. "Hardly. This estate boasts one working water closet on the ground floor, but water is at a premium here as you can imagine, given our irrigation requirements. But we have a system here that is both sophisticated and simple to use. Mr. Paine is quite proud of it. Apparently Thomas Jefferson had one very similar in Monticello."

"You seem very well-educated for a servant," I said. The words escaped my mouth before I could stop them, but I couldn't help it. I wondered how someone like Antony came to work for Akiva Paine. The butler thing seemed like a front of some kind. In fact, all of this did. And a badly constructed one, at that. They didn't have time to prepare for such a large party. That had to be it.

The hum of unease in the back of my mind increased in pitch, and I wondered if the others were feeling it.

Antony showed his creepy gap-toothed grin once more, but it didn't come close to touching his eyes. "Nice of you to observe so. I think. But you are correct. I'm no mere servant. I guess you could say I'm Akiva Paine's rightmost hand. Follow me."

After showing us the "Thomas Jefferson toilet," which was

basically a system of pulleys that helped to move the privy's chamber pot from the first floor to the cellar where servants cleaned it out and raised it back up, Antony showed us back to our rooms.

"I'm sure I don't have to tell you Mr. Paine doesn't like people roaming the grounds without chaperone. He has considerable investments to protect. I'll be happy to give a tour if you wish, but otherwise, we ask that you don't poke around without escort. Breakfast will be served soon." He turned on his heel and crept back downstairs.

Kaya, Genevieve, Harry, and I were in one room. Turpin, Christoph, and Ezekiel were in the other. The quarters were bare. A small mirror hung above a table that held a ceramic washbowl and a pitcher full of water. There were two rickety chairs and a tiny closet with a few wire hangers. White lace curtains hung limply from the room's single window, which faced the rear of the home and gave way to a field of pink and red poppies scattered amid scores of green bulbs. A few dozen workers picked the bulbs from their stems and stuffed them into burlap shoulder bags. They wore the same flat-brimmed straw hats as their master. I didn't see any corn, but there was a lot more land out of sight.

"This place is creepy, Dad," Kaya whispered behind me.

"We'll be out of here soon, kiddo."

The others joined us, all of them grave-faced. Particularly Turpin, who spoke in hushed tones. "I have to say, I don't like the look of Paine. I ain't seen him in years, but he looks as old as me, and he's younger by a decade."

"How do you know him?" I asked.

"Brother of the long dead Mrs. Turpin. History best left

buried, boyo, but that's the long and short of things."

If only we'd had time for that story. "Can we go into town?" I asked. "I feel like we need to check the state of things there." And I also wanted to get the hell out of this house for a little while, though I think that was stating the obvious.

Genevieve nodded. "Sure, but you're not going without me. You don't know a lick about Old Babylon customs. Even under ordinary circumstances, they're suspicious of outsiders and more superstitious than the Hand of God. You'd probably get yourself strung up by the neck by noon."

"Thanks for the vote of confidence," I muttered.

She went on as if she didn't hear me. "Kaya and Daddy should stick around here and try to get a look around the place while we're gone. The rest will have to see about getting the supplies."

Christoph set Ezekiel in one of the bunks and covered him up before we headed downstairs. "Turpin and I will go."

We followed our noses to the kitchen where Paine was sitting at a heavy plank table, sipping at a bottle of beer and smoking a pipe filled with Turpin's tobacco. A trio of dark-skinned women in stained whites scurried among simmering pots, sizzling fry pans, and clattering dishes. He looked up when we walked in, but didn't smile. "Hope you're hungry. The Amy sisters put on one bloody helluva breakfast spread. Dontcha, girls?"

The women at the stoves barely glanced in our direction before heading back to their cooking. It was clear by their timid reactions that despite Paine's attempt to be gregarious, he ran a pretty grim ship.

"It smells delicious," Kaya said.

Paine offered us chairs. All but Christoph and Turpin took one. "If ya don't mind, Mr. Paine, Christoph and I would like to retreat to the old church to secure the supplies we promised. We were wonderin' if ya could spare one of yer hands or a couple of barrows for the errand."

"That'd be fine. *Antony!*"

The anemic man glided into the kitchen like an apparition waiting to be summoned. "See these fellows get carts and one of the workers to go with 'em to the outskirts." Antony nodded wordlessly and bade Turpin and Christoph to follow him. When they were gone, Paine turned his attention to Genevieve. "So tell me where you're headed, and what you want from me other than a place to stretch your legs before you go there."

Genevieve cleared her throat and glanced at her father, who gave a flicker of a nod. "We intend to go to Donum Dei to retrieve Mr. Welland's daughter."

Paine, who had been taking another sip of his beer, spurted amber liquid from his mouth. Some dribbled from the corner, which he caught with his napkin and winced when it brushed against the red sores there.

"So it's suicide you're aiming for, eh? What're you planning to do when you get there? Knock on the christing door and ask Urban the Fourth for your kid back?"

"We're crazy, but we're not stupid," Harry said. "We're going to need a small army to get in."

"And where do you think you're going to get one?"

Harry cleared his throat and spoke three words that made my jaw drop: "From a Cradle."

The silence between us was nearly suffocating as Paine's

eyes narrowed. "You have to be out of your christing mind."

"I disagree," Harry said. "All we ask is for a few extra hands, or maybe some of your supplies here to play for it properly. Christoph has been working out a way we can storm the compound closest to here with minimal—"

Paine slapped the table, making the plates and silverware jump. His eyes were wide and angry. And afraid. "That's enough! It's not gonna happen, you hear?"

"Don't pretend we don't know your conflict of interest," Genevieve said. "You aren't only growing poppies and wacky grass for the Sin Bins. The Hand of God uses opiates to keep the Sentinels sedated, and you're probably supplying them too. This is a threat to your business. Admit it."

The old man blinked at her from behind his spectacles, but he was no less defiant. "So christing what? I worked my bloody hands to the bone for my keep! I had enough business sense to deal with the right people, unlike that spineless Turpin who holed up in his little compound after my sister Maggie died, churning out free booze for the locals and sending you people up to interrupt my operation a few times a year on some crackpot rebellion mission. I ain't gonna feel guilty for trying to get ahead in this world and cutting off dead weight when I see it."

"That's unfair, Paine, and you know it," Genevieve said. "We've always paid our way and run a clean business with you. And you yourself have always stood behind the principles of our movement."

"That may be, but you ain't got enough to pay for what you're asking, young lady. I can get you on a boat like always, but I ain't gonna risk my own neck to get you into a Cradle.

You'll just have to find another way to conduct your little suicide mission." He wiped at the flowering sore in the corner of his mouth and winced again. I winced with him. It did look painful.

Harry spoke this time. "You don't have to get us into the Cradle. We're just asking for fuel, heavier provisions, and time. You don't have to play any sort of active role."

"Pfft. Active role. You're asking for the bloody keys to go and take out my biggest meal ticket. And what in christing hell is in it for me, exactly? That is if they don't trace you back to me? I oughta kick you lot outta here now. You want to go to a Cradle? I can arrange for it pretty quick if you want to go in the easy way."

While Harry's face grew even redder as he geared up for one wallop of a response to Paine's taunt, I reached into my breast pocket and pulled out the wooden whistle Anansi handed me earlier and held it up for him to see.

"How about you help us, Mr. Paine, and you get to keep your crops?" I didn't need to look at the others to know I'd surprised them. Genevieve gasped behind me.

The old man squinted at the object, sat back in his chair, and started dabbing at the sore next to his mouth again; only his hand trembled a little this time.

"Am I supposed to know what that is?"

"I think you know. Frankly, I think you know a lot more about things than you're letting on. But I'll level with you. We have a friend not far from here. If I blow this whistle, it'll summon one hell of a locust plague that will whittle your poppies and cannabis and God knows what other abominations you're growing out here down to nothing in a matter of minutes. That'll level the playing field a little bit between us, won't it?"

If Paine had grown paler, I would've been able to see right through him. "So that's how you do business, is it, bucko? The low ballin' dirty way?"

I leaned forward. "Who's the low baller here? Is it the people who are asking for your help, or you who sit there threatening to turn us in to the Hand of God?"

Paine's jaw worked, like my words were a particularly tough piece of cud to chew. "All right. It'll be done, God cuss it."

"I'm sorry, Mr. Paine. I couldn't hear you," I said.

"It'll be done! It'll be bloody done," he shouted. "You'll get your christing things and in two days you'll go on your christing way!"

"Thank you, Mr. Paine," Genevieve said quietly.

"Don't thank me, girlie." His lips stretched back in a black grin. One lightly scabbed sore near his mouth broke open and spilled out a trickle of cloudy white fluid. "You probably noticed some of us don't look too good around here. I can't promise you won't catch it yourselves."

"What's wrong with you?" Kaya asked.

"Dunno exactly. We're no doctors, but we're working on figuring it out."

"Is it just the, you know," Harry asked, gesturing to the corner of his mouth.

"I had a full head of hair three months ago." He ran his hand across the top of his head, which retained only a few wisps of white hair amid the brown age spots. "I also had most of my teeth. We're workin' on a treatment, though."

The Amy sisters interrupted the conversation by arranging several steaming platters of food on the table before them. A mountain of fried shredded potatoes with chopped vegetables mixed in was on one. Thick sausages piled on another. "Wild buffalo. Made 'em myself," Paine boasted. Others contained familiar preparations of barley and Lazarus pilaf. The final platter, stacked high with flat, round golden cakes and a little side dish of amber colored honey, gave me pause. Their aroma was intoxicating.

"What are those?" I asked, pointing to the plate.

Paine grinned again. "Those're Johnny cakes. My great-granny's special recipe."

A look passed between Genevieve, Kaya, and I, a silent knowledge relating back to the warning Anansi had given us that Paine was growing corn here, recalling a vision I had not long ago about acres and acres of the stuff stretching on for miles beneath a moonlit sky, about so many lessons gleaned in the Divine Rite Academy as children regarding the "Devil's Grain" and how to spot it and its many forms by sight and smell, so that we would always avoid it if it should ever reappear on this earth. That yellow sweet temptress. Its siren song was near impossible to avoid, even though I'd never once tasted it. But somehow I knew exactly how it would taste, how its rough grit would crunch between my teeth like grains of sand, as if it had been imprinted into my genes from so many ancestors going back thousands of years who were gluttons for those kernels of gold. We could drive it to extinction or turn it into a monster that would drive *us* to extinction, but it would always be a part of us, waiting for resurrection. I could tell by the way the women gazed at the platter of golden medallions that they were having a similar fight in their minds. Just one bite. One little taste. It wouldn't be so bad. And then we could move on.

But something told me Paine would want that. That he was counting on it.

With a lot of physical effort, I looked away, and so did the girls. Paine, meanwhile, gummed several of his Johnny cakes down with obvious relish on his face. I thought of what else might be growing out there on all that land of his, and my heart grew heavier.

Chapter 17

After lunch, Genevieve and I prepared for our trip into town. Paine voiced his objections through a fog of booze breath. "You got no business going there. You'll bring attention to yourselves and to me."

"Nonsense," Genevieve said. "I've been doing business in Old Babylon for years. I blend in well enough. I also would like to look in on the proprietor of the General Store. John will be my silent companion. Won't you, John?" She beamed up at me, but her unsmiling gaze was all the admonishment I needed.

"Is Saul Andrews still well, Mr. Paine?"

"I wouldn't know," he mumbled and dropped his eyes. "I don't do my own shopping these days."

"I suppose you wouldn't. Let's go, John." She turned with a flourish of skirt and the lightweight brown poncho she borrowed from Paine's closet in order to blend in better with the Old Babylon town folk. I wore a poncho as well, and hated how the wool made my neck itch.

We only waited for a moment outside the home's main gate before the groom arrived with a cart and mule. Another victim of whatever ailment was attacking the Paine residence, the young man's pale complexion was the worst I had seen yet. The clusters of sores on his face looked like raspberries. The boy said nothing to us, but the sunken-in look of his mouth suggested he too was missing most of his teeth.

A few moments later, Genevieve drove us down the wheel-rutted dirt path of the Paine stead's main driveway. I had no experience using animals for transportation. Living close to the center of God's Hope, I usually walked on my errands, or rode a bicycle that Linny's dad had resurrected from some ancient pre-Blight dumping ground. I kept its chain oiled, its tires pumped, and it still sat on my front porch as far as I knew. But Genevieve rode with confidence, guiding the animal with little clicks out of the side of her mouth.

"By the way, we're married," she said.

I startled a bit. "Excuse me?"

"When we get to town, if anyone asks, we're married. Newlyweds. Visiting Saul Andrews's store on an errand for my father."

"Got it. Anything else?"

"Hopefully nothing. I doubt word about us has traveled this far so soon. We just want to take a quick trip up and down the main avenue and observe. See if they're sporting the same sores as Paine and his people. If Saul's store is open, we'll pop in and check on him. Just let me do the talking."

"Yes, ma'am," I said. We rode in silence for a bit longer before I finally decided to ask her about something that had been on my mind since the night she showed up on my doorstep. "Why are you so different now than you were before?"

She glanced at me sideways. "What do you mean?"

"You know what I mean. You used to flirt with me all the time in the store."

She gasped in fake exasperation. "I didn't flirt!"

"So you offer cooking lessons to all the guys, then?"

She threw back her head and laughed. "I was just being friendly. And, I suppose part of me wanted to cheer you up a little. You looked so lost when you came into the store those weeks after your wife died. I wanted to reach out and brighten you up a little. But I guess you're right. That Genevieve was more of a character trying to keep up appearances as a bubbly, happy-go-lucky shopkeeper. I may have overdone it in some cases, especially if I genuinely liked someone." She glanced at me and blushed.

I breathed a little internal sigh of relief. "I can understand that," I said.

"Do you? I hope you aren't disappointed."

Now it was my turn to laugh. "You're about the farthest someone can ever get from being disappointing."

"So the cooking lessons aren't out of the question, then?"

"Never." I edged in a little closer and put my arm around her shoulders. She leaned against me the rest of the way into town, and for the first time, I didn't wonder what Linny would think.

We passed no one on the road into town. The houses off to either side were quiet, their dark windows giving them a disused look. "That's odd," Genevieve said. "This road is usually a good bit busier by this time of day with people coming and going." She sat up stiff in her seat and looked around us as the donkey's hooves clacked hollowly along the cracked pavement. Her face had that same drawn look as the night we fought the Hand of God. "Keep your eyes open, John."

We rode closer to the cluster of buildings that made up

Old Babylon proper. They were tidy wooden structures, none taller than two stories. A few people ambled along the sides of the road. I noticed they wore the same types of ponchos Genevieve and I wore. Some also sported the same flat-brimmed hats that the folks did back at the Paine farm.

We passed the first building, which housed a small clothing store and a trading post. Both shops were dark. Their broken windows and emptied merchandise told a disturbing tale of businesses that had been looted and ransacked. A bakery across the street with the quaint name of Patsy's Pastries and Such stood with its doors propped open, but I saw no one conducting business inside. The shop's front window, which probably once displayed delicious wares to entice passersby, now showed vacant shelves covered with crumbs and a film of dust.

The few townsfolk we passed as we made our way up the unkempt avenue shielded their faces from view by tilting their hats just so. The apothecary was open for business, but a short peek in its windows also revealed rows of bare shelving and a floor littered with broken glass and other merchandise. Outside, an emaciated woman poured water into a window box filled with dead plants. She gave us a sidelong glance, and I noticed those familiar red sores covering her face. I'm sure if she had reason to smile, I would have seen toothless gums as well.

Another block up, the flyblown, bloated hulk of a dead mule lay in the street. It was about a week gone by the look of it, and no one had bothered to remove it. Thankfully we weren't downwind from the stench.

"This place is forsaken," I whispered.

Genevieve gave a minute nod and kept her eyes fixed ahead. "Do you notice something missing?" she asked.

"You mean other than thriving businesses, animals, and human beings?"

"Children," she muttered. "There are no children. Old Babylon used to be filled with them."

A chill settled into my gut as I continued to survey the wasted and empty town. Faint outlines of bodies and white faces appeared in a few of the upper-story windows. The ones I saw milling along when we arrived had cleared out as we rolled up the main boulevard. "They know we're outsiders," I said.

It wasn't hard to pick us out. We looked the way they would have about a year ago. Now we looked too healthy to be one of them.

Then I saw something that made both Genevieve and I cry out. She pulled the cart to a halt and we both stared. Ezekiel's prophecy ("Babylon is burning") pulsed inside my head like an infected tooth. "Oh my dear God," she whispered. I had nothing to add.

Ahead was a rather odd five-way intersection. Cut into it like a wedge of wood and stone was the familiar shape of a Divine Rite Fellowship. Only, the familiarity ended there, for it had been gutted by fire. Shards of sooty stained glass lay on the street, and I could still smell the campfire tang of smoldering wood. Three blackened bodies hung from the singed oaks that graced the church's once-green front lawn. Though fire had incinerated their clothes and flesh, the ornate golden crucifixes around their necks gleamed in the sun.

The buildings adjacent to the Fellowship, though blackened, had barely escaped the fire's reach. A miracle must have stopped the whole town from going up like a pile of dry firewood.

The town had gone mad, as we had all feared when we saw the abandoned gate at the town's net, but it apparently still had some semblance of self-preservation. Was Akiva Paine the mastermind of all this, or had he lost whatever influence he was holding here? The burning of a Divine Rite church would seem to be against his best interests. This told me this place was fast becoming a no-man's land, and we were sitting right smack in the middle of it.

"We need to get out of here," I said.

Genevieve shook her head. "Not yet. Saul's store is just one more block up. If he's still alive, he can tell us what happened."

"What makes you think we can trust him after all this?"

"Because he's a dear family friend."

"Yes, but—"

She turned to me, trembling, eyes glassy with unshed tears. "Right now, we trust the few people we can until we can't trust them anymore. I'm all ears if you have any actual ideas, John."

I bowed my head. "I only suggest we be careful."

She sighed. "Saul and my father go way back. He's a good man. If he's turned . . . Let's just say I'd rather he be dead than whatever these people are."

She guided the donkey to a stop outside a long building with Saul's General Store painted on the sign in large, blocky letters. The scene didn't inspire much hope. It looked as looted and abandoned as all the others did. "Let's just check it out," she said. The animal seemed content enough to stay put as we hopped down.

The door swung on creaky hinges and we stepped inside, our feet crunching on shards of broken glass, dried beans, oats, and other random litter. The light was dim and gloomy, the air thick with the cloyingly sweet stench of garbage, rotted produce, and an even less pleasant under-smell of rotting meat. A broken jar of honey lay on one shelf with its contents dried to a viscous amber glaze dotted with the bodies of the insects it had trapped.

"Look there," I said, pointing to a dull maroon pool of blood on the floor near the ancient cash register. It wasn't exactly fresh, but it still looked like it was relatively recent. A trail of quarter-sized droplets led from there through the swinging double doors of the store's back room.

"Someone hurt him," Genevieve said, making for the doors with her gun raised.

I followed close behind her, feeling stupid without a weapon of my own. I'd left my own gun back at the house; it was harder to conceal. "Wait a second." I yanked a piece of sturdy wood from a broken shelf. A couple of nails jutted from it. Better than nothing. We pushed through to the back room. Genevieve found an oil lamp hanging from a nail, and turned it on. Its meager yellow glow gave us just enough light to see around the place. Whoever had emptied the front of the store also did the same to the back, save for a couple of torn open bags of salt. The trail of blood led directly to them, and its source.

A man lay slumped among a few remaining sacks of Lazarus grain.

"Saul!" Genevieve ran to him. "Help me turn him over." I set down my weapon and took him by the shoulders. His body was cool and clammy. A moan and a raspy rattle escaped his mouth when Genevieve checked the pulse in his neck.

"He's alive, but just barely. Someone stabbed him." She pointed to the handle of the knife jutting high from his right side.

"Sonsabitches," he muttered. His lips and teeth (I was relieved to see he still had his teeth) were coated in a veneer of blood.

"Saul, it's Genevieve. Can you hear me?"

He grunted. "You don't see a knife comin'... outta my ears, do ya?"

She looked up at me. "He's always been a little salty."

Saul tried to laugh, but instead sprayed a fine mist of blood from his mouth that Genevieve narrowly avoided. "You'll be salty on your deathbed too, missy."

"Enough with that kind of talk. We're getting you out of here," she said. "John, help me lift him."

He raised his hands and weakly batted at her like someone swatting at a fly underwater. "Don't bother. You're a little late for that. You shouldn't be here, child. Town's gone..."

"Gone what? Crazy? We noticed," I said.

He nodded but never opened his eyes. "The nutters ransacked the place and one of 'em planted this in me... must've been a couple days ago, maybe a little more. Who... who's the feller?"

"He's my friend," Genevieve said. "We were going to ferry him and his daughter out of God's Hope through here, but our plans changed. We're staying with Akiva Paine right now."

Saul's eyes flew open. "You can't stay there. He's crazier than all of 'em. He caused all this. He and that Antony fella did. Started growin' this new type of corn. *Corn!* Of all the bedeviled things. Made everybody sick. Killed most of the children first, but all the rest'll be joinin' 'em soon." He rolled his eyes over to me. "It's forsaken."

I shivered and the goosebumps made my hair stand up. "Goddamn," I whispered.

"Got that right," Saul said. "God damned us all. Watch yer women close."

I leaned closer. "What do you mean by that?"

"The corn, and God knows what other experiments those bastards did made all the women go sterile. Paine'll use your women if he can. He's trying to breed babies who can take the stuff he's growing. Thinks he can save the world and go up against the Rite. Probably be even worse. Crazy fucker."

"Oh God. Kaya," I said. "Genevieve, we have to get back right now. Let's get Saul and hurry."

Saul protested. "I told you I was dyin'."

"Quiet," I said. "You're not going to die. Trust me."

Genevieve looked at me, frowning. "What did you have in mind?"

"What do you think?"

Her eyes widened. "You don't think . . . Ezekiel?"

"Of course I do." I didn't know how we would do it, but I had an inkling that we should try it. If we could channel the kid's power to break bracelets, why not use them to heal knife wounds?

"What will Paine do when he sees Saul?" she asked. "He knows what happened here. Hell, he probably orchestrated the whole thing himself."

"Damn right he did!" Saul cried, and then winced.

"He'll keep his mouth shut, if he knows what's good for him and his crops," I muttered and patted the breast pocket that held Anansi's whistle. "We have reinforcements on call."

Genevieve nodded and grabbed Saul's feet while I looped my arms through his damp armpits. The old man squawked and broke wind as we hoisted him up. "Oh gawd, you're rippin' me in half!"

"That wasn't us," I said, quickly clamping down my teeth to keep wild laughter at bay. It would have been inappropriate, but I was more afraid of dropping him. Genevieve and I quickly carried him through the destroyed store and out the front. After we loaded him onto the cart, I removed my poncho and wrapped him in it. We'd brought along a canteen of water and I gave him a few sips, which seemed to have an immediate effect on him. He was still badly—perhaps even gravely—injured, but I felt a little more hopeful that we could fix him.

Genevieve also removed her poncho and bundled it into a little makeshift pillow to place under his head. I had just enough time to check myself and register that I had left my little impromptu club behind in the store, when something hard hit me on the back of the head. Stars exploded in my vision and I soon felt a warm trickle of blood dripping down my neck.

I turned around to see three women standing just ahead. *The Sisters Ugly*, I thought immediately. It was random and had no basis in anything else I knew, but the name fit. They were toothless, sore-riddled hags with hair hanging like dirty kelp down their bony shoulders. The one on the right wore an eye patch and held a rock about the size of a potato in her hand, as did the one on the left. The middle sister had no rock, but instead stood with her stick-like arms folded across her emaciated chest. Cunning danced in her eyes. I figured her for the leader.

The other two raised their stones to throw. Their biceps trembled under the weight, but they looked determined and would probably be accurate enough to seriously hurt one of us.

"We don't want any trouble," I said. "We're here to take the old man for some help. Someone hurt him badly. Was it one of you?"

The middle sister cackled. "I'm afraid it weren't our handiwork. Does that mean we can be friends then? I'll take ya to our house 'n you can wag yer wee little worm for us." The three of them laughed together, their atonal giggles grating in my ears like shards of glass.

"What do you want?" Genevieve asked.

The middle sister turned her gaze to Genevieve, and the look of greed that stole over her face was chilling. "Truthfully, we could take or leave the men. What we really want is you, ginger girl. Come with us, and we'll let your man and the whoreson grocer leave on their merry little way."

Genevieve took a few steps forward. The one with the eye patch said, "That's a pretty wee girl. Come now, with us." She reached out to touch Genevieve's hair, and Genevieve seemed to bear it, though the stiffening of her shoulders told of her revulsion. I was about to rush forward and put an end to this when I saw Genevieve hold up one finger behind her back.

Wait.

"I have a better idea," Genevieve said. I didn't need to see what she was doing. She'd stuck her pistol in the back of her pants when we went to help Saul, and now it was right where she wanted it.

The middle sister, the leader, was no dummy. "Show me your hand, ginger girl!"

"Gladly." Genevieve's hand moved in a blur. Before I could see what happened, the gun's report filled the street along with the acrid stink of gunpowder. A single shot. The leader of the Sisters Ugly dropped to her knees with a blackened bullet hole branded into the center of her forehead and a slack-jawed expression of surprise on her face. Her blood painted the shocked faces of her companions in a bright red stipple. They dropped their rocks and gaped at the blazing redhead with the smoking pistol in her hand.

"Go now, and you won't die with her," Genevieve said.

The sister with the eye patch gazed at Genevieve as if she were crazy. "We're already dying. But since you took away our Tatum, you should kill us too." The other sister nodded in agreement.

Now it was Genevieve's turn to look shocked. "What is the matter with you people?"

"Mr. Paine promised he would fix us if we brought him new ladies," she said.

Genevieve's tongue seemed to be struck dead by that. I, however, wasn't suffering from the same problem. "Mr. Paine is a lunatic. And he's dying just like the rest of you."

The other sister, the one without the eye patch, began to weep. "You killed Tatum! You should kill us too! Please, I beg you. Don't let us live this way no more!"

Genevieve looked back at me, her eyes imploring me to say something to them. I looked down at the two women who resembled tragic mockeries of small children and I offered my hand down to the one with the eye patch, for she seemed the most coherent of the two. She took it and gazed up at me.

"We're going to fix this one way or another. I promise you that. But your work here isn't done yet. Your job is to spread the word and tell the people that Akiva Paine will pay for what he's done. If we meet again, and you still want to die, I'll do you the mercy."

She nodded, her good eye sharp in spite of the tears that filled it. "All right then. But only 'cause you promised to come back and finish us. We've become an abomination 'fore God. I s'pose we've earned this."

"No. No, lady you haven't. It's the abomination who did this to you, and we plan to deal with it."

I let her hand go and watched as she gathered her remaining sister close. Her one eye seemed to shine with cautious hope as we left them standing in the middle of the lonely street.

"Thank you, John," Genevieve said.

"They're still damned," I muttered and set about making Saul more comfortable. "And we need to get back before those bastards hurt my daughter."

We raced back to Paine's house in silence.

Chapter 18

It was mid-afternoon before we rolled back up the plantation's drive, and by then Saul was unconscious and taking shallow, rattling breaths. We agreed not to pull out the knife, because he would almost certainly bleed out. I just hoped whatever we could do through Ezekiel would make the knife a non-entity.

On the way back, I'd become so certain that something happened to Kaya that when I saw her jogging up with Harry to greet us, I almost thought she was an illusion.

I jumped off the back of the cart before it even stopped moving and ran to her, hugging her just to remind myself of her substance and vitality. I stood back and looked at her. "Are you okay? Did anything happen?"

Kaya frowned. "I guess I should ask you the same question. What's going on, Dad? You have blood on you."

"I'll tell you in a minute."

Harry, meanwhile, was climbing into the cart. "Saul? Buddy? Who did this to you?" His face was red with dawning rage.

"We'll talk about that in a bit, too," I said. "Take him to Ezekiel's room and wait for me there."

Genevieve looked torn over whether to go with her father

or stay with me. "Go ahead and help get Saul comfortable. I'll talk with Kaya and we'll be up soon."

"What happened?" Kaya asked.

I wasn't quite ready go to into the ruin that was Old Babylon and its female population. Or the Sisters Ugly. Instead, I deflected. "You first."

"Look, I'm fine, but . . . things are wrong here. Worse than we thought. And it isn't just with that weird butler or those corn cakes at breakfast, either."

I nodded. "Paine is up to some sinister stuff, all right. Women in particular are vulnerable."

She bowed her head in thought, chewing on her thumb nail. Her mother used to do that, and both our daughters had inherited the same habit. My heartstrings gave a sickening tug.

"That's interesting, but I guess it makes sense given what I've found. I need to ask Genevieve about some of the others she brought here from God's Hope."

"Why?"

She sighed. "I had Harry run some interference while you were gone so I could do some snooping around the house." She must have seen my face, because she held out her hands. "Don't freak out. I was careful. I found this room up on the third floor. It was locked, but I got in."

I gaped. "Who taught you to pick a lock?"

She shrugged and then gave me a sheepish grin. "Just something I played around with when I was younger. I used to try to sneak into Beth's room to read her diaries. Total waste of time. No juicy details at all. Just normal, sweet Beth stuff."

We both let that hang between us for a second. I knew she missed her sister, but I think that was about as close as she would ever come to saying so aloud. "What did you find in the room?" I asked.

"It was full of junk, mostly. But then I found a bunch of personal things like jewelry, rosaries, brushes, clothes. Many things were still in knapsacks that had been tossed into a corner."

"Where do you think those things came from?" I already had a sickening idea, but I wanted to hear her say it.

"I recognized one of the rosaries. A strand of rubies with a mother of pearl cross. Really beautiful and rare. Greta Abernathy, a girl I went to school with, had one just like it, and she loved that thing more than life itself. Said it was her great-great grandmother's, and she had her initials engraved on it. I tried to remember when I last saw her. Maybe a year ago. I always thought she'd moved away, but that rosary said she was here. She never would have left something like that behind if she were alive."

I knew the name Abernathy. I used to see her parents, Tom and Margret, in church. Margret sang in the choir with Linny. She was a fine soprano. Tom made shoes. I didn't see them at all after Linny died, but I didn't remember seeing much of anybody after that. Justification must have gotten to them when I wasn't looking. I couldn't think of why, but then again, the Rite never needed much of a reason.

So they came here with Genevieve and never made the next stop in the journey. Or perhaps they did, but Paine robbed them first. There was no real way of knowing for sure, but it didn't seem like Paine was interested in collecting trinkets from passengers on the Absolution Railroad. He was interested more in the passengers themselves. I would have to talk to Genevieve about this.

"Have you seen Christoph and Turpin yet?"

She nodded. "They were back pretty quick, but then Christoph said he had an idea about something and they left again."

"Whatever they're doing, I hope it doesn't take long. We need to be out of here soon."

We went into the house. But for the ticking of an ornate grandfather clock in the parlor, the place was silent, almost as if it were waiting for something to happen. Upstairs, Saul lay on a lower bunk in Ezekiel's room with his shirt off. Genevieve cleaned Saul's face with a wet cloth while Harry examined the knife wound. He looked up at us. "If I pull this out, he'll bleed to death," he said. "He also has a punctured lung and is in shock. I'm not sure I'll be able to fix this."

"We'll use the Sentinel the way we did with Anansi," I said.

Harry shook his head. "John, I don't know. You didn't handle the last trip so well. It might kill you this time. Or him."

I looked at Ezekiel and remembered the visions I had when we were connected, and I knew for better or worse this wasn't my time to die. Genevieve and I also gave each other a knowing look. "I'm not so sure about that, Harry. I want to try."

The redheaded man sighed. "You seem to have a way with this stuff that I don't quite understand yet. If you think it'll work, let's do it."

He got up, fetched the unconscious boy from his bunk,

and set him on the bed next to the half-conscious Saul while I prepared myself for another trip into the *Élan Vital*.

I braced myself for that wallop of energy, but this time it was different. While the power was no less brilliant, it was gentler, almost sweet. In it, I heard a choir of voices singing. The light swelled to the intensity of a white sun and I closed my eyes against it as I let its warmth and life flow through me and into the man I hoped to heal.

When the brightness waned, I opened my eyes again. The scene was pure déjà vu. I sat beneath the flowering plum again with Ezekiel, only this time, Saul sat just to my right. We formed a tight circle. The grocer was uninjured; the knife that had been jutting from his side was now sitting in his hands, and his face had a hearty vitality that made him look almost young again. I looked over to my left and saw a blackened pit where Turpin's house once stood. Black-clad men raked through the still-smoking mess. Divine Rite men. My heart kicked into high gear.

"They cannot see us. Be calm, John," Ezekiel said.

"Where the hell am I? Heaven?" Saul asked.

"We are gathered for what will be my final meeting here," said the Sentinel.

"Why final?" I asked.

"I am dying, John. I think you know this. You felt it. My energy is weakening and it will not last much longer. I must save what I have left for the end."

"Will you be able to heal Saul?"

"As you can see, he has already been healed. I have brought him here with us because he too is part of this and he has a job to do."

"What job?" asked Saul. "Where the hell am I?"

"You are going to become a great leader of your people here in Old Babylon. You and the survivors will mend this land and start gathering together to stand against your foe."

He frowned. "Survivors? What survivors? No offense little fella, but you probably haven't noticed they're all dying from the corn sickness."

"Not all will die. Their illness can be cured with the right medicine, as your Samaritan, Harry, will soon discover. Many more are just hiding until the storm passes. They will come to you soon seeking aid, and you will give it. It will not be easy, but this must be your burden, Saul Andrews. You have received many favors in your life, and it is now time to return them. This is your place."

He shook his head. "I'm no leader," he said.

"You are, but you will not lead alone," Ezekiel said and turned his attention to me.

"You and your friends are in danger and must be prepared to fight when we leave here. Akiva Paine has decided to take his chances and alert the Divine Rite to your presence. The Hand of God will soon arrive."

My stomach lurched. "How long do we have?"

"Not long. I have done my best to share this vision with the others through dreams, but you must lead them. Prepare to be tested, my brother. Your band of allies will experience great trials and tragedy, but you must stand strong." The Sentinel's body began to evaporate before me, and I could see Turpin's old garden through him, burnt to ash. My hands were losing substance, and I looked at Saul as he faded to little more than a pair of bemused eyes and a few wisps of his graying hair.

Then, it was only the light.

I awoke on the bedroom floor, gazing at the dust bunnies under the bed. I reached up and felt under my nose; my fingertips came away smudged with only a faint streak of red. Thankfully, I hadn't pissed myself.

"John, get up." It was Genevieve, tugging on my arm, her voice edging on frantic. I sat up slowly, fighting off a little dizziness but otherwise feeling okay. It seemed I was becoming a little more acclimated to my exposure to the boy's power.

I looked over at Saul, who sat up in the bed looking very much alive, but grim. The knife from his wound was still in his hand. I don't think I ever saw him without it after that. Our eyes met and we seemed to acknowledge what we had shared. Ezekiel lay beside him, taking in tiny sips of breath. He was so gaunt now, his cheekbones looked as if they could cut right through his papery skin. It hurt my heart to look at him, but the sound of Harry cursing under his breath pulled my attention away. He was trying to jimmy open the lock on our bedroom door.

"What's going on?" I asked.

"Antony bolted our door from the outside when you were away," Genevieve said. "Dad nearly lost a hand trying to stop him, but the bastard moved fast."

A stone fell in my gut. "The Hand of God is coming for us. Paine alerted them. Ezekiel said."

"That turncoat son of a bitch!" Harry cried. "Well at least Turpin and Christoph are still out there. If they haven't been captured already."

We were stuck in the one bedroom that didn't offer a window. If we'd gone into my room, our chances may have been better, but then again maybe not. We were on the third story, and someone surely would have spotted us dangling from the building like a strange band of monkeys. Easy targets for anyone to shoot down. But at least I would have been able to use the whistle to summon Anansi. It was important we got outside fast.

"Any luck at all with the lock?" I asked.

"Goddamn thing won't budge a millimeter," he grumbled. "These are state of the art. Probably pre-Blight, but built to last a dozen lifetimes."

"They probably keep their prisoners in these rooms," Kaya said.

"What if we try shooting the lock?" I asked.

Harry shook his head. "That never works. Trust me. Especially on locks like these. Besides, we only have Genevieve's pistol. Our high-powered stuff is in the other room. Or was. They probably took what we brought with us."

Saul spoke up. "You think this magic kid's got any juice left in him?"

"No. He said he was storing up for the end. Whatever that meant."

"Maybe this *is* the end," Kaya said, a flutter of panic in her voice.

I shook my head emphatically. "No. Not this. I'm pretty sure he meant something else."

Genevieve stepped forward. "John, have you ever felt any residual effects after being in contact with the Sentinel?"

"You mean apart from being covered in blood and urine?"

She didn't appear to see the joke. "You know what I mean."

I thought about it for a minute, but I shook my head. "None that I know of. But I've never really been in good enough shape afterward to figure it out. I'm usually unconscious for hours."

"You weren't this time," she said. "You were only out for a couple minutes. It's possible you could break the lock, with my help."

"Oh, I doubt that," I said. I felt like someone had just told me I could walk through a brick wall. Separated from Ezekiel, I was a mere mortal.

She put her hand on my shoulder. "Just try it, John. If it doesn't work, we'll figure some other way out of this box."

I looked at Harry and he shrugged. "There might be a little reverb of it left in you. That was one of the things we—or the Rite, really—wanted to test when they conducted experiments with the Sentinels, but seeing as you're the only one who ever lived after linking up with one, we never found out. Couldn't hurt to try."

Kaya patted my shoulder. "They're right, Dad. Do it."

"Yeah, what have we got to lose, right?" I said, stepping up to the door and exhaling. Stupid waste of time is what I thought it was, of course.

"Can you feel it in you?" Genevieve whispered. I felt the firm press of her breasts against me. "It's like a white doorway just out of the corner of your eye. If you focus on it hard enough, it'll become clearer."

"Easier said than done," I muttered, but I exhaled again and concentrated. There was something there, or at least I thought there was. It wasn't much. It reminded me of an imprint on my retina after staring at the sun too long. But seeing it was like trying to grab at empty air, and the harder I tried to snag it with my mind, the more insubstantial it felt.

"I can't do this," I said. Beads of sweat ran down my forehead and temples.

"There is no can't," Genevieve whispered. "You just need to focus, and believe."

"Easier said than done," I repeated, "I stopped believing in most things months ago."

Her hands, small but strong after years of working at her father's store, squeezed my shoulders. "Enough of that crap. Doubt isn't going to get you anywhere. You've gone farther against the Rite than anyone else ever has. Now keep going."

I bristled at her tone, but she was right. I pushed the bad thoughts away and focused.

"When you get to that light, it will try to consume you. Just remember what you did when you freed Anansi. Imagine the lock, channel the energy outward from your body. Be the conduit, John. Control the energy. Do not let it control you."

I nodded impatiently. "I got it. Just be ready to fight, because it might be a pretty loud bang." I edged closer to that ball of light, my mind extending a hook like a lure in a pond. Soon I realized I wasn't fishing for it. It was fishing for me. I understood what she meant about it controlling me, and how I might bring the paltry remainder of human civilization to its knees under such power. The vision I'd had, the mad man atop the mountains as the world bled, made more sense than ever, but the influence of my daughters, of Ezekiel, held it in check.

I called up the image of the lock while I breathed in the

light and let it fill me with its sweet chorus. It soon surged through my veins, and every capillary was alight with it. I was a human torch waiting for a breath of wind to release a spark.

I breathed, and the spark flew through the keyhole.

It didn't shatter with the same time-splitting supernova of intensity that Anansi's bracelet had. Instead, I heard nothing more than a faint click.

I opened my eyes, and the *Élan Vital* vanished, leaving a palpable despair in its place. Everything felt so . . . mundane. Mortal and fragile, like dried leaves. I turned the knob, and the door opened. The long metal bolt that had been holding it shut lay in two pieces on the rug. Satisfied, I closed it again.

"Well that was easy enough," I said, my voice shaking.

Genevieve hugged me. "Wonderful work, John."

"Yeah, you're pretty amazing, Dad," Kaya said and joined in the hug.

"Well I think you're all nuts," Saul muttered.

"Where are we going from here?" Harry asked. "They probably have every exit from this place covered."

I already had an idea in mind. "Anyone here need to use the privy?"

Chapter 19

We crept down the hall in a single-file line, hugging close against the wall. The privy was three doors down, but under the circumstances, where we were certain Antony or some other stooge of Akiva Paine's was going to jump from the shadows, it felt closer to three miles. Harry adjusted the sling Christoph had made, and he now carried Ezekiel on his back. His legs hung lifelessly at Harry's sides and his head lolled a little, but he otherwise looked secure.

The five of us crammed into the tiny room and I squeezed the door shut and flipped the lock for good measure.

"Now what?" Harry asked, his brow covered in a heavy mist of sweat.

I pointed to the modest wooden bench sitting on the far end of the room. "That's our ticket out of here," I said.

"Ugh. The toilet?" Kaya groaned.

"It's not a toilet, at least technically speaking. It's more like a dumbwaiter for human waste," I said.

"That doesn't make it sound any better, Dad."

"Do you know where this goes?" Genevieve asked.

"It goes clear down to the basement," Saul said. "I used to make deliveries out here, and sometimes asked to use the facilities just because I was so damn impressed with the thing.

Paine liked to show it off every chance he got. You do your business into the chamber pot and yank the pulley. Some peon down below takes it, cleans it out, and raises it back up."

"So there could be people down there?" I asked.

Saul shrugged. "Maybe, maybe not. If so, it's probably just a slave or two. Could probably take him out myself if I had to."

"What we really want to know is if we're doing ourselves any favors by going deeper into this place rather than just storming out the front. We could end up stuck down there with no way out," Genevieve said.

"Doubtful," said Saul. "Basement likely has a coal chute. Most of these old houses do. That would at least get us outside. After that, who knows."

"Perfect," said Kaya. "Down the poop chute and out the coal one."

"We only need to get outside," I said. "After that, I can call Anansi."

"Who?" Saul asked, and then shook his head. "Never mind."

We opened the seat on the box and peered into it. The ceramic chamber pot inside was clean, so at least we didn't have to worry about combating any additional stink. The hole was not much more than a foot wide. I worried it was going to be an extremely tight fit for Harry and I. Saul was a very slight man, not much more in height or weight than Kaya. We stopped worrying when Harry noticed hinges on the backside of the bench. The entire surface opened, revealing an additional few inches of diameter to the hole. Better, but not by much.

Because he would need more room to maneuver himself and Ezekiel down, Harry agreed to go last. Genevieve had a gun and refused to take no for an answer, so she went first. She removed the ceramic bowl from the privy and stepped into the little wooden box that held it. "God, this stinks," she whispered.

"Just hold your nose, sweetheart," Harry said and yanked on the rope that sent the pot down the shaft. It wasn't designed to hold the weight of a whole person, but it was constructed well and didn't seem at all like it was going to give. She gave us all a sardonic little salute as she disappeared into the hole. It seemed Harry pulled that rope for at least a minute before it reached the bottom, with us all cringing at the racket of the squeaking pulley the whole time. A few seconds later, the rope jiggled and Harry raised the box back up again.

Saul went next. "I guess my day really has gone into the crapper," he remarked without an ounce of irony, and Kaya snorted a giggle.

"See you on the other side, my friend," Harry said, and quickly lowered him. When the box was back up a couple minutes later, Harry looked at me. "Your turn, comrade."

"I want Kaya to go now," I said.

"She'll be right behind you. You need one of us looking after Genevieve. Saul's a good man, but he's old and weighs a buck twenty soaking wet. I'll look after things up here."

I wanted to argue the point further, that Genevieve had a gun and could look after herself, and that I would feel better if I knew Kaya was in front of me, but there wasn't time. Soon they would discover we'd escaped the bedroom, and this door would be knocked down. I stepped into the box and waved at them both. Kaya gave me an encouraging smile that glinted white even in the dim lamp-lit room and said, "See you in a few, Dad."

I think part of me, the part tied to Ezekiel, must have known that would not be so. Or maybe that's just what I tell myself, because I need to feel guilty.

I descended into the stinking blackness that had for years served as the main freeway for Akiva Paine's shit and piss. Years' worth of stench from the traversing chamber pots had sunk into the walls, made worse by stifling heat and lack of air circulation. The ropes slid easily enough along the pulleys, but they were beginning to fray a little with the extra weight. I looked up and saw the meager light from the bathroom getting smaller. Nothing was visible below me, but I estimated I was about halfway down. I took measured breaths and tried not to touch the stinking walls. A moment later, a pounding thud from up above echoed down the chamber. The movement of the box paused, and I heard Harry whisper, "Ah, shit," and the ropes lurched faster. My hand brushed against the wooden wall, and splinters whispered into the skin of my palm.

"Come out of there now!" said a muffled voice from behind the privy door above me. Antony's, perhaps. We'd run out of time, and there were still three of us left up there. Namely my daughter. But my descent was unstoppable at this point. A few seconds later, I hit bottom, and I saw Harry's head fill the opening. "They're coming. I'm sorry, John. I'll take care of this." I caught a brief glimpse of Kaya's profile, a terrified sliver, before the lid to the privy closed and the darkness filled the shaft. I screamed as heavy thuds and commotion swarmed above me.

I heard Kaya scream next.

"*KAYA!*" I cried. "I have to get back up there! Someone help get me back up there!"

"*Shhhhh!*"

A calloused hand clapped over my mouth.

"You tryin' to get us all killed?" Saul whispered into my ear.

I yanked his hand away. "They have my daughter up there!"

"They have my father too," Genevieve said. "They'll have the rest of us if you don't be quiet." I couldn't see her—my eyes had not yet adjusted to the darkness—but I heard her just to my left. Her words made a small dent in my hysteria, but my mind was awash with my daughter's name, and that last tiny glimpse of her terrified face. I heard an army of footsteps over our heads. We had but a few moments to make our escape.

"Where's the coal chute?" I asked.

"Should be along one of the outside walls, but I can't see a goddamn thing down here," Saul said. We crept along, my night vision finally beginning to kick in. I saw humped, shadowy shapes to my right. Furniture draped in sheets, perhaps. My nose registered the faint aroma of human waste mingled with the sour stench of the ancient packed earth floor. There was something else as well: a putrescence worse than shit. I had a feeling there were corpses of some sort down there, human or otherwise.

We formed a line with Saul in the lead, me in the middle, and Genevieve bringing up the rear. I jumped when my shoulder nudged something hanging against the wall. It had a familiar shape. "Stop," I said, and reached out for it. I felt the glass and metal certainty of a lantern, and my fingers fumbled to turn it on.

The room filled with a dim glow, and my breath stopped. The basement was a labyrinthine tangle of junk with no clear exit in sight. But space had been cleared for at least a dozen long metal tables, beside which were trays of surgical tools. Most were knives, tweezers, clamps. Others were decidedly more barbaric looking. There were other machines I didn't recognize, but Genevieve identified one of them as a microscope.

"For seeing things up close," she explained. "Turpin had one." There were glass bottles and tubes filled with colorful liquids varying from yellow to green to blood red. Unspeakable things floated in those fluids, but I averted my eyes before they could confirm what my mind was already sure of.

Those are babies. Dead babies.

The far end of the light's circle of illumination revealed a series of long wooden boxes, about eight across, four deep, and right up to the ceiling. *Coffins.* I clamped down on a scream.

A door opened in the opposite corner and boots thudded down the basement stairs. I also heard the click of the hammer pulling back on Genevieve's pistol and looked back to see that familiar gleam of impending battle in her eyes. "We have to hide," she whispered and opened the door to the room directly behind us just as we heard the familiar grumble of Akiva Paine's voice not twenty feet away.

"They got to be down here. Only christing place they can

be," he muttered.

Genevieve threw the bolt on the door and we surveyed the space. It was a tiny storage room lined with shelves and boxes of miscellaneous junk. There was a distinct chemical odor. In the meager light, I examined the shelves and found the source of the stink: glass jars filled with pinkish fluid and more mind-numbing horrors. I recognized a liver in one, a heart in another. More dead babies. Some barely fit and were crammed in until they resembled something more like globular lumps of flesh with lidless, cloudy eyes pressed against glass. One of them had a series of flippers for appendages. Another had a cyclopean eye in the middle of its stark white forehead. "Good Christ," I moaned, gagging.

Saul took the lantern and moved it away from the jars. "We've seen about enough of that," he whispered. I listened outside the door and heard people rustling around in an effort to find us. There were many places to look, but eventually they would get to this door, and they would break it down, or Akiva Paine would open it with a key. I heard a sniffle next to me and a shaky intake of breathe. Genevieve wept quietly. I put my arm around her, but I said nothing. We both knew what we'd just lost and what we needed to do, and getting caught up in our emotions was only going to slow us down, but at the moment, locked in a room full of horrors with the Divine Rite goons on the other side, it felt like things were about to wind down to a gruesome end.

"Pssst!" Saul whispered. "Over here." He was grinning, though I didn't know why. "Girlie, of all the rooms in this hell pit you could have picked, you definitely picked the right one." He shined the lantern on the wall behind a table littered with empty jars, books, and playing cards of all things. I saw a circular black metal grate about three feet wide. The coal chute. Salvation.

After a quick effort to move the table out of the way, Saul used his pocketknife to loosen the screws and we pulled the grate free, loosing a century-old cloud of coal dust into the air. I clearly heard Akiva Paine outside the door now, but just to the left of our room.

"Let's try this one," he said.

"Appears empty. Dirty, but empty," Saul said. "I'm going up. Hopefully I can get the door open topside." His top half disappeared up the chute, and when his feet were gone, we waited, listening to his grunts echo down the old aluminum tube. A minute later, we heard a loud metallic squeal and saw moonlight spill from the chute.

Genevieve bade me to go next. I shook my head, determined not to leave someone else behind. "Not this time. You go."

"I have the gun, and you have the whistle," she whispered fiercely through gritted teeth. "Get in there or I swear to God I'll shoot you myself."

Without stopping to think, I reached for her, pulled her to me and kissed her hard on the mouth. She stiffened at first, but softened and touched my face just before I let her go. I didn't wait for her reaction before entering the second strange, dark tunnel of the night. It was easy enough climbing, only about six or eight feet at most.

Saul reached his hand down and helped midwife me out of the house's dank recesses, and I breathed a grateful double lungful of the fresh night air. As he dove down to reach for

Genevieve, I heard Paine's muffled voice and a jiggling door-knob. "They're in here. They locked it. They won't get far. Go outside 'round the side of the house . . . goddamn coal chute."

"Got her!" Saul cried and yanked as hard as he could. I saw Genevieve's coal-blackened hands clasped in his, and then her head.

Then she screamed and Saul was yanked forward. "Son of a bitch! John, help me!"

I was there before the words were out of his mouth, and I saw a white hand in the darkness, clasping Genevieve's ankle.

"Go! Run!" she yelled.

"Not a chance," I growled, grabbing her other hand. "Saul, when I say pull, you goddamn pull. I'm not losing anyone else in this hellhole, you understand?"

"Loud and clear, fella."

Genevieve screamed again as another hand grabbed her, this one higher up inside her skirt. Perhaps her thigh, but no place a man had any business touching a woman without permission.

"Down you come, my dear soft girl," I heard one of them say. I could almost hear him slobbering.

My fright became a bitter rage. Hypocrites! I didn't care if we dislocated her shoulders, we were going to free her from these animals.

"*Pull now!*"

I dug in my heels and launched myself backward with my legs. After an initial moment when I felt sure we were going to tear her in half, she came free with a howl and we stumbled to the ground. I wanted to inspect her, make sure she was unhurt, but she was already up on her feet and running.

Paine's furious bellows echoed up the chute after.

"Get her! Curse you christing bastards! Get her!"

We followed her around the house and toward the perimeter fence. I looked back and saw a few black-robed figures, thankfully not Hand of God, running from the front door and around the corner from where we'd just escaped. The roar of a pistol, close enough to make my ears ring, filled the air, and all of them dropped. I fell with them to avoid the line of fire and glanced back to see gun smoke, and Genevieve's fury bordering on madness. Her hair flew in every direction, eyes reddened and filled with tears, face smeared with coal soot, but she was beautiful. "John, blow the goddamn whistle!" she cried, firing off two more shots with one hand while she dug in her bag for spare ammo.

I sat up and groped for the tiny wooden instrument in my breast pocket, but it wasn't there. Everything seemed to slow down, the sound muffling like my ears had been stuffed with cotton. Invisible hands clamped around my lungs, and I couldn't breathe.

Somewhere, in all the commotion of our escape, I'd lost the only lifeline we had left.

A line of Divine Rite stooges were heading for us and they would mow us down in a matter of seconds. I saw the swirling blue of electric sticks in some of their hands. Hand of God weapons. My mouth went dry.

Best to just lie down in a fetal position and let them take us. At least then I'd be reunited with my one daughter. Perhaps Beth too. The thought was so tantalizing that I might have done just that if Genevieve hadn't grabbed me by the hair and shaken me out of my stupor.

"There! There in the grass in front of you! Grab it!"

I don't even know how she saw the slim hollow of dark wood in the twilight, but there it was. It must have fallen from my pocket when I hit the deck.

Before I could hear another second of the tempting lullaby of surrender, I snatched it up out of the grass with numb fingers and blew into it hard enough to make my cheeks tingle. It didn't make a sound, but it wasn't supposed to. It was meant only for locusts' ears. An entire, swarming plague of them.

We darted toward the fence that bordered the property. It was electrified, of course, but I figured there was probably an easy enough way through if we disabled the solar panel. The pistol erupted again, and that very panel shattered, spilling out a rain of sparks like fireflies. The woman was dangerous with that revolver.

"I hope that whistle worked," she said, as we climbed over the fence and staggered over to the same stand of trees we'd waited under that very morning that seemed like a year ago. No one had spotted us over here, at least yet, and we took a moment to catch our breaths.

"It will work," I said, though I couldn't hear anything yet.

"Maybe you should blow it again."

"Trust me, I know how to blow a damn whistle," I snapped.

Saul looked at me with his eyebrows raised. "Anyone gonna clue me in here?"

"Our friend is a Heretic. A shapeshifter that used to work for the Hand of God," I told him.

"I know what a Heretic is. I just want to know how the hell you befriend one of them."

"Long story," I said, and then I heard a man cry out.

"They're over here! Over the fence!"

I was too tired to run any farther. My legs felt like a couple of sticks that had been snapped into pieces and taped crudely back together. But maybe there was a shortcut back to town. Maybe we still had a chance. Where the hell was Anansi?

"We need to get to your store, Saul. Do you know a faster way?"

"Well, I think if we go up yonder . . ." Saul began. Then I spied a pair of bobbing headlights up ahead. I wasn't close enough to see the whole vehicle, but I recognized the roar of the engine, and my heart sang with joy.

"Come on!" I cried. We ran for it, a stitch in my side and a knife in my heart over everything we had lost since we last saw this part of our group.

As we drew closer, and as I heard the sound of footsteps on the fence behind us, the night grew darker, as if a cloud had passed in front of the moon. Only it wasn't a cloud of vapor. Relief unlocked my knees and I would have fallen to the ground if Saul hadn't been there to catch me.

"Anansi," I whispered, feeling ever so grateful to have such a terrifying ally.

The swarm drew close, compacted, and began its descent about fifteen feet away. I reached him just as I saw his green and orange eyes materialize in his face.

"I heard your call, my man. I am at your service."

"The Rite has Harry and Kaya. You were right about the corn."

"Yes," he said. "I spied the Rite moving out of here on the road that goes to the Cradle fifty miles northwest." He stopped with an expression of deep sorrow painted on his face. "I wanted to stop them, my man, but I hadn't yet heard your call. If I had gone for them, I would not have been able to answer your signal. I hope you can forgive me."

I reached out and grabbed one of his strangely rigid shoulders. "Anansi, you did right. I did not expect you to rescue them. We need you here. Can you destroy this cursed piece of land?"

Anansi's eyes shone with the carnal gleam of a predator. "With great pleasure, my man."

"We'll be on the road heading toward the Cradle. Meet us when you're done."

"I am sorry, but that will not be," he said faintly.

"Why not?"

"What this evil man grows here will surely kill me as it has the others. What I do here, will be the last thing I do."

I felt my heart break all over again. "Oh, Anansi," I said.

"Do not fret. What I do here could save the world. It would be a most honorable way to meet my maker."

I swallowed the lump that rose in the back of my throat and offered my hand to the shapeshifter, who took it and gave two decisive pumps. "Your ride is here," he said. "Act with haste, my man. Your party will not last long in the Cradle. Now, I must fly."

"Godspeed, my friend," I croaked as Anansi broke apart and took to the sky for the last time.

Christoph's truck roared to a stop in a cloud of dust and Turpin's wizened head popped out of the window. "Get in the back," he said, and the three of us jumped into the cargo area. By the time we got going again, the scream of a billion hungry locusts filled the world.

Chapter 20

Unlike the very first vision I shared with Ezekiel, Christoph's truck was not overrun by the swarm. In fact, we never came close to any sort of collision, because we drove off in the opposite direction. Any scenes of agricultural destruction were left strictly to my imagination, and that was good enough.

When we arrived at Saul's, the sound of the bugs carried on long into the night from the northeast, and Genevieve and I held each other's hands and listened to Anansi's ultimate sacrifice with heavy hearts for a little while before we headed inside.

"It looks like I've got some cleaning up to do," Saul said.

"Yes," I said. "You have to prep for your own little rebellion. The Divine Rite isn't going to forget about this place." I thought of the burnt out church and the hanging bodies and was grateful it was all shrouded in darkness.

"Maybe, maybe not. I have a feeling the net's been disabled by the locust swarm. We might not be able to stay here for long before the weeds start taking over."

My heart sank a little. I hadn't considered that. If Old Babylon was exposed, it was only a matter of time. It could be days, months, or years before the weeds appeared, but they would. They always did. And when they did, there was no hope of living where they lived. I thought, wildly, that maybe there was something I could do about that with Ezekiel's power at my hands, but I wasn't going to get too far ahead of myself. The boy was unlikely to even survive the night, if he was even still alive at all. Thinking about Ezekiel naturally led to thoughts of Kaya, and I stopped that short real fast. Despair was waiting to pounce, like a hungry stray dog.

Saul looked at me for a moment. "You're thinking what I'm thinking, aren't ya? About the boy?"

"I guess so, yeah."

"I can still hardly believe it, ya know? That kid brought me back from the dead and I feel twenty years younger. We'll cross the weed bridge when we come to it. Maybe if we can get the net back up and running . . ."

"You never know," Genevieve said. "Maybe nothing will germinate. At least it's not spring. It's always worse in the spring."

"You got that right."

"And there are people here still worth saving," I said. I thought of the Sisters Ugly. At least the two who were remaining. I hoped they were still alive, and had done what I asked them to do.

Saul sighed. "Let's hope so. Listen, I'm all cleaned out of goods in here, but I got a hidden stash the looters probably didn't get to with some food and supplies if you need them for your journey."

Turpin finally spoke after what seemed like years of silence for the normally talkative old man. "That's mighty generous of ya. Thanks, Saul."

"It's the least I can do." He led us through the store into

the backroom where Genevieve and I had found him on the verge of death just a few hours ago.

"Do you know how we intend to break into the Cradle?" Genevieve asked.

"Yeppo," Turpin said. "Christoph has a way with poppies and chemistry."

"Yes, but it may kill them," Christoph said flatly.

"Wait, what?" I said. "Killing them is exactly what we don't want. Our people are in there."

"Which is why we must move quickly," Christoph said.

Saul led us up a set of stairs to his personal quarters, which were still thankfully locked and apparently had survived the looting. It was a modest apartment, but equipped with the bare essentials, and it felt good to get the soot, sweat, and fecal stink off my skin. After that, I was at least able to think clearly again.

I hadn't expected Saul to have anything in his wardrobe that would fit, but he handed me a pair of jeans and a button-down flannel shirt he said were Harry's. "They're about ten years old. He was skinnier then. They ought to fit you."

Back in the living room, I saw a freshly washed and braided Genevieve in a pair of jeans and a man's shirt that might have also once belonged to her father. She gave me a sad grin, before turning back to Christoph, who was unzipping a large canvas shoulder bag and pulling out small objects that looked like hand grenades.

"What are those for?" I asked.

"I retrofitted these flash-bangs with a homemade opioid chemical that will make the people in the Cradle sleepy."

"How will we keep from passing out ourselves?" Genevieve asked.

Christoph reached into the bag and pulled out a cylindrical metal tube attached to a clear plastic mask. "These are filled with about thirty minutes of air. We'll use these to get in. There are enough for our friends inside and a few others. If we move quickly enough to get people out into the clean air, they should revive soon after."

"Where did you get those masks?" I asked.

"One of Paine's workers gave them to me in exchange for some tobacco. They used them when they sprayed the chemical fertilizers on the corn."

"I guess they won't be needing them anymore," I muttered. "Do you know anything about how a Cradle is guarded? How will we get inside to disperse the chemicals?"

I looked at Genevieve, as she was the only one remaining in our group who had any real familiarity with such places.

She shook her head. "My own memories of that time are mostly blank, though sometimes I dream about it. Or at least I think I do. The only real accounts I have are my father's, but even he didn't talk much about it in detail."

"Just tell us what ya think ya know," Turpin said.

"People are organized according to their uses. Sentinels stay sedated while not engaged, and they are heavily guarded when they are. It's quiet and sterile in a Cradle, at least in the Sanctuary where the Sentinels are kept. Like a church during a prayer session. In my dreams, I remember a lot of white. Where they keep the prisoners, though . . . I can't say. I never saw those places, and my father never talked about them much. Because of my mother and all. But I imagine it's pretty bad. The people there don't usually last very long."

My rage kindled at thought of my daughter in such a place. "Will we be able to break in, do you think?"

"It won't be easy. Heretics likely guard the fences, and as you know, they see far and wide. We would likely be spotted before we got within half a mile of the place."

"That won't help us at all," I said.

"No, but I encourage you to work on your connection with Ezekiel. Maybe see if he can reach you from a distance. He's really the one person who can help us. You said he was saving himself for something. Maybe it was this," Genevieve said.

"I'll work on it," I said, though not too hopefully. I had never felt so severed from the *Élan Vital* as I did right then. Maybe it was the exhaustion.

"You'll know more when ya get there tomorrow," Turpin said. He was sitting on a stool with his head bowed, looking almost meditative.

"Where will you be?" I asked.

"Here. Saul is gonna need some help gettin' this place back in order again after the actions of my dearly-departed former brother-in-law. Ya can't have an old fart like me slowin' ya down. I work best when I can sit still."

I thought of how Ezekiel had said that Saul wouldn't have to lead on his own and I wondered if this was what he meant. "I think that's a fine idea, Turpin," I said and stood up. "We should get going." I was so exhausted and sore from the day's exertions, but I was eager to press on. The longer Kaya was away from me, the worse her chances.

"There is just enough night left to cover the drive and stage your attack at dawn," Saul said. "If you go now, you should make it."

"I think doing it just before daybreak, during the guards' likely shift change, is the best idea," Genevieve said. We all agreed, and set about gathering our things and saying our goodbyes. We left Turpin and Saul with the bulk of the weapons and supplies we had remaining with us. They would need them to help secure the town. Old Babylon now officially belonged to us, the first real outpost of our little rebellion.

"We'll be back soon," I said and shook Turpin's hand just outside the cab of Christoph's truck.

"I know ya will, boyo," the old man replied.

"Is that confidence speaking or are you trying the whole prophecy thing on for size?" I asked with a grin.

He cackled. "I don't need to play fortuneteller to know there's destiny written all over ya. I think it's in yer blood."

"I think that's your bourbon talking."

"Well, yer right to be scared. If ya weren't, you'd be a damn fool. But I've seen some things lately that are makin' me question everything I thought I knew about this world, and I've dreamed some things too. This whole business with that Sentinel has got me thinkin' yer link with him is more than just coincidence. But I guess ya already know that."

I nodded. "Yeah, I guess I do."

Turpin stood there looking at his scuffed shoes for a minute, his face working like he was either fighting off an urge to sneeze or cry. "Ya know, ever since I saw that boy, my gears have been turnin' so much I can't even drink it away. I guess ya noticed I've been a little quiet."

"A little."

"I get that way when I'm thinkin'. There's so much information in this old head of mine that I have to crawl into the back of my brain and curl up for a little while to sort things out, if ya get me. This time, I was mostly thinkin' about yer parents, and the siblin' that never was." He sighed and turned his rheumy eyes up to mine. "And after a few days of tryin' to find every which way around this puzzle, I think I figured it out . . . I think Ezekiel could very well be yer brother, boyo."

I was thunderstruck. My mouth moved, but no sound came out at first. When it did, it was a croak. "Why would you think that?"

He shrugged. "Just connectin' the dots. Yer mom and dad left town just before she gave birth. Divine Rite probably spared her for the baby she was carryin'. Fresh meat they could turn into one of their own. Only it ended up bein' a lot more valuable than they anticipated."

"There's only the problem of his age," I said.

Turpin shook his head. "Ya heard Anansi. Ezekiel is older than he looks. His abilities have probably stunted his growth. I asked Harry about this too. He remembers that boy. Watched him grow up. He was born in the Cradle around the same time as Genevieve, and the two of them are about the same age."

So many questions were flying through my mind, but time was slipping away like a fish in the hand, and I could see Genevieve's impatient face in the passenger window.

"Why wouldn't Harry have mentioned something to me about this?"

"Questions you'll want to ask him when ya find him, boyo. My guess is Harry saw so many kiddos, so many mothers, he probably just didn't make the connection to you until he and

I compared notes."

I wasn't sure what to believe, but Turpin's theory was so tantalizing, and it explained so much. Like maybe why the Divine Rite took Beth to Donum Dei. They were trying to lure me there, but what good was I to them? It was Ezekiel they should want, not me.

"Why are you telling me this now, Turpin?"

"It means more to ya now. If strengthening yer connection to that boy is the one thing that'll help ya rise to the challenge of savin' them folks, and yer girls, then it might help if ya looked at Ezekiel as yer own. We fight harder for our blood. For family." He reached out and gripped my shoulder. "If ya got even a sliver of what Ezekiel's got in him, you'll be able to make all the difference. But be careful. They'll want ya even more when they realize what ya can do."

With that, he turned and walked back toward the store, leaving me there with so many questions running through my mind like nasty gossip.

Interlude

I'm still grazing at my depressing feast as I tell my tale, trying to stretch each bite until such a time comes when I'll have to decide between the last morsel and the last word. It won't be much longer.

It's strange how precisely concocted the poison is to match your specific body chemistry, which is of course obtained during Justification exams. It's only after the last bite that you actually die. Sure, a few errant crumbs can be left, but finishing the last laborious bite is essential to ending the agony. I imagine if you don't take that last bite, someone will eventually come and force it down your throat, but more likely you'll just want to get it all over with by then.

The steak's taste did not match its initial aesthetic. It had a spongy texture and a watery, sweet flavor that reminded me of eating peaches just before they begin to rot. The experience was in every way completely counter-intuitive to eating meat, but I've learned to expect disappointment from the things in this world. Nothing is as it should be.

The Rite designs these meals to be eaten rather quickly, and I have languished in eating mine as I've been writing this. Over time, the illusion has begun to wear off, and the illusion of a feast most illustrious has now given way to the depressing banality of the inedible tripe beneath. In that sense, The Last Supper is a gastronomic representation of the Divine Rite itself.

But the Supper is a pretty kind death when you think about it. I think that's part of the reason why most people never fight it when they get one. If after a year of breaking most every rule and precept in the book, shy of becoming a full-blown Nil, the worst you could expect was a full meal followed by an eternal nap, don't you think you'd stay pretty placid about the whole thing too? Yeah, I thought so. Linny was right when she said the Supper was a mercy, and she didn't have to venture outside God's Hope to realize it. Of course, I was always the stubborn one. Kaya and I both.

I guess the truth is I'm stalling on writing the rest of this tale, and I suppose anyone who has read up until this point would feel comfortable waging a guess on how it all turns out. After all, I'm writing from a place of confinement. The specific circumstances that brought me here have not been easy to even think about, let alone tell, but I consider what I'm doing a necessary duty. The Rite calls confession one of the most necessary actions of the faithful, but relating one's sins and fallacies to a faceless entity in a darkened closet is as easy and perfunctory as swallowing a pill. Confronting oneself is always the bigger challenge, and most fail at it. If in the confessional we had to stare into a mirror, we would all be carrying a heavier load of untold sin on our backs.

I suppose I will just forge on like I always have, and in the meantime butter a slice of bread.

Chapter 21

After about two hours of traversing the ruined roads of the countryside northwest of Old Babylon and a harrowing river crossing where the water nearly crested over the hood of the truck, Christoph decided it was time to stop for a break. He found a small wooded grove about twenty miles shy of our destination and parked us there, urging us to try and get a little bit of sleep. Even a half hour, he said, would do us a world of good. To that end, he made a pillow out of his jacket, leaned back in the cramped truck cab, and immediately fell asleep.

Such logic did little to soothe my or Genevieve's nerves and we soon found ourselves walking among the trees, still well within sight of the truck. We found a soft spot to sit and I leaned against a trunk and gazed at the stars that peeked through the canopy. The weeds weren't so bad here, though I guessed it would only be a matter of time before they found this spot too.

"Do you think this is going to work?" I asked.

"I really don't know," she said. "But we have no choice. Doubt does us little good at this point."

"Stand up for yourself, even if your knees shake," I said. The old quote floated up into my head like a bubble. I hadn't thought of it in years.

"Nice. What is that from?"

"I had this teacher once. Miss Grafton, I think her name was. She would have fit in nicely with our little group here. After years of teaching school for the Rite, she basically snapped. She spent an entire day teaching us all the banned subjects and contraband literature she could fit into six hours. I remember feeling like she was talking right to me, like she was sending me a message. It wasn't long after my parents left, and I was so alone and confused and angry. She made me feel like there was a reason to keep going. At the very end of the day, in front of all those kids who were fascinated, amused, and scared to death of all the wonderful and marvelous things we'd learned about human history and the universe, she looked at me and said those words. Stand up for yourself, even if your knees shake."

Genevieve was looking at me, fascinated. "What happened to her?"

"She was gone the next day, replaced by a woman old enough to fart sand."

She burst out laughing, and leaned against me. "Incredible. And sad, too. But I bet her lesson was valuable."

It was. I didn't realize it until right then. Didn't even remember it until that very moment, in fact, and most of the information she shared with us was a garble, but those last words stuck with me. "I'm scared to death, Genevieve. But I'm fighting anyway. I've messed up a lot, but I'm still going. I was too blind to realize my little acts of rebellion would affect my daughters. When Linny died, I didn't comfort either of them. I went off on my own, thinking they'd care for themselves. Now Kaya's imprisoned in a concentration camp and Beth is all the way up in Donum Dei, and your dad . . . it's all my fault. All of it. Everything we've had to deal with, from leaving God's Hope till now has been because of my selfish grieving. And it's enough to make me want to collapse and die, but I can't do that, because I have to fight, and I won't stop until I'm dead."

Genevieve was quiet for a bit. When she did speak, she was restrained. And maybe a little hurt. "You are noble and you are brave, and the pain you've experienced is something I can't even begin to comprehend. But don't speak for the actions of me or my father, John. We knew exactly what we risked by even daring to go against the Rite, and we were willing to risk it all on you as we did for everyone we've tried to save. I can't tell you to stop blaming yourself where your daughters are concerned. I know you well enough to know you'll carry that to your grave no matter how this turns out, but when it comes to me and my father, let it go."

"I can't do that," I said.

"Then we're doomed. You may not have asked for this. You were engaging in some child's game back in God's Hope and it got out of hand. I get that. But if you don't embrace the good that's come of it or recognize the scope of change you can enact in this world by empowering people who feel just as defeated and powerless as you once did, then we all might as well quit now. You're the key in all of this. I don't know how yet, but I believe it anyway. And your self-pity is getting in the way of you seeing that."

Her words bit me, but I refused to get angry with her. "Look, I never said I wanted to quit. That was the whole point of this discussion."

"But you're acting like someone who has already lost. You're shouldering burdens that don't belong to you, and for what? So you can reinforce your defeatist thinking? Nobody has more power than you to make this thing work or fail. I can't speak for Beth, but Kaya knew what might happen by going into this."

"She's just a kid!"

"And a damned brilliant one, too. She knew, probably better than anyone on our team, the cost of fighting for a better world, and she took it without complaint. You need to let her decisions be her own, and you need to start making decisions that speak to what you believe in. Are you in this because you're being pulled along, or are you in it because you want to stick it to the bastards that ruined you and your daughters' lives long before they even got started?"

Turpin had once said that anger and vengeance were the closest cousins of grief, and he was right. Only after a time, my overall losses muddied the bigger goals. The only thing on my mind was rescuing my daughters, but I'd forgotten the kind of world they'd have to live in. If we failed, perhaps Kaya and Beth were better off dead. It was the sort of thinking that would have horrified Linny, but I bet my parents would have understood. "You're right," I said. "For better or worse."

Even in the darkness, I could see she was smiling. "I'm glad you're finally talking sense." She sat up on her knees, facing me. "Now, I want you to try to reach Ezekiel. Your link with him is part of the puzzle."

"I know, but I just can't see. I've tried since we left, but it's like something is blocking me."

"I want to try something. It's a hunch I have."

"Okay."

She took my hands and scooted closer until our legs touched, leaned forward, and caressed my cheeks, kissed my forehead, and pushed off my jacket. So far, I was liking her hunch. Her scent, spicy, musky, floral—from her sweat and the remnants of the perfume she wore—filled my nose. Her lips made the base of my spine tingle, and in that tingle was my old friend guilt. *Cheatin' on your wife*, it said, and I felt a familiar pang in my chest.

"Close your eyes," she whispered.

"I'm not sure I can do this," I murmured.

"You can do this. *We* can do this. We need each other—I need you." Her voice shook, and I could feel her heartbeat. She took my jacket and spread it on the ground, and removed the clip from her hair, letting the flaming waves cascade down her shoulders. I wanted to hide there and never come out.

She removed her shirt, exposing her ivory skin in the dappled moonlight. I swallowed the lump in the back of my throat and drank in the beauty of this woman who represented so much to me now. She was the future and the strength I so desperately needed to push forward. She was the woman I'd once envisioned as the faceless object of my grief-fueled lust in those furious journal entries all those months ago but she had become so much more than that. She was now the warrior at my side and the only thing I had left in that dark moment, the only one who knew me.

I got onto my knees and pulled her close. Her body—soft, curvaceous, warm—molded itself perfectly against me. "I love you," I whispered, but I didn't wait for her words. Just kissed her. She answered by pulling me closer.

And as I entered her with a sigh in the darkness, there was that light again, distant but palpable. It grew brighter with every thrust. A ball of hot lightning opened in the center of me, held by the most tenuous bonds as it began spinning, growing. I pushed even harder, speeding up, feeling her grow wetter, moan louder. She bit the hollow of my shoulder, and that lightning began to throb faster until it finally burst like a supernova. All the strength ran out of me and into her, and she held me as I nearly collapsed on top of her from exhaustion.

The light faded, the darkness returned, and in that darkness, against the sweet swell of her breasts, I slept.

—

I fumbled through a dark tunnel clogged with the detritus of a long-dead civilization. Rusted cars tangled together in what must have been a failed *en masse* escape attempt, the bodies of their drivers long since turned to dust, all consumed by the weeds. An ethereal light illuminated my way, but I didn't question its source. I knew I was dreaming. I was also naked, just as I'd been when I fell asleep.

I emerged from the tunnel's maw to more heaping wreckage that marched in a standstill down the road farther than I could see, and looked up at a glowing rectangle of light perched high on a metal scaffold in a field of swaying corn. It was a sign reading: *"DON'T MAKE ME COME DOWN THERE"*—GOD.

Another one behind it featured something called Jose's Taco Shack and the gigantic likeness of meat, cheese, and lettuce enveloped in a speckled yellow shell. Beneath this read, *Corn Tortillas Made Fresh Daily!*

I continued walking along the side of the road, skirting rusted bumpers and broken suitcases with rotting clothes spilling out like the guts of long-slain animals. A breeze lifted my hair from my sweaty brow, chilled my naked chest, and made the leaves of the cornstalks whisper. The road sloped upward and curved slightly. When I reached the top, I saw where the line of cars had come to a stop. A twisted pile of metal and glass lay at the base of a giant wall that spanned from left to right and up to the sky in an eternity of brick and mortar. Serpent weeds clung to the face of it, but it hadn't been fully consumed just yet.

The end of the line, I thought.

When I reached the wall, I ran my hand along its craggy surface and tiny pebbles came away in my hand. A thin carpet of moss thrived between some of the bricks where the weeds hadn't touched yet, and I peeled it away, running my finger along the moistened groove left behind. It was as pliable as wet sand, and I scooped out a clump of it and let it fall to the ground. Compelled to dig deeper, I scooped out more until I couldn't reach in any deeper, and the brick above it moved like a loosened tooth. It pulled free easily and a beam of light shot out from the gaping hole. The compulsion to break down the wall took over, and I reached in and grabbed for another brick, and another. The structure of the wall began to tremble as my face drank in the warmth of that glow. My hands, covered in gloppy grit, trembled and bled as I worked, but I didn't feel any pain.

I tore off a fingernail as I pulled at another brick, but it came off as easily as a piece of dead skin. No blood or sensation. Soon there was a hole big enough for me to crawl through, and I dove into it, seeing nothing, yet seeing everything, as the wall began to fall to pieces behind me, its structural integrity too compromised to remain standing. It rained down in a barely audible thunder, like a storm still fifty miles distant.

"Hello?" I called out, unsure who or what would answer. The ground here was soft and pliant, like pillows of silk, making it difficult to move.

Whispering voices flooded my mind. *He hears us . . . who comes . . . John sees . . . feels all . . . who are you . . . who comes here . . .*

"*Daddy?*"

I felt the purest jubilation at the sound of that voice. "Kaya? Kaya, where are you?" I tried to stand, but the floor wobbled and grabbed at my feet, and I went sprawling. Crawling was equally futile; my hands made suction sounds as I pulled them up out of the floor. I managed to gain a couple more feet before my limbs stuck for good, and I began sinking into the strange, ethereal quagmire.

"Don't go to Donum Dei, Daddy. That isn't the right place. Not anymore. They're using . . . using . . ." Her voice was fading away.

"I'm coming to get you, Kaya! Daddy is coming to get you out of there."

Silence followed, and then so faint I could barely hear, "I'm already out. Free as free, Daddy. I'm even floating . . .

Ezekiel still waits for you."

"*Kaya!*"

I tried to wrest myself from my bonds, and my shoulder popped out of its socket. It was the first real pain I'd felt in this place, but I was losing consciousness, and the pain along with the light was fading fast. I fell forward and the floor consumed me.

—

I was lying on the ground, shivering from the breeze drying the sweat off my naked body. Genevieve was gone. My clothes and Christoph's truck were also nowhere in sight, and I realized I must have walked in my sleep. I jumped up and began fumbling my way around the woods, wincing at the pain in my hands and the bloody and raw patch where the nail on my index finger used to be.

"Genevieve?" I cried out, but no answer came. Panic was gnawing at the edge of my mind as I wandered through the woods, alone and naked, with the residue of my strange dream still lingering in my mind like silt from a drained riverbed.

I had absolutely no bearing on my direction until my foot caught beneath something and I fell flat out on the unforgiving undergrowth of the forest floor.

"John? What are you doing?"

I looked behind me and saw Genevieve sitting up, rubbing the sleep out of her eyes. Her full breasts came into the path of the moonlight and turned the skin into porcelain.

"I, uh . . ." I trailed off trying to think of where or how to begin.

"Were you sleepwalking?" she asked.

"We have to go. Now."

"What happened?"

"I believe I broke through to the *Élan Vital* in my sleep," I said.

"That's great! What did you see?"

I swallowed a lump in my throat, but it felt like razor-blades. "I think my daughter is dead. Kaya is dead."

Genevieve got up immediately and knelt beside me. "Are you sure it wasn't just a nightmare? You're under a lot of stress."

"Yes, I'm sure."

"Not all visions are accurate, you know that."

I wanted her to shut up. All she was doing was building up my hopes just to have them dashed again. Already I could feel my mind detaching, going to a place to protect itself from the warhead that was about to go off in my heart. It wasn't at all unlike how I dealt with Linny's death, only this was worse. I was trying to escape the pain, then. This time, I was also outrunning madness.

If Genevieve had tried to convince me again that Kaya was still alive, I didn't hear. After we dressed, and before we headed back to the truck, Genevieve gripped my forearm and pulled me to her in an embrace. She said nothing more about it, and I knew she understood.

Chapter 22

An hour before dawn, we saw a band of light in the distance. The closer we got, I realized it was actually a white wall. I felt a sudden nausea and began to shiver. Genevieve put her hand on my leg.

"Calm down. Tell me what you see."

"I see a wall," I said.

"No, what does your mind see?"

I closed my eyes and tapped into the light that had lurked ever-present just in the corner of my vision like a twinkle of sunlight off a shimmery pond ever since we'd made love. Christoph had bandaged my scraped and bloody hands, and they sat throbbing in my lap, but I tried to ignore them.

A large concrete chamber and a circle of hammock-style beds suspended from the ceiling came into focus. Sleeping in each one was a pale, thin child (or grown man; it was hard to tell), with their arms outstretched as they held the hands of the ones on either side of them. White tubes ran from their foreheads and into a larger tube, which jutted from the base of the skull of the one who sat in the hammock in the center of them all. Ezekiel. "They're feeding off of him," I whispered. "They're like cannibals."

As if they heard me, the Sentinels opened their eyes.

I pulled back and felt a shooting pain in my head.

"John? Are you okay? What did you see?" Genevieve shook my shoulder.

"How did you get your powers as a Sentinel?" I asked her, trying not to sound accusatory but feeling tendrils of it seep into the question anyway. She'd known this but never told me.

She frowned. "I don't know what you're talking about. We were born that way."

"It's not that simple, and you know it," I muttered. "They kept you hooked up to him and he fed you. He's like a human battery. He's the real deal. The rest are basically throwaways, aren't they? Maybe they had glimmers of talent, like you did, but they weren't like him."

Genevieve sat back in her seat, unable to meet my eyes. "I didn't know. Not until recently. And even then, I didn't know Ezekiel was the one. Not until I started putting things together in my mind. My father didn't want to tell me, but I made him."

My anger faded at the look of complete despair on her face. Besides, Genevieve and her father weren't the correct targets. It was the Divine Rite all the way. "Harry wanted to protect you," I said. "Probably didn't even want to admit out loud what he had witnessed."

"This also means the Sentinels will be useless without Ezekiel, if or when he dies. And they won't be of much use to us in our fight, either. Some of them will likely die with him."

"Maybe that's why they want me. And my daughters."

She frowned, and I realized she didn't know what I meant. Didn't know the crux of this whole issue.

"Ezekiel is my brother, Genevieve."

Her eyes widened with shock. "What? But ... how do you know?"

"Turpin figured it out."

"But if you're his brother, why didn't they take you sooner? Why did they allow you to live freely in God's Hope?"

All good questions, but I found myself growing irate again. "How should I know? Maybe they didn't realize it until I brought myself to their attention. Maybe the other Sentinels saw something through Ezekiel. At any rate, I feel a lot like I'm being manipulated through this whole thing from afar. I wouldn't be surprised if they were waiting for us in that Cradle right now."

"Then what should we do?" she asked.

"We do what they want, of course. We have to rescue our people. And someone has to make them pay." Fury coursed through my blood like jagged ice chips.

Christoph pulled off the road into a thicket of trees, still well shy of the Cradle's walls. There were no weeds or nets from where I could see. Maybe it was special technology. Maybe it was psychic power. Christoph dropped the tailgate, pulled out the bag of grenades, and handed us each one of the small air tanks, which we slung over our shoulders. Genevieve loaded her pistol and put spare bullets in her pockets. I took a pistol as well, though I didn't feel I would need it for long. My weapon of choice was inside my head, and my ammunition was behind those walls.

Christoph pulled a green metal case from the truck and opened it up. A large tubular gun, about two feet long, rested inside. "What's that for?" I asked.

"How did you think we'd get the grenades behind the walls?" he asked.

"Oh." I hadn't thought that far ahead.

"How are we going to deal with the Heretics?" Genevieve asked. "They may not be susceptible to the gas."

Something occurred to me. "I think we'll be able to handle them just fine. Their loyalties are not with the Rite. They're prisoners too, remember." I pulled out the wooden whistle Anansi had given me and felt a pang of grief over his loss, but I understood what his sacrifice meant and intended to let that legacy continue to do its work for us.

"Let's go," Christoph said, and we followed him into the field of high grasses toward the Cradle.

—

Fifteen minutes later, we lay huddled three hundred yards shy of the Cradle's looming gate. Christoph gave me a small pair of binoculars, and through them I saw four dark-skinned Heretics who looked every bit as foreboding as Anansi had. They stood in towers overlooking the surrounding landscape, but by some miracle, they hadn't spotted us yet. Or maybe they weren't on duty. They clasped their hands before them in the classic "at ease" position and appeared to be speaking with one another. Around each of their wrists was the same bracelet of red and green twinkling lights like Anansi had worn, that no longer existed.

What happened next would ultimately determine the success of our mission, and I said a little prayer—force of habit, even for a newly minted non-believer—before closing my eyes. I felt no doubt this time.

"Be ready with that launcher," I said to Christoph, and set about concentrating on those bracelets. The light grew stronger, and deep in my mind, I knew I was glowing and that I would be giving away our positions. A buzzing drone sounded just as I felt their bonds obliterate.

The sound of a single Heretic swarm was deafening; my last memories of Anansi would forever be imprinted on my brain. Four of them together made my teeth rattle and tears stream down my face. The sky, which had only just begun to show the first signs of the coming dawn, darkened with the looming insect storm. Genevieve buried her head in her arms, her screams soon lost amid the buzz. The locust cloud, which I estimated to be at least a mile across, barreled toward our position, and paused overhead. The wind from their wings generated enough force to violently ripple our clothes. Christoph pointed the bazooka upward, prepared to fire the first of his grenades at the swarm, but I grabbed his arm and shook my head while mouthing the words, "Not yet."

I braced myself for whatever would come next. Either this was the end of the line, or they would realize I had freed them and they would let us go.

"*Johhhnnn Wellllannnd.*"

The collective voice issuing from the swarm made my insides hurt, and I was certain I could feel blood trickling from my ears.

Twitching, I stood as straight as I could and gazed up at the shifting ocean of insects hovering over head.

"*Showwww ussssss the sssignalllll.*"

The signal? At first, I was at a loss. Was it some sort of

sign language or a magic trick they were looking for? Then it slammed home. Anansi. He was still helping me from beyond the grave. I reached into my pocket, brought out his whistle, and held it up and out to them.

The pitch of the swarm's sound changed, as if to acknowledge what they'd seen. Then, a moment later, the cloud broke up into four distinct groupings and retreated west, where the coming sun had not yet touched the land.

"Thank you, Anansi," I whispered, and then exhaled a great sigh of relief.

We took a few minutes to gather our wits again, and to wait for our hearing to improve a little before moving closer to the gate, not feeling nearly as inclined this time to conceal ourselves. No alarms had been sounded yet. Perhaps the people inside hadn't realized their watch had departed for good. Either way, we were in it for real now. No backing down until we could claim victory.

"Christoph, you'd better go with that launcher," Genevieve said. The big German didn't hesitate. He got down on one knee and loaded his bazooka. Leaning back slightly to get the right trajectory, he fired just as the warble of the Cradle's alarm rose into the purple sky. He didn't wait to see if it landed before loading another into the chute and firing again. He shot four of them before giving us the nod to go ahead. Already, a cloud of white mist was rising up into the air, and we could hear people screaming.

There was no question about how we would get in. That's what they needed me for. I reached out with my mind, felt for the gate's lock, and heard a thundering crash as it, and the gate itself, an immense expanse of wood planks and steel hinges standing approximately twelve feet high, blew apart into a rain of splinters and shrapnel. We fumbled our masks over our faces and climbed through the gaping hole and into the Cradle.

I nearly stumbled over a tangled mass of black-robed bodies just behind the gate. It was hard to tell how many of them were unconscious from the drug in the grenades, or knocked out by the shockwave that took down the gate. A few dismembered body parts lying amid the carnage told me it was probably a mixture of both.

I looked up and saw a group of agents already wearing masks blocking the way in. Red spears glowed in their white-gloved hands.

Genevieve fired her gun before I did, but I was close behind. The men fell in a spray of bullets to join their brothers, their spears clattering to the ground and losing their crimson glow.

The first thing I noticed was that the Cradle compound was a cluster of large, round huts with louvered windows, which had been opened to let in the air and now, to our advantage, the opium gas. Straight back was a stucco building that looked a bit like a Divine Rite Fellowship, with a large crucifix on top. A little more than just raw intuition told me it was also where they kept the Sentinels. I could feel Ezekiel's call from in there.

A few more unmasked Rite stooges ran out from between the buildings and directly into the mist of gas from a nearby grenade. Christoph raised his gun and waited to see if they would fall without his help. They did.

We walked a little farther and found a number of HOG

agents sprawled in open doorways, even with masks on. "That's odd. They have masks, but the gas got them anyway," I said.

"Those aren't gas masks. Not exactly," Christoph said, but he didn't stick around long enough to elaborate.

"Halt, you filthy Nil. Repent before you die!"

I whirled around to see another member of the Rite, his face clad in a black respirator. In one hand he held an electric stick. In the other was an enormous silver cross with a long blade at one end, a blasphemous weapon if there ever was one, but I wasn't surprised to see it in a place like this. His cold blue eyes reminded me of Reverend Blackwell from way back in God's Hope, the one who had been so offended by my one-dollar tithe contribution that he'd gotten this whole show running by siccing the Hand of God on me. But this wasn't Blackwell. This man had a lot more gray hair, and gold piping on his robes that spoke of a rank much higher than a small town sermon-giver.

"What did you do with my daughter? Where is Kaya?"

The man frowned for a moment and then the corners of his eyes crinkled with what I could only assume was a smile. "Ah yes . . . The girl in the Sanctuary. Last I saw her, she was repenting, crying out to God Himself."

White filled my vision momentarily like a flashbulb, and a warm chunky spray covered my face. When I could see clearly again, I saw the stooge lying on the ground, his head looking like a burst melon.

More gunfire erupted from the other side of the compound, cutting into the shock over what I'd just done. I ran in that direction first, even though my mind was screaming at me to find Kaya. She was here, somewhere. Dead or alive. Please, I prayed to whoever was listening, let me be wrong about the worm of dread wriggling in my gut.

I ran between two of the huts to find Genevieve gunning down two more Rite officers while jabbing one behind her with an electric stick she must have acquired during the fight. The old man quivered from the voltage and fell to the ground with smoke rising from his smoldering robes. It wasn't the first time, nor would it be the last, that I was grateful she was on my team.

"I think that's the bulk of them," she said, her voice muffled by the blood-spattered mask on her face. "Let's search the huts. Beware any stragglers."

I ducked into the nearest building and found scores of unconscious, emaciated people lying in bunks. A younger man in a black robe knelt in the center of the room. An enormous gold cross hung from his neck, and he wore a respirator on his face.

"Please, don't kill us! We're defenseless!" he begged. I thought of all the lives his people had destroyed, what had happened to my daughters and my wife, and how this man—this *captor*—was using these people as cover to save his own life. Coward. I felt no urge to give him quarter, but he would have a better death than he deserved. I leveled the pistol at his head and pulled the trigger, grateful the women and children lying only feet away weren't awake to see. His eyes rolled like marbles as blood ran like a teardrop between them, and he fell backward.

I examined the emaciated prisoners more closely. There seemed to be no organization in terms of ages or genders.

Just shaved heads in tattered uniforms with identification numbers on the breast pockets. The little girls looked every bit as frail as the old men did. No Harry and no Kaya, though.

I checked the pulses of each one and found some to be very faint, but they were all alive. Most of the gas had dissipated by now, so I thought they would be okay until we got them out. I left the doors open in the hopes the fresher air would circulate.

Outside, I found Christoph busy busting in the door of the main building with one enormous shoulder. Genevieve was already diving into another hut and I took the one beside it. This one was worse off than the first. More bunks stacked to the ceiling, filled with starved bodies, many covered in cuts and stitches and surgical scars. They'd been experimented on, I realized with mounting rage. Many were too weak to move, let alone acknowledge my presence. A few lay with their glassy eyes staring at the ceiling. They still breathed, but they likely wouldn't survive the effects of the gas.

"Daddy!" I heard someone cry.

I jumped, at first thinking it was Kaya, and darted from the hut and into the one across the way, where Genevieve stood above Harry, trying to affix a spare air canister to his sleeping face. I was happy to see the man was still alive, but part of me hated them both a little right then.

Harry looked as if someone had taken to him pretty hard. His face was puffy and bruised, and dried blood crusted in his beard and mustache, but at least he was still alive. My hope, however meager, that I would find Kaya alive, was waning by the second. She would have been here with him if they'd intended to keep her alive.

"You stay here with him while I go and find Kaya," I said. "And take out any of the ones in black robes who have enough life in them to beg for mercy."

Genevieve looked at me, eyes wide with fright, likely from the gore covering my face, but she nodded. "Absolutely. I'll be here."

When I got to the main building, Christoph was just stepping back outside. His face was pale and drawn, which was saying a lot for him.

"Is it clear?" I asked.

He seemed to think about it for a minute, but then he gave his head a nearly imperceptible shake. I moved to rush past him when one implacable hand gripped my shoulder and held me back.

"Let me pass," I warned. I didn't know if the flashbulb thing would happen again, and I didn't want it to, but I was a time bomb right then.

"I took her down," he said. "So you wouldn't see what I saw." His face softened and I saw the briefest glimpse of what was in his mind, and I leaned over and threw up, barely managing to rip the air mask off my face in time.

"I'm coming with you," he said, but I shooed him away.

"No. No, this is all me. I own this. She's my daughter. See to the others."

I didn't wait to see if he listened. I just staggered into the building, mindless of the robed bodies I stepped on just inside the door. The cavernous interior opened on to an enormous sanctuary flanked with hard, white pews. Banks of tiny candles stood to either side of a monolithic dais, behind which hung a gigantic, rustic cross that appeared to have been hewn from a single piece of wood. Garlands of ivy grew around it in thick, green spirals, reminiscent of the serpent weeds, and perched in the center was not Jesus, but a grim-faced oil portrait of Holy Uniter Urban the Fourth, a sickening display of idolatry.

Three hallways branched off the sanctuary, but I took the one going toward the back, which I believed would lead me outside, where Christoph's vision had been. I stumbled over a few more bodies on my way—they'd been shot—and my shoes crunched on something brittle. Perhaps fingers.

The dark, narrow passageway ended at a wooden door standing open just enough to let in a crack of new daylight. I pushed it open and felt the strength fall out of my knees. I hit the stone-flagged ground of a large circular courtyard. Three mammoth, bloodstained crucifixes stood in the center, and Kaya, my beautiful fair-haired girl, lay beneath the center one. Her shirt and jeans were drenched with blood, but her face, ghostly white in this light with her colorless lips and bloodless cheeks, was placid, almost indifferent. It betrayed none of the great pain and fear she must have felt in her final moments. How many times had I seen that same face poking out above a heap of blankets as she slept away these same morning hours in her own bed?

In my moment of pure agony, I didn't see Kaya as the fierce grown woman she'd been when she died, but the pudgy infant I'd raised and bathed and tossed into the air on wings of laughter. I saw the clenched jaw and dagger-like eyes staring down at me the morning after her mother died, challenging me to answer why the world was this way, why things like this should be allowed to happen. I saw that same girl who so wanted to be a grown woman weeping and calling me "Daddy" when she saw the nightmare that lay beyond the net that had sheltered her since birth. And they took this gentle, brave girl and they . . . they crucified her. And for what? For their amusement? To get answers about me she didn't have?

A sound was coming out of my mouth, a dreadful, high-pitched moan that wanted to be a scream if I'd had the strength to make it so. I fell to my knees and crawled to her on my ruined hands and pulled her into my arms. She felt like a block of ice, and her body had already begun to stiffen. I saw the holes in her shirt where they'd stabbed her and forced her to bleed out. A pool of blood lay at the foot of the cross like spilled paint. Her dainty hands and feet had gruesome stigmata driven through their centers, and I saw the huge, crude nails lying nearby. Christoph must have pulled them out, and for that I was grateful. I couldn't have done it.

I drew her closer, wrapping her in my arms as I had on so many sleepless nights during her infancy, when the world and all of its sensations proved too overwhelming for her, and rocked her back and forth, but it was like hugging a piece of granite. The lightness of her human spirit had departed.

Free as free, Daddy, she had said in the dream that hadn't been a dream at all. It had been her calling to me from a place far beyond my reach, where I couldn't go. Not yet. Not as much as I wanted to right then.

The dry twist of my rage helped me gather up whatever power I could to give to her—to fill her again with the abundance of life to which I'd finally gained access. What good was the *Élan Vital* if it couldn't resurrect my dead daughter? But try as I might to channel the light into her, she was impervious. It was like trying to penetrate rock with a feather.

I struggled to my feet with her draped across my arms and walked with her into the sanctuary, where Christoph, Genevieve, and a newly conscious Harry stood waiting for me. Genevieve's face broke apart at the sight of her.

"Oh, John," she murmured, her voice hoarse with tears. But I had no time to acknowledge her. As had been the case after Linny's death, I had no time for anyone else's grief. They would have to console themselves.

I strode past them all, ignoring any offers of assistance, and carried Kaya down the other branching hallway that led to the Sentinel quarters, where Ezekiel still waited. He was alive, and by God, he was going to fix this. Maybe I didn't have the power to do it myself, but he was going to make it right. Make *her* right again.

"John. John ... what are you doing?" Harry asked. His voice was hoarse and weak, but he sounded vital, and I hated him and Genevieve for it. They had each other again, but I was left with nothing and nobody.

"I'm taking my daughter in to get fixed. It's not too late. It hasn't been too long. I heard her last night. She spoke to me."

"It doesn't work that way, John. You're going to—"

I rounded on him, and the look on my face made him stumble backward. He later told me my eyes were burning white. "Stay away, Harry. You really don't want to mess with me right now. Trust me on this."

The big man stood aside and let me pass without another word.

The heavy stone doors into the Sentinel's quarters swung open freely of their own accord and I stepped in to a blinding white chamber. It was just as I'd seen in my vision and also how Genevieve had described it. Sterile and white, with hammocks stretching clear to a vaulted ceiling, each one containing a sleeping, tiny body feeding into Ezekiel, who sat facing me, his eyes—blue like mine, not white—open and staring solemnly.

"What you plan to do will not work, John," he said in a voice barely above a whisper, as if he didn't even have the energy to operate his vocal cords.

"I don't believe you. You healed Saul, you can fix her."

"Her spirit is no longer with her. It cannot be restored."

"Liar!" I screamed. "You think I don't know what you're capable of? They think you're some kind of Messiah! You can fix this, and you will!"

"I am not a Messiah, John. There is no force in this universe that can fill a dead vessel with life. She has gone to the same place I will soon go. It's a better place."

"And where is that?"

"I do not know. Nor does it matter."

"But I saw it! In a dream, I broke through a wall, and she was on the other side. In the . . . in the light."

"Your mind will create whatever path is necessary to achieve enlightenment. What you saw was your brain's way of interpreting something incomprehensible, but you do not know where that is any more than I do, or if it even truly exists. We see what we want to see. Feel what we want to feel. The part of you that knew Kaya was no longer here longed to communicate with her, so you did. Her voice was an echo from your subconscious."

"I don't believe that."

Ezekiel nodded, as if to say that was quite all right with him. "I have one last thing to do before I go."

"Yeah? What?"

He held up the end of one of the tubes that connected to the bigger one running into the back of his head. "I believe in the previous age, they would have called this a download."

"I'm supposed to drill a hole in my head and stick that thing there? And then what? Become like you? You don't look too healthy. Brother."

Ezekiel gave me a weak and terrible smile. "I have not been used very lightly, either. Don't worry. You will never wind up like me." He gestured to the sleeping bodies around him. "You originally wanted to come here for them, but you can do everything they can do, only better. You were meant to do it. I'll give you nearly everything you need. These poor souls ... They should be taken somewhere and nurtured back to health. Your beloved, Genevieve, would be of great service to you this way. She was such a wonderful child, but sad."

He spoke as if he were so much older than her, even though chronologically, they were only maybe a year apart.

"I don't know if I want this," I said. "I'm afraid of what I might do with it." I looked down at Kaya, and the sorrow that washed over me was so great, I nearly blacked out with rage. "I'm so angry."

"Your anger has gotten you far in this fight, but look at everything you have lost along the way. It will destroy even more of the things you love if you don't let it go."

I placed Kaya's body in an empty hammock, and sat before my brother, the strange vessel of great power who would never grow to be a man, who would never know the love of a woman as I had, who was forced to live a life of detachment in the service of unspeakable evil. I felt great sadness wash over me again. It all seemed so damned unfair. I never knew my brother as he should have been, and though I didn't know the sequence of events that led to him being here, I hated my parents for it anyway.

"You and I were meant to share this," he said. "You were the second half of the puzzle, but the Divine Rite could never figure that out. They thought they could wield me through any person who showed any hint of telepathic ability, but that wasn't so. If they had known how vital you truly were, they would have taken you too. But they watched you, waiting for you to show even the smallest trace of ability. You never did, and they gave up on you. Thinking you were normal." He cracked a weak grin. "You sure showed them."

"But what am I supposed to do? Just blow Donum Dei to shreds? My other daughter is in there."

He shook his head. "It doesn't work quite that way. You don't use the power of life to bring death to others, just as you cannot use the power of death to create life, as The Divine Rite has been doing for over a century by killing off those whom they believe do not fit their strict moral construct. The *Élan Vital* can break physical bonds and cause destruction, as you have already demonstrated, but doing so in excess will only hurt you and take away your ability to wield it. Instead, the power should allow you to sow the seeds of compassion, and from compassion comes wisdom. You will use that to lead people down the right path, to heal this planet. What grew here once before will grow again. Perhaps not in your lifetime, but you will set things into motion. You will show the Divine Rite the true path."

"But they would never allow that!" I exclaimed. "They will see me as a threat to their power and try to kill me or use me. They must be stopped with force."

He smiled again, and I felt my years and size dwindle, just as an adult must feel when he tries to usurp his grandfather's wisdom. It was hard to believe he was my younger brother. "I realize I cannot change your mind now. The answers for what you must do will present themselves, when it is time. It is more likely you will find a way I haven't even seen yet."

I had so much more I wanted to ask him, but I could tell he was growing wearier by the minute, and my time was limited. I couldn't let this time pass without knowing something else. "When we broke Anansi's bond, you shared a vision with me and Genevieve, but they were two different ones. Which one is correct?"

"As I said before, we often see what we want to see, or what our minds think we want to see. The future I envisioned showed you standing on a hill. Your respective minds filled in the blanks."

"Oh," I said.

"It is up to you to fulfill what my visions cannot." He shifted a little in his bed. "Our time grows short, John. Is there anything else I can tell you before we proceed?"

I thought for a moment. So many potential answers were right at my fingertips, but I could only pick one question. And it had to be a good one. For instance, could I use the *Élan Vital* to destroy the serpent weeds, or at least find a way to make them work for us instead of against us? Was Beth still at Donum Dei, or was there some truth to Kaya's warning in my dream to stay away?

But of all the questions I could have asked, I chose the only one my heart wanted to know the answer to.

"Do you remember our mother?"

The cool serenity left Ezekiel's face, and he looked every bit the small and defenseless child. "Not in the way you might, I am afraid. They allowed her to stay here and nurse me after I was born. No normal infant would remember this, of course, but I do. Afterward, I'm afraid they did not have much use for her. I see small glimmers of her. I remember how she smelled of cinnamon. I remember her heart and how it hurt for us both. I missed her when she left. Our father . . . I am afraid I know nothing more of him. He did not come with her, and I have never been able to reach his mind." He held up the tube again. "It is time, John."

I sat down beside my brother and took the tube from his hand. "Where do I put this?"

"Not in your head. I am afraid that was another thing the Hand of God had wrong. They were under the impression that the power flowing from me must go into their brains. It works as a temporary measure, but our brains can only hold so much. The *Élan Vital* must flow to you as it flowed from our mother into me."

I was bewildered for a moment, but it soon became clear. "The belly button?"

He nodded.

"Why didn't you suggest that with the others?"

"Because it wouldn't have worked. Think of it this way. Even a man may be stimulated to make milk for his child, to carry it on the outside and care for it as if he gave birth to it. But only a woman holds the true vessel. You and I hold a similar vessel. And it is in there, in your gut."

I couldn't help but be a little amused by the metaphor, as I imagined myself with a uterus in my belly. I placed the tube into my navel and immediately felt it expand to accommodate the small space. It stung, but otherwise felt warm. My insides hummed a little. "I'm ready."

"Goodbye, my brother. Perhaps we'll see each other in greener times," he said. And the light filled the world.

Chapter 23

I awoke with a searing headache that throbbed right behind my eyeballs, which reminded me of the first hangover I had after a night on Turpin's homemade bourbon. The room was pitch-black, and for the moment, I couldn't remember where I was. It was only when I moved a little hard to the left and spilled out onto the cold stone floor that I realized I had been lying in a hammock, and the memory of everything that had just happened slammed into me.

My hands flew to my abdomen, prepared to find blood, a larger hole, a pregnant, distended lump, or at least a whole heap of pain, but none of that was there. I searched for Ezekiel's body, but I found nothing but a tangle of empty fabric where he once sat. The darkness precluded my ability to see more, and I crawled toward a wall, intent on finding a switch, or better yet, the door. After a few minutes of futile searching, a phantom voice wafted up from the deep recesses of my mind. My voice.

You *are the light, stupid.*

"Oh, right." I closed my eyes and thought of the room as I last remembered it, bathed in that effervescent glow that once came from Ezekiel's mind. When I opened my eyes again, I saw that same light. And it was good.

The place where Ezekiel and I had sat was empty, save for the clothes the boy had been wearing, which lay in a puddle as if they'd dropped right from the body they'd been covering. I thought of the way Linny's nightgowns looked lying on the bathroom floor after she'd stepped into a hot bath. The thought of her naturally led to Kaya, who laid in the hammock just as I'd left her. The sight of her brought another wave of grief and anger that not even my solidified conduit to the essential life force could wash away. But then again, the *Élan Vital* was not necessarily composed of all things happy and good. In life, there is also pain, sickness, death, and grief. I would find no relief there.

I wrapped her in some of the blankets lying around and was just gathering her up into my arms again when I heard a loud crash. I stole myself for the possibility of a HOG agent, but it was only Christoph using his body as a battering ram again. He dusted splinters of wood off his shoulder as if he had merely used it to pass through a bead curtain. "We should go soon," he said and let his blue eyes briefly flit down toward my daughter's body.

"We need to take these others too," I said.

"We will make separate trips. Some of the prisoners are awake. The stronger ones are helping us move the weaker ones. Or bury them."

"How many died?" I asked.

Christoph's grim face grew even grimmer. "At least half. They were already too weak."

I nodded. The guilt just kept piling on. "How many do we have?"

"Twelve, not including the sleeping ones here."

"Let's load up as many as we can. I can remain here with the rest until you return," I said.

"Where am I taking them?" he asked.

"Old Babylon. It's ours now."

Christoph bowed his head in agreement. He reached for Kaya too, but I held him back. "I can handle this," I said.

"Yes," he said and paused to pat me on the shoulder before he turned and left the building. I followed close behind and emerged into the dusty street. It was full daylight, but under a gunmetal blanket of clouds, I smelled rain in the air. I prayed to a non-existent God for a flood in the vein of Genesis.

The Cradle's remaining survivors lingered with Genevieve and Harry near the wreckage of the gate. Many of them staggered drunkenly or simply leaned against the wall. Genevieve saw me and jogged over. "I'm staying to help you," she said, and the way she said it left no room for argument.

"I'd like that," I said. "Where are the other bodies?" I was referring to the black-robed goons who had run the place.

"Christoph piled them in the sanctuary."

"Good. That will make things easier." I had a plan, but I wasn't going to say anything yet and she didn't ask. Instead, I just walked with her toward the survivors gathered near the Cradle's entrance, still cradling Kaya's body in my arms. Ordinarily, I would have strained with the effort of holding so much weight, but I refused to let her be a burden to me.

"Have you had a chance to see yourself yet?" Genevieve asked.

"No. Is something different?"

"Well, your hair is completely white now," she replied. I

wasn't surprised. Everything about me felt old.

The survivors looked at me with a mixture of caution and wonder, and I detected a thread of hope in them all. They also appeared to be waiting for me to say something. Why not? I was their leader now. I set Kaya's bundled up body down with care. "You'll all find a safe haven in Old Babylon," I told them. Of course, how safe it would remain was a mystery, but it was best not to give them anymore to worry about for the time being.

One of them, a girl not much younger than Kaya had been, stepped forward. "Will my ma and da be there?" she asked.

I shook my head. "I don't think so, hon." The girl nodded as if that was what she expected and returned to the fold.

Christoph spoke up. "I will get the truck and load everyone up. You will stay here while we are gone?" he asked.

"Absolutely not. This place will cease to exist once everyone is outside," I said. I'd no more use a Cradle for temporary shelter than I would have danced on my daughter's soon-to-be grave. "Genevieve and I will bury my daughter some place to the west and then head toward Old Babylon on foot. After you drop off these people and help Saul and Turpin figure out who is who, you can head back out and meet us part way."

With orders in hand, he gave me a slight bow. "*Auf Wiedersehn*," he said, turning on his heel to head back through the gate. Harry came over next.

"I can't thank you enough for everything, John. You are every bit the man I estimated you to be from the first time we met."

"You knew Ezekiel was my brother," I said to him.

He stared at me for a minute, his bushy brows knitted

in the center of his forehead as tears welled up in his eyes.
"Yeah, I guess I did. Not at first, but I put two and two together not long after we moved to town and I learned your
name. I'm sorry I didn't tell you. I just didn't think it was my
place."

"It's okay. You're right, and I'm not sure I would have believed you anyway. I learned when I needed to learn. Just tell
me one thing. Did my parents . . . did they go easily?"

He struggled with the question. Not like someone trying
to lie, but like someone trying to figure out an easy way to
deliver a hard truth. I admired him for it, but there would be
no worse truth than the one lying dead at my feet.

"Your mother was a lovely woman. It was her who I think
eventually convinced my Esther to join the resistance. When
she gave birth to Ezekiel, she and Esther both were busy
making plans to escape, but then they were caught . . . I don't
think you need me to tell you what happened next."

He was right. Neither woman died well. The Rite's toler-
ance for defiant women was evident even before I found my
crucified daughter.

"My father? What of him?"

Harry shook his head. "I'm sorry, John. I never saw him.
He never came in with your mom. I don't know if he was sent
off to a separate Cradle, or . . ."

"Or if he cut himself a deal and turned her in," I said. I
didn't want to believe such a thing, but I only knew him
through a child's eyes, and my memories of him were spotty
at best.

"I guess that's possible," Harry said. "I'm sorry I didn't
have better answers for you."

"Not your fault, my friend. I just appreciate any answers at all at this point." And the main answers I was taking away from that conversation were that my mother was dead, but my father might still be out there. An old man, to be sure. Not much younger than Turpin. I was going to find him.

Harry touched my shoulder. "You okay, friend?"

"I'm fine. Let's see about getting these people to safety."

"You got it. They'll receive the best possible care in Babylon. Maybe they can learn to fight the old-fashioned way."

"Will they live?" I asked.

The big man beamed over at his daughter. "If this one is any indication, John, I think they'll be fine." He pulled Genevieve to him and gave her a tight squeeze. I tried to quench my jealousy, and bent down to pick up Kaya. Harry's face fell when he saw her.

"I'm so damn sorry, John," he said. "She was a hell of a young woman."

"It's not you who should be sorry," I said savagely. "Best of luck on the journey back." I stepped past him and the gawking survivors with Genevieve close behind. I had to get out of there and away from Harry's pitiful gaze before I threw up.

We walked long and far through the fields west of the compound, the high grasses bristling against our legs the only sound. Craggy mountains lay against the horizon like a fallen Goliath, and I felt their pull. Donum Dei was somewhere up there.

We crested a hill and I came to a stop. The land fell away in a graceful slope and opened up to a small, green-brown valley below, free of the serpent weeds. A few houses dotted the landscape, but even from this distance, I could see their peeling paint, overgrown grasses, crooked or missing shutters; they had long been abandoned. "Here. This is a good spot," I said, and placed my daughter gently on the ground. Genevieve wept silently.

"It's a beautiful place to put her," she said. "And you can't see that cursed place from here either." I looked behind me, and she was right. The Cradle was lost to our backs. She asked if I'd need help, but I shook my head. We hadn't brought shovels, but who needed shovels when you could move things with your mind?

I reached my hand toward the ground. I wasn't sure if that was absolutely necessary for what I needed to do, but it felt natural, and I had no one to teach me otherwise. I saw each individual particle of soil, each blade of grass, as something light and malleable, and as I moved my hand, a section of the earth parted, creating a deep brown gash. I thought of Moses and the Red Sea. I also mused over how a week ago I couldn't even cook dinner without help. Now I was digging my daughter's grave with little more than a thought and the swipe of a hand.

A wild and inappropriate urge to laugh at the sad absurdity of the whole thing bubbled up in my chest, but I buried it, as I was now burying one of the few sources of joy I had left in this world. I placed her into the hole and we stood there beneath the cruel sunshine, gazing into my Kaya's new and permanent home.

"Would you like to say a few words?" Genevieve asked, her voice choked with tears.

I shook my head. "She knows." I knelt down and began pushing the damp earth back into the hole.

"Don't you want to do it the other way?"

"No. Not for this. I want to get my hands dirty. Need to."

Genevieve didn't argue, but hunkered down and started helping me move the soft and yielding earth not yet sucked dry by serpent weeds. Before I sent in the handful that would hide Kaya's form forever, I told her goodbye for the last time. The rest was a blur.

Working together, we filled the hole quickly. There wasn't quite enough to fill it back in all the way. There never is.

"Would you like to gather some stones? For a monument?" Genevieve asked.

I spotted something familiar in the distance and pointed. "Right there," I said. "Come with me."

She followed me for the next ten minutes toward the stand of trees where, against all odds and expectations, a flowering plum tree was growing amid a coarse tangle of serpent weeds, the first of both I'd seen in a while. I pulled off a branch of blossoms and carried it back, where I planted it in the dirt of my daughter's grave.

It was small, but it wouldn't be for long. Kaya would make it grow.

"It's beautiful, John," she murmured and clasped my hand. Our filthy fingers intertwined just as the skies opened up above and let loose a curtain of rain. I was grateful. It allowed me to cry as much as I wanted to in secret.

Genevieve led us down the other side of the hill toward the darkened houses. "We'll be able to sit this storm out, at least," she said. I was in no hurry to get out of the rain. It made me feel cleaner than I had in days, but I needed somewhere to sit. I was more tired than I had ever been in my life.

Soaked through our skin, we reached the nearest house after a few minutes. Thunder rumbled overhead, and I knew it was going to get worse before it got better. We dodged under the porch overhang of the tiny ramshackle that once had been white, but was now the color of sun-bleached wood with flecks of white paint clinging to the boards.

Genevieve knocked on the door. Although the place looked empty, and I could feel no one's presence, common consideration still felt necessary. Civilization might have been dead, but we were still civilized folks. I peeked in through one window and saw the humped shapes of furniture highlighted by meager light spilling in from another window farther in. There was a fine coat of dust on everything.

"Try the door," I said.

It swung open easily, and we ducked inside.

The front room was tiny, the air stale, but it was a good enough place to dry off. I closed the door and we stood listening to the torrential shower thrum away on roof. "I'm going to find some candles," Genevieve said, but I held her back.

"No need." I illuminated the room's dust-coated light fixture by touching the glass.

"Good trick," she said, pleased. "I bet you could dry our clothes too."

"Good idea."

I raised my hands and put them on her shoulders. Water sluiced from us both and landed on the floor in an unceremonious smack. Her eyes widened with awe, and I think I detected a little bit of fear in them as well.

"John . . . do you even know how you're doing it?"

I shook my head. "It's like breathing."

The accomplishment did little to marvel me. Whatever abilities I'd gained from Ezekiel felt almost banal to me now. What use was such power if it couldn't bring your dead daughter back to life?

Genevieve headed into the kitchen and began rummaging through the cupboards. They were mostly empty but for a few errant jars of green beans someone had put up for the winter some years ago. There was also a tin of dried tealeaves rendered nearly to dust, and a package of jerky. "Looks like breakfast," she said. After popping open one of the jars, she sniffed cautiously. "The beans haven't gone over." She plucked one out, ate it, and handed it to me. "I'll make some tea."

She opened the kitchen's small black stove, saw there was still some wood inside, and lit it with one of the matches in a jar near the back burner. After filling the kettle with rain water and sitting it on top of one of the burners, she came back and sat down.

"You should eat, John."

"I had a few beans," I told her. They had a strong brine flavor, and a few of them went a long way. Paired with the salted meat—I assumed it was venison—my body felt a little less taxed, though I imagined one of Turpin's concoctions would go a long way toward making me feel better.

"What do you imagine happened to these people?" she asked.

It was a silly question, but I knew she was only trying to make conversation. "I don't think you could ever live so close to a Cradle and not become one of its first inhabitants," I said.

She fell silent again, the gaping chasm between us feeling all the deeper. How do you fill such moments with words, like so much dirt into an open grave? Instead of talking, I just pulled her closer and buried my face in her hair. "What comes next?" she asked.

I thought for a moment. Going to Old Babylon had been part of the plan, but I didn't want to go back the way we came, not when we were already out here. Sure, we could procure weapons and support there, but I needed to push forward. Our goal was what lay in the mountains, and I no longer needed a guide. That information now lay in my brain as securely as my ability to light a room without having to flip a switch. But we had one thing to do before setting off for Donum Dei to rescue my one remaining daughter.

"We're going to finish what we started," I said. Before Genevieve could respond, the kettle began its high whistle, signifying that its contents had reached the boiling point.

—

"Are you sure they're all gone?" Genevieve asked as we stood on the breast of a hill overlooking the walled-in cluster of huts we'd stormed early the previous morning. Our vantage point allowed us to see its deserted streets and the crushed gate. I could also now see the crucifixes behind the church, and I forced myself to swallow more angry fire.

The place looked about as lifeless as the house we'd just left. Christoph and the remaining survivors were well along the road to Old Babylon, if they weren't there already. I wasn't sure how long it would take for any Divine Rite reinforcements to arrive on the scene, or if they even would. We'd killed or set free anyone who could raise a distress signal.

"The place is dead," I told her.

"Is there anything I can do?"

"Yes. Close your eyes." Ezekiel had told me that I couldn't use my (our) ability to kill, but I didn't think it applied to inanimate buildings that had once housed so much misery. I preferred to call it a cleaning job. I raised my hands toward the cursed facility and directed my energy toward the ground, which began to shake. The huts, which were shoddily constructed, fell into piles of matchsticks. But I wasn't after that one. I wanted the big white stone abode just beyond it. The House of Lies and Death.

I pushed harder.

Soon, an explosion ripped apart the early morning, throwing up an enormous wave of dirt. Genevieve hit the ground and screamed. Large chunks of stone and debris flew a mile into the sky, as if the site had been struck by a giant meteor. The shockwave from the blast knocked me off my feet. The veins in my temples throbbed painfully, a freshet of blood poured from my nose and down the back of my throat. Nevertheless, I struggled back up to inspect the damage.

A few minutes later, the dust cleared, revealing a smoking black pit where the Cradle once stood. The only thing visible among the rubble was the enormous crucifix from the sanctuary's steeple, broken in two. A few chunks of concrete the size of boulders lay just a few feet away from us in the grass, but we were otherwise unscathed.

"You can open your eyes now," I said.

Genevieve's face went white when she saw the destruction. "My God," she whispered. She became more afraid when she looked at me and saw the blood from my nose making a bib on the front of my shirt. "John, you're bleeding!"

"It'll pass. It's just a bloody nose."

"It's not just your nose," she said. "Your eyes . . . The whites are red. Your ears are bleeding too. What did you do?"

Another jolt ripped through my head, and my knees buckled. Genevieve handed me a towel we had taken from the house we'd slept in. She also gave me a canteen filled with water. I drank deeply and rinsed out my mouth before lying back with the towel over my nose.

"You can't do that again," she said. "You've only just started doing this. We should have just gone in there and burned it down ourselves."

"I would have rather died than set foot back in there," I muttered. She didn't argue, but instead helped clean me up. I put on a different shirt and a few minutes later, we set our backs to the place for good, toward the mountains.

Chapter 24

We walked for nearly two days before I realized something was very wrong. We passed through entire towns and neighborhoods where nets were torn down and every house and place of business was empty. Weed-choked roads nearly impossible to walk on were equally deserted of vehicles and fellow travelers alike. We were able to stock up on some provisions in one abandoned store that was barely standing after years of exposure to the weeds, but it was clear the Rite or nature itself had eaten away at the countryside until not a single soul, righteous or otherwise, lived in it.

But it was the morning of the second day that I came to the conclusion we were lost. It wasn't that I had simply made a wrong turn at a bend. I had no directional bearings whatsoever. When I asked Genevieve if we were still heading northwest, she looked at me with her brows knitted together, as if she too just realized we were completely turned around.

"I assumed you knew where we were headed."

Yes, I did. Or I *had*. Donum Dei was glowing in my mind like a homing beacon right up until I realized it wasn't any longer. Problem was, I hadn't noticed exactly when that happened. It was like a slow leak in a tire. One minute you had air, the next you were flat. Until that morning, *Élan Vital* had been like an open doorway between regular and heightened perception, but now something sat in its way, like a stone blocking a road. Or the moon eclipsing the sun. I was now a mere mortal, every bit as weak and unseeing as I was before I ever met Ezekiel, and I suddenly felt overwhelmed and naked.

"It's gone," I told her, sitting down on the side of the road. "I got nothing."

She sat down too. "When do you last remember having it? Calm down and just think back."

"I'm pretty sure I still had it after destroying the Cradle, but . . . maybe not. I wasn't doing so well after that."

"That's putting it lightly, John."

She was right. My nose had bled for over an hour and I had a headache so terrible I could barely hold my head up. We ended up setting a general course west and walked for the rest of that day, but most of it was a complete daze. Genevieve found us an old barn to sleep in, and the next morning (after stuffing anything remotely edible from the property's mostly-empty root cellar into Genevieve's satchel), we continued on the same path. Sleep had improved the headache, but I hadn't even questioned my lack of extra perception. My mind was occupied by other things, like my dead daughter and the sound of her voice and the way she used to look at me with her crooked grin when I was being silly. And the last moment I saw her alive, that terrified sliver of her face in Akiva Paine's house before Harry closed the privy lid and the Rite took her away from me forever.

Also, on a more pragmatic level, it hadn't become much of a habit yet to have such abilities, and so I hadn't grown to miss them when they were gone. I told Genevieve all of this as we sat on the side of the road.

"This has all been too much for you. Between everything you've lost and not knowing how to control these abilities, I think it's understandable that you're feeling blocked right now."

"Do you think it will be back?" I asked.

"I can't say for sure, but I think it will be. Ezekiel imbued you with his abilities. They're a part of you now. I would tell you to relax and not worry about it, but I realize what a waste of time that would be. Still . . . I think you should try."

"Relax. Got it."

She sat silent for a moment, her hand resting beneath her chin in that classic posture of deep thought. "I don't know how you do it or if it's even possible, John, but you have to find peace somehow. It's the only way you'll ever be able to control this thing you have, that you were given. Just find moments of peace however you can."

"I don't think I've had that since all this started. Well . . . except for a certain night in the woods." I looked at her and grinned, hoping that would smooth some of the tension between us a little.

She blushed and tipped me a wink. "Cheeky. But that's beside the point, dear. I think there's something to be said for being natural about it. Maybe that's another reason the Sentinels were always kept sedated. The *Élan Vital* is like a feisty little dog that struggles to get away if it's held too tightly. The more you try to control it, the less you can. I think you just need to let it flow through you and stop trying. But I'm sure you know that."

Her use of the phrase "flow through you" reminded me of the one time I felt most in touch with the light. It was when she and I had made love. We hadn't done it again since then, but then again, neither of us had much been in the mood. The weight of my grief far eclipsed my lust, even the needy kind.

"I think you're right," I said. "I need to get hold of my emotions a little, although I don't think I could ever be like Ezekiel was."

"No, you will definitely never be like Ezekiel, and I wouldn't want you to be. He was like a butterfly raised in a jar. He was given air and food, but he was never allowed to fly among the flowers and sunlight. Your passion drives you. But I do think you need to find some silver lining in all of this mess, John, or you might never find your way back to the light again."

I placed my hand on her leg. "If anything good has come out of this whole horrible mess, it's you. You're the only one keeping me sane right now." We kissed briefly, and when she pulled away, reluctantly, she was watching me closely with a grin on her face.

"Did that work? Do you see the light now?" she asked.

I laughed. It had been so long since I'd done it that it felt almost foreign. But it also felt genuine and good. "Afraid not."

She slapped her leg in playful frustration. "Shucks. Better luck next time, I guess."

She stood up and stretched and then reached down to help me up. "I believe we're still heading west, so at least there's that," she said. "We can keep walking until we hit the ocean, but I have a feeling we'll need to turn northward at some point. Let's hope we didn't miss our chance back there somewhere."

"I don't think we're that far off track. We'll come upon something soon."

We walked on. The sun was long past its zenith by the time we came to another stop in the road. I could see a structure through the trees that looked about as out of place as an ice rink in the middle of the desert. For the life of me, I couldn't remember a time I had ever seen something so colorful. I stopped Genevieve and pointed to it. "What do you suppose that is?" I asked.

She peered a little closer. "It's . . . a house, I guess. How do you suppose someone got away with painting it that way? The Rite would never have allowed it."

"Well, who's to say they did? It could be vacant like the others." However, as soon as I said that, I knew I was wrong. As we drew closer to the place, I noticed how green and well manicured the lawn was. I also noticed neat rows of tulips springing out of the dirt and mentioned to Genevieve how odd that was. Tulips never grew so late in the season, and they rarely grew outside of the nets.

It was a squat, one-story brick structure, but each brick had been painted a different color in random order. Red, green, blue, yellow, white, gray. The roof was a vivid green sheet of aluminum, and so clean it gleamed in the sun. Whoever lived in the place had cleared the surrounding foliage and built fences around all sides but the front, with each plank painted a color to match the bricks. There was no question someone inhabited the house. It was far too maintained, and it just had the feeling of life all around it, unlike every other desolate hovel we'd passed on our journey.

"Are we going up there?" I asked.

"Of course we are. We need all the help we can get."

"How do you know it won't be a trap?"

"Look, anyone who paints their house like this is definitely not Divine Rite."

"Yeah, but the person is probably a lunatic. Didn't you ever hear of Hansel and Gretel?"

"Just come on!" she said and hiked up the driveway to the front door, where more flowers grew from colorful glazed pottery. We looked at each other for a second before she raised a fist to knock, but before she could make contact, the door flew open. A stocky man with a shock of curly hair and a long, shaggy beard stepped out wielding a long, white staff that looked suspiciously like the ones used by the Hand of God.

My heart sank.

"Who the hell are you?" he demanded. "Not like any goddamned Divine Rite puke I've ever seen. What is this? A new tactic? Plain clothes? Smoking hot redheads?" He glanced at Genevieve and gave her a crooked grin and a wink. "Not that I mind, gorgeous."

I cleared my throat. "We're, uh, not Divine Rite."

"Prove it," the man said.

"They killed my wife and daughter, and kidnapped my other daughter. I destroyed the Cradle to the east of here, and I'm headed to Donum Dei to kill the Holy Uniter myself." The man studied my face for a moment to see if I was either telling the truth or more crazy than he was. Then he lowered the staff.

"Shitty deal, man. I thought I had it bad." He eyed Genevieve again. "You two wanna come in? I got tea, cookies, potato chips, burgers, steak. Just kidding. I wish I had a burger. If I'd wished for one more thing, I would have wished for endless burgers. Also, something else you should know, I don't get much company these days, so I'm probably not gonna make much sense to you." He stopped, realizing that Genevieve and I were still standing on the porch staring at him. "Well? What're you standing there for? Get on in before the bugs follow you."

We stepped inside and found it to be just as colorful as the outside. Large pictures hung on the walls. Some were of mountainous desert landscapes. Others were abstract streaks of color on canvas. But it was the mass of paper covering every horizontal surface that really caught my eye. Maps, drawings, more paintings. Some looked like they were ripped out of books while others were on big rolls I didn't think existed anymore.

"Sorry for the mess," he said, as if we hadn't just dropped in on him unannounced. He gathered up the papers covering the two chairs flanking an ancient Victrola. Turpin had one very similar, or he used to.

"I do have tea and cookies. I didn't lie about that. Would you like some?"

We both nodded our heads, still too shocked to say anything. We'd never seen a house like this, and the man who lived in it was unlike anyone we'd met so far. He was too thick, for one thing. People in our world didn't usually grow plump. There wasn't enough good food to go around most of the time, and the Rite tended to frown upon the sin of gluttony such that things like weight and waist measurements were factored into Justification results.

"You two got names?"

"Oh. Uh, my name is John Welland, and my companion here is Genevieve Camden. We came from God's Hope."

The man reached out his beefy hand and shook each of ours. His curly hair fell into his face as he did, and he flipped it back with the air of good practice. "Zehnson Braxtany at your service." He looked at our bewildered expressions and laughed. "Just call me Zehn. I'll never forgive my parents. They were a little too New Agey for their own goods." He retreated to his small kitchen, put water on to boil and began arranging small, round cookies on a plate.

Genevieve was the first to ask the question we'd both been wondering about. "If you don't mind us asking, Zehn, where are you from?"

He poked his shaggy head out of the kitchen and gave her that playful grin again. I wanted to be jealous of his flirting, but I was too caught up in the new surroundings. Besides, Genevieve was plenty good at holding her own.

"You don't think I'm from around here? The ladies do say I'm out of this world." He winked again. She blushed a little and shifted in her seat.

"Either that, or you've found a great way to avoid the Divine Rite."

Zehn's smile faded just a bit. "No, I wouldn't say that. But you know how they are. They figure they'll just nab me in Justification, send me a Supper, and have done with the whole matter in less than a year, and if that's the case, I might as well live it up a little. Like being in a Sin Bin, but without being surrounded by stinking drunks."

"So you know about the Suppers at least," I said.

He came out of the kitchen holding a tray with a teapot, saucers, butter cookies, and dishes of stuff that looked like honey and jam. "Well yeah, I know about the Suppers. Saw all of my neighbors get taken down by them over the last ten years or so. Then my own family one by one. My wife died a decade ago. About five years later, they got my two sons. They never did get over their ma dying, and started cutting up almost immediately. Teenagers are hard enough to control as it is. Add something like the Divine Rite into the equation, and it's a wonder any of them make it out alive."

I swallowed my grief as best I could in a sip of tea. I wasn't going to break down in front of this man, no matter how easily he'd just salted my wounds.

"The dogs and cats went not long after my boys. The Rite didn't take them. They just keeled over when everyone else left. Probably couldn't take the loneliness, or living with me. I'm a snorer. Drove the wife crazy."

He reached forward and grabbed a handful of cookies and started popping them into his mouth one after the other. Sandy crumbs dropped down the front of his gray shirt. I understood something immediately about Zehn. He had to be either moving or talking constantly to avoid thinking about the things that really hurt him. I would have bet he talked a lot to himself just to fill in any moments where quiet reflection could occur.

He washed back his cookies and kept talking. "A few months after my second son died, I went and painted the house. I ate what I wanted. I stopped going to church of course. Justification's coming up in just a few short weeks, but I've already decided I'm not gonna do it. I painted the house like Turner's favorite blocks. Turner was my youngest. The flowers were for my wife. I planted them in the spring, but they're still alive for some reason. The posters were for my other boy who loved to paint. I'm going to hole up here until my time passes, and I'll see if I can fight them off when they come for me."

"With that?" I asked, pointing to the white staff now leaning against the wall next to the doorway. The other man nodded.

"Oh yeah. That's one of theirs. Found it embedded in a tree in the woods here behind the house. It doesn't glow or anything. If it did, they'd probably have homed in on me by now, and I wouldn't be gracing you lovely people with my company. I can't wait to use it on one of them."

"It's a good feeling. I've done it," Genevieve said. Zehn looked at her like he wanted to simultaneously worship her and rip her clothes off. She shifted in her seat again, a smile touching her lips.

"What are all these papers for?" I asked, trying to change the subject.

The man's eyes softened. "Those are my stories. My secret art, as I like to call it."

I thought longingly of my red leather journal. "I did a little writing once."

"It's a tough profession to break into nowadays, what with the Rite scooping up and killing any author whose books don't exclusively deal in the holy thees and holy thous. But it's the one remaining artform you can still carry on with relative safety from the lookie-loos, provided you have a good hiding place. But I was a map-maker in my regular life, so I had plenty of excuses to have a lot of paper and pens around."

He grabbed more cookies and shoved them in his mouth. It seemed like he was doing it to hold back tears.

"You know how I said if I'd had one more wish, I would have wished for endless burgers?" His mouth was full of crumbs, but I could understand him well enough.

"Yes," I said.

"I once wished for my wife and kids to leave me alone forever so I could just write. And I can't tell you how many times I wished those damn cats would kick the bucket when they were meowing up a storm or begging for food during a particularly intense scene. They were secret, dark wishes, the kind of thing a person only pulls out when they're too busy not appreciating how lucky they are. But they came true anyway, one by one, little by little. And then one day, I was all alone. Ever since, I've been trying to see if it makes it easier for me to do what I want."

"Does it?" I asked.

He shook his head. "No, man, it doesn't. But I'm making the best of it. I asked for it, after all."

"You're being too hard on yourself," Genevieve said.

"Not at all. I'm just owning my hand."

"I also understand that," I said.

"Yeah, something tells me you do. Can I ask where you're headed? I feel like I've been in the spotlight long enough."

"We told you. Donum Dei," Genevieve said.

"Yes, I know that, gorgeous, but you're not taking the most direct route either. I mean, if you want to take the scenic tour through God's Country, that's fine and all, but if you want to get there before the next decade, you'll need to backtrack and head north."

"I had a map in my head, but I lost it," I said, realizing how absurd that sounded when I said it aloud. Zehn threw back his head and barked hearty laughter.

"Everyone thinks they know the way to Donum Dei." He paused and tilted his head. "That could almost be a song. Anyway, people's sense of direction starts to get funny the closer they get to the place. Don't ask me why. I've had in a lot of pilgrims over the years trying to get to the place, and they're none too pleased to find their maps are no longer accurate, whether they're in their head or on paper. They either start reading it funny, or the lines change direction. Compasses don't work particularly well over here either. Weird, huh?"

Genevieve and I frowned at each other. "Yeah, really weird," I agreed.

"Let me go and see if I can find a good one for you. I mapped that part of the country several years ago, before things really started turning odd. In fact, I had the privilege of going right to the gates of Donum Dei itself. If I'd known then what I know now, I would have firebombed the place while I was there." He got up and went into the other room. I grabbed one of the cookies from the tray and took a bite. It had considerable chew, but it contained lots of nuts and honey. It was delicious.

"He said he could get us a map, John," Genevieve whispered, excited.

"Seems pretty damn serendipitous, doesn't it? We get lost,

and we stumble on a mapmaker's house."

"Deus ex Machina," she murmured, and I was just chewing on those words when Zehn crowed from the other room. "Ah-*ha*!"

A few seconds later, he skipped into the room with a long roll of parchment under one arm. "It's a beauty, my friends. Not that I love to brag or anything, but honestly, I was amazing at my job." He handed me the roll of paper and I spread it across my and Genevieve's laps. The whole northwestern part of the country opened up before my eyes. Mountains and trees stood out in stark relief with blue rivers and squiggly black lines running through and around it all. In the high left corner, nearly off the map, was a large cross with a circle around it, and the words Donum Dei. Even on paper, it looked imposing.

"So this one stays accurate, then?" Genevieve asked.

Zehn put his hands on his hips and pretended to be insulted. Then he grinned again. "Does it stay accurate, she asks. Well, it does when you're using the right tools. I positioned all my maps by the stars. As far as I know, those haven't started moving out of pattern yet. And when they do, God help us all."

I touched the cross that marked our final destination. "Beth," I whispered, shivering. For a moment, I thought I saw the light of *Élan Vital*, but it was just the setting sun coming in through Zehn's front windows.

He cleared his throat. "So as you can see, you have a good long trip ahead of you."

I looked to the southeast and tried to estimate about where we might be. The Cradle wasn't marked on the map.

Maybe the place hadn't been there when Zehn had made it. "So we're about here, then?" I pointed to a section about three inches shy of Donum Dei, and by the scale, I estimated it to be about a hundred miles or so.

Zehn laughed again, though when he looked back at me, he apologized. "I don't get much time with people anymore, forgive my manners. Anyway, no. You're much farther away than that," he said and moved my finger another four inches to the south. "That's about a three-hundred klick detour you've taken, my friends. I hope you aren't doing all that on foot. It's very rough country."

We both looked at him with desperation in our eyes. "There is no way we could have walked that in two days. No way at all," Genevieve said.

Zehn nodded. "Yep. Like I said, time and distance get funny out here. I wish I knew how to explain it better than that, but I was never one of the egg head kids."

She looked like she wanted to cry, and I couldn't blame her.

"Aw, darn it, don't give me those doe eyes now!" Zehn cried and looked at me. "You do know she's pretty goddamn irresistible, don't you?"

I managed a smile despite the hunk of lead sitting in my gut at the news. "I do."

"Well, Uncle Zehny happens to know of a truck about a mile from here that could probably use a little bit of a tune-up. Fella also made his own fuel. Most of 'em do, if they run vehicles like that. I don't know if there's much left or how far it can get you, but I do know the truck is still there. I always pass it on my daily walks."

I looked at him. "How come you never used it? Didn't you ever think of running?"

He appeared to really think about it before he answered. "I didn't know where else to go, I guess. Never saw myself anywhere else. Not the adventuring kind, really. At least not in life. I save all the swashbuckling for my pages."

"Thank you for all you've done, Zehn," I said.

His blue eyes gleamed again in the darkening room. "You ain't seen nothin' yet. I felled a prize stag yesterday. Got meat coming out of my armpits. What say we have some juicy venison steaks ala Zehn followed by a steamy threesome?" He broke up into hearty guffaws again, and we joined him.

"Steaks sound good," I said. "We'll pass on the threesome."

"I got booze too. You never know what'll happen when we got whiskey in our veins."

Chapter 25

Zehn took us out back and gathered up an armload of vegetables from his massive garden. He had carrots, cucumbers,
zucchini, and tomatoes, and all of them looked like prize-
winners. I asked him how he grew such a hearty bounty, and
how he kept the weeds away without living under a net, and
he shrugged. "The soil here has always been pretty magical.
The weeds never did take very well up here. Vegetables always grow huge, the grass is always green, and the flowers
never die. Heck, I bet you could even grow corn here. The
good kind."

"That's amazing," Genevieve said.

He sighed. "Yeah, it's just a lucky patch of ground, I guess.
I think there are a few left on this earth. Maybe more than
folks realize."

"I guess we're in good company," I said and we all went
back in. Zehn insisted we sit down while he did all of the
cooking, and I watched him chop vegetables and add them to
a large wooden bowl along with torn lettuce leaves. From his
icebox, he pulled out a large hunk of dark red meat, grabbed
a long knife, and started slicing off thick steaks. I felt the first
stabbing pangs of real hunger in days.

"So, John, how do you and Genevieve—that's a gorgeous

name, by the way—plan on taking out Urban the Turd? Two folks against the world is stoic and romantic, but a little unrealistic."

"We're out of our minds, and we will likely die," I said.

He shrugged and tossed three steaks into a hot cast iron skillet. The meat gave a loud hiss. "You seem pretty confident in your lack of confidence, but it's still confidence."

"I had a weapon I could use against them, and I temporarily lost it," I said and pointed to my head.

"Lost your mind, huh?"

"Something like that."

"Well, maybe you just need to relax and not think about it too hard. If you start thinking you're going to lose your, uh, power every time you go to use it, it'll never come. That's what my wife used to tell me on the very, very rare occasions when I couldn't, you know."

"I get you," I said.

"Or maybe," he suggested, sliding the sizzling steaks onto a large plate and sprinkling them with some fresh herbs, "what you need is some good food and drink. Pardon me for saying, but the two of you are looking a little skeletal." He placed the platter on the table along with the bowl of salad, which he'd tossed with oil, vinegar, and herbs. "Eat well of the vegetables. They do wonderful things for the health. You'd be shocked if you knew I was nearly old enough to be your father."

My and Genevieve's jaws dropped simultaneously. "You are not!" she exclaimed.

He looked at us for a minute and burst out laughing. "You're right, I'm not. They are really good, though. Eat up."

He was right. The vegetables were crunchy, sweet, and addictive. I ordinarily ate such things out of obligation rather than enthusiasm, but I couldn't get enough of these. Even the best ones from God's Hope were often stunted and dull. Putting them in soups was the only way to eat them. With each bite, I felt a little more life flow back into my veins. The steak was medium rare, cooked to perfection. It was so seldom that I'd had any meat other than fish and poultry that I could eat only a portion of it before begging off.

It easily outshined every meal I ever ate in my life, or would ever eat again, and I now realize that my Last Supper is a poor attempt at recapturing that magical meal again. If only . . .

"And there is plenty more where this came from. I'll send you along with a doggie bag," Zehn said. He got up and went back into the kitchen to retrieve a tall bottle from the cupboard. It was filled with an amber colored liquid. "And now, the pièce de résistance!" He poured us each a bit, swirled his around in the glass, took a sniff, and finally an indulgent sip. I followed suit, and welcomed the familiar bloom of fire in the back of my throat.

"You've officially outdone yourself," I said.

Zehn laughed. "Now you see why I don't want to leave here. A man gets used to good living."

"Unheard of in this world," Genevieve reminded him.

"Ain't that the truth, sweetheart," he said. "It's pretty brave what you're doing, though, and I wish you the best." He gulped down the last of the whiskey in his glass and poured another measure. "Got a joke for ya. Did you ever hear the story about Zehn the Divine Rite Stooge?"

An icicle stabbed through my heart, but I finally managed to utter, "No."

"Well, he lost his job awhile back. You know what they call him now?" He looked back and forth between the two of us, a playful smile turning up the corners of his mouth. When he saw we were waiting for him to answer, he said, "Zehn," and burst out laughing. He swallowed the contents of his glass at a draught and poured another. He reached forward and topped off our glasses as well. "Yep, just Zehn now. Just regular old Zehnson."

"What's that supposed to mean?" I asked.

"I was only a contractor for those bastards, but it was enough to make me feel guilty. I tried to tell myself I was just making maps, but the truth was, the Hand of God used 'em on their hunting missions. Maybe still do. At any rate, you got my fullest support in taking on the Rite, and I'm damn glad you got rid of that Cradle. A place like that has no earthly business among civilized men and women." He swallowed more whiskey and grunted as something funny occurred to him. When he spoke, he slurred his speech. "Didja know that if you ask the Divine Rite for a Lass Supper, they won't give ya one?"

"What?" I was completely dumbfounded by what he'd said, not only because it was so out of the blue, but because the idea of someone actually asking for a Supper had never occurred to me.

"I requested one after Turner and Gabe died. Didn't think I could hack it on my own. I got a response saying some blithering nonsense about how 'the determination for the distribution of Suppers occurs only at Justification,' and that granting requests was no different from suicide, which was a mortal sin. Can you believe that? They're killing people willy-nilly, but when someone actually *wants* one of the damn things . . . It's all about control. It isn't about whether or not you wanna die. It's about them having the final say."

Genevieve reached out and put her hand on his. "Did you ever try to, you know . . ."

"Kill myself anyway?" He shook his head. "Thought about it plenty, but I lack the stones to put a gun in my mouth. I only know I won't be dying under their terms."

"Why did your sons eat the Supper?" I asked.

Zehn grunted again. "Why does anybody eat the goddamned Supper? If you think I don't stay awake every night thinking of how else I could have saved my wife and boys, you'd be wrong. I couldn't have stopped them if I tried. They wanted it. That's the thing. They got the meal and ate it without question, even when I tried to take it from them. Why, I bet I could sit one of those boxes in front of you two right now, and you'd eat it. It's like they put some kind of pheromone in it."

I wanted to contradict that, but then I thought of how easily Linny gave in to her fate, how she managed to coax me into letting her eat it, even while I became more and more enraged with every bite.

"You're probably right," I said and drained my whiskey. It burned going down, but I needed it.

Chapter 26

We talked the sun down and the whiskey bottle nearly empty, but soon Genevieve and I were yawning politely into the backs of our hands. Zehn set us up in one of his spare bedrooms. The two of us enjoyed a night in a real bed, and we made the most of it. After we made love this time, I didn't fall into strange dreams about brick walls and the worlds beyond them. I didn't dream at all, though the question of whether I would ever be able to touch the *Élan Vital* again, and what I would do if I couldn't, never left me.

The next morning, we woke to the smell of cooking food and Zehn singing boisterously in the kitchen. His eyes lit up when he saw us emerge. "Good morning, compadres! Come get your share of Uncle Zehnny's Breakfast Gruel." He filled two bowls with a steaming grayish, gloppy mixture, topped it off with honey, a handful of chopped walnuts, and fresh blueberries. "It tastes a heck of a lot better than it looks. Trust me."

He was right. The mixture was nutty and satisfying. "Is this Lazarus?" I asked.

"I'm gonna pretend I didn't hear that," he said. "It's barley mixed with father's own proprietary hybrid of spelt that he developed and tried to sell to the Rite years ago. They took it, stripped it of most of its nutrition and bran, and did some other genetic whackadoo magic on it to make it more impervious to the weeds. And that my friends is what they called Lazarus."

I was shocked. "If Lazarus tasted anything like this . . ."

"People would be fat and happy, like me. Alas, they are undernourished and miserable, just how the Rite wants them."

"Good point," Genevieve said.

I noticed he wore a pair of battered blue coveralls and I asked him what he had planned for today. "We're going to see about fixing up that set of wheels for you and the missus. I know my magical little patch of land, not to mention the dashing fellow who lives on it, is going to be hard to say goodbye to, but you can't take on the scum of the world from here."

I scraped my bowl clean of its delicious contents and resisted the urge to ask for seconds. "I understand. I just don't know how much help I'll be. I don't have much experience with motors." I suddenly wished Harry or Christoph were here.

"No worries," Genevieve said. "I've worked on a few of them with my dad. You and I can do it, Zehn." She burst out laughing at the perfect O of surprise the other man made with his mouth.

"Marry me, lady. Come on, I'll cook, I'll clean, and I'll never kick you outta bed for eating crackers."

She continued laughing as we all headed outside. The sun dazzled on the grass's morning dew, giving the blades a diamond-encrusted sheen. Zehn's eccentric house looked as out of place as ever, but it also put a great smile on my face.

I realized how easily I'd become accustomed to a drab existence. The Blight had robbed the world of so much color, both through biology and the resulting tyranny.

We walked companionably down the dirt road for about fifteen minutes before arriving at another single story brick house, this one far more conservative with its faded red hue and chipped white trim. Jutting from the side was a covered garage area, inside of which sat a truck of a much older vintage than Christoph's. Flowers of rust bloomed on its grill and near-colorless fenders. The windshield had a long, jagged crack running across it like lightning frozen in time, and it sat lopsided from the flat front passenger-side tire. I followed Zehn to the driver-side door. He opened it and a smell of apples and old leather wafted out. A small dreamcatcher hung from the rearview mirror, an odd place for such a thing if you really think about it. I noticed the keys still dangled from the ignition.

"You sure these people are no longer here?" I asked.

He nodded. "Yep. We were pretty good friends with the Sturgesses. Then Lee kicked the bucket not long after my wife. Natural causes, at least. Ruth—well, she was luckier than most. Suicide, about three years later. This house has been sitting untouched since she died. No family so much as came and emptied it out." Instead of waiting for me to do it, he hopped into the driver's seat. "You never know, maybe we'll get lucky," he said, and cranked the key.

There wasn't even a click. It was deader than the Sturgesses. Zehn popped the latch that allowed access to the engine and hopped out. "Probably the battery," he said and lifted the hood. He and Genevieve started inspecting the guts of the car like a couple of veteran surgeons.

"Is there anything I can do?" I asked, feeling very much the third wheel.

Genevieve looked up. "I bet if you looked around the property, you could find some extra fuel for this thing."

"Yes, there's a utility shed out back," Zehn said as he yanked up some piece of black tubing and sniffed it.

"I'm on it," I said and walked around the back of the house. The yard was a travesty of overgrown, mostly-dead foliage and broken fencing. The shed stood to the far back. Constructed of dark, moss-covered wood with a single window cut into the front, it looked like some square Cyclopean creature hunched beneath the trees catching some shade between meals. I didn't want to go inside, and I berated myself for being such a coward. After everything I'd seen and been through, I couldn't believe I was about to surrender to an old tool shed. Before I could let that single eye leer at me any further, I strode across the backyard and pushed open the shed door.

Inside, from one of the beams, hung the putrefying body of an old woman in a dowdy, flowered dress. Her white tongue jutted from her mouth like an albino slug, and her eyes bulged from her skull, as if even in death she were screaming for help. I cried out and stumbled back toward the yard. My foot caught on the bottom edge of the doorway, and I went sprawling into the grass. I heard Genevieve call my name from the front of the house.

"John? You okay?"

It took me a second to untangle the knotted words in the back of my throat, but I managed a semi-convincing, "Yeah!

Doing fine!" I stood up and looked back into the shed. The body wasn't there.

"I'm losing it," I muttered to myself, though I was unable to believe that what I'd seen was a hallucination. Maybe some sort of residue from the mental exertions of the last several days. I would have to ask Genevieve about it later.

Inside the shed, I found several canisters of fuel and a toolbox so heavy I had to lift it with both arms. On a workbench were several chunks of wood, some of which had been formed into little animal figurines. One was a whale, its large tail breaching some invisible sea. Another was a horse cropping imaginary grass, but it wasn't the animals that held my attention. The knife lying near a pile of wood shavings did. It had a filigreed ivory handle, and the edge of the blade was so honed it looked nearly invisible. Mr. Sturgess must have been one hell of a whittler. I picked up the knife, folded the blade back into the beautiful handle, and placed it into my pocket. Then I hoisted up the toolbox and went back out front.

"He's alive! And walking!" Zehn exclaimed as I walked over. He came and helped me with the toolbox, and we both carried it over to the truck and set it down with a grunt. "Now we have tools. Was there a battery back there, by chance?" I thought for a minute, but didn't recall seeing one, and I said as much. He shrugged. "Looks like we're gonna have to push it to get it going. Good thing the driveway is on an incline." He took one of the wrenches from the box and started loosening the bolts on the flat tire. The spare, which he'd retrieved from the truck's cargo bed, leaned against the door waiting to be attached.

Genevieve closed the hood. "Plugs and hoses look decent, but the oil is pretty low and it's filthy."

"Where do we get oil?" I asked.

"Every vehicle owner gets an oil ration. You didn't see one back there?"

I shook my head and bit down on what I wanted to say: nope, no oil ration, but there appears to be a ghost ration of some sort.

"Well, we'll gas it up, get it started, and see how far we get. I think we'll be able to get a good piece on it before it goes tits-up."

Zehn tapped me on the shoulder. "Listen to that. She talks like a man when she's up to her elbows in a car's guts."

She snickered. "Can't help it. Reminds me of my dad."

"Where is he?" Zehn asked.

I answered, "He's in Old Babylon trying to hold down the fort with an eighty-plus year old man, a bunch of emaciated Cradle survivors, and some corn mutants created when some crazy coot tried to feed the town a Blight contaminated strain."

"Jesus! Sounds like a real party."

"You don't know the half of it," I said. "Look, Zehn, there might be people looking for us, and by the sound of it, the Rite will be breaking down your door sometime soon anyway. Why don't you head out to Old Babylon? We could use a strong hand to help out our people and be ready to stand."

He appeared to think about it for a minute, but he shook his head. "I don't know, John."

"Hey," Genevieve said. "You were the one talking about dying on your own terms and taking Divine Rite scum with you."

"Yeah, so?"

She sighed. "So, you'd have a heck of a better chance of doing that in Babylon."

"And I also think there is some additional good you can do there. I think whatever makes your grass and your garden grow has nothing to do with the soil. It's you," I said.

He laughed. "Me? You're joking, right?"

I smiled. "I've seen a lot of different people with different abilities lately. Whatever caused our world to end up this way, this messing with nature, has resulted in some things that I can't even begin to explain. Some people have abilities and don't even know it. I've learned that from experience. At any rate, I'm sure the people there would love to see that strain of spelt you have here." I looked at Genevieve. "Imagine if Akiva Paine had had someone like Zehn by his side."

"I'm afraid to," Genevieve said.

"Who is that?" Zehn asked

"I'm sure you'll hear all about it in Old Babylon," I told him.

"If I go."

"Yes, if," I said. "Let's gas this thing up and get her rolling."

Zehn went to grab the cans. I turned to Genevieve.

"You think he can really do what you say?" she asked.

"I might not have all of the ability I had before, but my intuition is still pretty strong. Yeah, he definitely has something. Someone who can make the ground on which he stands thrive. I doubt he even knows he does it. I think it has something to do with his good nature."

She sniffed. "I like to think we're all good-natured."

"Okay, maybe it's because he's so perverted." I laughed, and she joined in.

"You two sharing jokes without me? I thought I was the joke guy," Zehn said as he finished topping off the tank and putting the spare canisters in the truck bed. "Let's see . . . I guess it's convenient you're not much for driving, John. We can give Genny here a good push and she can operate it."

"I like the sound of that," she said.

After a few preparations, Zehn and I stood together, our hands pressed against the truck's tailgate, and began pushing. After a few effortful heaves, the truck started to roll. Our feet dug into the packed dirt, which gave us just enough traction. Genevieve turned it onto the road toward Zehn's house, which was downhill. After a little correcting, we gave the truck another long push, and the momentum took over. "Come on, you son of a bitch," I heard her mutter from behind the wheel.

"Drop the clutch!" Zehn called.

A few seconds later, the truck roared to life. Blue smoke burped from its tailpipe. It didn't sound pretty, but it was alive.

"Success!" Zehn cried. "Come on, slow poke. Let's hop in back before she takes off and leaves us here."

"Don't tempt me!" Genevieve yelled back as we boosted ourselves up into the truck bed. We all laughed as she drove us back to our new friend's house. It felt good to win something for a change.

Genevieve stopped the truck in front of Zehn's house, but kept the motor running. It had a throaty rumble, but it seemed steady enough. Zehn hopped out and jogged toward his front door. "Be right back!" he yelled. I climbed out, opened the passenger side door, and peered in at a grinning Genevieve.

"Going my way?" I asked.

"Until I stop breathing," she said, and then blushed a deep red. I slid into the truck, and kissed her on the cheek.

"Sounds good to me," I told her. What I didn't tell her was how hopeless I felt about our future, despite the bright moment we just had. When I tried to look beyond the now, I saw only darkness, madness, or death.

After a couple minutes, Zehn came out of the house with his arms full of stuff. I got out to help him. "You don't want to forget your doggy bags," he said and handed me a sack filled with wrapped portions of meat, vegetables, and more of his cookies. He also handed me a long, thin paper tube. "The map. You really don't want to forget that."

"I can't thank you enough, Zehn," I told him and reached out my hand.

"Aw, come on now, I've at least earned one of these." He pulled me into a bear hug that made my spine pop.

After we let go I decided one more time to coax him. "I'm sure you know how to get to Old Babylon from here, right?"

He rolled his eyes. "Silly question to ask a map maker. Will you be there?"

"I don't know," I said, though I had an idea if we made it to Donum Dei, the answer would be no. "Look for a man named Turpin. Tell him where we're going. Tell him I said we're going to take care of the elephant in the room."

"If I go, I'll tell him."

Zehn walked over to Genevieve, who stood against the open truck door. "Take care of yourselves. And watch out for your man. We're stupid creatures and need all the help we can get."

She kissed him on the cheek. "I will. And you stay safe. Thank you for everything."

A few minutes later, we were heading west. Both of us waved goodbye to our strange friend as he grew smaller in the rearview mirror. I still don't know if he ever made it to Old Babylon.

Chapter 27

A little while later, a glum silence fell between Genevieve and me as we drove along the broken road leading up into the mountains. The landscape grew stranger the farther we went. A carpet of fog swirled around barren trees and towering rock formations that looked like melting globs of wax. Without Zehn's joviality to distract us, we were faced with the reality that we were running headlong into the darkness, with no plan. It was a certain recipe for death.

The refusal of my abilities to show themselves over the last couple days despite the rest and good food was particularly frustrating, and I was sure Genevieve was feeling it too, despite her show of confidence that things would eventually return. But rather than hash it out, we sat ruminating in silence, both of us probably waiting for the other to ask the obvious question. What the hell were we going to do when we got there?

It made me feel like a savage to admit it to myself—makes me feel like one right now just writing it—but I wasn't thinking about Beth so much as we neared the place where she was being held captive. I probably wasn't thinking about her through any of this as much as I should have, and it wasn't just my preoccupation with keeping Kaya safe and later over her death. My other daughter had never been as close to me. She'd always been Linny's girl. The two of them shared their bonds over God and duty, and while the unfairness of Linny's death ignited a rebellious fury in Kaya and me, I think it only deepened Beth's devotion, and that made us more distant than ever.

I know what that must sound like, and I don't blame anyone reading this right now for hating me because of it, but in the spirit of confession as I take my Last Supper, I feel I have no choice but to admit what was in my heart: my main motivation for going to Donum Dei wasn't necessarily to rescue Beth, although I had every intention of doing so. It was to avenge Kaya.

"You seem quiet," Genevieve said as she guided the truck along the winding road. There were parts where cliffs dropped off into foggy chasms beside me, and I closed my eyes and pushed away images of us plunging into unknown depths.

"I guess I feel quiet. A lot to think about."

"Yes. Like what we're going to do when we get there, besides get ourselves killed."

There it was. All our doubts were about to be hashed out, at which point we'd either turn back or split up. I knew which it was going to be, even if she didn't. I'd go on alone if I had to. Would have preferred it, to tell you the truth. How many more people was I going to get killed before this was over?

"Do you have any ideas?" I asked.

"I'm afraid not. Aside from hoping by some miracle you find your abilities again. Without them, I don't think we stand much of a chance."

"I think it's still there. It's just . . . playing with me."

She glanced over. "What are you talking about?"

"I saw something, back at the house when you and Zehn were working on the truck." After some debate, I'd decided to tell her about the body hanging from the shed ceiling, and how it had disappeared. It was a phantom thing, sure, but proof that maybe the *Élan Vital* was still lurking.

But Genevieve didn't look particularly thrilled by that. She looked distressed. "Have you had any other hallucinations since that happened?"

"Not that I know of."

"Tell me if you do. It could have been a fluke. That's what I hope, anyway, because the alternative isn't good."

A stone dropped in my gut. "What's the alternative? That I'm going mad?" My mind briefly fled to the vision of the madman on the mountaintop.

She took a breath. "It's happened with a few Sentinels, but you're not like they were. Their minds were not meant for that kind of power. Yours might just be making a few adjustments."

"But you don't really mean that, do you?"

"Are you saying I'm lying?" Her voice took on a confrontational edge, and I knew then that I'd read something in her mind. It wasn't telepathy. Just simple intuition. And Genevieve was clearly ready to battle something out.

"What I mean is you're trying to bullshit me so you don't scare me. You're worried that I might be losing my mind."

The old truck skidded to a halt in a cloud of dust and a series of squeals from the brakes and she turned to me, her green eyes blazing. "I never bullshit anyone. You think I got as far as I have in my life dodging death at every turn by flitting around the important words?"

"No. But I think you're doing it now."

I wasn't going to let her rile me up or distract me with hyperbole. Her anger was of her own creation, and my calm in the face of it only seemed to make her madder, which told me I was right.

"I can't believe how arrogant you're being. Why am I even here? You're just off on some crazy revenge errand that's going to get both of us killed, and will do nothing to help our friends, not to mention my *father*, back in Old Babylon who are fighting for you!"

At least we were getting close. It wasn't about my hallucinations or any potential madness at all. "Do you want to go back? Is that what you're saying?"

"Yes! Why are we here, John? How exactly do you think we're going to be able to beat these people when we have no weapons and no plan? By the looks of things, we're marching right into a place that doesn't even look like our planet, for crying out loud. Have you really looked at what's out there?"

Of course I had looked. It was all I'd been staring at since we'd set off on this road. And she was right, of course. The rocks, the fog, the scrubby brush. There were no serpent weeds that I could see, but a few birds circling out in the gray sky were unlike any I'd ever seen before. They weren't flying so much as lumbering.

"There are a lot of problems with your suggestion, but I'll only name the two biggest ones," I said. "First, we need more fuel. We won't even make it back to Zehn's house on what we have. Second, we can't turn around on this road. If you nudged over another inch, we'd go tumbling off into a bottomless pit."

Her face fell with every word, but she didn't fight it anymore. "Okay. So we go to the next town, get fuel, and turn around. How close are we to the next place? Check the map."

I grabbed the roll of paper from the dash and spread it open. After studying it for a minute, Genevieve pointed to a small cluster of buildings nestled in a little valley with the word Purgatory printed above it in elegant script. "Looks like it's about fifteen miles or so away. We can make that."

"Purgatory. Sounds charming."

"I don't know a whole lot about it, but I have heard there's a Sin Bin in these parts. I bet it's there."

I couldn't tell if the slight tremble in her voice was fear or excitement.

"Makes sense, given the name of the place. Are you sure you want to go there, though? It's probably heavy with Hand of God patrols. We don't want that kind of attention."

She sat silent for a moment, tapping her finger errantly on the map. I noticed she dropped into these brief spells of quiet before making any major decisions, her brain weighing all possible options before coming to a conclusion. I loved that careful thoughtfulness about her. "I think we should go. If we're careful, we can avoid capture. And maybe get some fuel. Or a new vehicle altogether. There are probably all kinds that people drove in but will never drive home again."

I swallowed my disagreement. This felt like the wrong step, but what choice did we have? Even if we'd elected to keep going, we would have had to face down Purgatory anyway. It was in our road. If anything, it showed how badly prepared we were for Donum Dei. We were better off heading back to Old Babylon. We could train a small army and take on the Divine Rite battle by battle until we could bring our fight right to the gates of Donum Dei.

As for Beth . . . I had to swallow that loss for the time being. She wouldn't be served well by us rushing in without a plan. And for all I knew, I admitted with a sick stomach, she might already be dead. The Hand of God certainly hadn't wasted any time killing Kaya. Why would Beth be any different?

"To Purgatory we go," Genevieve said and eased the truck back into gear after a little bit of fiddling with the stubborn clutch. I asked her if she was hungry, and we agreed that some pieces of meat would do us both some good. I dug into one of the bags for the packages containing the food when my fingers brushed against something hard and leathery. I grabbed it instead and pulled out a Bible. It was black and scuffed, its pages rippled around the edges, as if it had once been wet and dried again. The book had seen a lot of action. A purple ribbon bookmark stuck out of the top, and I opened it. The pages fell open to Chapter 3 of the book of Peter. Someone had circled verses 18-20 in red ink:

For Christ also died for sins once for all, the just for the unjust, in order that He might bring us to God, having been put to death in the flesh, but made alive in the spirit; in which also He went and made proclamation to the spirits now in prison, who once were disobedient, when the patience of God kept waiting in the days of Noah, during the construction of the ark, in which a few, that is, eight persons, were brought safely through the water.

I read the verses aloud to Genevieve. They sounded familiar to me, but I couldn't remember where I'd last heard them. "What do you think that means?" she asked.

"It's one of the few biblical mentions of purgatory. Reverend Blackwell loved that stuff, remember? The whole basis of the Rite dogma rests on the belief that after the Blight, we were put into purgatory." She glanced at me for a second before turning back to the road, which was just starting to lead downhill. "Interesting coincidence, don't you think?"

"I'm not so sure there are such things as coincidences," I said.

We fell into another silence. This one was more comfortable than the last, but I detected some stuff there still unresolved. Still, she seemed more at ease now that we'd agreed to hold off on the suicide mission.

We'd had the strangest courtship, if one could even call it that. There were so many things I wanted to ask her. You know, those intimate but trivial things that all couples know about each other, like what they liked in their tea or what their favorite book was, but we never seemed to have time for that kind of talk. And even though we'd shared a deep and sort of desperate intimacy that told me more about her than any small talk would, I wanted the rest of the stuff too. Maybe when we had the luxury of actual rest, it would happen.

Night fell as we dropped deeper into the valley. The road narrowed, and the walls of the cliffs were mere inches from my window as we squeezed through certain passages. The fog completely enveloped us, and Genevieve flicked on the truck's headlights only to find they did little to cut through the opaque mist. On her side of the truck was a stratum of rocks, dirt, and scrubby foliage that looked like dead hands popping up out of the ground. Gooseflesh rippled my skin. The sight through the windshield was no less frightening, however, so I simply trained my eyes on the Bible lying open in my lap, seeking solace in old familiar verses.

There had been a Bible in my hand since I was a boy and I had a pretty decent grasp of the contents, but Linny's memory of the passages had been nearly verbatim. I could throw out a random book and verse, and she'd recite the words down to the letter. Or you could give her the verse, and she'd name the book and chapter. Not for the first, and certainly not for the last, I thought I was the one who should have gotten that Supper. She'd followed every goddamn rule, and it still didn't matter.

"How much longer do you think it'll be?" I asked.

"At this speed, maybe an hour. You never know on a road like this." Her brusque tone told me that she would like to talk as little as possible while she navigated through the difficult terrain. I obliged her and continued flipping pages. I had just gotten to the Sermon on the Mount when Genevieve cried out and the truck came to another grinding halt.

I jerked forward in my seat and my head thumped painfully on the dash.

"John? Are you okay?" Genevieve leaned over and patted my cheek. "You weren't wearing your seatbelt, were you?"

"Seatbelt?" I asked and closed my eyes. There were swimming speckles, which had begun to coalesce into a single entity of light floating before me like a distant galaxy. There it was. *Élan Vital.* I wanted to ask why it had forsaken me, but a sharp sting yanked me out of the dream, or whatever it was.

"Wake up, John," Genevieve said. Her voice was a frantic whisper, and I opened my eyes in the dark truck cab to see her leaning over me. Her hair hung in her face, and I wanted to brush it away and pull her to me. I was reaching up to do just that when she took my hands into hers. They were shaking.

"The road ran out."

"What do you mean the road ran out?" I sat up to look out the windshield. A few feet in front of us, the road ended at a ravine, where gray mist wafted up like steam from a hot bath. If she hadn't stopped just in time, we would've gone over. I felt my stomach lurch.

"We're very lucky," she said. "There must have been a bridge here that let go. Let's get out."

We walked to the edge of the drop-off. The fog parted in some places and I could see a suggestion of the ruin below. Pairs of thick concrete columns, which were likely supports for the bridge that once stood here, jutted out of the fog like broken teeth. A piece of road still stood defiantly on one set. Bent rebar, pitted and scarred with rust, jutted out from its ends. Across the divide, which I estimated to be about 500 feet, I saw the thick concrete supports that once held the other side of the bridge. It didn't look like something that had just given away over time. The end of this bridge's life looked more violent. "What happened here?" I asked.

"Who knows? Old age, explosives, a troll? Looks like we're hoofing it from here."

"And then what? We now know we can't go back the way we came."

Genevieve sighed as if she were speaking to a willfully ignorant child. "That's why we have a map, right? We can still get to Purgatory and find another car, and another road that will take us back to Old Babylon. These mountains are probably full of other little roads and passages."

We went back to the truck and grabbed the map, holding it in front of the truck's lights so we could study the landscape. There were other roads branching off the main one before reaching Purgatory, but we'd still have to cross the bridge to get to them.

I still didn't like it. "I think this is a sign we should stay the hell away from whatever lay on the other side of this bridge."

"We don't have time for omens. We either find our way across, or we walk back the way we came. Do you want to do that?"

I thought of the weird landscape and what might be lurking under all that fog when the sun finally baked it away. If it did. "No, but . . ."

"But what?" she asked, sounding more testy by the second.

I bent down and studied the concrete wall on the other side. The truck lights and the relatively generous moonlight revealed a familiar shape. "Look over there at that wall." I pointed, hoping she would be able to see it too.

She squinted her eyes in the direction of my finger. "Is that—?"

"A ladder?" I finished. "Yeah, I think it is."

"Well if there's one over there, there might be one over here." She went over to the edge and leaned over to get a look. "I see the first few rungs, but it's too dark to see past that."

"Good. We at least have an easy way down there and up the other side," I said. I didn't want to bring up the possibility of breaking a leg trying to find our way through all the ruin down there. She was irritable enough.

"Okay then. We'll sleep here tonight and make our way over in the morning. No way in hell we're going to cross through that crap in the dark."

We set up camp in the bed of the truck. Genevieve made us a nice dinner out of the vegetables and some more of the venison steaks that Zehn had packed for us. After that, we lay down shoulder to shoulder. The sky was pregnant to bursting with stars, and I tried to remember the last time I ever just sat and admired them. I thought of Kaya, Beth, Linny, and me staying up all night for meteor showers around this time of year, late summer when the only use for a blanket was to protect us from hungry mosquitoes. Linny would beat me at cribbage and we'd take turns breaking up spats between the girls. Times were simpler then, and I was not surprised to find myself missing them. Life under the Rite's shadow can feel sunny with enough love to go around, I guess.

Now I ruminated over the fact that even if I got Beth back and we managed to escape capture, things would never be the same. Of course, they stopped being the same the day Linny died. As Genevieve snuggled up against me, I did my best to remind myself that the end of one life was the start of a new one.

Chapter 28

It was a restless night. The wind whined and moaned around us as we took turns lying across the truck's bench seat while the other kept watch with a pistol at hand. At some point, a wild animal began to howl in the distance. They were mournful cries that sounded almost human, starting with a low moan and ending with a glass-shattering crescendo that turned my blood to icy sludge. Neither of us could peg the species but agreed it sounded both big and hungry. It never seemed to get any closer, but every time it started up, we were both bolt upright, glassy-eyed and trembling with terror, wondering if it would eventually cease with the howling and just jump at us from the shadows, shattering the truck's windows and turning us into its midnight snack.

Eventually, we both agreed the animal wasn't growing any closer and the howling ceased, but we gave up the ghost of sleep just before daybreak, groggy and grumpy and anxious to be on our way. We gathered as many of our things as we could carry on our backs or fit into Genevieve's bag. Our guns didn't have more than a few rounds of ammo each, but they were better than nothing.

The fog was still thick in the ravine, and we wanted to wait for the sun to burn some of it off before making our descent, but our impatience won out. It was just too damn creepy there to stay for another minute. Not with that howling creature from the night before possibly roaming around in search of breakfast.

"We'll probably be able to see better once we get down there," I said, and she agreed even though I think we both knew we were just rationalizing.

Genevieve stood before the precipice, arms folded across her chest, and we both looked into the murky chasm for a minute. Birds—normal enough looking ones—dove into the cloud, but didn't come back up. I also heard no singing. That was a little disquieting, but I tried to tell myself they were just down there looking for food.

"You sure you still want to do this?" I asked.

She turned to me, her face drained of color, but for those green eyes of hers that looked almost feline. "Look . . . Before we go down there and face whatever might be ahead, I want to tell you something."

"Yeah?" I always dreaded conversations that started this way, and this one was no different. Especially this one.

"I think I might be pregnant."

The words acted like a blow to the head. "How could you possibly know something like that? It's only been a few days since—"

"I know. It's far too early to know for certain. I'm not due to start my period for another two weeks. But I trust my intuition. I think I knew even the moment it happened. I'd been hoping that maybe you'd even be able to tell me yourself. You know, given your abilities. But then everything that happened afterward was so terrible and fast. It sounds crazy, and I don't blame you if you want to doubt me, but I think if anyone could understand crazy, it's you."

I squatted down and rubbed my face. This changed everything, of course. But it also explained why she'd been acting so funny. She'd been carrying around that worry for days, too afraid to bring it up because of everything I'd been through. I was glad she'd told me. It at least gave me more incentive to get her out of here and back to Old Babylon, where she'd at least have a fighting chance of getting through the pregnancy safely. Provided there was a pregnancy. And a considerable part of me wasn't ready to believe it. Not yet. It was just too much to take in all at once.

"I'm sorry about all this, John. Maybe I shouldn't have told you." I looked up to see her weeping silently. Standing up, I pulled her into a hug.

"You have absolutely nothing to be sorry for, and I'm glad you told me. It helped me pull my head out of my rear. Besides, we kind of knew this might happen way back in the beginning, right? Even if we didn't exactly know how."

"I just didn't expect it would happen now. Not this way. I can't think of a worse time for something like this."

I held her face in my hands and kissed her. "That doesn't matter, and we can't think about it like that. We have even more reason to get you to safety. I'm not going to lose anymore of the people I love if I can help it."

"But Beth . . ."

"Let me worry about Beth." If she's even still alive, I thought.

Genevieve must have detected some of that in my voice, because she looked up at me with a frown. "You're not giving up on her, are you? You don't think she's already dead."

I wanted to lie, but I was terrible at it. "You saw Kaya. Tell me you haven't been having similar thoughts."

"It crossed my mind, but John . . . they took her to Donum Dei for a reason. They must think she's special."

"Or they're using her as bait to get to me."

"I suppose it's possible. But you can't lose hope yet. We're going to find her and get her back. I feel very strongly about this. I've . . . I've even had dreams about her. She's out there."

My heart started pounding and I grabbed her arms. "You've had dreams? What dreams?"

She shook her head. "I can't really remember them. Just fleeting images of her face, the sound of her voice. Honestly, I haven't put much stock into them, other than to remind myself she's still out there."

I let her go and turned to face the ravine. Some of the fog had gone down, and I could see more of the twisted wreckage from the fallen bridge. It wasn't exactly reassuring. "I haven't had any dreams about her. Not a single one since we started this whole thing. Why do you think that is?" I felt guilty even saying that out loud, as if it was like admitting I was a failure of a father.

Genevieve put a gentle hand on my shoulder. "It means you're so worried about her that you are afraid to even think about her."

That couldn't have been it. But I appreciated her attempt to make me feel better. "The last dream I had of Kaya, she was warning me not to go to Donum Dei, that it wasn't the right place anymore."

"And do you think it was just a dream, or does it mean

something?"

I shrugged. "I don't know. We have to go there eventually, anyway. But if Beth isn't at Donum Dei anymore, where the hell could she be?"

Genevieve didn't have an answer. A few minutes later, we both decided it was time to move on.

She was far smoother at getting down to the ladder than I was. She simply grabbed onto the top rung and swung her legs over the edge until they found purchase on the one below it, making it look about as easy as a kid climbing a playground slide. I didn't realize how terrified I was until I reached down to grab the top rung. A cold sweat broke out on my brow when I saw how high up we were. It was a good thirty feet, at least. Maybe not quite high enough to kill me in a fall, but only if I didn't happen to land on my head or on a jutting piece of rebar.

"Don't think about it, John," she called up from below. Already she'd reached the ground, and the fog concealed her. She was just a disembodied voice. "Just slide down feet first until you feel the rungs. That way you don't have to look down."

"Heh. Good idea," I muttered and did as she instructed. My feet dangled into space as my sweaty hands first gripped the concrete ledge and then the pitted iron rung. Any wrong move at that point would have been the end of my burgeoning world-saving career. Finally, I found the rung about three feet down, and descended to the bottom. When I pulled away from the ladder, flecks of rust coated my hands, and I wiped them on my pants. "Well at least the hard part's over," I said.

I looked at Genevieve, whose face was nearly the same color as the mist. "I wouldn't be so sure about that," she said.

The fog was still thick down here, the air acrid and moist. I could only see vague twists of steel and concrete from the shattered bridge. The ladder we needed to reach on the other side was lost in the cloud.

"It's worse than I thought," she said. "If you don't want to go on, we can think of something else. I bet we can turn the truck around."

I grabbed her hand and whispered, "Don't worry. We'll get through this." It didn't occur to me then why I whispered, but in retrospect, we might not have gotten as far if I hadn't.

We put our backs to the concrete wall and kept as straight a course as we could, knowing that we would hit the other side eventually. However, we had to keep our eyes on our feet as we navigated through the bridge's graveyard. There were hundreds of holes and other traps just waiting to snare an ankle, snap a bone, or puncture skin with disease-carrying shrapnel. Serpent weeds were woven through all of it, and they were some of the biggest specimens I'd ever seen. Some of the vines were as thick as my forearm and their orange flowers were an angrier shade, almost fluorescent, and about the size of my fist or larger. A newborn's head, maybe. Upon closer inspection, it looked as if one of them was leaking some kind of milky sap. No, those weren't serpent weeds. Or if they were, they were mutants of some sort. I wanted to point them out to Genevieve, but she was already upset enough, and she had probably already seen them and was doing her best to ignore them and push forward.

It was about fifteen or twenty paces before I began seeing

whitened bones of animals and other creatures far too long to be anything other than human femurs. A skull nestled within a pile of twisted metal and broken glass confirmed that fear. Tattered clothes and a few crushed automobiles also lay among the carnage. A tiny, skeletal hand still clutched a one-eyed teddy bear that had miraculously survived at least a few years' worth of seasons.

It was another thirty paces before I became certain we weren't alone. Not that I saw or heard anything directly, it was just a certainty we were being watched or stalked. There was a stillness in the air that felt almost like the holding of breath.

Genevieve clasped my hand tighter. "This is a graveyard, John," she whispered, her voice shaking with borderline panic.

I shushed her, not wanting to disturb our stalker. That was when I notice streaks of that milky sap on the windshield of a crunched green station wagon, like the trail of a giant slug. But it was definitely no slug.

Something rustled amid the debris to our left, and Genevieve squealed, fully in the grip of her terror now. I expected her voice to echo, but the fog swallowed it whole. Still, I pulled her close and whispered, "We need to be very quiet."

The rustle moved a little closer, and we picked up our pace, realizing that running any faster would likely result in one or both of us injuring ourselves. But we had to get to the ladder. There was no choice. I heard a flat whip crack just behind us, close enough that the wind of its impact blew across the back of my neck.

Genevieve fell down. "John! Help me!"

I yanked her wrist, but she didn't budge, and I was reminded of the hands gripping her in the coal chute at Akiva Paine's place. Something was holding her.

I looked back to see a thick, green vine wrapped around her ankle. Blood was already welling up as it dug into her skin. I pulled her again, but she screamed even louder, the opposing forces threatening to rip her to pieces. Already, I could feel her shoulder dislocating, and my shoes losing grip on the sloped chunk of concrete.

"You have to let me go this time, John," she cried.

"Not a chance. Just hold on!"

"Please! This hurts so bad!"

I slowly bent my knees down so I could reach the strap on her bag. If I could get her gun . . .

My foot slipped and I nearly lost my grip. I heard rubble crumbling, debris shifting, and soon, and soon a new vine, about a foot in diameter at its thickest point, appeared out of the fog. It was a toxic green that darkened progressively to purple and finally to black at its tip. As it slithered toward us, I noticed the orange flowers aligned like suckers on the underside of a tentacle before I slipped again and came down hard on my knee. Genevieve slid another foot or two forward under the force of the thing's pull, taking me with her. I jabbed my cheek on a tip of protruding rebar and felt warm blood run down my jaw.

"I can't hold this much longer, John. I can't do this."

I ignored her, flailing my hand out for the nearest object I could grab. Something pointy or sharp. My hands closed on a piece of broken off rebar. Stabbing downward with the jagged end, I punctured the thick meat of the tentacle vine.

Something screamed in the fog—sounded almost like steam coming out of a kettle—and the vine loosed its grip on Genevieve. Wounded as she was, she fumbled away quickly enough to avoid being recaptured.

I snatched her shoulder bag as she passed and opened it to find the pistol resting right on top.

"Get up! There's no time for that!" she cried, yanking on my arm.

I fought her off. "Wait! I'm trying to find the gun!"

Another tentacle flew out from the fog, and I rolled down the concrete slope into a pile of loose pebbles. Thankfully no jagged metal or glass was waiting there to shred me open.

The appendage missed its mark by mere inches, landing on a slab of blacktop just to my left. As it drew back, it slithered across my lower legs and stopped. I imagined it wrapping itself around them and pulling me toward some gaping, tooth-lined alien maw. It was the image of that mouth, so clear in my mind, that got me moving again. I raised the pistol, aimed down the site, and pulled the trigger.

The bullet went into the thickest part of the tentacle.

Yellowish-white sludge oozed out of the hole like pus, and the thing cried out in another piercing wail. I fired a couple more shots and then leapt to my feet.

Genevieve took the lead. Her adrenaline was probably too high to feel the pain in her cut ankle, but at least none of the muscles appeared to be severed. The outline of the wall finally loomed ahead, and the ladder, our salvation, jumped out at us soon after. The tentacle thing's shrieks were dying down and I dared a look back.

I wish I hadn't.

Only the silhouette of its form was visible in the murk, but it towered at least ten feet high, a wavering blob with the outlines of flowers jutting off it at random angles. It grunted as it pulled itself closer, and soon it would no longer be shrouded by the fog blanket and the full sight of it would drive every coherent and sane thought from my brain.

"*Go go go!*" I screamed. "It's right fucking behind us!"

A sound I could only compare to some giant, sick man bringing up a big ball of phlegm from the back of his throat filled the air. A second later, a glob of yellowish, snot-colored muck flew past our heads and splattered onto the rock wall ahead of us. It immediately began to sizzle and stink.

Genevieve pushed me toward the ladder first, snatching her gun back. "You go first! I'm going to take it down."

"I don't fucking think so. Not this time! Get up the ladder and let me shoot it."

She shook her head. "No, you don't—"

"*You're pregnant!* Get up there now!" I roared, and she must have seen something in my face, because she thrust the pistol at me without another word and climbed the ladder.

I turned to face the lumbering abomination, raised the pistol and pulled the trigger three times. The fog insulated my ears from the report, but the shriek from the wounded thing was another story. Only the sound of the locust swarm hurt more. After it fell silent, leaving me only with the sound of my pulse hammering away in my ears, I waited another minute before turning again toward the ladder. Genevieve reached the top and I saw her pale face looking over the edge. I stuck the gun in the waistband of my pants and began climbing.

The pain in my knee was excruciating, and the going was slow. Too slow. I felt like an old man.

Genevieve cried out again just as I felt another tentacle wrap around my ankle. The twist and pull on the joint was agonizing, but the skin began to burn immediately and I understood that whatever it had spit at us could also excrete from this thing's skin. I wrapped my arm around the rung, for my hands had become too slippery with sweat to hang on. Something had to give. Either I would be ripped free of the ladder, or my leg would be ripped free of my hip joint. The pistol tumbled from my grip and into the mist-blanketed pit below.

Genevieve was screaming my name from another universe. *"John! Oh my God, John! Use the gun!"* I didn't have the strength to tell her that was no longer an option.

I looked to the cloudless morning sky and prayed. I don't know who to. Not God, necessarily. I think maybe Kaya. And my brother, Ezekiel, whom I knew better than anybody else, but not at all. Then I felt a hot pop as my hip dislocated, and I screamed until my throat was raw. I screamed until I drowned out the pain. I screamed until the world shook. I screamed until the white light filled my vision.

The white. Finally, the white. The reassuring brilliance of *Élan Vital*, so warm, so fluid, so effervescent.

The creature's wails threatened to burst my ear drums. Then, almost inexplicably, the sound began to decrease in volume, as if someone at a master switch were turning a knob. And the quieter it became, the less it pulled. As the shriek dwindled to a near-inaudible drone, I was able to pull my leg back to myself. The charred, deflated remains of the tentacle were twisted around the lower cuff of my pants like any average dried-out vine. I shook it loose with a grunt of disgust and continued to climb.

It wasn't until I reached the top that I realized I was no longer injured.

Chapter 29

When I surfaced from the ravine, Genevieve rushed to me and covered my face, including my newly healed cheek, in kisses. "You're okay? You're really okay?" she asked, and then proceeded to run her hands over my chest and down each arm, checking for wounds, to reassure herself that I was indeed alive and unscathed. Regardless of the reason, I was happy to oblige it for a few minutes until I finally pulled her into a long embrace.

"It's okay," I said. "It's going to be okay."

But then I opened my eyes, and I knew we would never travel another step together.

The men, if one could accurately call them that, wore the familiar black robes with red piping, white gloves on their right hands. Perhaps among them there was a Sentinel, but I couldn't tell just then. Unlike previous Hand of God agents we'd faced, these didn't carry the Holy Staves or electric sticks; they had guns, and the chests of their robes were heavily armored. But they still wore masks. Molded black things with sophisticated hoses and tubes running in and out of them. I couldn't see their eyes.

One of them stepped forward. "State your names, sinners." His voice rippled and grated, like it was coming out of a very old machine. I thought of Turpin's intercom back in God's Hope.

I was at a loss for words, but Genevieve didn't seem nearly as fazed as me. "Do exactly as I do. No funny business," she whispered and stepped forward.

"I am Alaina Frizzell, and this is my husband Thomas. We are seeking the Sin Bin in Purgatory."

I wanted to gape at her, but I kept my face passive.

"Please provide identification," said the agent.

Again, I had to hold back my shock. I was positive they would know who we were on sight, but maybe news didn't travel equally among the different groups. And of course, given our recent encounter with the local wildlife, it was clear things were different up here.

Genevieve held out her hands. "I'm afraid we don't have any. Our belongings were lost to harriers on the road, and we nearly died attempting to cross the ravine. We seek refuge in the Sin Bin. We have surrendered to the truth of our futility as citizens and will not pass Justification." She got down on her knees, and a second later, I followed suit.

The HOG agents marched forward in a wave of black cloth. The horror of being so close to so many of them made it easy enough for my knees to buckle. Genevieve had said no funny business, which I presumed to mean she didn't want me using any of my ability to slay these people, but I doubt I could have anyway. There were too many of them for me to be sure we could get off any attack cleanly. Furthermore, the power seemed to have eluded me again.

"On your feet, sinners."

Iron strong hands wrapped around my biceps and pulled

me up to my feet as if I were made of straw. I looked one of them in the face, but only saw smoked glass lenses looking back at me. The mask's hoses hissed with every breath.

"Will you take us to Purgatory?" I asked.

"You require ample currency to gain entrance into the Sin Bin." The agent pulled a small black device from inside his robe and pressed the button. "However, women usually have ways of paying from within." He yanked Genevieve close and my skin went cold.

"No, no we must stay together!" I cried.

"Don't worry. You'll be together again soon."

The buzz of a coming locust plague stopped any remaining begging in its tracks. The sky soon went black, and my screams were drowned in the descending swarm. Millions of beating wings and crawling appendages surrounded and finally filled my clothes and then my mouth, barely allowing me the air to breathe. Every muscle in my body soon became paralyzed. The bugs even nestled in my eyes, blocking my vision. My feet left the ground, and I soon detected the sensation of flying. This happened to Beth, I thought. This is what happened to everyone who ever took a ride to a Cradle.

My terror threatened to consume me completely as the locusts carried me away. I saw not so much as a glimmer of the *Élan Vital* within my reach, not even enough to comfort me. But soon enough, my consciousness showed me a mercy and fled.

—

I awoke in a bed to the sight of sunlight filtering in through white lace curtains. I sat up, my skin still crawling with the memory of the locusts, and for a moment I was sure they were still crawling through my hair, along my arms and the back of my neck. I rubbed furiously at every part of myself. My mouth tasted of something closely resembling dirt.

"No more of that, boyo. The locusts left ya near three days ago."

I looked over to see Turpin sitting in a chair beside the bed, his cane propped up between his legs. Surely he was an apparition. My mind had detached from itself permanently, and I was in a dream or the *Élan Vital*. Had to be. He must have seen this doubt on my face, because he cackled.

"I'm as real as real can be, boyo. Yer back in Old Babylon, certain as the sunshine coming in through yonder window."

"But . . . how?"

"Yer decision to befriend the Heretic was a wise one. It seems they are all loyal to him now. Him that was, anyway, bless his soul. If he has one."

I swung my legs out of the bed and stood up. Immediately my head began to swim, and I sat back down. "We have to get her. She's in the Sin Bin. In Purgatory."

"I know it, boyo. The shapeshifter brought everyone up to speed on that."

"Where is he? I want to speak with him."

"You'll be able to do that soon enough. Right now, just take it easy. Our boys are on the case, and as soon as we're ready to go, you'll be on yer way to rescuin' Harry's girl. Christoph has experience with these things, as ya know."

Christoph. It felt good to hear that name again. To see

Turpin. So much had happened since we left them behind. I never thought I'd see any of them again. Had already said goodbye to them in my head, in fact.

The old man was about to get up, but he stopped and bowed his head. "I was damn sorry to hear about Kaya. She was a good girl. Strong and fierce like her dad."

I swallowed the lump in my throat. Up until Turpin had mentioned it, I had forgotten that Kaya was gone. I guess part of my mind still imagined she was around somewhere, that she was going to burst into the room and tell me to get my ass out of bed. But the weight of reality gradually settled in, and I found it even harder to hold myself up.

"She was better than me," I said with a throat that felt lined with broken glass. "I'm sure she gave them hell till the very end."

"We're gonna get yer other girl back too."

I felt as disconnected from Beth now as I did from the *Élan Vital*. But I couldn't tell Turpin that. He'd think I was a monster. "I hope so."

A knock sounded at the door and an old woman came in bearing a tray of food. I almost didn't recognize her at first, but for the eye patch. Then I recalled. She was one of the Sister's Ugly. In the days since I'd last seen her, she'd cleaned herself up quite a bit, and had even put a few pounds on her emaciated body. I also noticed the clusters of sores that had been around her mouth were clearing up.

She placed the tray, which held a bowl of steaming soup, on the table beside my bed then shuffled meekly toward the door.

"Thank you, Miss," I said. "I . . . I remember you. But I

don't remember your name."

She turned to me, her head bowed. "I'm Tessa, my Lord."

Turpin rolled his eyes. "Tess, old girl, ya need to stop dispensin' the Lords and Sirs." He looked at me. "She's doin' that to everyone 'round here. Don't matter how many times we tell her we ain't in charge o' no one."

Tessa didn't seem swayed by Turpin's words. If anything, she bowed her head deeper. "You saved our lives and set us free, Lords. We owe thee our deepest respects."

Turpin sighed. "Thee? Now yer spoutin' off like Shakespeare. See what I mean?"

I sat up. "Tessa, can you come here, please?" I held out my hands, but for a moment she seemed almost afraid to come too close. Somehow I'd been elevated to God status since the last time I took her hand. On some level, I couldn't really blame her for being afraid. My hands had done a lot of frightening things lately, and she could probably sense that. But she finally came around and placed her hands in mine.

"Look me in the eye, Tessa. Chin up."

After a moment, she raised her eyes. This close, I could see the cloudiness in her one good eye. A cataract, likely, though I couldn't tell if it was coming or going. Lines grooved every square inch of her skin, but she was beautiful to me. Like a statue that had weathered the worst nature could throw at it, but still stood defiantly against it. I wondered what stories those wrinkles could tell.

"You don't owe us your fealty, Tessa. Do you understand?"

Her mouth quivered a bit, but she didn't break her gaze as she shook her head no.

I sighed. "I came from a town that wasn't much different

from this one. The reason my friends and I are fighting this fight is because we want a world where no one should have to call anyone else Lord or anything like it. Those names make us feel like we haven't succeeded. We just want to be equals, Tessa. Does that make sense?"

Her eye seemed to grow a little clearer at that. She nodded. "Yes. Yes, I think so."

"Good. Now be sure to spread the word, because I know you're good at doing that. We're all equals here. We act as one." I kissed her hands and let them go. When she left the room, she was no longer shuffling.

Turpin stared at me for a moment, jaw dropped. "Ya really are a miracle man, boyo."

"Hardly. I'm a guy who's lost his whole family. Two of them by fault of my own. I don't feel too comfortable being treated like a god."

"She would've only taken that kind of advice from you, though. Yer principles are noble, but like it or not, yer the leader here."

My head started throbbing. A leader was the last thing I ever wanted to be, but Turpin was as stubborn as Tessa. I decided to let it drop. Turpin got up and gave himself a bone-cracking stretch. "I suppose I should get back to things. There's a lot of sick people in this town we're tryin' to fix. Dunno if the medicine Harry's makin' is gonna heal all of 'em, but we're gonna do our damndest. We need as many folks as we can to hold the Hand of God at bay when they come."

"Do you know if they're coming?" I asked.

"No word just yet. There's a lot of ground to cover, and takin' out that Cradle and freein' the Heretics probably slowed them down a lot, but it's inevitable."

"How do you feel about our chances?"

"I don't know that we'll win against 'em. Their numbers will be greater than ours. But we got a few tricks up our sleeves, and we won't go down easy."

"I never saw us going down any other way, Turpin."

I stood up again. This time, I was a little less woozy and a little steadier on my feet. "I'm coming with you. I want to see our new shapeshifter." I was afraid he was going to try to stop me, but he didn't. I guess now he saw me as the leader too.

Chapter 30

Saul's store had been cleaned up since I last saw it. One of the other Sisters Ugly (I reminded myself to actually learn both their names and stop calling them that) was sweeping the wood plank floors. The sound of hammers hitting nails seemed to echo all around me as people repaired and rebuilt the parts of the town damaged from the looting.

Although a few items were on the store's shelves, things were haphazard and disorganized. It didn't look much like Saul was doing real business anymore. He waved at me from behind the counter, where he sat writing something down. "Welcome back, John! Good to see you up and around."

"Thanks, Saul."

Harry and Christoph were sitting at a table behind him studying the map I'd gotten from Zehn. I was surprised my belongings survived the trip. When they saw me, they both got up. Harry was beaming, despite his red-rimmed eyes. He looked like he'd been crying, and I couldn't blame him. Even Christoph's mouth twitched in a ghost of a grin, which was an enormous display of affection for him. I shook the big German's hand and reached out to do the same with Harry, but he bypassed it and gave me a big hug. He held on for a minute, and I could feel the tremor beneath his skin followed by the sound of his big wet sobs. Seeing the big man weeping had me tearing up as well.

"We're gonna get her back, right, John? We're gonna get our girl."

"I'll stop at nothing," I said. I knew his agony all too well. He pulled back and wiped his wet face on his shirtsleeve.

"Sorry about that," he said. "I haven't been able to stop ever since Kaya, and now this. I can't believe those sons of bitches have my baby girl in one of those places."

"She's one of the strongest people I know," I said. And she has a baby to fight for too, I thought. It would give her a reason to keep going. I wondered if I should tell Harry his daughter was carrying my child, but I had a feeling that might only make him break down again.

The two men led me over to their table, where I saw far more than just Zehn's map. I was a little disheartened not to see the actual mapmaker with them, but perhaps he was still making his way here.

There was also a hand-drawn layout of Old Babylon, and lines drawn over it in red. "What's this?" I asked.

"Our defense plan," Christoph said.

"Yep," said Harry. "We got the net back up and running right away, which is good. Christoph and I have been working some extra defensive measures into it. We're also constructing a wall around the main part of the city, using lumber from Akiva Paine's property. We all agreed that the house should no longer stand. It's cursed."

"You'll get no argument from me there," I said. It was the last place I'd seen my daughter alive. I remembered how she'd urged me to go before her down the privy. If I hadn't, if

I'd been more forceful, things would be very different now. "I need to speak with the shapeshifter. Can you tell me where he is?"

"You mean Chitin?" Harry pointed out the door. "He's out there. Doesn't do indoors if he can help it."

I thought of Anansi, who was also wary of being inside. But he had sat with us in the old church that night, enjoying bourbon and the stories Turpin told.

I walked outside and looked up and down the dirt-packed main avenue that Genevieve and I had not too long ago traveled with Akiva Paine's cart and mule. The town that had looked abandoned and haunted on that day was now surging with life. People dashed up and down the wooden sidewalks carrying tools and wood from the direction of Paine's deconstructed plantation. Others were sweeping out the ashes and debris from the burnt Fellowship. Thankfully, someone had taken down the bodies that were hanging there and disposed of them, along with the dead mule that was in the street.

A few people were eating their lunches on nearby benches or resting beneath the dappled shade of the hickory trees. I heard bright bubbles of their conversation floating around, but most importantly, I heard laughter.

It was a feeling both simple and beautiful, but revolutionary, a sense of peace I don't think I ever felt during my most torpid days in God's Hope, where everything was green and nothing else mattered. The threat of Justification put a strain on people. It was subtle but palpable. People were afraid to have much fun. Every action, no matter how small, had to be checked and re-checked, and would often haunt a person long after. With that threat gone, however, it was as if a giant invisible hand had been lifted from the throats of these people. Though their troubles were far from over, they were enjoying their moments here under the sun, free of charge for the first time in their lives. Even if it only lasted a day, it was worth it.

When I stepped off the porch, there was an obvious break in the commotion. The conversation and laughter faded as everyone looked in my direction. Soon, the only sound was of the leaves rustling in the light breeze. Then the two people standing closest to me, a pair of men in overalls with planks of wood hoisted on their shoulders, set their load down on the ground, and began to clap.

More people joined them, and the applause began to swell, with hoots and even whistles joining the chorus. Soon, most of the town was gathered before me, including Tessa and her sister. I wanted nothing more than to turn on my heels and run, but my feet were more or less glued to their spot. I couldn't turn my back on these people, as much as I didn't want their accolades, as much as I thought I didn't deserve them. Genevieve should have been here for this. It was her damn Railroad that led us here. Even Harry, Turpin, and Christoph were better for this than I. They'd worked tirelessly for years to subvert Justification and ferry people to safety. I was just a passenger. Worse, I felt like a fraud.

I couldn't take the applause any longer. I raised my hands. "Thank you. Please, please, I don't deserve this," I tried to say, but their cheers overrode me.

"You DO deserve it!"

"Hail, John Welland!"

"Bringer of the Light!"

I looked behind me and saw Harry and Christoph flanking either side of the door, grinning, their arms folded across their chests. There was no help there. I turned back to the crowd and raised my hands again. This time, the applause began to die back. The last to stop was Tessa, whose eye was shining with a form of adoration that made me feel ill. "Thank you everyone for your kind words, and for your support." My stomach and my knees were quivering like jelly, and I couldn't keep the shaking out of my voice, but I pushed forward anyway. Most of these people had lived here their whole lives. Others had lived in the Cradle, being starved and tortured day after day. All had suffered, and they craved hope just as they craved any other nourishment.

I cleared my throat one last time, took a deep breath, held it, and then let the words flow from me, as I did the energy from the *Élan Vital*.

"I am more grateful for your support than you will ever know. Therefore, I will not do you the disservice of being less than brutally honest. The road to our freedom is going to be long and hard. Many of you, including myself, will likely die to protect what we've started here. I've already lost my daughter Kaya, and may yet lose my other daughter, Beth. My mother and father fought against the Divine Rite long ago, and they too gave their lives. And there are many more who have died along the way trying to usurp these tyrants. Their struggles were great, but ours will be even greater. I have seen what is out there, and I am here to tell you our foe is bigger and stronger than we feared."

No one reacted to this. They knew we were fighting an impossible fight. The bald and emaciated ones we had rescued from the Cradle knew better than anyone. Their solemn eyes told more stories than I had years to hear. I pushed on, feeling more at ease as I went.

"If we're willing to do the same as my parents, if we don't back down even when the tide turns against us, if we continue to fight as our blood mingles with theirs on the streets of Old Babylon and beyond, we may just prevail. I will understand if you turn back from this call, if you'd rather live your lives as quietly as you can. I will say nothing. I will not force you to take up arms. You may even turn away right this second, if that's your wish."

I waited for people to start falling away from the crowd, but no one moved. No one even flinched. In truth, I wasn't surprised. These people knew the lives that were waiting for them if they quit now, and they didn't want to go back. Or maybe they realized they couldn't even if they wanted to. If they fell back, they would certainly die. Might as well take the honorable route.

"I will soon be taking the fight to them myself, in Purgatory, where they are holding Harry's daughter Genevieve captive. They will not hold her for long, however, once they discover she's one of us. They will kill her."

Several gasps escaped the crowd. One of the gentlemen who had begun the round of applause and cheers earlier stepped forward. "What can we do, Sir Welland?"

I cringed inwardly at the address, but there wasn't time for that. I still had to find Chitin and speak with him. "You will hold the town here. Christoph and Turpin will show you all the ways of the gun, if you're unfamiliar. But if you're not comfortable with combat, there will likely be many other jobs to do. The important thing is that we stand together."

Tessa's sister stepped forward. Her shoulders were hunched, but her eyes were aflame with passion. "No quarter for the pious sons of bitches!"

The crowd erupted in raucous applause and cheers, and I felt a hand on my shoulder.

I turned around and met a pair of bright orange eyes flecked with green. His coffee colored skin and tight black curls reminded me painfully of Anansi, but this was not Anansi.

Chitin was taller, for one thing, and his face longer, with gaunt cheekbones and a dimple in his chin. But most noticeably, he lacked the spirited mirth of his brother-in-arms, or whatever they called each other. This one looked grave. "We must speak, John Welland," he said. Beneath the words ran that same restrained buzz unique to Heretics.

I nodded. "Yes."

Harry stepped forward to finish talking to the group as we walked off. I was relieved to be getting away as Chitin led me down the sidewalk and around the backside of the building, where a couple of chairs had been set up. On a small table sat a deck of playing cards laid out in a game of solitaire.

"Please, have a seat," he said. "My accommodations might not look like much, but compared to living under the Rite, it is a palace."

I sat down and looked at his wrist. There was no bracelet. "Who freed you?" I asked.

"A group of children from the Cradle, still strong enough in their ability. Harry instructed them in the ways of it, as he remembered from when you freed my swarm brother from his bonds."

Swarm brother. I liked that. "Is he the one who told you about all this? Why you brought me here?"

Chitin reached into his shirt pocket and pulled out a familiar looking whistle. "Word spreads quickly among our kind. Others will be coming here soon. They will help your people against the Divine Rite."

"I appreciate that," I said. "But will you take me to Purgatory? I need to get into the Sin Bin."

Chitin's orange eyes were penetrating. It was hard to hold that gaze for too long. "Getting in is easy. It's getting out that's the problem."

"Yes, I know. Are they heavily guarded?"

"In a manner of speaking. But not in the way you're thinking. The people in those places are held in thrall somehow. A queen bee of sorts who isn't much different from the Sentinels, but extremely rare and far more powerful. As I understand it, she bonds with their minds and puts them into some sort of trance."

As outrageous as it sounded, I wasn't surprised by any of it anymore. Not after everything I'd seen and done. The queen bee was just another tool of the Rite.

"What happens if we release them anyway? Kill the queen?" I asked.

"Almost no one could survive separation from the psychic bond."

"Our friend Christoph, he and his family escaped a Sin Bin once. He's the only one who made it."

Chitin nodded thoughtfully. "That is interesting. I imagine it changed him greatly."

I thought of the big German's stony, nearly expressionless

demeanor and didn't argue.

"I can see no other way to go about this."

Chitin didn't have any eyebrows, but I could see that part of his forehead rise in a similar expression. "What's your plan?"

"It's simple, really. We free everyone. Queen bee included."

Chapter 31

I spent the remainder of that day in my room, deep in a sort of meditative trance, in the hopes that it would allow me to reopen my connection to the *Élan Vital*. It was like trying to grab a single strand of hair blowing in the wind, but at least it was there, which was an improvement. After fighting the creature in the ravine, I knew I still had the capacity to wield it, but it was going to be difficult to control and predict. I decided the best way to deal with the problem was to just stop dealing with it. Stop trying.

Chitin and I decided we would leave that night in order to decrease our chances of being spotted. Turpin and Harry were apprehensive about me going in alone, but Christoph reminded them that the more people who were with me, the higher the likelihood of something going wrong. Aside from the support of the Heretics, this was going to be a solo mission.

I slept what was probably the last real sleep I remember having, and it couldn't even rightly be called that. Faces swam in and out of my vision. Kaya, Genevieve, Linny, Beth. However, Beth's face was the least distinctive. The vision I had of her was simply a longer-haired version of Kaya, but my mind insisted—outright scolded really—that Beth was different. Was it the slight bend in her nose? That had to be it. There was also a birthmark on her right shoulder.

Or was that Kaya? Kaya with the tiny birthmark that looked a little like a one-winged butterfly? She'd even named it when she was three or four. Matilda, wasn't it? Where had she come up with that name, anyway?

I sat up in bed, sweaty and ashamed. Any parent with twins should have known better. Linny would have been ashamed of me. I promised to myself that if I ever got Beth back, I would never again let her go. I would never forget.

It was past midnight when I made my way downstairs. Saul had retired, but Harry, Turpin, and Christoph were pulling sentry duty on the front porch. Or rather, the big German was. Harry and Turpin were lounging in rocking chairs, sipping at a familiar looking amber liquid. I had a sudden craving for a bit of it myself. I almost denied myself the pleasure, but then I considered where I was headed. And how I was going to get there.

"Mind if I have a bit of that?" I asked.

"Yer damn straight," Turpin said and topped off the shot from the bottle he kept at his feet like a faithful dog.

"Thank you," I said, relishing the woody sweetness of it.

"Happy to help, boyo. There'll be more waitin' here when ya get back."

I nearly said, "If I make it back," but I couldn't with Harry sitting there and hoping beyond all hope that he'd see his daughter again. Instead, I just finished my drink and handed him back the glass. "I'll definitely need it."

"The town's likely going to be facing a battle of its own when you return," Harry said. "They aren't going to take too kindly to you laying waste to another one of their facilities."

"How many will be able to fight?" I asked.

"Not enough." Christoph's deep voice stomped into the conversation like a big heavy boot. "We need more. I will be having other Heretics scouting for more recruits in the towns downriver."

"Yeppo," Turpin said. "Eudora's been ripe to go rogue for awhile now. Won't take much to turn 'em."

"Assuming the Rite hasn't turned them into soldiers by now," muttered Harry.

"They can do that?" I asked.

"They can do whatever they want. And they'll do whatever they can to boost their numbers to fight a war. It would be different if we could use these Sentinels we rescued from the Cradle. I've been working with them, but they're weak without Ezekiel and growing weaker. It took three of them to break Chitin's bracelet."

It seemed we were all growing weaker. Perhaps my brother had been key to it all. But then there was this queen bee figure at the Sin Bin. What was powering her?

Chitin walked around the side of the building. If it hadn't been for the torches lit around the structure, he would have been nearly invisible. At least if he'd kept his strange eyes closed. "Hello, men. Pleasant night, is it not?"

"As pleasant as things get these days," said Turpin.

"Indeed. I've noticed you have your perimeters manned. Will they hold until my swarm brothers can arrive?"

Turpin shrugged. "They'll have to. We'll get by as we can and hope that John will create enough of a distraction to the west that they'll forget about us for a little bit longer. Every extra day we have counts."

"Yes. Each day is a blessing. You have given the people here something to fight for. You have already helped free my people. Not all of them may come. They are afraid. They do not know their own power. But I do believe that most of them will be unable to resist the siren call of freedom."

"Most of us can't," said Turpin.

Chitin turned to me. "Are you ready to travel to Purgatory, John Welland?"

Goosebumps rippled my skin. I remembered my last trip all too well. The thought of being enveloped by more swarming bugs did little to settle my nerves. "I'm about as ready as ready can be."

The two men rose from their rocking chairs and approached me, hands out. None of them would say what was obvious, that this would likely be the last time they'd see me alive, but we knew it anyway. "You give 'em hell, John," Harry said. "Bring my girl back to me."

I felt incapable of making a promise that I didn't know I could keep, but I met his eyes and gave him a nod. Turpin clapped me on the shoulder. "Last time ya left here, I didn't think I'd be seein' ya again, boyo. So I'm thinkin' if I treat it the same, I'll not be testin' the fates too much."

"I hope you're right, Turpin. Thank you for everything you've done." I shook his hand, careful of the old and brittle bones, and stepped down to the street, where Chitin was waiting. I think I dreaded the experience of flying with him more than the prospect of storming the Sin Bin. "Let's get this show on the road," I said.

"I promise to go easier on you this time. You will ride as

passenger rather than prisoner."

"I appreciate that," I told him, though I didn't think it would be much better. Chitin took several paces back until he stood in the middle of the wide, empty avenue. He looked to the sky and spread his arms wide like a man receiving the spirit of God.

"Lift up a banner in the land! Blow the trumpet among the nations! Prepare the nations for battle against her; summon against her these kingdoms: Ararat, Minni and Ashkenaz. Appoint a commander against her; send up horses like a swarm of locusts!"

I chilled at the words, plucked from the book of Jeremiah when God summoned the people to rise against Babylon. In a split second, he burst outward in a nova of insects made sentient from their feasts upon this cursed land. I closed my eyes and lost myself in the drone. The bugs, mercifully, did not fill my mouth this time while they surrounded me like a tickling coat that lifted my feet gently from the ground.

I dared to open my eyes and witness my body moving ever closer to the stars ahead. Below, the torches of Old Babylon burned into the night. Those watching at the gates, at least the ones I could see, waved their hands. I could see Akiva Paine's dismantled house and the devoured wasteland that surrounded it. The place where the corn had once been was a bare patch laid to waste by Anansi as his final gift to the earth. It would be some years before anyone could plant there, but the land would produce again. It always did.

Chitin turned a full one hundred eighty degrees, and we were now facing the direction of Purgatory. Darkness shrouded the land, though from this height, a few small clusters of light were spread about in tiny villages and steads that had managed to spring up over the years in places not consumed by the weeds. Places like Zehn's. The Divine Rite and Justification still held sway over them, of course, but perhaps they could be convinced to fight.

The locust swarm protected my body from the chill of the wind, but my face was soon numb from it. I closed my eyes and tucked my chin in the hopes of averting the chill. Soon, I was asleep and floating in darkness, free of the locusts. A pinpoint of light lurked ahead and I swam toward it. Eventually it grew to an all-encompassing sun, the warmth enfolding me in its embrace, caressing my skin. It was limitless, so beautiful and pure and free. I reached out and felt a soft, invisible give, as if the light itself was a malleable force. Ethereal putty.

But of course it was. That had always been the beauty of it, hadn't it? The gift of the *Élan Vital*.

I took both hands and began to sculpt a face. My fingers worked without much guidance. They knew what my eyes wanted to see. Soon, Kaya was gazing at me. "Daddy, don't forget her. She needs you."

At first, I didn't know what she was talking about, but then a brief image popped into my head. Beth. My sweet Beth. How could I have ever forgotten that face? It was the longer nose like mine, the freckles on her cheeks, her eyes the same light blue as her mother's.

"Can you see her? Is she in Donum Dei?"

"I can't reach her. She's beyond me . . . I am beyond me . . ."

Her face was losing definition, but I reached out, trying to sculpt again, only the light would not yield to my fingers. "Kaya! No, don't leave!"

Her features swam like a reflection on a rippling pond, turning her mouth up into her trademark crooked grin before it dissolved completely.

Desperate, my hands went back to work, this time sculpting the same face, but with the features slightly elongated, the hair longer. Beth. My Beth.

"I still remember you," I whispered, gazing at my creation.

But this was not right. A black thread was corrupting the landscape of her face, first breaking apart her forehead in a jagged line and then her left cheek. The blackness filled her eyes with pools of brackish ink that spilled out in big, wet drips I tried to wipe away, but only succeeded in smearing into a substance like war paint. She opened her mouth, and the sound of her screams filled my head, threatening to shatter my skull from the inside out. The force of it pushed me out of the light, tumbling me backward into the cold darkness.

"Beth, no!"

My eyes flew open, and I was struck by an immediate disorientation in mid-air. Thankfully, I could not see the ground, though maybe if I could, I might not have felt as out of control. In the darkness, I couldn't tell whether I was up or down. My body contorted in its insect shell, and the monotone hum of the swarm warbled a bit as it pitched and yawed.

Finally, I caught sight of the half-bloat of the moon just above me, and my mind asserted some control again over my rogue body. I stilled and breathed in and out, thinking the same disconcerting thought over and over.

Beth is in trouble. Beth is alive, but she's also in trouble.

But didn't I know that all along? Didn't I know it and

abandon her anyway, from the very beginning when I fled God's Hope?

Then, just as I'd settled back into the course, a new light appeared far below, nestled amid the mountains like a pearl in an oyster. This was no tangible, ethereal illumination, but a hard white beam slicing right through the night. A cluster of brick buildings lay below, with the unmistakable movement of bodies, ant-like from this height, milling about them. Whether they were agents of the Rite or residents themselves, I couldn't tell. And although I had never before seen even a picture of one of these places, I was certain I was looking at a Sin Bin. I could hear the barest whisper of its lullaby calling to me, promising bliss and secret pleasures within its walls.

Genevieve was somewhere in there.

The swarm veered away from this sight and began to descend well shy of the compound, presumably so we could avoid detection.

Once my feet hit the ground, the bugs immediately dispersed, letting the chilly mountain air hit my skin in full. I wondered why I hadn't thought to dress in warmer clothes. The landscape here was a lush huddle of firs smelling strongly of pine. Patches of snow nestled at their bases, and I could hear the trickle of a stream somewhere nearby. No serpent weeds near here, at least that I could see.

Chitin took form quickly nearby and walked the rest of the way up the slope to join me. In the lack of light, he was just a pair of floating orange eyes. "You nearly lost me, John Welland. Why the struggle?"

"I fell asleep. Had a bad dream."

"Doesn't surprise me this close to a Sin Bin. This is bad ground."

I looked around. "I don't see any weeds, at least."

"What's here is worse than weeds." He stepped to one of the tower firs. "Come, touch this tree trunk."

I did as he asked and placed my hand upon the wood. I was immediately filled with a sense of revulsion. The trunk of the fir didn't feel like wood at all. It felt like . . . flesh. Cold, bumpy flesh, almost like that of a reptile. I yanked my hand away, feeling violated. My stomach roiled in disgust. "My God! What *is* that?"

"An abomination," Chitin said. "We are very close to Donum Dei, and whatever it was that perverted this land. Some of my swarm brothers say it is a place where a hole has been ripped through the fabric of all things, and it is that from whence the weeds came. And all that followed."

"Did you see this? This hole?"

"Fortunately, no. But I don't need to. As you can imagine, my kind has never been of this world. What world, I do not know. I was born here. But it's a strange evolution, wouldn't you say? A little too strange? Even time is funny around here."

I thought of the strangely long detour we took that brought us to Zehn's house and agreed.

"But they said the Blight came from science gone amok. That we brought this fate on ourselves through tinkering with creation."

"That may have once been. Perhaps it was science that opened that gateway. I'd say by accident. But the Rite is mad. They believe these things are now the works of the true god. If there is indeed a hole torn in the fabric of our universe, they believe it speaks to them and only them. Everything else is just simple control, John Welland. And plucking out those who exhibit the characteristics of a brand new race."

A cold horror filled me. No matter how hard we fought, there would be no victory until that doorway was closed. If it even could be closed.

"Donum Dei will have to wait, John Welland. Yonder Sin Bin is where we must go. And you need to listen, for I think I have a plan to get you inside."

Chapter 32

"You're going to feel the siren call from the moment you emerge from these trees," Chitin said. "You may want to fight it, but it is a waste of time and will only force you to expend too much energy. Surrender is the only true way through."

I could already hear it. It was fainter than it had been overhead, but it was giving me a tingle that felt almost like a budding orgasm.

"Do you feel it?" I asked.

Chitin shook his head. "Our minds are not wired that way. The temptation for you to remain there will be strong, and it won't be long before the spell she weaves sticks for good. In fact, I suspect I may never see you again once you go inside."

"You know, that isn't very encouraging."

"I am sorry, John Welland. I speak only truth."

"It's okay. I'd rather hear honesty."

"Just get to the queen bee. If you can rescue her or find a way to sever her connection with the thralls, your chances will improve."

I had no idea how I was supposed to do that. "Of course, right."

"I will create a diversion to bring the front guards toward the gate. They will likely not even see you get in. Remember, it isn't getting inside that's the problem."

"Yes, yes. It's getting out. I know. Now can we go?" I sounded a little more impatient than I'd intended, but it probably had something to do with standing in a forest filled with fleshy trees.

Chitin handed me Anansi's whistle. "The Bin is about a mile from here. You won't need a map, because the call of what's inside will guide you. Use this when you get to the outer fence. You shouldn't have trouble climbing it, since they don't usually worry about people trying to sneak in or out. I only hope to hear the whistle again, when you've made your escape. By then, I will have more of my swarm brothers ready to assist us." He slapped my back with his hard hand. "God be with you, John Welland."

"And you as well, Chitin."

He quickly dispersed into the night. Although I could see the light just over the hill, I didn't need it to guide me. The song of the queen bee inside was pulling me along like a dog on a leash.

Come to me come to me come to me come come . . .

The closer I got, I could hear music. Strings and drums in a syncopated beat, accompanied by the crooning of a deep male voice. *A well I bless my soul, what's wrong with me? I'm itching like a man on a fuzzy tree. My friends say I'm actin' wild as a bug. I'm in love. I'm all shook up.*

I'd never heard the song, or anything like it, but it was nothing at all like the organ powered hymns played during mass at the Fellowship every week. The Rite had a list of approved songs and musicians, all of it religious propaganda of some sort. This certainly didn't sound religious, in spite of its mention of blessing souls, but I liked it. A lot.

I realized with a distant sinking feeling that I wanted . . . no *needed* . . . to see the inside of the Sin Bin, and not only to rescue Genevieve. It was more of a carnal demand.

Chitin had been correct about the fence. It was five-feet of wrought iron, with easy places for footholds. It was almost as if they'd designed it to be scaled, but strategically placed temptation was something the Rite had always excelled at. I could smell roasting meat mingling with other enticing scents. Tobacco, possibly even some of Akiva Paine's cannabis.

I hunkered down in the grasses lining the fence and closed my eyes against the swell of the music and the even stronger call of the queen bee inside as she sank her psychic hooks into my mind. I was dimly aware of an erection stirring in my pants. Getting inside was all I could think of, so to speak. The urge to tumble over the fence now, leaving Chitin and all other obligations behind, was nearly overwhelming. There was real food in there and the bourbon flowed like water. I was certain of it. Real bourbon too, possibly hoarded from the previous generation when corn was as common as air.

And there was sex. I couldn't shake the obsessive certainty that there were people fucking in there. Probably in groups. I remembered a term Reverend Blackwell always used to describe sinful decadence. *Bacchanalian.*

I grasped the bars of the fence. My thoughts
(*I need . . . I want . . . I must . . .*)
in swift competition with the queen bee's
(*come to me . . . come . . . come . . .*).
If a mosquito hadn't lit upon the back of my neck, I might

never have blown the whistle to summon Chitin. I might still be in the Sin Bin even now, in spite of the horror I discovered once inside its inner sanctum.

But I reached back and slapped my neck free of the feasting bug, and in turn brought myself back from the brink, at least just enough to remember my part of Chitin's plan. I put the hollow reed to my lips, and for the second and final time in my life, I summoned a plague.

The swarm was immediate. My mostly unimpeded view allowed me to see the commotion of black robes heading toward the main gate. I heard first one scream, then several, but finally my yearning could no longer be held back. I had to go now.

Needed to go.

I grasped the top of the fence and vaulted myself over. Easy. Too easy. Of course it was. It wasn't as if I'd expected any different. I headed toward the nearest building, but I was immediately caught up in a school of people—not Hand of God, but regular looking men and women. They weren't exactly in a panic. In fact, they didn't look particularly interested in the nearby chaos. They just wanted to get to their next destination in the funhouse.

The music changed to a throb of deep bass that wormed its way into my head and down my torso before settling into my groin. The group of people (or school of fish, more like) cheered out in unison and began pumping their fists. Most of the women were only half dressed, their glittered breasts spilling out of their skimpy tops. Their skirts were little more than scraps of cloth hanging from their waists. I saw faces dusted with glitter, painted in rouge and kohl, their lips dyed various shades of red and pink and blue, hair puffed up and dyed in brilliant colors of red, pink, turquoise.

They were like living erotic paintings.

The men were thankfully not dressed so differently from me, so I could blend in. Sure, there were a few in full makeup and leather body suits, spikes, or chaps. I also spied plenty of face jewelry. But most were wearing short-sleeves and pants, overalls, jackets and hats.

I followed the school through the enormous revolving door and into the Sin Bin.

The music was louder in here, bone shaking. Bodies pressed together beneath tendrils of smoke colored pink and green and blue by the hypnotically pulsing lights. The smell of sweat was primal, meaty. The warm press of flesh jettisoned nearly every coherent thought from my head. But the voice of the queen bee overrode it all. That divine jingle settling in, making itself at home. If I didn't finish this quickly, I would come to depend on that feeling the same way I depended on my heartbeat.

I looked up and saw at least two levels to the space. People were leaning over the rails, holding colorful beverages and cigarettes. Others danced, kissed, or performed even more daring acts out in the open. I nearly tripped over a woman who had her head buried in one man's trousers.

She pulled her head away and looked up with a scowl on her face. Her eye makeup was a black and blue glitter smear. "Watch where you're fookin' goin'! I nearly bit off his member!" She pronounced "member" as "membah." I couldn't really place the accent, but she must have come from afar.

The man, whose penis was jutting out of his fly like the

head of some curious animal, didn't seem to notice me at all. He just pushed the woman's head down and his eyes glazed back over. I envied him a little.

That made me think of Genevieve. Beautiful Genevieve with the red hair and green cat eyes, the soft curves that melded so perfectly against me. I didn't just want to find her to rescue her. I wanted to find her so I could have her. It was a purely animalistic motivation by that point, as my brain soaked up the music and the atmosphere. I hadn't had a thing to drink or smoke, but I felt almost drunk with the libidinous urges surging through the place.

As I moved deeper into the room, the voice in my head grew more urgent.

"*come ... come ... come ... COME ... come ...*"

Phantom hands explored my chest, my ass. Another—it could have belonged to a man or woman, I couldn't tell— tugged at my erection, which had been prominent since I vaulted the fence outside. My vision went white for a moment and the room faded back little by little.

There was knowledge in that whiteness. A room I had to go to. I thought I could see the inside of it, but I needed more light. I needed to find that room. I needed to know ...

My eyes scanned the dance floor until they settled on a likely woman. She danced alone in a white gauzy dress. Through the flimsy cloth, I could see the pink-brown circles of her nipples. Her hair cascaded down her back like chocolate silk. As her hips swayed to the music, she brought her hands up to her nipples and squeezed. Completely lost in the beat, my erection strained at my pants. The primal need took over. But it was more than that. It was the only way I could see what I needed to see.

"COME... COME... COME..."

I stepped up to the woman and pulled her to me. She fell against my chest, no resistance. Her eyes were the brightest blue. Her lips tasted like fresh strawberries dipped in cream and sugar. She wasn't shy with her hands, and soon, I could feel her stroking me, skin on skin.

"I want it in me," she whispered. Her voice was velvet in my ear, and I nearly came right then.

I lifted her up and felt her long legs wrap around me as I carried her to a nearby post, pressing her against it, letting her hands loosen my pants the rest of the way. I was free for only a second before I drove myself up into her.

I'd never taken a woman in such a way before, but it felt like the most natural thing in the world.

She tightened her legs around my hips, countering my every thrust, driving me deeper. Her breath was hot on my neck as she pulled at my hair, and finally began to claw at my back. People pressed against me as they passed, and I felt more random hands as people tried to take a piece of the experience for themselves, and I let them, if only because it would make me come faster.

So close.

The room grew brighter. Everything took on an intense white halo that built more and more as the intensity of our fucking increased with the *thump-thump-thump* of the music. I knew when I came I would see. I would *know*.

Just as I knew this nameless woman would take my seed, and it would be the last seed she ever took in this place, or anywhere else for that matter.

"Come . . . come, baby . . . come in me."

Not the voice in my head this time, but hers, hot against my ear. I didn't need another invitation. I exploded with an orgasm that made everything in the room dazzle. Somewhere deep in the background, people were crying out in surprise and fear, but I couldn't tell over what. Not yet anyway. I was too busy seeing into a brightly lit room with silver walls, and an enormous vertical tank in the center. A body was floating in a viscous fluid, but I couldn't see a face. Only strands of golden hair floating like tattered streamers in stasis.

And on one bare shoulder, a birthmark that looked like a butterfly with one wing.

Matilda.

My soul began to curdle as every last bit of sexual excitement fled my body. It wasn't Kaya who had that birthmark. It was Beth.

Beth.

"Oh . . . Oh God no . . ."

I backed away from the woman who only moments ago I'd been fucking as if she was the only thing that mattered. She was looking at me with wide eyes and flaring nostrils, but she wasn't the only one. All eyes were on me, and in the mirror on one wall, I could finally see why. A pair of white beams was shooting from my eyes.

Chapter 33

The sea of bodies parted before me like I was Moses. Many of them fell into one another, spilling drinks, interrupting impromptu coitus sessions. I heard cries of pain and rage as people stumbled over one another to avoid my iridescent gaze.

"Who is this freak?"

"He's ruining my fuck!"

I had to move. Whoever kept watch over this playpen would be after me soon, but I knew where to go now. There was a door in the far corner marked Restricted Access, but that would be no problem for me. I ran, pushing any who stood in my way. Beth was here. *Here!* How in God's name?

The door lock cracked and fell away at my touch. No effort on my part; none was needed. I was mired in the *Élan Vital*, for better or worse. I dashed up a dank stairwell, footfalls echoing. There might have been darkness, but I couldn't detect it through all of the white light that was pouring not only through my eyes, but my very pores.

"Beth! Where are you? *Beth!*"

I didn't know if she could hear my voice, but I called out even louder with my mind.

BETH!

It was followed by a faint *Daaaaa* . . .

As I climbed the stairs, I could feel the Hand of God in my mind and in the pit of my stomach like a mass of squirming maggots. When I reached the door, I kicked it in and watched it slam into one of the agents, knocking him out cold. The other two jabbed out with their electric sticks, but I felt nothing. The power already surging through me was exponentially greater than what their weapons could wield, but the blowback was enormous as the electric sticks shattered in their hands, rendering their pristine white gloves into gory red stumps.

They screamed behind their masks and stumbled back. I booted one in the chest, sending him flying to the end of the hallway and into the big metal door there. It was not just any door. It was *the* door. Stainless steel, with a keypad lock. No light could escape its heavy-duty seal, but I saw it anyway. Felt it.

The other Hand of God agent was still rolling on the floor, screaming over his lost limb. I knelt over him and ripped off his gas mask. The face I saw filled me with a revulsion so great I might have lost my sanity right there if I didn't have my daughter's pleas swirling in my head.

This was no human man, though he might once have been. He was bald, but for a few patches of gray hair that curled at the ears. Or where his ears were supposed to be. Brown scales covered his head and neck, and his baleful red eyes had vertical pupils that were fluttering open and shut, likely due to his injury or panic. A black cross was branded on his forehead. He opened his mouth in a hiss and a white tongue, forked and barbed, shot out at my face. My reflexes saved my eye, possibly my life. I jerked away, but stumbled over the body of the one lying unconscious behind me.

The snake-man sat up, a cold grin spreading across his deformed face, revealing needle-like fangs dripping something undoubtedly venomous. But already, his breath was labored. The air outside his mask was poison to him.

"*Lie ssstill . . . sssinner . . .*"

I leapt at him. He hissed and bucked beneath me, but he was losing strength. I could hold on a little longer, and he would simply suffocate, but he didn't deserve to go out so easily. I pressed my thumb against the cross on his forehead. The area immediately began to burn, the smell like scorched and infected flesh. He screamed with his remaining breath, and his eyeballs popped like poisonous cherries. I dropped his head and relished the sound of it thudding against the carpet.

While I still had the presence of mind to do it, I also ripped the mask off the unconscious one. This one was a mutant like the other, but he was no snake. He was covered with scraggly brown fur and had a deformed snout filled with yellow teeth jutting haphazardly out of his head. The same cross was branded on his head.

Immediately, he began to seize and convulse, and I knew I wouldn't have to worry about him.

The last agent lay crumpled at the foot of the metal door. I kicked off his mask—he was more of the reptilian persuasion like the first one—but he didn't stir. His neck was broken. Finally, I turned my attention to the lock. The wheel resisted at first, but the metal soon began to glow red in my head. I didn't feel any heat, but the metal bent anyway as if it was in a furnace.

The keypad lock beeped a few times before it began to melt into a drizzle of black goo. I gave the door a good shove, leaving the imprint of my body in the softened metal, and it swung open.

The windowless room was not much bigger than a large closet, but it was lit brightly enough to hurt my eyes. Machines with banks of buttons and blinking lights lined each wall. Hoses and tubes ran from these machines into two fluid-filled tanks that stood in the center of the room. The nearest tank held the naked and wrinkled husk of a woman floating in cloudy fluid. Her mouth was frozen in an eternal scream, and her hair floated behind her like burnt straw. All that remained of her shrunken eyes was the barest hint of white that almost seemed to accuse me for not arriving in time to save her.

And then there was the one in the other tank.

Beth.

Just like in my vision, I could only see her from behind. I feverishly wished for it not to be her, but the birthmark on her shoulder told me everything I needed to know. I cried out her name and ran around to the front of the tank, stumbling over the naked body of the one I'd originally come here to rescue.

Genevieve was laid out on a metal table at the tank's base. Tubes ran from her head, nose, and mouth and into the tank's ports. I screamed in horror when I saw another tube running up in between her legs, to the place our child was growing. If it was still growing at all. I placed my hands on her belly, but I could detect nothing more than a flicker. Perhaps because the life inside was still so small and fragile.

Her eyes flew open at my touch. Islands of green in a sea of red. They saw nothing. "Come . . . come . . . come . . ." she murmured, and I realized it was her voice I'd been hearing in my head, guiding me.

Then I forced my eyes up to my daughter.

"Beth . . . oh my dear baby girl . . ."

She had more tubes feeding into her head than Genevieve had, and the two women seemed to be working in some strange psychic tandem. Beth floated freely in the liquid, which I imagined was a conductor of some sort. A catheter bag was strapped to her leg to catch any urine that might make it unclean. Her skin was as white as Ezekiel's had been before he died, her fingers so pruned that bits of flesh were lifting off of them as the fluid broke her body down. I now understood the used up husk floating in the other tank. There was a limited shelf life for the queen bees, and they were trying to use Genevieve, and whatever residual Sentinel ability she might still have in order to feed her.

"John . . . come . . . Joh-Joh . . ." Genevieve called out. Beth jerked awake, revealing eyes bleached completely of their blue. Only a hint of gray was left around her pupils to signify that color had even been there.

"Daaaaaa . . ."

Bubbles flew up from her mouth as she tried to speak. She began to choke and spasm in the fluid, her hair floating around her face in ghostly tendrils.

"No, sweetheart! Don't talk!" I pressed my hands and forehead against the glass.

Don't talk, sweet girl. It will kill you.

Good. Yes, good.

No! No, Beth. I'm going to get you out of here! You're coming home with Daddy. We're going back to Old Babylon together. You, me, Genevieve.

But . . . they'll all die, Daddy. I can't let them die.

Rage surged through me. Indignant rage, the kind I felt when Linny so insisted on eating that damn poisoned feast. I wanted to smash the glass with my fists, but I tried to remain calm. For her.

These people came here to die, sweetheart.

They said I had a greater purpose. I was a shepherd . . . I served well. Kaya would be . . . proud . . .

Hot tears squirted from my eyes, angry and oh so bitter. My throat hurt with the sobs I was holding in. I wanted to save her, but why? For whom? For me? I didn't deserve her. She was more like me than I'd ever known, and I never bothered to notice. And even now, after everything they'd done to her, she thought she was doing right. I couldn't take that from her, no matter how much I wanted to.

I'm so proud of you, honey. You have . . . a good heart.

I had to force those last words out no matter how badly they hurt, because I didn't want her to die with such a heavy burden on her. I hadn't been much of a father, but I knew it was my job alone to carry those burdens for her.

Love you . . . Dad . . .

I love you, Beth. I'm so sorry.

I pressed the glass and felt warmth beneath my hand just before it shattered. The clear fluid, thicker than water, whooshed out in a huge wave, but I grabbed Beth before she could tumble onto Genevieve, and we both fell to the floor.

Her eyes were wide and bulging as she struggled to breathe. She was like a fish out of water.

I turned her over and pounded her back to help her expel the fluid. Frantically, I tried infusing her with the light from my mind in the hopes I could heal her, but she started convulsing.

"Oh God no, no! Please don't let her suffer anymore!"

Below me, I heard the blare of sirens and the terrorized screams of thousands of condemned souls suddenly cut off from their queen. More Hand of God agents were storming down the hallway. They would be here within seconds.

I wrestled her against my chest and whispered into her ear.

"Come to me, Beth. Bring me all your flock. Daddy will care for them now. Then you let go. Fly free." I clasped her soggy hand in mine as I cradled her the way I did the day she was born. "Come to me. Come to me, sweet girl."

The force of her power slammed into me with the heat and light of a million suns. An explosion rocked the building and I was soon looking up into the night sky. Dawn was coming, but the stars hadn't yet retreated. The last vestige of me still attached to this physical world called out for Chitin. I'd lost Anansi's whistle, but this signal was stronger.

As I faded away, the last thing I heard was the locust plague.

Chapter 34

My Last Supper is now nothing more than a colorless, odorless paste, reduced to its component parts, primordial clay. I don't think it was ever intended to sit this long. But I still have to eat it, for it's the only way out I've created for myself. There isn't much left, so I guess I can choke it down.

Afterward, I suppose I will go to sleep. I just don't want to wake up again. I've seen what I have to come back to, and it's only grown darker and scarier since I arrived on this strange little plane of existence, my own little self-imposed Purgatory if you will. But Genevieve says I have to do what's right. I can't stay here forever, and I don't much think she'd care to stay with me if I didn't go back. Besides, I wasn't made of lazy blood, as much as I'd like to be, and I can't wallow in my grief forever.

She and Matilda have been spending a lot of time away lately, probably to give me space to think about what I need to do. But I think it's also because Genevieve knows that she herself will have to make a similar choice very soon.

Matilda has grown so fast in our time here, or so it seems. Time is speedier on this side of things, that much is certain. Her hair is red, but she's Kaya all over again with her scabby knees and perpetual smirk. She has Beth's generosity and inner calm, though, and it warms my heart to see both of my girls in her. Oh how they would have loved their little sister.

News regularly comes down from the pipeline through a little radio I designed to pick up the signals. It's mostly Turpin doing the talking, but Harry will sometimes speak as he keeps vigil over Genevieve and her growing belly. Old Babylon survived its first siege not long after I departed for the Sin Bin, but only just barely. Most of the ones we rescued from the Cradle died or were recaptured by the Hand of God. I can only hope they were given a swift execution thereafter, but I shouldn't expect such mercy.

The day was mostly won by Christoph's expert knowledge of explosives, and the Heretics also did a lot of the heavy lifting. Harry took three spears in the back and laid in a coma for a few days. I fully expected him to come knocking on our door. Lord knows he'd love to see his little girl and his granddaughter, but he managed to pull through with the help of Tessa and Nessie (now I know her name, at least) and he's already up and around again, gearing up for the next wave.

Everything here feels so goddamn tangible, much like my time with Ezekiel under the plum tree. In fact, I have one of those growing on the north corner of our yard. Its petals fall in an endless snow, and when I sit under it, I think of my brother. I had hoped to see him again while here, but I don't think I ever will. Not in the form he once was. He's in every blade of grass, every speck of dirt, every flower petal. The grass and flowers grow freely. The fruit from the peach trees is sweet and juicy. But best of all, there are no serpent weeds, and no Justification.

You might be wondering why my daughters aren't here, if this is a world of my own creation. Why didn't I imagine back my wife? My only guess is that Linny, Beth, and Kaya are dead. They're on a plane I can't reach or reconstruct. As for Genevieve and Matilda . . . They're just asleep. I get the sense that Genevieve will be waking soon, when it's time to bring our daughter into the world for real.

I only hope they make it. My heart can't handle losing another.

I asked Genevieve this morning if she was ready, but she won't answer. She's become more and more distant of late. I don't think she wants to go if I don't go first. And that's why I have this meal sitting in front of me now, with its dull insipid food that I imagined for myself, because I guess that's all I think I deserve. And maybe if I can't eat it I can stay here.

Of course we'll have to go at some point. I don't have any notion that this little paradise I've created for us will last. Already, some of the flowers are beginning to wilt around the edges. Not a lot. Not enough that you'd notice at first glance. But things are winding down. I can feel the ebb in my bones.

I'm going to finish this colorless lump of food. And then I'm going to retire to my bed for one final sleep in this waning paradise. And when I open my eyes, I'll be ready. I'll have the strength I need to see this through. I might have been down for a bit, but I'm pooling my energy, healing my body and spirit for the next round. The Divine Rite may think they know everything there is to know about me, and that may be. But they missed one important detail.

I have only just begun to fight.

THE END

About the Author | Allison M. Dickson

Allison M. Dickson writes dark contemporary fiction, covering both speculative and realistic realms. Her debut psychological horror novel, *Strings*, released to rave reviews in 2013 and has topped Amazon's horror and crime bestseller lists. She is also the author of several short stories, such as "Dust" and "Under the Scotch Broom," as well as the 1940s sci-fi noir *Colt Coltrane* series. She currently resides with her husband, children, and two four-legged ginger beasts in Dayton, Ohio.

For the latest news about our authors and events, or to learn more about upcoming releases and other projects from Hobbes End Publishing, visit:

www.HobbesEndPublishing.com